Professor Bernard Knight, CBE, became a Home Office pathologist in 1965 and was appointed Professor of Forensic Pathology, University of Wales College of Medicine, in 1980. He is the author of twelve novels, a biography and numerous popular and academic non-fiction books. *The Grim Reaper* is his sixth novel in the Crowner John series, following *The Tinner's Corpse, The Sanctuary Seeker, The Poisoned Chalice, Crowner's Quest* and *The Awful Secret.*

THE GRIM REAPER

Bernard Knight

POCKET
BOOKS

LONDON · SYDNEY · NEW YORK · TORONTO

First published in Great Britain by
Simon & Schuster UK Ltd, 2002
This edition published by Pocket Books, 2002
An imprint of Simon & Schuster UK Ltd
A CBS Company

9 10

Simon & Schuster UK Ltd
Africa House
64–78 Kingsway
London WC2B 6AH

Simon & Schuster Australia
Sydney

A CIP catalogue record for this book is available
from the British Library

ISBN-13: 978-0-67102-967-8

Typeset by Palimpsest Book Production Limited,
Polmont, Stirlingshire
Printed and bound in Great Britain by
Cox & Wyman Ltd, Reading, Berkshire

Acknowledgements

I would like to thank the many people who have given me historical information for both this and the five previous Crowner John books, especially the staff of the West Country Studies Centre at Exeter Public Library, Professor Nicholas Orme, University of Exeter, and Mrs Angela Doughty, Exeter Cathedral Archivist. Mr Frank Gent, of the Exeter Synagogue, was kind enough to refer me to Professor Adler's article, which gives what little is known about the Jewish community at that period.

Dr John Morgan-Guy, University of Wales College, Lampeter, and Mr Thomas Watkin, Cardiff Law School, University of Wales, have been particularly helpful in clarifying some of the complexities of religious and legal life in the twelfth century, though any errors of interpretation are mine alone.

Fellow mystery-writer on fourteenth-century Devon Michael Jecks, author of the Sir Baldwin Furnshill series, kindly sent me a copy of the 'Crown Pleas of the Devon Eyre of 1238' (Devon & Cornwall Record Society, vol. 28, 1985) which was invaluable, as well as fascinating, and can be recommended to anyone who wants to read an actual account of medieval justice in Devon.

Finally, my thanks to Gillian Holmes and to the editorial staff of Simon & Schuster, especially Kate Lyall Grant, for their encouragement and efficiency.

Historical Foreword

As the Crowner John Mysteries always strive for historical accuracy, a few matters should be mentioned, especially as much of this story concerns the priests of Exeter. First, although in 1195 that small city had at least twenty-seven churches, parish boundaries were not drawn until 1220–22. However, for convenience, the term 'parish priest' is occasionally used.

The period was, of course, centuries before the advent of paper or printing, and 'Bibles' were handwritten volumes on parchment. Most were the Latin 'Vulgate' version, often incomplete, though some vernacular copies existed. These scriptures were continuous, not divided into 'chapters' until after the work of Stephen Langton, Archbishop of Canterbury, who died in 1228. Chapters were not subdivided into 'verses' until much later, when printing began in the fifteenth century. However, the term 'chapter' for the ruling body of canons in a cathedral like Exeter existed from an early date, as a 'chapter' of the Scriptures was read before each meeting – but this is a translational twist, as 'chapter' in that sense meant a *capitulum* or 'passage'. Though this might sound academic, it has some relevance to this story!

There was a Jewish community in Devon before 1177: in that year it was allowed its own cemetery outside the wall of Exeter. In 1188, the Jews had to pay a fine for resorting to the Beth Din or Jewish Court in the city. In 1290, they, with all of England's sixteen thousand Jews, were expelled from the country.

Any attempt in novels to give modern dialogue an 'olde worlde' flavour is as inaccurate as it is futile, for in late twelfth-century Devon, most people would have spoken Early Middle English, which would be unintelligible to us today. Many others would have spoken western Welsh, later called Cornish, and the ruling classes would have used Norman French, while the language of the Church and all official writing was Latin.

Many of the churches mentioned in the book, as well as the gatehouse of Rougemont Castle, survived Hitler's blitzes on Exeter and can still be visited.

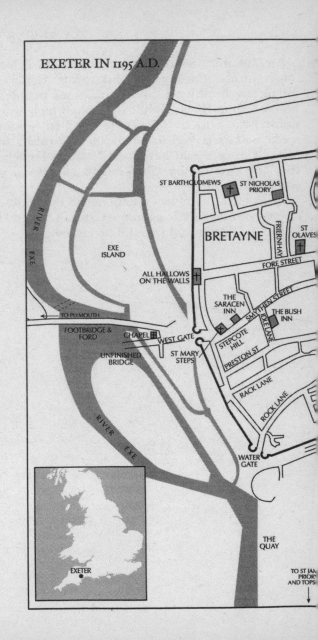

EXETER IN 1195 A.D.

RIVER EXE

ST BARTHOLOMEWS

ST NICHOLAS PRIORY

BRETAYNE

FRIERNHAY

ST OLAVES

FORE STREET

EXE ISLAND

ALL HALLOWS ON THE WALLS

THE SARACEN INN

SMYTHEN STREET

IDLE LANE

THE BUSH INN

TO PLYMOUTH

FOOTBRIDGE & FORD

CHAPEL

WEST GATE

STEPCOTE HILL

PRESTON ST

UNFINISHED BRIDGE

ST MARY STEPS

RACK LANE

ROCK LANE

RIVER EXE

WATER GATE

THE QUAY

EXETER

TO ST JAMES PRIORY AND TOPS

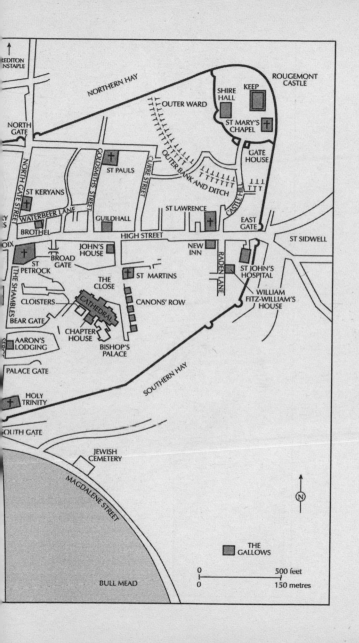

CREDITON
BARNSTAPLE

NORTHERN HAY

ROUGEMONT
CASTLE

OUTER WARD

SHIRE
HALL

KEEP

ST MARY'S
CHAPEL

GATE
HOUSE

NORTH
GATE

NORTH GATE STREET

ST KERYANS

GOLDSMITH'S STREET

ST PAULS

CURRE STREET

OUTER BANK AND DITCH

CASTLE HILL

WATERBEER LANE

GUILDHALL

ST LAWRENCE

EAST
GATE

ST SIDWELL

BROTHEL

HIGH STREET

ROIX

JOHN'S
HOUSE

NEW
INN

BROAD
GATE

RADEN LANE

ST
PETROCK

THE CLOSE

ST MARTINS

ST JOHN'S
HOSPITAL

THE SHAMBLES

CLOISTERS

CATHEDRAL

CANONS' ROW

WILLIAM
FITZ-WILLIAM'S
HOUSE

BEAR GATE

AARON'S
LODGING

CHAPTER
HOUSE

BISHOP'S
PALACE

PALACE GATE

SOUTHERN HAY

HOLY
TRINITY

SOUTH GATE

JEWISH
CEMETERY

MAGDALENE STREET

N

THE
GALLOWS

0   500 feet

0   150 metres

BULL MEAD

GLOSSARY

ALB
A long tunic worn by a priest during Mass

ALE
A brewed drink, before the advent of hops – derived from an 'ale', a village celebration where much drinking took place.

APPEAL
Unlike the modern legal meaning, an appeal was an accusation by an aggrieved person, often a relative of a victim, against another for a felonious crime. Historically it preceded (and competed with) the Crown's right to prosecute and demanded either financial compensation or trial by combat or the Ordeal.

AMERCEMENT
An arbitrary fine imposed on a person or community by a law officer, for some breach of the complex regulations of the law. Where imposed by a coroner, he would record the amercement, but the collection of the money would normally be ordered by the royal justices when they visited at the Eyre of Assize.

ATTACHMENT
An order made by a law officer, including a coroner, to ensure

that a person, whether suspect or witness, appeared at a court hearing. It resembled a bail bond or surety, distraining upon a person's money or goods, which would be forfeit if he failed to appear.

BAILEY
Originally the defended areas, sometimes concentric, around a castle keep ('motte and bailey') but later also applied to the yard of a dwelling.

BAILIFF
Overseer of a manor or estate, directing the farming and other work. He would have manor reeves under him and be responsible either directly to his lord or to the steward or seneschal.

BOTTLER
A servant responsible for providing drink in a household – the origin of 'butler'.

BURGESS
A freeman of substance in a town or borough, usually a merchant. A group of burgesses ran the town administration and in Exeter elected two Portreeves (later a Mayor) as their leaders.

CANON
A priestly member of the chapter of a cathedral, also called a prebendary (qv). Exeter had twenty-four canons, most of whom lived near the cathedral. Many employed junior priests (vicars) to carry out their duties for them.

CHAPTER
The administrative body of a cathedral, composed of the canons (prebendaries). They met daily to conduct business in the Chapter House, so-called because a chapter of the Gospels was read before each session.

COIF
A close-fitting cap or helmet, usually of linen, covering the ears and tied under the chin; worn by men and women.

CONSTABLE
Has several meanings, but could refer to a senior commander, usually the custodian of a castle, which in Exeter belonged to the King – or a watchman who patrolled the streets to keep order.

CORONER
A senior law officer in each county, second only to the sheriff. First formally established in September 1194, though there is a mention of the coroner in Saxon times. Three knights and one clerk were recruited in each county, to carry out a wide range of legal and financial duties. The name comes from *custos placitorum coronas*, meaning 'Keeper of the Pleas of the Crown', as he recorded all serious crimes, deaths and legal events for the King's judges.

COVER-CHIEF
More correctly 'couvre-chef', a linen headcover, worn by women, held in place by a band around the head, and flowing down the back and front of the chest. Termed 'head-rail' in Saxon times.

CURFEW
The prohibition of open fires in towns after dark, for fear of starting conflagrations. Derived from 'couvre-feu', from the extinguishing or banking-down of fires at night. During the curfew, the city gates were closed from dusk to dawn – one thirteenth-century mayor of Exeter was hanged for failing to ensure this.

DEODAND
Literally 'a gift from God', it was the forfeiture of anything that had caused a death, such as a sword, a cart or even a

mill-wheel. It was confiscated by the coroner for the king, but was sometimes given as compensation to the victim's family.

DESTRIER
A large war-horse able to carry the weight of an armoured knight. When firearms made armour redundant, destriers became shirehorses, replacing oxen as draught animals.

EYRE
A sitting of the King's justices, introduced by Henry II in 1166, which moved around the country in circuits. There were two types, the 'Justices in Eyre' or 'Eyre of Assize' which was the forerunner of the later Assize Courts, which was supposed to visit each county town regularly to try serious cases; and the General Eyre, which came at long intervals to scrutinise the administration of each county.

FARM
The taxation from a county, collected in coin on behalf of the sheriff and taken by him personally every six months to the royal treasury at London or Winchester. The sum was fixed annually by the king or his ministers; if the sheriff could extract more from the county, he could retain the excess, which made the office of sheriff much sought after.

FLETCHER
A maker of arrows

FRANKPLEDGE
A system of law enforcement introduced by the Normans, where groups or 'tithings' of ten households were formed to enforce mutual good behaviour amongst the group.

HAUBERK
A chain-mail tunic with long sleeves to protect the wearer from neck to calf; usually slit for riding a horse.

HUNDRED
An administrative division of a county, originally named for a hundred hides of land or a hundred families.

JUSTICES
The king's judges, originally from his royal court, but later chosen from barons, senior priests and administrators. They sat in the various law courts, such as the Eyre of Assize or as Commissioners of Gaol Delivery. From 1195 onwards, 'justices of the peace' recruited from knights and local worthies, dealt with lesser offences.

LEAT
An artificial channel for water, leading it into an ore-washing system

MATINS
The first service of the religious day, originally at midnight

MARK
A measure of money, though not an actual coin, as only pennies existed. A mark was two-thirds of a pound i.e thirteen shillings and fourpence (sixty-six decimal pence)

MUTILATION
A common punishment as an alternative to hanging. A hand, foot or genitals were amputated or blinding carried out.

ORDEAL
A test of guilt or innocence, such as walking over nine red-hot plough-shares or picking a stone from a barrel of boiling water or molten lead; if burns appeared, the person was judged guilty. For women, submersion in water was the ordeal, the guilty floating!

PREBENDARY
A canon of a cathedral, deriving an income from his 'prebend', a tract of land granted to him (see CANON)

PYX
A box or container for the wafers used during the Mass

RULE OF ST CHRODEGANG
A strict regime of a simple communal life, devised by an eighth-century bishop of Metz. It was adopted by Bishop Leofric, who founded Exeter Cathedral in 1050, but did not long survive his death. The canons soon adopted a more comfortable, even luxurious, lifestyle.

SECONDARIES
Young men aspiring to become priests, thus under twenty-four years of age. They assisted canons and vicars in their duties in the cathedral.

SURPLICE
Derived from 'super-pelisse', a white outer garment worn by a priest during services.

TERCE
The fourth of the nine services of the cathedral day, usually around nine in the morning.

TRIAL BY BATTLE
An ancient right to settle a dispute by fighting to the death. Usually, an appealer (qv) would demand financial compensation from the alleged perpetrator or be challenged to battle. Women and unfit persons could employ a champion to fight for them.

VICAR
A priest employed by a more senior cleric, such as a canon, to carry out some of his religious duties, especially the many daily services in a cathedral. Often called a 'vicar-choral' from his participation in chanted services.

PROLOGUE

Exeter, May 1195

The cathedral Close was never totally silent, even after midnight. There was the scrabble of a stray dog rooting in a pile of butcher's offal and the rustle of rats in the garbage that was strewn along the muddy paths that crossed this episcopal heart of the city. The wind moaned between the two great towers that reached to the sky, where thin clouds raced across a haloed moon. Its pale light made the shadows cast by the huge building all the blacker and the flickering light of a flare stuck on a wall near Beargate did little to penetrate the gloom along the cathedral's west front. From beyond the great doors came faint chanting: Matins, the first Office of the new day, was being celebrated in the distant quire.

Across the precinct, from the direction of little St Martin's church, came a new sound, the slap of leather soles on the wet soil, as a figure threaded its way through the tomb mounds and piles of earth from newly opened graves. As the walker came out of the shadows, the moonlight shone on the long black cloak and cowl of a priest. However, the devotions of the early hours were not his target, for he walked purposefully past the west front and the cloisters that lay on his left.

The pitch-soaked brand burning at Beargate threw its

yellow light down on him as he strode beneath, but it failed to reveal the grim intent on the face hidden by the deep hood.

CHAPTER ONE

In which Crowner John visits a moneylender

A thunderous knocking on the street door dimly penetrated Sir John de Wolfe's consciousness and triggered a throbbing headache that told of too much wine the previous evening. He groaned and turned over, pulling the sheepskin coverlet over his ears. Angrily his wife jerked the coverings back over herself.

'See who's making that noise, John!' Though she was half-asleep, Matilda's voice held its usual belligerent rasp.

De Wolfe sighed and levered himself up against the faded tapestry nailed to the wooden wall behind the bed. The movement jarred his brain, which felt as if it was swinging around loose inside his skull. He rubbed his bleary eyes and saw the dawn light peeping through the cracks in the shutters. The knocking stopped and he heard distant voices through the slit that penetrated the wall of their solar into the main hall of the house.

'Mary's answered them,' he grunted, closing his eyes again and running a hand through the long black hair that covered his aching skull. The previous evening, he had been dragged, at Matilda's insistence, to the Spring Feast of the Guild of Cordwainers. It was part of her campaign to get him to associate more with the great and good of the city and county. An enthusiastic social climber, it galled Matilda that, as sister of the sheriff and wife of the coroner, she missed out on many of the upper-class events because her husband did all he could to avoid them. Last night, he had sat glumly at the top table in the Guildhall, doing his best to drown the idle chatter of the burgesses, barons and clergy with a considerable excess of ale, cider and Anjou wine. He had managed to totter the short distance to their house in Martin's Lane, oblivious of the tight-lipped disapproval of his grim-faced wife, but this morning he was paying the price.

'Get up and see who's there, I said,' she snapped, jerking the bedclothes even further, leaving him partly naked in the cold morning air. Gingerly, he climbed out of the low bed – a thick feather mattress set on a plinth on the floor – and stumbled to a wooden chest against the opposite wall. He sat down heavily and pulled on the long black hose he had worn the previous evening. Then he hauled his long, stooping frame up again and searched in the chest for a clean undershirt and a dark grey tunic that came just below his knees, slit at the sides for sitting a horse. He stood up and cautiously opened a shutter, then squinted at the early-morning sky. Though spring was well advanced, it was cool and, as an afterthought, de Wolfe groped in the chest again for a pair of worsted breeches, which he hauled on and tied with a drawstring around his waist.

'Go on, then! See who it is that disturbs God-fearing folk at this hour,' goaded Matilda.

Slipping his feet into a pair of house-shoes, John opened the door and stepped shivering on to the platform outside. The solar was built high on the back of the narrow timber house, like a large box supported on wooden piles. Steep steps went down to the backyard, where several thatched sheds housed the kitchen, wash-house and privy. Mary, their cook and housekeeper, slept on a cot in her kitchen, and

Simon, the aged man who tended the fires and the night-soil, lived in the wash-house. Under the stairs to the solar, another cubicle housed Lucille, Matilda's rabbit-toothed French maid.

When de Wolfe reached the muddy yard, he could hear voices through the narrow covered passage alongside the house, which went through to the front vestibule that lay behind a massive oak door to the street. As he bent his head to go through, his old hound Brutus came towards him, tongue lolling and tail wagging in welcome. He stooped to fondle the dog's ears and saw that Mary, a dark-haired, handsome young woman, was coming towards him, followed by a massive figure that almost filled the narrow alley. Backing out, he waited for the maid and his henchman to join him in the yard.

'Gwyn, I might have known it was you, trying to hammer down my front door.'

'We've got a body, Crowner. A strange one, this time.'

Gwyn of Polruan was an untidy Goliath of a man with a mass of ginger hair and a large moustache of the same tint that hung down over his lantern jaw almost to his collar-bones. Bushy eyebrows and a bulbous red nose framed a pair of twinkling blue eyes. He was dressed in a faded brown worsted tunic that came only to mid-thigh, girdled by a wide leather belt that carried a sheathed dagger. His brawny legs were covered with baggy fawn breeches held to his claves by cross-gartering above ankle-length leather boots. Around his shoulders was a frayed leather cape, with a pointed hood that hung down his back. De Wolfe had rarely seen him dressed in anything else, summer or winter. A former Cornish fisherman, Gwyn had been de Wolfe's bodyguard and companion for almost twenty years, in campaigns in Ireland, France and the Holy Land.

The coroner groaned at the news, his head still

thumping like a water-hammer in a forge. 'Don't tell me we've got a long ride. I doubt I could sit a horse before noon.' His jurisdiction covered the whole county of Devon and it could take two days' riding to reach the more distant villages.

Gwyn grinned and shook his head, his tangled hair bouncing like a red mop. 'You don't need your horse, Crowner! It's only a few hundred paces away, across the Close.'

Mary stood listening, her hands on her hips. 'Do you want some breakfast before you go gallivanting?' she demanded.

Before the ever-hungry Cornishman could open his mouth, de Wolfe had shaken his head. 'If it's that near, you can get something ready for us when we get back – say an hour.' He jabbed a finger into his disappointed officer's chest. 'Go and rouse that miserable little clerk of ours while I go up and tell Madam where I'm going. She'll give me the length of her tongue if I disappear so early without some good excuse.'

Ten minutes later, John stepped from his house into Martin's Lane, the short, narrow alley that joined the cathedral Close to the city's high street. As he stopped to swing his mottled wolfskin cloak about his shoulders, he looked up at the dwelling he had bought ten years ago with loot from Ireland. Tall and narrow, with a steep roof of wooden shingles, the house-front was blind apart from the door and two shuttered windows at ground level. Alongside it stood an almost identical house – the only other building in the lane, apart from the farrier's stable and the side of an inn opposite – which was empty: the silversmith who owned it had been murdered a few months earlier.

And now de Wolfe was off to see another corpse, though Gwyn had not said what kind of death it was – he had an exasperating habit of spinning out any story to keep the listener in suspense. Now he was striding towards the coroner, his cape blowing in the brisk breeze. 'I hauled Thomas off his pallet, Crowner. The little turd will follow us down when he gets some clothes on.'

The coroner's clerk was Thomas de Peyne, a disgraced priest from Winchester, who had been given the job by de Wolfe as a favour to his friend the Archdeacon, who happened to be Thomas's uncle.

The coroner and his officer set off across the Close, the patch of ground around the cathedral which was an ecclesiastical enclave independent of the city, and outside the jurisdiction of the sheriff and burgesses. Although it was supposed to be policed by the cathedral proctors, it was an eyesore, not only because of the squalor and rubbish but because hawkers, beggars and loutish youths made a nuisance of themselves there in front of the more respectable users of this busy space in the middle of the city.

However, at this early hour, only a couple of optimistic hawkers rattled their trays at the pair as they strode purposefully from the end of Martin's Lane towards one of the several exits from the Close, a beggar sitting on the cathedral steps opened his mouth to whine for alms, but shut it again as a waste of breath when he saw who the two men were. Though Gwyn of Polruan was a huge fellow, his master was barely an inch shorter, but where the Cornishman was massive John de Wolfe was lean and spare. His posture was a little hunched and his head stuck out like that of some predatory bird; his long black hair, jet eyebrows and great hooked nose enhanced his resemblance to a raven. He had no beard or moustache, but the dark stubble on his long face and the fact that he invariably dressed in black or grey had earned him the nickname 'Black John' in campaigns across Europe and the Levant.

'It's just past Beargate,' rumbled Gwyn, beginning grudgingly to leak information, 'in a dwelling around the corner in Southgate Street.'

'Not in the cathedral precinct, is it?' snapped the coroner, mindful of the Church's jealous hold on its property and all that happened in it.

'Well, the back wall comes to the Close, but this is a room rented out by one of the cloth merchants in the Serge Market.'

Beyond Beargate, the Close funnelled into a narrow lane, which opened into Southgate Street. This was one of the four main thoroughfares in Exeter, built over the original Roman plan, in which a quartet of roads radiated from the central crossing at Carfoix to each of the gates in the town walls.

'Down this way, Crowner.' Gwyn turned left and thrust his way through the early-morning traders, who were putting up their booths along the street and lowering the shutters of the shops to act as counters. This was the Serge Market, where the cloth dealers held sway. The road dipped down steeply towards the South Gate, and through the big arch they could see a slow procession of cattle, sheep and pigs being driven up to the Shambles near St George's church, where the upper part of the street acted as a slaughteryard to supply the butcher's stalls. Soon the morning would be rent by the wailing of cows and the scream of pigs, as poleaxes and knives left the cobbles awash with blood.

John followed his officer for a few yards down the street until they came to a knot of people squeezed between two cloth stalls, the traders still struggling to fix up the gaudy striped awnings in the fresh breeze. The small crowd was huddled around a tall, fair-haired man holding a pike, who blocked a doorway into the building behind. He banged the heel of his weapon on the ground in a salute to the King's coroner. 'These here are the people who found the body, Crowner,' he said, in a thick country accent. 'I reckoned I had better keep them here until you came.' The lanky fellow, his cheeks ridden with old cowpox scars, was one of the town constables, a Saxon named Osric, and was employed by the burgesses to try to safeguard the properties of the merchants. As there were only two constables in a city of more than four thousand inhabitants, they were somewhat ineffective, but had some use in keeping order among the scuffles and fights that broke out hourly in the streets. De Wolfe turned to Gwyn. His patience had run thin. 'Now, are you going to tell me what happened?' he snapped.

Gwyn smiled amiably and laid a huge hand on the shoulder of a small man trying to look inconspicuous among the witnesses. 'This fellow here is the First Finder. He came as it was getting light to call upon the man who lived here, but found him dead. He called the constable and Osric sent someone up to the castle.'

'How did you get to know about it so quickly?' demanded de Wolfe. Gwyn lived in St Sidwell's, a village outside the city walls.

Gwyn grinned sheepishly. 'While you were enjoying your feast in the Guildhall last night, I did some gaming and drinking with Sergeant Gabriel and some of his men. I slept in the gatehouse overnight and was there when the constable sent the message up.'

'So who's dead, damn you?' snarled his master.

'Best come inside and look for yourself, Crowner.' Gwyn was determined to spin out the suspense as long as he could.

The skinny constable stood aside and John followed his officer through a doorway into a dark passage with a damp earthen floor. Ahead, it went off somewhere into the gloomy nether regions, but in the left-hand wall of limed wattle there was another doorway, hung with a large sheet of thick leather to keep out draughts, its bottom green and mottled with damp. Gwyn held it aside for the coroner to pass through. There was a strong smell of mould and stale urine, but it was so dark that de Wolfe could see almost nothing. 'Open those damned shutters, man,' he barked.

The pale daylight flooded in and a row of heads appeared over the front sill, until the constable prodded them away with the end of his pike and stood guard there himself. John turned slowly to take in the whole room.

'Who is he, do we know?'

In the centre of the uneven floor, a man was lying flat on his back, deathly still. His head was enveloped in a brown leather bag, the drawstrings pulled tightly around his neck.

'No doubt about it – he's well known in the markets here. It's Aaron of Salisbury, a Jewish moneylender,' said Gwyn.

From outside the window, Osric added some detail: 'He's lived here about half a year, Crowner. Rents this room for his business, and eats and sleeps in the one behind. Keeps to himself and causes no trouble. I did hear his wife and son died in that terrible trouble in York in 'eighty-nine, after which he moved to Salisbury, then came here. I think he has a married daughter somewhere, maybe in Honiton.'

De Wolfe stood and looked slowly around the room. The only furniture was a rickety table, a folding chair with a leather back and a couple of milking stools. The table had been against the back wall, but was now on its side, one of its legs broken. On the floor was a small balance for weighing coins, a scattered heap of silver pennies and a tattered book, consisting of a wad of ragged parchment sheets sewn between two thin wooden boards. In a niche in the timber wall was a seven-branched candlestick, green with verdigris. In the corner was another doorway, with no door or screen in its mouldering frame.

De Wolfe and his henchman crouched on each side of the body, postures in which they had plenty of practice in the last eight months since John had become coroner.

'Call that First Finder in here,' de Wolfe growled at the constable. A moment later the small man came in from the street and stood apprehensively inside the doorway. He was a furtive figure, with a pug nose, dressed in a mouse-coloured tunic and a pointed woollen cap, its tassel flopping over one ear.

'Was he like this when you found him? Did you move him at all?'

'Yessir – no, sir! I ran out of here as if Satan himself was after me.'

'Why were you here at all, so early in the day?'

The man hesitated, not from guilt but shame. 'I wanted a loan, Crowner. Never before have I needed to borrow, but my business as a fletcher has been so bad with the King's army away in France for over a year that I needed money to tide me over.'

'You need a good war to get you back on your feet,' suggested Gwyn to the arrow-maker, not unsympathetically.

De Wolfe gave one of his throaty grunts, which might have meant anything, and turned his attention back to the dead man. 'That drawstring around his neck, Gwyn, is it tight enough to strangle him?'

The Cornishman poked a large forefinger between the neck of the money-bag and the collar of the black woollen tunic that shrouded the money-lender. 'Feels loose enough to me now, though it might have been pulled tight earlier.'

'But it's not knotted to hold it in place,' growled John. 'Let's have it off his head.'

His officer pulled the neck of the bag as wide as it would stretch and slid it up over the face and head of the Jew. A full grey beard was revealed first, then a pale face with closed eyes. Long iron-grey hair, parted in the centre, framed strong features with a peaceful expression.

'Anything in the bag?'

Gwyn peered into the strong leather pouch, which had neat, tight stitching along the seams. He put in a hand and studied his fingertips when he withdrew them. 'Blood – not much, but it's fresh.'

The fletcher was still standing inside the door, gaping at the scene, and the Saxon guard peering in through the window, as de Wolfe put a bony hand under the neck of the cadaver and tried to pull it into a sitting position. The whole body moved, resting on its heels, and the coroner let it drop back. 'Stiff as a bloody board! Must have been dead a good few hours. Pull him over – I want to see the back of his head.'

Gwyn grabbed a shoulder and effortlessly turned the corpse on to its side. He held it there while John felt under the armpits, then prodded at the scalp with his fingers. 'Matted blood in the hair. Can't feel any broken bone underneath. There's still a bit of warmth under the arms, so he must have been killed during the night.'

Gwyn lowered the body back to the floor and they both crouched silently for a moment, staring at the moneylender as if waiting for him to give them some answers.

'Give me that bag,' commanded de Wolfe. He turned it over in his hands, pulled at the drawstrings, then tested the strength of the seams. 'Good enough to be airtight, with the neck of the bag filled with his collar and that mass of beard. Must have cut off his breathing well enough.'

'He's not blue in the face, Crowner,' objected Gwyn.

'Doesn't need to be, it's not like being garrotted. I've seen a few smotherings and they weren't blue.' John vied with his officer in considering himself to be an authority on all modes of violent death, after twenty years in a dozen campaigns across the known world.

They went through their usual routine of pulling up the dead man's tunic to examine the rest of his body. As they moved his arms, a scrap of folded parchment fell from his fingers. John opened it, but could make no sense of the crabbed writing upon it. He was learning to read and write but this script defeated him, and everyone else present was even less literate than he was.

The corpse wore long woollen hose held up by strings attached to an underbelt and had a shawl-like garment around his shoulders, over his long tunic. He had the wrinkled skin of an elderly man and the brown moles and blotches of advancing age, but there was no sign of injury, other than the blow to the head. De Wolfe stood up, and looked around the room again. 'You say he lived in the next chamber?'

The Saxon outside the window nodded. 'He rents the rooms from Edmund Pace, a cloth merchant who uses the rest of the house as a store for his bales. I think it's a sub-letting, as the building belongs to the Church.'

'Let's have a look next door,' commanded the coroner, and led the way through the other doorway into the back room. This was as black as pitch, but de Wolfe saw a crack of daylight in the back wall and, stumbling over a dead fire-pit in the centre, reached a small window with a tight-fitting shutter. When he pounded on it with the heel of his hand, it flew open to reveal a narrow alley at the back of the house, which opened twenty paces on into Palace Lane, the next connection between Southgate Street and the cathedral Close.

'Like a damned rabbit warren, this city,' grunted Gwyn.

His master was looking at the surround of the window. 'I doubt any killer came in or out this way,' he grunted. 'The shutter was jammed tight and the dirt on the sill hasn't been disturbed for years.' He turned to view the room, as mean a chamber as the one where the dead Jew lay. A ring of stones in the centre surrounded a depression lined with clay, filled with ashes. A blackened cooking pot sat at one side and a three-legged stool bore a wooden tray with a dented pewter plate and an earthenware cup. Against one wall was a table, with a loaf of bread, a jug of milk and a few shrivelled apples, alongside a knife and a horn spoon. Two rough shelves hung on the wall above the table, carrying a pot of salt, some dried herbs and a dish of oatmeal.

On the opposite side of the room, the moneylender's bed consisted of a long hessian bag stuffed with hay, lying on planks supported by four large stones to keep it clear of the damp floor. The only other furniture was a large oak chest, secured by a stout hasp and a padlock.

De Wolfe looked around with distaste mingled with pity. 'Fancy having to live in hovel like this. He must have come down in the world – he can't have been making much profit from his usury.' He bent down and rattled the lock on the chest. 'Best have a look in here – did he have a key on him?'

Gwyn went back to the other room to search the corpse. When he came back, he was followed by a small, painfully thin figure dressed in a long black threadbare tunic. The new arrival had one hunched shoulder and walked with a slight limp. 'Look what's blown in, Crowner – our noble clerk!'

The Cornishman's sarcasm was laced with affection, for Thomas de Peyne was going through a difficult time. Last month he had attempted to kill himself during a fit of depression over his continued failure to be re-admitted to his beloved Church. Even that had turned into a fiasco, when his clothing caught on a water-spout as he jumped from the cathedral parapet.

De Wolfe nodded curtly at Thomas, then held out a hand for the key Gwyn had found tied to the money-lender's belt. He used it to open the chest, when he found two bags, similar to the one that had been over Aaron's head. They were both filled with coin and there was another thick book filled with lines of neat writing: de Wolfe handed it to his highly literate clerk. 'I presume this is a record of his business, eh?'

Thomas rapidly scanned a few pages. 'Yes, Crowner. He has names, dates and the amount of the loan, as well as when it was paid back.' His reedy voice ended in a whistle. 'A good business to be in, judging by the difference between the loan and the repayment.' He handed the book back to the coroner, who was peering inside the money bags.

'Quite a few pounds in here – robbery certainly wasn't the motive.'

'Maybe the killer was disturbed before he could find the key?' countered Gwyn.

'Then why didn't he grab the coins from the floor next door? There must be a few shillings' worth there.'

De Wolfe locked the chest, stood up and slipped the key into the purse hanging from his belt. 'Let's have another look next door.'

They trooped back into the front room, where the constable was still stationed outside the window to keep away curious eyes. The fletcher had vanished, and the three members of the coroner's team stood around the body, staring at it as if urging it to tell them what had happened.

Thomas's eyes roved around the room, taking in details of the bare chamber. Always insatiably curious, his long thin nose seemed to point like that of a hunting dog, and the squint in his left eye was accentuated as he turned his head slowly back and forth. Though unfrocked from the priesthood several years before, he still affected a tonsure, the shaven patch surrounded by lustreless black hair.

'Better get the body carted up to the castle,' growled the coroner. 'It can go into one of the store sheds until we hold the inquest.'

His officer looked puzzled. 'What do we do with Jews, then? They can't be buried in the Close.'

Everyone who died in Exeter had to be buried in the cathedral precinct, unless their relatives purchased a dispensation to inter them at some other church outside the city. The cathedral jealously guarded this additional source of revenue for the funeral Mass and the sixpence for the grave-pit digger, but of course it could not apply to the body of a Jew.

'Let's see what his relatives have to say. He has a daughter, according to the constable. We may have to bury him temporarily outside the walls, in the Jew's plot, if he's not claimed within a day or two.'

De Wolfe turned to leave, but Gwyn pointed to the overturned table, where coins had slid on to the floor. 'What about that money? We can't leave all those split pennies on display in an empty house.'

De Wolfe ran a hand over the black stubble on his face as he considered the matter. 'Best collect them up and put them in that chest next door.'

As he fished in his purse for the key, de Wolfe remembered the scrap of parchment in the dead man's hand, rooted again in his pouch, then handed it to his clerk. 'What does this say, Thomas? Is it something more about lending money?'

The little clerk walked delicately around the stiffened corpse. The familiarity with violent death that had been forced on him since his appointment as coroner's assistant had not lessened his squeamishness. He studied the brief note, then crossed himself and looked up at his master with a puzzled expression. 'It's a quotation from the Bible, Crowner – if I remember rightly, from the Gospel according to the Blessed St Mark.'

CHAPTER TWO

In which Crowner John listens to the Gospel

Half an hour later, the three men climbed Castle Hill, which led up from the eastern end of the high street to Rougemont. This was the local name for the fortress of red stone built by the Conqueror at the highest point of the city, in the north-east angle of the old Roman walls.

The coroner and his officer strode energetically across the short drawbridge over the dry moat, while the clerk limped despondently behind. Once under the raised portcullis of the tall gatehouse, they turned left into the guardroom and climbed a narrow staircase in the thickness of the wall to the topmost floor, where de Wolfe had his office. This was the smallest and most uncomfortable chamber that his brother-in-law, Sir Richard de Revelle, the sheriff, had been able to find for him. It was still early, less than two hours after a May dawn, but as usual Gwyn was ready to eat. Though John was himself a good trencherman, his appetite paled into insignificance alongside that of his officer, who needed to stoke his huge body at frequent intervals.

This morning, with a halved penny from the coroner, Gwyn had bought three meat pies, a loaf of barley bread and a chunk of hard cheese from the stalls on their way back from Southgate Street. Now he spread these on the coroner's trestle table, pushing aside some parchment rolls of recent inquests as he did so. A bench and two stools made up the whole furniture of the bare chamber, which had two slit embrasures looking down on Exeter. The doorway at the head of the stairway was hung with sacking to block some of the draughts.

By the time Thomas de Peyne entered, the other two were working at the food, washing it down with rough cider that Gwyn produced from a gallon crock that stood in a corner. The sad-looking clerk refused the pie Gwyn pushed towards him and contented himself with a slice of bread and a pottery cup half filled with cider. While the jaws of the other pair champed rhythmically, Thomas sat on his stool and stared glumly at the rough boards of the table, his lips working in some silent conversation with himself.

Gwyn broke the rejected pie in two and gave half to his master. There was a further delay until the last of the food had been washed down with the acidulous cider, then after a final belch, de Wolfe got back to business. He turned his dark, glowering face towards his clerk. 'Now then, Thomas, explain to me again what you meant about that message – from the beginning.'

Rousing himself from his reverie, the former priest fumbled in the brown leather shoulder bag that held his writing materials and came out with the ragged scrap of parchment. Though John could now write his name and read a few simple sentences in Latin, anything more than this was meaningless to him and he waited for his clerk to explain.

'As I thought, the writing is a direct quotation from the middle of St Mark's Gospel,' said Thomas quietly.

De Wolfe nodded, but Gwyn was mystified. 'So what does that tell us – the name of the killer?'

For answer, Thomas again burrowed in his bag and brought out his most prized possession, a leatherbound manuscript Vulgate, given to him by his father when he was ordained, long before his shameful ejection from the Church. He turned over the pages reverently until he found the place he wanted. 'I was right, my memory didn't play false,' he exclaimed, with a momentary return of his old enthusiasm.

Gwyn groaned. 'Have we got to listen to a damned sermon now?' he demanded.

De Wolfe was well aware of the Cornishman's antipathy to religion, though even after twenty years as a close companion, he had never discovered the cause of Gwyn's phobia for the Church.

Thomas ignored the interruption and began to read from the Gospel, translating the Latin as he went. ' "And Jesus went into the temple and began to cast out them that sold and bought and overthrew the tables of the money-changers." ' He closed the book and looked up at de Wolfe. 'A most appropriate text in the circumstances, Crowner.'

Gwyn snorted. 'The Jew was a money-lender, not a money-changer. And how does it help us to catch the killer?'

John was more appreciative of his clerk's acumen. 'It's near enough – and the table was overturned. Well done, Thomas.'

The little man's depression lifted a little: praise was rare from his master's lips, which made it all the more welcome when it came. 'As for being in the temple, that house does belong to the cathedral Chapter,' he said. 'It opens into the cathedral precinct at the back, which is near enough to having a money-trader and usurer on ecclesiastical premises.'

Gwyn drank deeply and wiped cider from his moustache with the back of his hand. 'Which tells us nothing about who did it,' he objected.

De Wolfe shook his head. 'You're wrong. It tells us

that the killer could read and write, *and* that he knew his Bible. Which strongly suggests a priest.'

Thomas nodded in agreement. 'And perhaps a senior cleric, for some of the ignorant parish priests can't put two words together and know as much about the scriptures as this hairy monster here.' He dodged a playful swipe from the Cornishman.

De Wolfe's brooding face stared ruminatively through the nearest window slit. 'But why would he want to leave such a sign behind him? And why did he want to kill the old fellow? It certainly wasn't a robbery.'

'Perhaps if he owed a lot of money to the Jew, it was a way to avoid repayment,' suggested Thomas, 'and the interest on the loan, which from that account book looked as if it was more than a fifth of its value per year.'

Gwyn whistled. 'At that rate of usury, I'd be tempted to kill, too.'

The clerk snorted. 'Some lenders charge much more than that,' Thomas averred. 'I've heard of as much as sixty pence in the pound – and not all from Jews, either.'

'I thought all moneylenders were Jews,' grunted the Cornishman. 'That's all they can do, isn't it, for they are banned from other trades? And doesn't the Church forbid Christians to become usurers?'

The coroner shook his head. 'The Templars are probably the biggest moneylenders in Christendom – though mostly on a grand scale to kings and princes. And there are some Englishmen, too. There was William Cade in old King Henry's time, and we still have Gervase of Southampton.'

Thomas was mumbling something under his breath and Gwyn grabbed the back of his collar, lifting him from his stool. 'What are you saying, dwarf?'

Shaking himself free, the clerk snapped indignantly, 'I was quoting the Bible again – Deuteronomy this time.'

'And how does that help us solve a murder?' chaffed the Cornishman.

'It shows that he wasn't killed by a relative or even another Jew – the Old Testament says, "Unto a stranger thou mayest lend upon usury, but unto thy brother thou shalt not."'

'Well, no one's suggesting that he was killed by a relative, fool!' Gwyn rumbled.

De Wolfe had grown impatient at this bickering between his helpers. 'Come, now, both of you, the man was killed during the night, so with the city gates shut, it has to have been someone in the city. And Thomas is right. It seems likely that some priest is at the bottom of this, with his writing and his knowledge of scripture.'

As an aid to thought Gwyn tugged at the ends of his drooping moustache. 'So we need a clerk who is either a crazed killer or who hates Jews or who owes money to one.'

'Plenty of the last two groups about – and senior priests are often borrowing money,' observed Thomas. 'But why leave behind a clue?'

The coroner eyed him piercingly. 'You know all the priests in Exeter – is there a mad one among them?'

Thomas shrugged his hunched shoulder higher than usual. 'There's a few queer ones, to be sure, but I'd be hard put to say that one was a murderer.'

De Wolfe hauled himself to his feet and leaned his fists on the table, like some great black eagle. 'We won't discover anything by sitting here, that's for sure. I'm off to tell the damned sheriff what's happened, not that he'll be too concerned about it. Gwyn, I want that inquest organised by the time the bell rings for High Mass.' He flung his cloak loosely across his shoulders, stumped down from the chamber and walked across the inner ward of the castle towards the keep, a two-storeyed block built against the further curtain wall. The ground had dried out after a long, wet winter and, as he walked, his feet kicked up red dust mixed with animal droppings.

The castle ward was a cross between a military camp, a farmyard and a village, with huts and lean-to shelters all around the inside of the walls, housing families, armourers, carts, stables and all the paraphernalia of a castle in time of peace. There had not been an arrow fired or a sword clashed in anger here for half a century, since the civil war in the time of Stephen and Matilda. The castle was now mainly an administrative centre for the governance of the county of Devon, under its sheriff, Sir Richard de Revelle, the bane of John's life.

The previous year, de Revelle had almost come to grief on a charge of treachery, for supporting the rebellious cause of Prince John, younger brother of the monarch, Richard the Lionheart. De Wolfe, a passionately loyal supporter of the King, had had it in his power to ruin the sheriff – perhaps even have him hanged – but the intercession of Matilda on her brother's behalf had saved him. Yet de Revelle was still on probation for good behaviour and he resented John's hold over him rather than feeling gratitude to him for saving his neck.

But however much the coroner despised the sheriff, he was still the King's representative in the shire of Devon, responsible for law and order as well as collecting taxes. As county coroner, de Wolfe was obliged to keep him informed of serious crimes within their jurisdiction.

The hunched figure swept across the castle compound, brushing aside squawking geese, dogs and urchins from the garrison families, and skirting plodding ox-carts laden with hay for the soldier's horses or blocks of stone for the endless repairs to the high walls.

He clattered up the wooden steps to the first-floor

entrance of the keep and went into the main hall, a large chamber roofed by smoke-darkened beams and lit by high unglazed slit windows. Along with eating and drinking, much of the business of running the county was conducted here, between harassed clerks, merchants, lawyers, soldiers and tax collectors.

A small side door guarded by a bored man-at-arms led to the sheriff's quarters. The coroner gave a perfunctory nod to the man and marched through into an outer chamber that served as de Revelle's office; his dining room and bedchamber were beyond an inner door.

His brother-in-law was seated behind a trestle table covered with parchment rolls. Richard was a dapper man, with wavy brown hair and a neat, pointed beard. Always fastidious in dress, he wore a showy green tunic with elaborate gold embroidery around the neck. A darker green pelisse of heavy wool edged with brown fur was draped over the back of his chair.

A bald-headed scribe sat at one corner, scribbling furiously as the sheriff barked at him. On a small folding table near one of the two narrow window embrasures, another clerk wielded a pen over what seemed to be long lists of accounts.

De Revelle looked up impatiently at the visitor. 'It's you, John,' he growled, his tone emphasising that the visitor was far from welcome. 'The Justices are due next week and I've got to get all these documents ready for them. I hope you're not going to interrupt me.'

Ignoring the rudeness, de Wolfe perched himself on a corner of the table, making it creak ominously. 'You're not the only one who has to appear before the King's judges, Richard. I was appointed for the very purpose of presenting cases to them, remember?'

'Bloody nonsense!' muttered the sheriff. 'We managed very well before this new-fangled idea of having coroners.'

De Wolfe sighed, but refused to rise to the bait. Last autumn, Hubert Walter, Archbishop of Canterbury and King Richard's chief minister, had appointed knights in every county as coroners, partly to keep an eye on the sheriffs, who were notorious for lining their own purses at the expense of the Royal Exchequer. Richard de Revelle was no exception: he had been up to all kinds of trickery and embezzlement and now strongly resented having John's eagle eye upon him.

'We complained long enough about the delay in the Eyre getting to Devon, Richard, so we can't complain now that it's actually coming.'

The sheriff nodded reluctantly. 'At least we can clear the prison – hang a few people and get them out of the way.' He shuffled his parchments impatiently. 'Did you come just to talk about the Eyre?'

De Wolfe ran his hands over his long hair. 'I came to tell you there's a strange killing in the city overnight – Aaron, the Jewish moneylender.'

The sheriff managed to look supremely uninterested. 'Never heard of him,' he said. 'Why are you telling me this?'

'Because I think a priest killed him. And the death was on cathedral property.'

Richard de Revelle scowled and tapped his fingers on the table in irritation. 'Then surely this is a matter for the bishop or his Chapter,' he snapped impatiently.

De Wolfe shook his head. 'In matters of murder and violence, you know well enough that Henry Marshal has handed his jurisdiction to us,' he said evenly. He explained about the biblical text and the fact that someone who could read and write must have been the culprit.

His brother-in-law frowned and pointedly picked up a parchment roll. 'Then you must look for a mad priest,

John,' he said offhandedly. 'Was there no hue and cry raised?'

'What was the point? His body was found almost stone cold this morning so it happened during the night.'

'The bishop has his proctors patrolling the precinct and the Portreeves have their constables on the streets. What do you expect me to do about it? I thought you and your inquests were meant to ferret out these matters,' de Revelle snapped.

The coroner sighed again and got up to leave. He could see that his brother-in-law had not the slightest interest in this particular item of law-enforcement, for which the sheriff was ultimately responsible in every county. He made one last effort as he made for the door. 'This is no ordinary killing, Richard. A priest must surely be involved and I feel in my bones that we haven't heard the last of him.'

De Revelle looked up at him, his cold eyes signalling his dislike. 'John, if it's a mad priest you're seeking, you needn't look further than your own clerk. I hear he tried to kill himself the other day, but maybe he's turned his attention to others.'

De Wolfe growled in his throat and slammed the door as he went out.

CHAPTER THREE

In which Crowner John visits the Bush Inn

De Wolfe had instructed Gwyn earlier to round up all those involved in the discovery of the moneylender's body and have them at the Shire Hall in Rougemont by the tenth hour of the morning.

He arrived at the bare stone building as the distant cathedral bell was tolling for High Mass, the sixth of the nine daily services. The hall was the venue for the sheriff's fortnightly County Court and would also house the long-awaited Eyre of Assize and General Eyre the following week. John used it for most inquests in the city: desolate though it was, at least it provided a roof over his head. An open archway led into a large barren chamber, with an earth floor and a knee-high wooden platform at one end, with trestle tables, stools and a high-backed chair favoured by the sheriff. De Wolfe hoped that de Revelle and the castle constable, Ralph Morin, would make some effort before next week to improve the place for the King's Justices. However, it was adequate for the brief inquest that he was obliged to hold on the money-lender.

As he arrived, Gwyn was marshalling a score of men in front of the platform, cursing good-naturedly and pushing them into a ragged line. These were the jury, dragged reluctantly from their daily work in Southgate

Street. As John climbed on to the dais and sat down, he saw that the fletcher who had found the body and the Saxon constable were present, along with a couple more faces he recognised as having been at the scene of the death. Thomas de Peyne was seated at a table, already pulling out his ink, pens and parchments.

De Wolfe yawned as he waited for Gwyn to get organised – he had been roused from his bed earlier than usual and was beginning to feel the effects. As the gingery giant harassed the motley crowd into some sort of order, a garrison soldier arrived with a small handcart, on which a long shape was covered with a coarse cloth. The man wheeled it into the hall and left it immediately below the coroner, where he sat in the centre of the platform. 'Here's the corpse, Crowner. I was told to bring him from our cart-shed.'

De Wolfe nodded and the man-at-arms left, passing a rather dandified figure in the archway. De Wolfe was surprised to see that the newcomer was Hugh de Relaga, one of Exeter's two Portreeves, the leaders of the city burgesses. Some cities were now electing mayors, but although there was talk of it, Exeter had not done so yet. The short, rotund merchant strutted to the platform and hauled himself up to sit on a stool alongside the coroner.

'What brings you here, Hugh?' asked John, with one of his rare grins. 'You should be in your counting house, increasing our fortune.' He and the Portreeve had a wool-exporting business with a warehouse on the quayside. De Wolfe played no part in the trading, but had invested in it much of the loot he had accumulated in foreign campaigns, and the burgess's skill in buying and selling made them both a comfortable profit each year.

The fat little merchant was puffing with the exertion of hurrying up to the castle and produced a yellow silk kerchief to mop his brow. 'I heard about Aaron's murder from our constable. He lent money to a number of tradesmen in the city, including one or two burgesses, I suspect.'

De Wolfe looked down at him from his chair. 'I doubt he was killed because of any money transactions, Hugh. He certainly wasn't robbed.'

De Relaga, resplendent even at mid-morning in a scarlet tunic and a blue mantle, with a close fitting helmet of red silk tied under his chin with tapes, dabbed at his face. 'Thank God for that, John. I was afraid that some debtor had decided to cancel the loan by beating him to death.'

By now, Gwyn was yelling for silence and when the jurymen and witnesses had quietened down, he yelled out the Royal Summons in a voice that sent the starlings flapping from the roof-beams: 'Anyone having anything to do before the King's coroner for the county of Devon touching the death of Aaron of Salisbury, draw near and give your attendance!'

The jurymen shuffled uncomfortably, raising dust which danced in the shafts of bright sunlight that struck through the archway. De Wolfe leaned forward, like some great black bird about to strike with the long beak of his nose. 'Let the First Finder step forward.'

The small man who had visited the Jew early that morning was prodded by Gwyn to stand alongside the death cart, just beneath the forbidding figure of the coroner. He confirmed that he was Rufus Fletcher, and when Gwyn lifted the cloth over the cadaver's face, he identified the dead man as Aaron of Salisbury. Then he repeated the story he had told de Wolfe a few hours earlier. '. . . I knocked up the four nearest householders, then sent for the constable,' he concluded virtuously. Here he paused to consider the safest course, then added, 'We didn't start a hue-and-cry, Crowner. It was pointless as the old fellow was as stiff as plank so he must have been dead for hours.'

This echoed what de Wolfe had told the sheriff, and after a few more questions, which produced nothing useful, the arrow-maker stepped back thankfully into the crowd, relieved that he hadn't been amerced for some legal transgression, which had become so common at inquests as to be almost a routine form of taxation.

The coroner looked over his shoulder to check that Thomas de Peyne was keeping the record, then turned back to his captive audience. 'As to presentment of Englishry, it is both impossible and unnecessary,' he barked. 'It is well known that the dead man was a Jew, which is sufficient for the law.'

Since the Conquest, anyone found dead was presumed to be a Norman and a heavy 'murdrum' fine imposed on the surrounding community as a penalty for assassinating one of the invaders. The process was fast becoming ridiculous, as it was well over a century since the Normans had seized England and it was increasingly difficult to define who was a Norman, rather than a Saxon or Celt. However, the fines were a lucrative source of income to the Crown and the only way they could be avoided was for the family of the deceased to swear before the coroner that he was English. De Wolfe took a fair, common-sense view of the issue, unlike some coroners who would do their utmost to extract the fine, especially if they could divert some of it into their own purse.

Now de Wolfe gestured to Gwyn, who again dragged the covering from the upper part of the old man's corpse, then walked to the edge of the dais, with Hugh de Relaga peering inquisitively alongside him.

'You jurymen, gather round,' he commanded, in his

sonorous voice. 'You have a duty to examine the cadaver with me, every one of you.'

The jury shuffled closer, some of them rheumy old men, others just lads; all males over the age of ten were eligible for this service.

'Gwyn, lift up his head!'

The officer grabbed the ears of the corpse and lifted it clear of the table. Rigor mortis had stiffened the neck and the shoulders rose from the cart, so that the matted blood at the back of the head was visible to the gaping jury.

'He has had a grievous blow to the cranium,' declared John. 'There seems to be no breakage of the bone, but certainly he would have lost his senses.' He motioned to Gwyn, who let the head drop with a thump.

'Show them the bag,' he commanded. Gwyn reached under the legs of the body, pulled out the leather money-bag and held it up to show the jury, pushing a fist inside to display how wide and deep it was.

'This pouch was over his head, the drawstrings tightened about his neck.' He gestured again to Gwyn, who handed the leather bag to the nearest member of the jury, who took it gingerly, as if it might bite him. As it was passed from hand to hand, de Wolfe continued, 'You will see that it is strong and has tight seams. It would easily have cut off the victim's air, especially if he was out of his wits from the blow on his head and could do nothing to save himself.'

Gwyn retrieved the money-bag, restored it to the cart, then covered up the old man for decency's sake. The jury gaped up at the coroner, waiting for the finale of his performance.

'I have no other evidence to offer you,' rasped de Wolfe, who had decided to omit the news about the Gospel text as being none of their concern. 'Now, does any man among you know anything useful about the death of this man?' He glared along the row of faces huddled around the handcart. He expected the jury to provide information as well as a verdict.

There were a few muttered denials. The less any man became involved with the law, the safer it was for him. Every step of the legal process was beset with penalties if things went wrong.

'Did any of you know anything of Aaron's life? Some of you were traders in that street and must know something of him,' snapped de Wolfe. He glared at the man Gwyn had appointed foreman, a cloth merchant from a shop near the Jew's house. 'You, surely you had some knowledge of him?'

The serge-trader shrugged dismissively. 'I knew him slightly, Crowner, just to pass the time of day. He kept very much to himself.'

'All his clients came to him so he didn't need to venture out much,' added a stall-holder from Southgate Street. 'Some of us borrowed a few marks from him when times were difficult. He was a fair man, given the trade he was in.'

There were murmurs of agreement.

'Anything else? Was there ever any trouble in his shop? Did anyone ever attack or threaten him?'

There was silence as each man looked at his neighbour and shook his head.

'Do you know if any priests were customers of his?' demanded the coroner.

This obscure question was met with some blank stares, and a few titters.

The stall-holder spoke up again. 'It would be a strange usurer who didn't have clerks as clients, Crowner. Some of our canons have expensive tastes in food and wine.'

'And women!' came a hoarse whisper from behind someone's hand.

'People who patronise Aaron and his like don't wish

to advertise their visits,' the foreman went on. 'They tend to slink into his doorway like a fox into a culvert, for there's shame in being short of money.'

A few more questions soon confirmed de Wolfe's expectations that nothing new would be learned, so he directed the jury briefly as to their verdict: 'This inquest has established that the deceased was Aaron of Salisbury and that he was not a Norman, even though no presentment of Englishry can be made. It is also obvious that he met his death in his domicile in this city of Exeter on . . .' He paused and cleared his throat noisily, while he turned to flick his fingers at Thomas who was writing busily. 'On whatever date it is, in the seventh year of the reign of King Richard.' He jutted his chin at the jury as if challenging them to contradict him, then concluded, in a loud voice, 'It is obvious that he died of a blow to the pate and mortal suffocation from that bag being tied over his head. That cannot be an Act of God, or an accident or self-inflicted, so it has to have been murder.'

He raised his voice almost to a shout at the end and glared at the cluster of citizens below him. 'Now give me your verdict, foreman.'

There was a hurried hissing of whispers. Then the cloth merchant raised his face to the coroner. 'We find it was murder, Sir John, by persons unknown.'

After the unsurprising result, the jury hurried away, eager to make up for an hour of lost business, while Gwyn trundled the handcart back to the shed on the opposite side of the inner ward. In the Shire Hall, John de Wolfe and Hugh de Relaga sat down at the trestle table to wait while Thomas completed the inquest roll in his impeccable script.

'This is a strange business, John, if you say that the old fellow wasn't robbed,' said de Relaga. He knew most of the commercial gossip of the city, being a Guild

Master as well as a leader of the council, and the abrupt cancellation of debts, now that the lender was defunct, might help several of his fellow merchants. 'Had you better go through his ledgers, John, to see if anyone might have profited considerably by his death?'

De Wolfe had already decided to ask Thomas to do this, but he felt obliged to tell his friend about the parchment found on the body. 'So it looks as if some aggrieved priest might have killed him,' he finished.

The wool-merchant dabbed again at his round, red face. 'That could be a bluff, John, making it look like some deranged cleric to cover up the real purpose of escaping from a money bond.'

John shrugged. 'It could be, I suppose. But how many of your burgess friends can read, write and quote the Gospels?'

'Many can pen a few words or have some clerk who is more proficient – not all accounting is done on tally-sticks these days. But I admit you have a point. Few of my acquaintances could quote you more than two lines from the Holy Book.'

When Thomas was ready to pack up his writing materials, the coroner and his gaudy friend stepped down from the platform and strolled outside into the spring sunshine. As they crossed the castle bailey towards the gatehouse, Hugh reflected again on the death of the moneylender. 'What will you do with the corpse? He obviously can't be buried in the cathedral Close like everyone else.'

'I'm going down to see the Archdeacon now. He's most likely to know about such things.'

'Has the old man got relatives? I seem to remember that the Jews have strict rules about quick burials. There are a few others of his faith in the city that could be asked.'

'There is a daughter in Honiton. The castle sergeant

sent a messenger this morning to seek her out, but even if he finds her, she'll not get to Exeter before tomorrow.'

They walked in silence, until de Relaga spoke again. 'This note from the scriptures . . . Is it possible to name a man from his penmanship?'

De Wolfe stopped in his tracks and looked down at the Portreeve. 'I don't know, Hugh – I've never thought about it. Isn't all script much the same?' As neither man could write more than his name, differences in handwriting were outside the experience of both.

'I'll ask that snivelling clerk of mine,' said John. 'He knows all about pens and parchment and suchlike. Though how we'd go about such a test is beyond me.'

It was approaching the time for the midday meal and when they reached the corner of Martin's Lane, de Relaga trotted off to his comfortable house near Carfoix to enjoy his usual large dinner.

De Wolfe walked past his own home, glancing furtively at the door in case Matilda appeared. He carried on past the farrier's opposite, where his horse Odin was stabled, then continued across the front of St Martin's church on the corner of the Close. Though he saw the small building several times a day, he looked at it now with renewed interest, as he had at every one of the parish churches he had passed that day. Did this one house a murderous priest, he wondered.

He loped past the first few houses of Canon's Row, which was the continuation of Martin's Lane forming the northern boundary of the Close, with the huge bulk of the cathedral towering above him to his right. His gaze rose unbidden to the narrow builder's gallery that ran along the outside of the nave, just below roof level and almost forty feet above the ground. Just before it met the massive projection of the North Tower, there was still a faint pale smear running down the masonry, where Thomas's cloak had rubbed off some of the lichen from the stones when he had made his unsuccessful suicide bid some weeks earlier. If that garment had not snagged on a protruding water-spout halfway down and broken his fall . . .

De Wolfe sighed at the memory, and forged on past the large, closely packed houses until he reached the dwelling of Archdeacon John de Alençon. There were four archdeacons, each responsible for one part of the huge diocese of Devon and Cornwall. De Alençon's responsibility was the city of Exeter, the most populous area with some four thousand inhabitants served by those numerous parish churches.

The house was tall and narrow, and stretched back a long way to the yard behind, with a privy, kitchen-shed and laundry-hut. The canons' houses were all different, with varying frontages and roofs, but all were spacious enough to accommodate a priest, sometimes his vicar, and a number of servants.

The canons were expected to offer hospitality to visitors and to hold regular feasts for the benefit of prominent citizens and senior clergy. Many enjoyed this festive existence, being fond of luxuries and good living. The Spartan precepts of Bishop Leofric who, in the previous century, had introduced the strict Rule of St Chrodegang had long been forgotten by most, but John de Alençon was an exception. An ascetic man, he kept his house simply furnished, had but three servants and, apart from a moderate appreciation of fine French wine, appeared free of vices.

His bottler showed de Wolfe into the Archdeacon's study, which was also his bedroom. The only furniture was a pallet in one corner, a plain table with two chairs and a large wooden crucifix on the wall. De Alençon rose from the table where he had been studying a bulky leatherbound book. His thin face broke into a warm smile as he greeted his friend, the lined brow and cheeks lit up by the bright blue eyes. He grasped de Wolfe's arm in welcome, and motioned to his servant to bring wine.

Moments later, they were seated across the table from each other, a cup of best Anjou red in their hands, with a stone jug between them for replenishment.

'How is that poor nephew of mine faring?' asked de Alençon.

'I sometimes fear for his sanity,' said John. 'He's taken to talking to himself a lot and he glares at the world as if he hates its very existence – but at least he's not tried to kill himself lately.' He took a long sip from his cup, savouring the flavour of the French grapes. 'I suppose you've heard nothing more about any possibility of his being received back into the Church?'

The Archdeacon shook his head sadly. 'As I told you before, John, it seems quite impossible. There are forces working against him because they wish to see you shamed.' There was a short silence as he refilled their cups then looked at his friend with a quizzical smile. 'But you didn't come here to talk about Thomas?'

The coroner shook his head. 'I have a couple of questions for you. You're always a fount of knowledge when I need it.'

The senior cleric smiled gently. Painfully thin, his plain black cassock fell loosely about his narrow shoulders. The short, crinkled hair that covered his head was grey, though he was barely a dozen years older than de Wolfe's forty summers.

'I'll do what I can, John. I doubt you wish to discuss theology.'

The coroner's first question was about the burial of the murdered Jew.

'I've heard about the killing,' replied the Archdeacon. 'That house belongs to our Chapter. The Treasurer's clerk was muttering this morning that, as a tenant, the cloth merchant had no right to rent out those rooms.' He rubbed his long thin nose. 'I claim no real knowledge of Jewish funeral rites. I expect you know as well as I that they do their utmost to bury their dead before the next nightfall.'

'That's impossible in this case,' replied de Wolfe. 'We're waiting for the daughter to come from Honiton tomorrow.'

'Is it really impossible?' answered de Alençon gently. 'If she has the body taken away, the delay will be even greater. Why not bury it today? There are other Jews in Exeter who would gladly see to the arrangements.'

'The daughter may wish to see her father's body. And where can we bury him? Surely your Church would not welcome him in one of their grave-pits.'

De Alençon smiled sadly. 'Certainly that would be impossible. Unlike some of my brethren, I feel great sympathy for his race, especially since the tragic disgrace in York and other cities, which followed King Richard's Coronation. But there is now a small plot outside the walls in Southernhay which those of the Hebrew faith have purchased for a cemetery.'

The coroner chewed this over in his mind. 'Maybe I'll do that. Then his daughter can decide later what she wants done with him.'

De Alençon prompted his friend to ask the other question he had mentioned.

'The same issue, really,' replied de Wolfe. 'This old fellow's murder last night.' As he related the story of the Gospel quotation he fished in the pouch on his belt and handed over the creased scrap of parchment.

After de Alençon had studied it, he handed it back and gazed steadily at his friend. 'You're wondering who could write and quote the Scriptures, other than a priest?'

The coroner nodded. 'As usual, it was your nephew who spotted that straight away. Then Hugh de Relaga suggested that whoever wrote this might be traced by his penmanship. Is that possible?'

The Archdeacon pursed his lips dubiously. 'I've never considered the matter before, John, but when I was in Winchester years ago, I was in charge of the scriptorium for a while and I could certainly have put a name to the writer of each document from the style in which he used his quill.' He looked quizzically at de Wolfe.

'But where would you start? There must be over a hundred clerics in Exeter, counting all the canons, vicars-choral and parish priests. Even the young secondaries and some of the choristers can read and write, you know.'

'I doubt we need to consider the juniors in this. You are the Archdeacon of Exeter, so you must know all the parish priests. Are any of them strange or unstable?'

De Alençon smiled wryly. 'We have our share of peculiar people in the Church, just as in any other walk of life, but no one that I would consider a potential killer.'

The coroner waved the parchment at him before he tucked it back into his belt-pouch. 'What do you read into this, then? Is the perpetrator following some godly command from the Bible that he casts out the moneylender from the temple? And is he likely to go on cleaning up the city, like some holy vigilante?'

The Archdeacon shrugged. 'Perhaps he just hates Jews, which is not uncommon now in England.'

They discussed the affair until the wine jug ran dry and John's stomach told him it was past time now for the midday meal.

He left the Archdeacon pondering on potentially wayward priests in his diocese and made his way back the short distance to the house in Martin's Lane. When he entered his high, sombre hall, Matilda was already well into her dinner, seated at one end of the long oak table that was the main item of furniture in the gloomy chamber. She was ladling more of Mary's hare stew from an earthenware pot into a wooden bowl, but paused to glower up at her husband as he sat down opposite. 'You were late, as usual, so I began without you,' she snapped. Along with religion, eating was Matilda's main interest in life. Her appetite almost equalled Gwyn's.

Mary came in with more bread and a quart of ale for her master, who drew a small knife from his belt and, with the aid of a large spoon carved from a cow's horn, loaded his own bowl with stew. They ate silently for a few minutes, until John felt obliged to start a conversation, if only to fend off the sulky cloud that he sensed appearing over his wife's head.

He told her about the murder of the moneylender that morning, which failed to grab her interest: Matilda classed Jews with Saxons and Celts as beneath the consideration of a Norman lady. Though she had been born in Devon and had spent but a few months of her forty-six years with distant relatives across the Channel, she acted as if she was a high-born Norman in exile in this inferior land. It was a matter of shame to her that even her husband was part Celt, his mother half Welsh and half Cornish.

However, when John came to the part of the story about the Gospel text, Matilda's ears pricked up, for Church business was her favourite subject. Suddenly he remembered that she had a compendious knowledge of Exeter's clergy, which might be useful to him. 'The Archdeacon agrees with me, that the most likely culprit is a priest. Can you think of any cleric in the city who might be evil enough to do this?'

He had phrased his question badly, for she bridled at his words. 'Indeed, I do not! They are almost all devout and righteous men – some are saints.' She was incensed that her irreligious husband should cast such aspersions on her heroes.

Then her tone became a little less harsh. 'Admittedly, there are some priests whose characters leave something to be desired. A few are fond of drink or women – though those failings are shared by most men,' she added sarcastically. 'But a murderer among our clergy? Never!'

But her husband sensed she was not as emphatic as her words implied and persisted in his question. 'But who among them might have some hidden vice, do you think?'

Flattered against her better judgement to be asked for her opinion about her beloved priests, she twisted her square face into a grimace of concentration. 'Well, Robert Cheever of St Petroc is certainly too fond of the wine cask. He has been helped to his lodgings more than once after falling in the street,' she answered grudgingly. 'And Peter Tyler of St Bartholomew's lives in sin with that old hag who cleans the church. What he sees in her is beyond my comprehension.' Warming to her theme she dipped deeper into the vat of gossip, filled by her cronies at St Olave's. 'I did hear tell, though there's no proof, that Ranulph Burnell of Holy Trinity was overly fond of the young choristers at the cathedral.'

She threw down her spoon with a clatter. 'But that's no reason to suspect any of them of being a killer. Maybe you and the Archdeacon would be better employed in looking among some of the canons and their vicars down in the Close – there's some odd characters there, God knows.'

Matilda glared at her husband and threw a final jibe at him, which echoed her brother's remark earlier that day.

'And if you are really seeking a weird priest, why look further than that perverted clerk of yours!'

There was a silence while Mary cleared the bowls and set down a dish of raisins imported from France. When she left, with a sly wink at John from beyond her mistress's back, he once again pulled out the piece of parchment from his purse and showed it to his wife, still hoping to coax her away from her threatened black mood. 'This was left with the corpse.'

She studied it, although like her husband she was unable to read it, as only one person in a hundred was literate. He explained the translation that Thomas had given him, that it was an apt quotation from the Gospel according to St Mark. 'You don't need to tell me, I know the passage well,' she snapped, but she held the scrap of palimpsest reverently for a moment, then handed it back.

'It may be possible to match the handwriting with whoever scribed it,' he observed. 'Only a priest would think of a trick like this and have the ability to write it.'

Grudgingly, she agreed. 'One of the law clerks or my brother's scribes could write the words but probably only a cleric would know the text.' Now hooked on the mystery, Matilda had a new thought. 'That's obviously a copy made from a Gospel, isn't it?'

Her husband stared at her, not understanding.

'Yes, there's blank space above and below it, nothing else,' he said. 'It's not an actual leaf from a Bible.'

'Then it must have been penned by a priest,' she brayed triumphantly. 'An unholy layman might have torn the page from a Vulgate, but a priest would revere the Holy Book too much to desecrate it. And he would know that copies of the Gospel are precious and expensive. He must have copied the passage out, even at the risk of having his script recognised.'

De Wolfe grunted his acceptance of her reasoning, though as he had assumed all along that the culprit was in Holy Orders, her assurance took him no further in identifying the villain. After a few more minutes of profitless discussion, Matilda abruptly pushed back her stool and announced that she was retiring to her solar for her customary nap before attending Vespers at St Olave's.

After she had stumped off to command Lucille to prepare her for her rest, John took his pot of ale to one of the cowled monk's chairs set alongside the hearth. Though the house was of timber, he had had this great stone fireplace, copied from one at a manor in France, constructed against the back wall. It was his pride and joy. Its tapering chimney rose up to the roof-beams to carry out the choking smoke that used to fill the chamber from the old fire-pit in the centre of the floor.

With his hound squatting alongside him to have his ears fondled, de Wolfe sat quietly until he judged that his wife would be snoring in their solar. Then, with a low whistle to Brutus, he left the hall, picked up a grey surcoat in the vestibule and let himself out into the lane. Taking the same route that he and Gwyn had followed at dawn, he went into the cathedral Close and strode along the rubbish-strewn paths between the grave-pits. Brutus loped hither and thither, sniffing at each pile of refuse and cocking his leg against every bush until they came through Bear Gate into the busy market street where the old Jew had died.

De Wolfe ignored the scene of the crime and dived into the lanes opposite, which led steeply down towards the river, where the West Gate and Water Gate lay. The alleys were crowded with the usual throng of porters carrying bales of wool, men pushing carts and barrows loaded with goods. Traders shouted the merits of their wares from their stalls, and hawkers pushed trays of sweetmeats, pies and trinkets under his nose. Beggars rattled coins in their bowls at him and cripples and blind men held out hands hopefully for alms.

As he went down the slope, the houses improved somewhat as the lane became Priest Street,* where most of the parish priests and many of the vicars and secondaries lodged. As he passed the narrow dwellings, John wondered if somewhere within them lurked a cleric of a murderous nature.

A short distance into the ecclesiastical ghetto, he turned right into Idle Lane, a short track leading across to the junction of Stepcote Hill and Smythen Street, where the smiths and metal-workers had their shops and forges. The lane's name came from the bare plot left by a fire some years ago, which had not yet been rebuilt. Only the Bush Inn had survived: its stone walls had resisted the fire that had engulfed its timber-built neighbours.

As he neared the tavern, de Wolfe's loping stride slowed and Brutus was now well ahead. De Wolfe, a tiger of the Crusades and a warrior afraid of no man, was fearful at the prospect of facing his former mistress, the landlady of the Bush. After falling out with her more than a month ago, he had avoided the tavern until now, but the thought of Nesta's sweet face – and an admitted ache in his loins – had helped him screw up enough courage to visit what had been almost his home-from-home. Yet as his dragging feet took him ever more slowly along the few yards of Idle Lane, he felt the unfamiliar signs of panic as he imagined a sharp confrontation with the comely Welsh woman. He stopped fifty paces from the inn and looked anxiously at it, as if he might be able to see through the walls and gauge what sort of reception he might have. The Bush was square, with a high steep thatch that came down

* *now Preston Street*

44

almost to head height. At the front there was a pair of windows, one to each side of the door, and along the wall nearest to him was a hitching rail for patrons' horses, which ran back to a gate into the yard behind. Here the kitchen shed, the brew-house and the wash-hut shared a dusty patch with the privy.

For a moment, he considered sneaking in through the back door to spy out the situation, but then his pride got the upper hand. With a muttered oath at his own foolishness, he strode to the heavy oak front door, over which hung a large bundle of twigs to indicate the tavern's name to its illiterate patrons.

With his dog at his heels, he ducked under the lintel and went inside. Immediately, nostalgia overtook him as he savoured the eye-smarting atmosphere of woodsmoke, spilt ale, stale sweat and cooking. When his eyes adjusted to the haze and the dim light from the shuttered windows, he saw that there were only a dozen or so people in the single big room: it was mid-afternoon and still quiet.

The murmur of conversation dropped as he walked to his favourite bench near the empty hearth. Heads turned, then drooped away to whisper to each other. The coroner's liaison with the inn-keeper was common knowledge, as was their recent rift, and his sudden reappearance was good fodder for gossip, but the other customers were careful not to whisper too loudly. They knew that the short-tempered knight was quite capable of cuffing the head of anyone he suspected of making personal remarks about him.

He dropped down on to the bench with Brutus against his knees under the rough table. Almost immediately, a clay pot containing a quart of ale was banged down on the scrubbed boards. 'Good to see you again, Cap'n,' wheezed the old potman, his one good eye swivelling independently of the horrible whiteness of the other, which had been speared, years before, at the battle of Wexford. De Wolfe had been in the same Irish campaign and old Edwin had great respect for him. De Wolfe grunted at him, though he was fond of the aged rascal, who was often a useful source of news.

'You're the only serving man here, these days, I hope?' he rasped.

Edwin grinned back, tapping the side of his pock-marked nose. 'She's not taken on any more young men from Dorset, that's for sure. Learnt her lesson, I reckon.' He looked furtively towards the back of the smoky room as he hissed the words.

'Where is she, then?' De Wolfe asked, gruffly to hide his unease.

'Upstairs, Cap'n. She spends a mortal lot of time in bed these days – on her own, though!' he added, with a leer, then limped away, his twisted leg another legacy of his days as a man-at-arms in Strongbow's army. John sat supping the ale, which was widely acknowledged to be the best in Exeter, thanks to Nesta's prowess in brewing. He turned on his bench to survey the room, half relieved that the auburn-haired landlady was not yet in sight. Most of the other drinkers, the majority of whom he knew well, were studiously avoiding his gaze, though one or two caught his eye and gave a nod.

As usual, there were a few strangers too, mostly merchants and craftsmen passing through the city. In a far corner, a few clustered around a table in the company of a couple of whores, who used the inns to pick up their clients. In a community of only a few thousand people, de Wolfe knew most of the harlots by sight, but one was new to him. She was a handsome, if somewhat raddled, girl of about twenty, noticeable because of her bright red wig, her low-cut scarlet kirtle, and the boldly striped hood of her green cloak, the trademark of a Southwark whore. He wondered why she was plying her trade so far from London. Still, he had had no need of strumpets since he had returned from the wars three years ago and his interest in her was merely passing curiosity.

His eyes moved to the back of the low chamber, where Edwin was drawing off ale and cider from a row of casks wedged up along the rear wall. Near him was a wide ladder that led to the upper floor beneath the roof. The sight of it triggered his nostalgia again. How many times had he climbed it, following Nesta to her tiny room, partitioned off from the open sleeping floor where the overnight guests rented a penny mattress? He had spent so many pleasant afternoons up there – and a few nights when he could arrange an alibi. He had even bought his mistress a fine French bed, a luxury indeed in a time when most folk slept on a palliasse on the floor.

The time went on, and de Wolfe was on his third jug of ale. There was still no sign of Nesta and soon his bladder complained of the quantity he had drunk. Rising, he went out through the back door and relieved himself against the rickety fence beyond the wash-house. On his return, he stopped alongside Edwin, who was pouring ale slops from a leather bucket back into one of the casks. 'No sign of the mistress, then? Does she often stay abed this long?'

'No telling what she'll do these days, Crowner. She's lost some of her spirit, I reckon, since that young bastard ran off with her money. She leaves much of the running of the tavern to the two wenches and myself.'

John rumbled in his throat, a sound that might have meant almost anything. 'I'll just finish my jar, then be off.' He decided he would stay until he heard the distant cathedral bell ring out for Vespers.

'Shall I tell her you were seeking her?'

De Wolfe shook his head, his face grim. 'If she's not down in a few minutes, forget I was here,' he said. When he slumped back on to his bench, even Brutus seemed to gaze up at him forlornly.

A few feet above his head, the landlady of the Bush was oblivious of his presence below her. She lay on the French bed in her shift, having pulled off her working gown and linen coif so that her mane of dark red hair flowed over the folded sheepskin that did service as a pillow.

As she stared up at the woven hazel branches that supported the thatch, her mind wandered for the thousandth time over the events of the past few weeks. Life seemed so flat and empty, a dull routine of brewing, cooking and chivvying the tavern servants. The brief excitement of Alan of Lyme had soon turned into shameful betrayal when he had run off with a week's takings and one of her maids. Her dalliance with him had been born partly of flattery from a smooth-tongued younger man but also as an act of defiance against John, whose devotion to his duties had come before his devotion to her.

She shifted uneasily on the woollen blankets, as she also admitted to herself that the break from him had been an acknowledgement of the hopelessness of their affair. He was a Norman knight and the second most senior law officer in the county, married to the sister of the sheriff. Though the marriage was a hollow shell, there was no way in which it could be broken – and even if Matilda were to die, what king's coroner would marry a lowly tavern-keeper?

Nesta tried to convince herself that she had ended the affair mainly for his sake, to rid him of the encumbrance of a common ale-house woman, but her heart told her that this was not true. She had been piqued that he had stayed away so much and for so long, and the sudden appearance of a good-looking young man, with his blandishments and flattery, had caught her at a vulnerable time.

Now she was regretting it deeply, especially as she had rejected John's clumsy attempts at reconciliation when Alan had decamped with her money and her prettiest servant. Her pride had provoked her into sending the coroner away, with a bitter message about their future. He had not been near her since and the passing weeks had made any hope of mutual forgiveness fade to nothing.

She was still young, barely twenty-eight, and knew she was as attractive a widow as could be found anywhere in the city. Had she so wished, she could have found a decent man without difficulty – one who would marry her and help her run the inn, as her Meredydd had done when they first came to Exeter. But the zest had ebbed from her life and as she lay staring up at the dusty rafters, she wondered if she should sell up and go home to Gwent, back to her own people.

Her eyes filled with tears of despair and self-pity, but she brushed them away angrily as she heard the cathedral bell tolling. It was time to pull herself together and get down to her neglected business. Swinging herself from the couch, she looped up her long hair and crammed it into the linen helmet, then stepped into her long green kirtle before trying an ankle-length hessian apron around her waist. By the time she had laced her shoes around her ankles and climbed down the ladder, the table near the hearth was empty.

CHAPTER FOUR

In which Crowner John rides to Sidmouth

The rest of the day passed peacefully enough for de Wolfe. While Matilda was praying at St Olave's, he went up to the castle again and spent a couple of hours on his reading lessons, which had been neglected during the busy past weeks. An older vicar from the cathedral had been coaching him sporadically for months, though Thomas de Peyne had achieved far more with him while de Wolfe had been laid up with a broken leg at the beginning of the year.

Now the coroner was trying to regain lost ground by silently mouthing the simple Latin phrases from the parchments supplied by the priest. Then he moved on to writing, but found that his lack of practice had set him back almost to where he had begun. He could still manage his name slowly with a sliver of chalk on a thin sheet of slate, but his attempts to pen the alphabet and Roman numerals on a piece of scrap vellum ended in a mess of ink scratches and splatter.

Impatiently, he threw down the quill and rammed the stopper back into Thomas's stone ink bottle. He stumped down the narrow spiral stairs to the guardroom below then went out into the city. He bought a hot pie from a booth at the bottom of Castle Hill and ate it between there and the Golden Hind, an inn on the high street near Martin's Lane. Since he had virtually abandoned the Bush as his regular drinking place, this had become John's local tavern and he stopped there for a pot of cider before going home to face Matilda's frosty face over the supper table. The midday meal was the main one of the day, but Mary always set out some hot gruel, bread, cheese and cold meat in the evening, with a jug of red wine, and this was waiting when he arrived home.

The pie had taken the edge off de Wolfe's appetite, but he sat down and ate a hunk of bread and a chicken leg to appease his wife, who was steadily working her way through everything on the table.

Depressed by his futile visit to the Bush, he studied his wife covertly from under his black eyebrows. What did the future hold for them, he wondered. Theirs had been a marriage of convenience and they had never been close, but as time had gone by, they had become more like two strangers lodging in the same house. His late father, Simon de Wolfe, who had two manors on Devon's south coast, had thought it a good move to marry his second son into the de Revelle family, who owned far more land. Matilda was six years older than John, and her father was happy to unload his plain daughter on to a young Norman knight, who was making a name for himself as an enterprising soldier. The deal was struck with little concern for the wishes of bride or groom.

That had been sixteen years ago and de Wolfe had regretted it ever since. Until recently, he had deliberately spent almost all of his time away, at the French and Irish wars and latterly at the Third Crusade, where he had become part of the bodyguard of King Richard himself. Until three years ago his time at home with his wife could be reckoned in months, but the catastrophe of the Lionheart's capture in Austria and long imprisonment had left John bereft of campaigns to fight.

Coming home, he had tried to settle down but boredom soon overcame him. He was comfortably off, due to his investment in Hugh de Relaga's wool business and a share in the profits of his late father's manors at Stoke-in-Teignhead and Holcombe, which were run by his elder brother William, but the tedium of this aimless life soon made him restless. Last year, he had even considered riding away again with Gwyn to find a war somewhere in France, preferably in the service of his king. Last autumn, though, a new opportunity had presented itself.

The huge ransom of a hundred and fifty thousand marks demanded by Henry of Germany for the release of Richard the Lionheart had thrown a massive burden on the Exchequer, added to by the King's constant demands for money to support his war against Philip of France. The task of raising these sums had fallen on the Chief Justiciar, Hubert Walter, who was now virtually Regent of England. Hubert had been the King's military deputy in the Holy Land and knew John de Wolfe well. The previous September, in a scheme to raise money, Hubert had re-established in every county the ancient Saxon office of coroner and had warmly supported de Wolfe's bid for one of the Devonshire vacancies.

In truth, de Wolfe himself had not been all that keen at first, but Matilda – as devoted to social climbing as she was to religion – had been adamant that he should grasp this chance to become a respected figure in the county hierarchy. As one of Hubert's objects in establishing coroners was for them to restrain the corruption of sheriffs, her brother was opposed to the whole idea, but Matilda had persuaded him that having his brother-in-law as coroner would be preferable to some more interfering stranger. Unfortunately for Richard de Revelle, the opposite turned out to be the case and ever since his appointment nine months earlier, de Wolfe had been a constant thorn in his side. His unswerving loyalty to his king and his refusal to indulge in the graft and embezzlement that was virtually a way of life to most senior officials, kept him endlessly in conflict with de Revelle.

All this marched again through John's mind as he watched Matilda finish her meal. She was a heavily built woman, with a short neck and a square face. Her small eyes had a slightly oriental look and the heavy pouches under them and the deep lines running down from her mouth gave her a permanently disgruntled expression. Matilda must have sensed his prolonged survey, for suddenly she looked up and glared at him. 'Are you any further with your latest murder?' she demanded.

He shook his head, his black hair bouncing on the collar of his grey tunic. 'The poor fellow's daughter is being brought in tomorrow morning. I had him buried in the Jew's plot in Southernhay until it's decided where he shall rest permanently.'

Matilda had no interest in dead Jews and abruptly changed the subject. 'I hear the Justices are due in the city very soon. I hope you'll assert the seniority of your office and not skulk in the background, as usual.'

'I'll do what my duties demand – no more, no less,' he grunted.

'I wonder where they will be lodged. Richard says there's no suitable accommodation for them in that miserable castle.'

That was true enough, thought John. Lady Eleanor, the sheriff's glacial wife, refused to live in that bleak fortress with her husband, preferring one of their manors at Tiverton or Revelstoke, which suited de Revelle well enough, as John knew that he was fond of entertaining loose women in the bedchamber behind his office.

Matilda clung to the subject of the King's judges. 'I trust that Bishop Marshall will give a feast in their honour. Certainly we would be invited – I will have a chance to wear my new brocade kirtle.'

De Wolfe sometimes found it hard to reconcile her religious fervour with her devotion to fine clothing, eating, drinking and her desire to be a county notable. Almost as if she was reading his mind, she added weight to his already considerable burden: 'Speaking of feasts, there was a message earlier, brought by a guildsman's servant. We are invited to a banquet at the Guildhall on Thursday night.' De Wolfe groaned at the thought of another evening jammed at a table with pompous merchants and their snobbish wives, to say nothing of the pious clerics and drunken craftsmen who gravitated to these celebrations.

'Who is it this time? *Must* we accept?' he muttered.

'Of course we must, John! It's your duty as the King's coroner to grace these events. This one is given by the Guild of Tanners, very influential people. A friend of mine at St Olave's is the wife of one of their Wardens.'

'Tanners? They stink, it's the dog turd they use in their fleshing vats.'

'My friend doesn't stink, I assure you,' snarled an outraged Matilda. She hauled herself to her feet and plodded angrily to the door. 'I'm going to get ready for my devotions. See that Mary has your best tunic washed for you to wear on Thursday night.'

As she slammed the door to the vestibule behind her, her husband sighed and dropped the remains of the chicken under the table for Brutus.

The church of All Hallows-on-the-Wall was empty, the few worshippers at Vespers long gone. The setting sun shone through the two slatted windows high up on the west wall, its beams almost solid in the dust thrown up by the angry strokes of the bundle of twigs that Ralph de Capra was using as a broom. The little building was paved with irregular stone slabs and though this was cleaner than the usual floor of beaten earth, the priest still muttered under his breath at the dried mud and wisps of straw and rushes that his parishioners had brought in on their shoes. He was a thin, miserable man, looking considerably older than his thirty-eight years. A hare-lip and a crusted skin ailment on his scalp, poorly concealed by his thin brown hair, did little to enhance his appearance.

The priest drove the debris towards the door and, with a few final flourishes, swept it down the two steps on to the narrow street that ran inside the city wall. Then he straightened up and walked down to the centre of the lane, besom still in hand. To his left stretched Little Britayne, with its criss-crossing mesh of hovel-lined alleys running up the hill towards the centre of the town. A night-soil cart pulled by a donkey was coming towards him, pursued by ragged, jeering urchins, who yelled abuse at the scarecrow of a man perched on the crossboard. A few pigs snuffled around the bottom of the high city wall and further up, where the wall turned at the Snail Tower, de Capra could see a small crowd gathered around two drunks who were futilely trying to fight each other, though they could hardly stand.

Directly across from the church, the bottom end of Fore Street climbed up to become High Street at Carfoix, the central crossing of Exeter. Clusters of towns-folk thronged it, some hurrying on errands, some buying and selling at the booths along its edges, others just lounging in the evening sun.

He turned to look at his little church which was now an integral part of the city wall, its other three walls projecting into the roadway. Like most of the many churches in Exeter, it was a simple oblong, like a barn. Some of the others were still timber-built, but many were gradually being replaced with stone – several even had little towers.

De Capra climbed the steps back into his domain, bent his knee briefly in the direction of the simple altar then went to the other end of the church where wooden screens partitioned off a small space against the far wall. Here he kept his simple vestments, an alb of heavy linen, a rather threadbare brocade stole and a maniple. A stone jar held some cheap wine and a small wooden box did duty as a pyx, to store the wafers bought at a cook-stall, which he used to prepare the Host for Mass.

He dropped the broom alongside a leather bucket and battered shovel, then went back down to the other end of the building. The chancel was merely a wooden platform, two steps up from the main floor. The altar was a small table covered with a white cloth, carrying two wooden candlesticks and a tin cross covered in peeling gilt. On the wall above, below the high window slits, was a large, crudely carved crucifix. The only other furniture was a kneeler for his own prayers and a heavy chair for the Bishop or Archdeacon, should they ever deign to take part in a service here. This was a poor church in the poorest part of the city, Britayne being so named because five hundred years ago, the 'Britons', the original Celtic inhabitants, had been pushed back by their Saxon conquerors into that least savoury part of Exeter.

De Capra turned his kneeler to face the altar and, after making the Sign of the Cross, lowered himself on to it and leaned forward, his hands clasped on the top bar, polished by years of use. He fixed his eyes on the image of Christ hanging on the wall, and his lips moved in earnest supplication, which gradually rose to an audible monologue. He had a secret that plagued most of his waking hours, and he desperately needed a sign to relieve his troubled conscience. He talked to himself for many minutes, becoming more and more agitated. Then his head fell on to his arms and he subsided into racking sobs.

The next morning, the Wednesday of an eventful week, the manor-reeve of Sidbury, a village some miles east of Exeter, rode in to report a fatal accident. He had left just before dawn and arrived at Rougemont a couple of hours later. The sentry at the castle gate sent him up to the coroner's garret, where Gwyn and Thomas were waiting for their master to arrive.

De Wolfe appeared when the reeve was halfway through his story, but soon caught up with the tragic tale. One of the boy labourers at the manor mill had been trapped in the machinery and was dead. 'Our bailiff knew that under this new crowner's law, we had to report it to you straight away, sir,' the village headman ended. He was a wiry fellow with a narrow but intelligent face, seemed somewhat in awe of the coroner and stood screwing his pointed woollen cap between his strong fingers as he spoke.

'You did right, man. I must come to view the body and hold an inquest – but it will be noon before we can set off.' The reeve was sent away for a few hours to fill his stomach and feed his horse, while de Wolfe settled his agenda with his officer and clerk.

'The Jews are coming this morning about the body,' Thomas reminded him, 'and you have an approver to hear at the Shire Court.' The coroner was required to take a confession from an 'approver', an accused or convicted person who was attempting to save his neck by turning king's evidence against his fellow accomplices.

Gwyn scratched his groin vigorously. 'That Ordeal is on, too,' he rumbled. 'The liar who claimed he bought that sword, not stole it.'

De Wolfe swore under his breath – he would be lucky to get away by noon, which meant he would not be back in Exeter before the gates were shut at curfew. Another night away from home would mean more whines and sulks from Matilda. Then a happier thought struck him: Sidbury was near Sidmouth, a coincidence that might prove interesting, especially if he was to be away all night.

But first the day had to be got through and the first chore was his brother-in-law's Shire Court. Normally it was convened every fortnight, but extra sessions were being hurriedly arranged in preparation for the arrival of the royal judges the following week, as all pending cases had to be presented before them.

An hour later, the trio crossed Rougemont's bustling inner ward to the Shire Hall, the bare court-house where de Wolfe had held the inquest on Aaron. Several cases had been dealt with already, either by Richard de Revelle or Ralph Morin, the castle constable, who sat on the platform in front of a posse of scribes. Also present was the obligatory priest, who today was the new garrison chaplain, an amiable monk called Brother Rufus.

Gabriel, the sergeant of the castle garrison, led in the next prisoner dragged from the stinking gaol under the keep. With rusty irons on his wrists and ankles, he was brought to stand below the middle of the dais. Lice were crawling on his neck and one ear-lobe had a festering rat-bite, signs of a prolonged stay in the cells.

The sheriff, lounging in the only chair on the platform, waved a hand carelessly at de Wolfe. 'This one's yours, John,' he drawled, managing to sound offensive even when the words were outwardly polite.

De Wolfe came to the edge of the platform to stand over the wretched prisoner. He hovered above him, his arms folded across his chest. 'Eadric of Alphington, you have been accused of robbing Roger Lamb on the high road near Alphington on the day of St Jude's fair, taking his purse containing seven shillings' worth of pennies, making off with his horse and causing a grievous wound to his head that almost killed him.'

The Saxon, a surly-looking man in his late twenties, glared up at the coroner through a mane of dirty blond hair that tangled over his face. 'I admit I was there, but I had no part in the robbery.'

There was a sigh of impatience from the sheriff, who was tapping his heel restlessly with a short silver-topped staff. 'Stop this mummery and send the damned fellow to be hanged!' he muttered audibly.

De Wolfe ignored him and glared back at the prisoner. 'You claim you wish to turn approver. You cannot do that unless you confess your crime to me.'

'How can I confess to something I didn't do?'

De Wolfe shrugged. 'It's your choice, fellow. You can go back to your cell and await your trial, if you so wish.'

Faced with the near-certainty of conviction and the gallows, Eadric took but a moment to decide. 'I can confess to my part in the affair, Crowner, but the others were the real villains.'

With Thomas de Peyne at the table behind them, writing as fast as he could, the coroner intoned the ritual formalities of the confession. Then the bedraggled Saxon grudgingly described how he and two fellow villagers had left the fair considerably the worse for drink. While they were stumbling along the main road between Exeter and Alphington, a merchant overtook them on a bay horse and abused them for getting in his way. According to Eadric's version, the rider struck one of the others with his whip and a brawl ensued. The merchant was pulled from his horse and hit his head on the road, being rendered unconscious. Eadric claimed that he was a mere spectator of this fracas and protested when his companions, afraid that they had killed the merchant, took his purse and horse and vanished into the trees.

The victim had recovered rapidly and denounced Eadric to a party of riders who appeared around a bend in the road.

'They seized me and beat me, holding me until the bailiff of the Hundred came. He bound me and I was dragged here to prison. But it was the others who did the evil, leaving me behind to take the blame. And I can name them!' Eadric declared.

'A likely tale!' sneered the sheriff. 'Send the liar back to his cell, John.'

Although, for once, the coroner was inclined to agree with his brother-in-law, he ignored his interruption and concentrated on the prisoner. 'An approver is supposed to challenge his accomplices to combat to the death. If you win, you can abjure the realm. But you'll have to fight two men, one after the other.'

Eadric scowled up at de Wolfe. 'I'll take my chances, Crowner.'

'There is another way for you. Instead of combat, which you are likely to lose against two others, you could choose to be tried by a jury of your fellows in the King's court before his Justices.'

There was a sudden scrape as Richard de Revelle pushed back his chair and jumped to his feet. 'Indeed he cannot! He must appear before this court – my court.'

De Wolfe glared down at the sheriff, who was half a head shorter. 'By my taking his confession, he has placed himself within the coroner's jurisdiction. And I have a duty, granted by our king through his Justiciar, to offer the justice of the royal courts to anyone accused of a serious crime, such as this.'

De Revelle's pointed beard quivered and his normally pallid face flushed with rage. 'Don't start all this again, damn you,' he hissed.

John was unperturbed by the sheriff's fury. 'This was a grievous assault, maybe even attempted murder. It should not have been dealt with in the Shire Court in the first place, but presented to the Eyre, as I have suggested.'

De Revelle glared around the hall, and saw the clerks' ears were flapping, and the few spectators waiting hopefully for a first-class row between the two most senior law officers in the county. 'I'll not bandy words with you in public, John,' he snarled. 'We'll thrash this out later in my chamber.' Abruptly, he turned and, with his smart green cloak flying behind him, hurried to the step at the end of the platform and vanished in the direction of the keep.

Sergeant Gabriel, trying to keep the grin off his face, prodded the Saxon towards the archway. 'I'll send him back to Stigand's tender care, Crowner, while he makes up his mind.' Stigand was the brutish oaf who tended the dreadful castle gaol.

There were no other cases and the participants broke up to go their various ways. De Wolfe found himself walking back towards the gatehouse with Brother Rufus, who held Masses for the castle inhabitants in the tiny chapel of St Mary across the other side of the inner ward. His black Benedictine habit bulged around his tubby body and his shaven head shone in the morning sun as if it had been wax-polished.

'Why the harsh words between you and the sheriff?' asked the priest, always ready for some gossip.

'Come up to my chamber for a jar of ale, Father, and I'll tell you.'

Thomas was still writing up his rolls in the court and Gwyn had gone down to the town to look for the Jew's daughter, so John was glad of some company at his morning libation.

After the rotund monk had puffed up the steep stairs in the gatehouse, they sat at the table with a mug each, filled from Gwyn's pitcher.

'I came to Exeter from Bristol only a month ago, so I'm not yet familiar with the local politics,' Rufus confessed. The garrison church of St Mary was given to three prebendaries who had brought him in to administer it after the death of his predecessor.

De Wolfe cleared his throat noisily. He had taken a liking to the new chaplain and felt he might make another ally in the castle, in addition to Ralph Morin, who covertly disliked the sheriff as much as John himself.

'De Revelle and I have a long-standing disagreement,' he began, markedly understating the situation. 'Last autumn I was appointed as county coroner. The sheriff agreed to this – perhaps because my wife is his sister – but he wanted someone he could control, and here I have grievously disappointed him.'

'I heard tell of this new coroner idea in Bristol. Was it not to raise more money for the Lionheart's ransom and his costly wars?'

'Partly that – but the King also wanted to curb the sheriffs, who have become more powerful and more corrupt of late. Some of them – one not far from here – supported Prince John in his treacherous attempt to usurp King Richard when he was imprisoned in Germany.'

'But what has this to do with you two sparring with each other in the Shire Hall this morning?'

De Wolfe sighed. 'It's a long story, Brother. When William the Bastard conquered England, he inherited such a complicated legal system from the Saxons, that all his successors have been trying to reform it ever since, especially the second Henry of glorious memory. Now Richard – or, rather, his Justiciar – is offering everyone royal justice, rather than the confusion of lower courts we have now.'

The fat monk took a pull at his pot and wiped his lips on the sleeve of his habit. 'That sounds very reasonable, so why are you at loggerheads with your brother-in-law?'

'That's an even longer story! The sheriff covets unchallenged power in his county and the chance to scoop as much profit as he can into his own purse. He sees the royal courts as a threat to his interests – and as the coroner is responsible for presenting as many cases as possible to the King's justices, he sees me as an interfering busybody, intent on thwarting his schemes.' The priest seemed genuinely interested and listened closely to de Wolfe's explanation of the varied functions he was expected to carry out.

'There were supposed to be three of us in Devon,' de Wolfe concluded, 'but one fell from his horse and killed himself in the first fortnight and the other was a drunken fool who lasted only a few weeks. I've been trying to deal with everything – though, praise be to God, a decent knight from Barnstaple is willing to take on the north before long.'

With the lubrication of another pot of ale each, de Wolfe and the monks chatted for some time, John explaining the multitude of tasks that a coroner was expected to perform, from taking the confessions of those abjuring the realm, to investigating house fires, burglaries and catches of the royal fish – whales and sturgeon – to witnessing Ordeals, viewing corpses, and enquiring into rapes and assaults.

The garrison chaplain proved to be an intelligent and astute fellow, asking sensible questions at intervals during the coroner's explanation, but eventually they were interrupted by heavy feet clumping up the stone stairs and Gwyn thrust his huge frame through the sacking that hung over the doorway. 'The Jews are waiting outside, Crowner,' he growled, looking askance at the fat monk who sat drinking his own ale.

De Wolfe downed the rest of his pot and stood up.

'Come with me, Brother. Perhaps you can advise me as this is a matter of religion – though a different one from yours.'

Two figures were standing just below the drawbridge of the castle, as the sentry under the gate-arch was unwilling to let them enter the bailey. One was a thin young man with a full black beard, his curly hair capped by a bowl-shaped helmet of embroidered felt. A long black tunic like a cassock enveloped him and a pack strapped to his shoulders gave an impression of a hunchback. He held the hand of a frail woman of about his own age, whose smooth olive face had the look of a sad angel. A Saxon-style coverchief was wrapped around her head, secured by a band across her forehead, the white cloth flowing down her back over a plain brown dress. In the background, a mule and a donkey with a side-saddle were being held by three men, their garb and appearance marking them as Jewish, presumably from Exeter itself.

Gwyn stepped forward and, in a strangely gentle voice, announced that the young woman was Ruth, Aaron's daughter, and the man her husband David.

De Wolfe explained to the silent and impassive pair what had happened. 'Had he any enemies that you know of?' he asked the daughter.

Ruth's brown eyes lifted to meet the coroner's. 'Almost everyone is our enemy, sir. Since my mother and brother were slain in York, we live in constant fear. But I know of no particular person who would wish to kill my father.'

'We saw him but rarely,' added David. 'Though Honiton is not far off, travelling is hazardous, especially for such as we Jews. Everyone thinks we carry great sacks of gold with us,' he added bitterly.

'Are you in the same way of business?' asked the monk.

'There is little else for us now. Since the Crusades

began, we have lost our chance to trade in commodities from the East. We are only allowed to be usurers, which is forbidden to Christians – though some seem to manage it. We are but sponges to soak up money from the people, then we are squeezed flat to return it into the royal coffers.'

De Wolfe did not wish the conversation to move into seditious paths so raised the matter of the burial. 'Your father was buried yesterday with dignity outside the city walls in the plot reserved for Jews. We understood that you prefer there to be as little delay as possible. I understand that several of your faith from the city were there to offer whatever last rites you use. You are free either to leave him there or to remove him elsewhere.'

David looked at his wife then turned back to the coroner. 'We thank you for your concern, sir. It is seldom that anyone accords us such consideration. We have decided to leave Aaron where he is, as we have nowhere better to take him.'

Brother Rufus laid a fatherly hand on the young man's shoulder. 'Do you need any further requiem to be said over the grave? Have you anyone who can help you in this matter?'

David nodded sadly. 'If we could be shown where the body lies, we can say our own few words over it. Then, later, we can bring some of our own elders from Southampton to join with the local Jews to carry out the proper ceremony.'

They thanked de Wolfe gravely once more and took their leave. John and the chaplain stood watching the pathetic little group walk down the hill from the castle gate, the woman perched on her donkey, the man leading his mule behind her as they vanished into the high street. 'He's right. Every man's hand is against them,' muttered de Wolfe. 'We use them badly in this country but they are far worse off in others. They are forbidden to engage in trade, and when they lend money, they are reviled by everyone, even though their customers are only too glad to use their services.'

'Did the wife say her mother died at York?' asked the priest.

'Yes, in that madness of 'eighty-nine, when most of England rose up in hysteria against them. Just because some well-meaning Jews in London wished to give presents to the new King at his coronation, a riot started that spread right across England. She must have been one of those hundred and fifty who died besieged in York castle – many by their own hand or by those of their menfolk, rather than be captured.'

The cathedral bell rang dolefully in the distance and reminded de Wolfe that he had another task to perform before he could ride to Sidbury. 'I have to attend an Ordeal now, Brother. I must collect my clerk to record the result.'

The portly monk turned back with the coroner to cross the drawbridge. 'I am summoned as priest too, so I'll walk with you. I hear that Rome is becoming more discontented with our attendance at these ancient rituals, saying they smack of necromancy, not justice. I suspect that before long the Holy Father will ban our participation in them.'*

'The sooner the better,' grunted John. 'They are complete nonsense, sheer black magic! Whenever I can, I try to persuade appealers to go for jury trial in the King's courts. It makes more sense and it's better for the Exchequer.'

He called at the Shire Hall on the way to drag the morose Thomas from his scribing on the empty platform and they made their way to the undercroft of

---

* *The Lateran Council of 1215 forbade the ritual of the Ordeal.*

the keep, which housed the castle gaol. It was a damp, squalid chamber, partly below ground level, with a wet earth floor beneath the gloomy arches that supported the building above. It was divided into two halves by a line of rusty bars, one of which housed a row of prison cells beyond a creaking gate. The rest was open, part-storehouse, part-torture chamber, ruled by Stigand, a grossly obese Saxon, who lived in squalor in an alcove formed by one of the arches. This morning, his task was to set up the apparatus for the Ordeal, a test of guilt or innocence that de Wolfe and many other intelligent people thought utter nonsese. But it was hallowed by time and still approved by most of the population, who were usually unwilling to exchange this unChristian soothsaying for the more logical process of a jury trial.

John swung round to the trailing Thomas, who trudged dejectedly behind, his writing pouch slung from the shoulder of his threadbare black tunic. 'Who did you say was the subject today?' he barked.

'A man accused of stealing a sword from the shop of Nicholas Trove, a burgess from North Street, who runs an armourer's business. Nicholas appealed him to the Shire Court last month, when he was attached with sureties of five marks to appear here today.'

'At least he didn't vanish into the forest in the meanwhile, so he must think he has a chance of proving his innocence,' dc Wolfe gruntd to Brother Rufus.

They went down the few steps into the dismal chamber and when their eyes had adjusted to the semi-darkness, saw a group of people clustered in the centre, below the low ceiling, which dripped turbid water from the slime-covered stones. The gaoler had a charcoal fire burning in a latticed iron brazier, which he was blowing with a pair of bellows. Stigand's breathing was almost as noisy as his bellows, as he bent over his vast stomach which was covered with a stained leather apron. His piggy features were contorted with the effort of blowing sufficient air into his fire to make the shaped lumps of metal on top glow red-hot.

Watching him with varying degrees of patience were Richard de Revelle, Sergeant Gabriel and two of his men-at-arms, the latter grasping between them the subject of the ghoulish ceremony, a porter from Bretayne by the name of Matthew Bezil. As de Wolfe, Thomas and the monk approached, they were followed by the complainant, Nicholas Trove. He was a red-faced, angry-looking man, short-necked and short-tempered. At that moment, his mood had much in common with the sheriff's.

'Stigand, for God's sake, hurry up!' snapped de Revelle. 'I've got better things to do than stand here while you puff away at the damned fire. Surely they're hot enough now?' He pointed impatiently at the iron ploughshares glowing on top of the brazier.

The gaoler hoisted himself upright with an effort, his bloated face almost purple. 'They'll do, Sheriff. I'll set them out now.'

With a long tongs, he took a glowing ploughshare from the fire and set it over a flat stone embedded in the mud of the floor. A line of nine carefully spaced stones, each a pace apart, ran across the undercroft and as quickly as his shambling gait allowed, Stigand set a series of the triangular lumps of hot iron on each one.

'Now, before they cool too much, damn you, get moving,' snarled the sheriff. Everyone present, except the accused, was yawningly familiar with the procedure and wanted the charade over as quickly as possible.

The guards jerked Matthew across to stand immediately before the first ploughshare and released his arms. Brother Rufus made the Sign of Cross in the air and murmured something in Latin as Matthew gritted his teeth and with a yell of defiance, ran as if the devil was behind him, jumping from iron to iron in a gliding, springing movement he had obviously been practising for weeks to make the least possible contact with the smoking metal. His banshee wail lasted the whole nine steps and at the end he stumbled and fell in a heap on the fouled earth.

Stigand had moved to that end, where he had previously left a leather bucket of dirty water, which he promptly threw over Matthew Bezil's feet – the fellow had paid him twopence in advance for the privilege.

The groups of observers moved towards him, carefully avoiding the sizzling ploughshares. Standing in a circle, they looked down at the man as if they were an audience after a cockfight, critically examining the result of the contest.

Bezil rolled over on to his back and Gabriel hoisted up both legs so that the soles of his feet could be seen. Stigand lit a bundle of rushes soaked in pitch at the brazier and held it near to give a better light.

There was silence while the experts critically regarded the calloused skin of Matthew's flat feet.

'They look clear to me,' muttered Brother Rufus at length.

'The man's been hardening them off for weeks, by the looks of it,' objected the sheriff.

'There's no law against that,' retorted de Wolfe, always ready to contradict his brother-in-law.

In fact, since electing to undergo the Ordeal, rather than a trial by jury, Bezil had spent a month in running the streets barefoot, had passed hours chafing his soles against a rough flagstone and rubbing in a concoction of oak-galls and tannin. As a result, the skin was twice as thick as normal and of the consistency of old leather.

'That's not legal, having feet like that,' howled Nicholas Trove. 'He should have undergone a different Ordeal – like that of water or molten lead.'

'He was given the Nine Ploughshares at the court, so that's what he got,' growled de Wolfe. 'You can't change the rules now, if they don't suit you.'

It was obvious, even to the sceptical sheriff and the outraged complainant, that Matthew's feet bore not a trace of burns – though perhaps Stigand's bucket of water had delayed the appearance of redness that was usually inevitable, even if scorching and blistering failed to appear.

De Wolfe called out to his clerk, who had squatted in readiness before an empty cask, on which he had spread his writing materials. Thomas had a ferocious scowl on his pinched face and his lips were moving in some soundless litany, unrelated to the events around him.

'Record that Matthew Bezil underwent the Ordeal of ploughshares and his innocence caused his feet to reject the hot iron,' he said, trying to conceal his cynicism.

Thomas scratched away with his quill, still muttering under his breath.

For a moment, John's mind wandered from the Ordeal to wonder why his clerk was acting so oddly these days, but then he recovered himself. 'Record also that Nicholas Trove falsely appealed the said Matthew Bezil in accusing him of the theft of a sword and is therefore amerced in the sum of two marks.'

The armourer howled in protest that he had not only lost his sword but now had to pay its value as a fine. Though the coroner felt some sympathy for him, he used the fiasco to promote his cause of encouraging the use of the king's courts – and to further irritate his brother.

'If the matter had been heard before the judges next week, you might have had a different result,' he snapped at the ironmonger.

Still protesting, Nicholas was pushed towards the doorway by Gabriel and stumbled out, shaking his fist at Matthew, who cheerfully made an obscene gesture at him. He had put on his shoes and was trying not to show that his feet were smarting with a growing pain that would be far worse by the time he had hobbled into the nearest ale-house to celebrate his escape – if burns had appeared on his soles for the witnesses to see, he would have been hanged that week for the theft of something that was worth more than twelve pence, which constituted a felony.

An hour later, John went to the stable opposite his house and climbed on to the back of Odin, his destrier. He had called at home to tell Matilda that he would be away for the night and was relieved to find that she was at St Olave's for noon service. Mary had fed him a meat pie, cheese and half a loaf, while Andrew the farrier saddled Odin, ready for the journey.

De Wolfe walked the stallion through the crowded high street to the Carfoix crossing, where he had arranged to meet the others, and the quartet, which included the manor reeve from Sidbury, made their way down South Gate Street, past the bloody mayhem of the Shambles, then the Serge Market to the gate. Beyond the city walls, the crowds vanished and they kept up a brisk trot along Magdalen Street, past the gallows, which today was deserted although a rotting corpse hung in an iron frame from a nearby post. They continued on the main highway eastwards, which was the road to Lyme and eventually Southampton and Winchester.

As usual, Thomas lagged behind, jerking awkwardly on the side-saddle of his reluctant pony, his features looking as if he expected to hear the Last Trump at any moment. The reeve, Thomas Tirel by name, pulled alongside the coroner to offer more details of what had happened in his village.

'This was a lad of thirteen, Crowner, the fifth son of

one of our villeins. His father offered him to work in the mill as part of the family's manor service, and he had been there almost a year, carrying sacks and cleaning the floor.'

'This is the lord's mill, I presume?'

'Indeed it is. Everyone is obliged to have their flour ground there and the fee goes to the bishop.'

De Wolfe was aware that the small village of Sidbury was one of the many manors that belonged to Henry Marshal, Bishop of Exeter.

'So what happened to the boy?'

'He fell through the floor, which was rotten, and was caught in the pinion of the mill-wheel shaft. His head was crushed, poor lad.'

John failed to visualise exactly what the reeve meant. 'I'll have to see the place for myself,' he growled. 'But what about this rotten floor?'

'Many a time the miller complained to the Bishop's bailiff that it was unsafe, but he was unwilling to stop the mill while new joists and boards were laid – he said the expense was unnecessary.'

The aggrieved tone of the man's voice suggested to de Wolfe that this was a source of discontent in the village.

Sidbury was about fifteen miles from Exeter and they reached it in less than three hours' easy riding. Thomas Tirel took them straight to the mill, a wooden structure astride a brook that ran underneath it. Upstream there was a deep pool formed by an earthen dam, and a crude sluice-gate controlled the flow to the wheel.

A rumbling noise came from the mill and John saw a cloud of dust drifting from an open door at the side. 'They are still grinding corn?' he demanded.

'The bailiff insisted. The gear was not broken, so he had the blood washed away and told the miller to carry on.'

'So where's the body?'

'Taken to the church, poor boy. We couldn't give it back to the mother in the state it was in.'

With Gwyn at his side and Thomas de Peyne trailing behind, de Wolfe followed the reeve into the mill, coughing at the cloud of dust and chaff that filled the atmosphere. In the single room, a large circular stone, four feet across and a hand's breadth thick, was slowly revolving below a similar but stationary wheel resting on top. A large wooden hopper fed grain into a hole in the centre of the upper stone and a circular tray around the moving lower quern collected the flour that dribbled from the joint between the stones.

The miller, a large, perspiring man dressed in a thin smock and a hessian apron, was adjusting the flow of grain from the hopper. Because of the noise, he was unaware of their presence until the reeve tapped his shoulder. Almost guiltily, the man turned around and, on seeing the coroner, tugged at his ginger forelock, which was almost white with dust.

'Turn it off!' yelled Gwyn, pointing at the stones.

The miller nodded and gestured at a young boy, who was up on a platform tipping a sack of grain into the hopper. Without a word, he ran out like a frightened rabbit and Gwyn, peering around the door, saw him racing up the bank of the stream.

'He has to close the sluice to stop the wheel. That's why we took so long to free the lad yesterday,' explained the miller, looking uneasily from the reeve to the coroner.

A few moments later, the rumbling beneath slowed, then stopped. The silence was almost as oppressive as the grinding judder had been.

'There's where the floor gave way, Crowner,' explained Tirel, pointing down at a series of loose boards laid across half of the floor on one side of the millstones.

De Wolfe stamped experimentally with his heel on the planks where he was standing. The edge of his riding boot made indentations in the soft surface of the timber.

'This whole place is decaying, for Christ's sake!' he exclaimed. 'How old is it?'

'My father was the miller here – and his father before him. It was here in their day, that's all I know,' said the ginger man defensively.

At the reeve's demand, the miller took them outside and down the grassy bank towards where the stream gushed out from under the building. He opened a low, rickety door and led them into a cramped chamber below the millstones. Looking up, de Wolfe could see a splintered hole a few feet across, with a length of rotten joist hanging loose. To his left was the now silent water-wheel, eight feet high, with a shaft like a small tree-trunk lying horizontally at his feet. This ended in a stout wooden wheel with projecting pegs which interlocked with similar pegs studded around a larger wheel at the base of the vertical shaft, which went up to drive the millstone.

'The poor little devil was caught in those gears, Crowner,' explained Tirel. 'Tore his throat open, it did. Blood everywhere by the time we got down here.'

'It stopped the wheel for a moment, the gears being jammed,' added the miller, with morbid relish. 'But then the pressure of water built up behind the wheel and it broke two of the pegs off, throwing his head aside – but by then he must have been dead. Had to make two new pegs this morning to get the mill going again.'

John peered more closely at the crude gearing. In spite of vigorous washing, part of the flat gearwheel and some of the pegs were ominously ruddy-brown. Straightening up, he made for the door, leaving Gwyn to squint inquisitively at the machinery.

'How much does the Bishop get for milling?' de Wolfe demanded.

'A ha'penny for five bushels, sir. Everyone in the manor must have their corn ground here, they've no choice. Anyone found using a hand quern is amerced at the manor court.'

This was usual: the lord had the monopoly of milling and guarded it jealously as a steady source of income. De Wolfe thought angrily of the mother mourning her youngest son, and determined to have some strong words with the bailiff – or even Henry Marshal himself. 'Then the Bishop can spend a little of his profit on a new floor – though he needs a whole new mill, before it collapses into the brook,' he said acidly.

A few hours later de Wolfe held an inquest, after Gwyn had rounded up enough men and boys from Sidbury and the neighbouring village of Harcombe, to form a jury. The proceedings were held in the graveyard of the old Saxon church, after John and the jurymen had solemnly inspected the mangled remains of the miller's boy. Although he had seen countless corpses on a score of battlefields and had been present at a legion of hangings, beheadings, castrations and mutilations, de Wolfe was affected by the sight of the weeping mother and distraught father standing at the edge of the small crowd in the churchyard. There was little he could do for them other than offer some gruff words of sympathy after he had passed the inevitable verdict of accidental death.

He could have declared the gears of the mill 'deodand', as many coroners would have done in those circumstances. This meant confiscation of the object that had caused the death, either for the King's treasury or sometimes as recompense to a widow for the loss of her breadwinner. In this case, it was physically impossible to remove the gears to sell them, as could have been done with a lethal dagger or even a runaway horse. As the boy was a fifth son and of tender years, his monetary value to the family was very small – he shrewdly guessed that the offer of a mark or two for the boy's life would be more of an insult than a gain to the family.

Instead, he took the opportunity to berate the bailiff publicly for allowing the mill to fall into such a dangerous state of dilapidation. The man, a pompous, self-important fellow, blustered that he was not responsible for spending the Bishop's money, but was soon deflated by the coroner's tongue-lashing and threats to consider attaching him to the forthcoming Eyre on a charge of manslaughter by negligence.

When the inquest was over, with the sun dropping over the trees, Gwyn raised the matter of a night's lodging. 'After the mouthful you gave the bailiff, he'll not be too co-operative in finding somewhere for us to stay,' he said. 'If we left now and put on a good pace all the way we might just get back to Exeter before the curfew.'

But de Wolfe had other plans. 'We'll keep clear of that puffed-up braggart, and clear out of this damned village. Sidmouth's only a couple of miles away at the coast. We'll find an inn there and go back to Exeter in the morning.' He was happy to pay for a penny meal and a mattress for his officer and clerk in the small fishing port down the road, but with luck, he hoped to find a softer, warmer bed for himself.

The sun was low in the sky when they reached Sidmouth. A single street went down to the strand, where a line of fishing boats was drawn up across the pebble bank. A score of huts built of cob and turf spread out from a nucleus of larger wooden houses and a few stone ones around the church. There were three mean ale-houses, full of fishermen, and two better inns that offered a sleeping place in their lofts.

After seeing to their horses in the yard of the bigger tavern, which had an old anchor hanging over the door, the trio settled in the smoky, sweaty tap-room to eat and drink. The food was more notable for its quantity than quality, which suited Gwyn's vast appetite, but even Thomas, after a day on a bouncing pony, managed to do justice to his grilled herrings, onions and cabbage.

De Wolfe ate well enough, although his mind was on other things. After eating his fill, he left the table and announced that he was going for a walk along the beach to watch the sunset – an intention that raised the eyebrows of both his henchmen, as he was not noted for his aesthetic sensibilities.

Ignoring their quizzical stares – and rejecting Gwyn's mischievous offer to walk with him – John grabbed his cloak and went out into the twilight. The sun was a deep red ball vanishing below the distant hills and the sea was a leaden sheet stretching out to a darkening horizon, but de Wolfe had no eyes for this kind of natural beauty, his mind on a different sort of pleasure.

He walked purposefully up the main street for a hundred paces, then turned into a side lane beyond the other tavern. A few yards further on, he stopped at a house with a stone lower storey, the upper part being timber. He knocked firmly on the heavy door and, with a twinge of annoyance at his own vanity, found himself running fingers through his thick black hair to brush it off his face.

The door opened a crack and an old man's face appeared in the shadows, looking fearful at a knock on the door at dusk. John's features slumped into a scowl at this sudden pricking of his pleasant expectations. 'Is not the Goodwife Godfin at home?' he demanded brusquely.

'Who seeks her at this time of the evening?' the old man demanded querulously.

'A friend – Sir John de Wolfe from Exeter.'

'She has left here these four months, sir. I rent the dwelling in her place.' De Wolfe cursed under his breath. His devious plans had obviously gone well astray. 'Where is she now? Still in the village?'

'She has married and gone away. To a butcher in Bridport.'

There was nothing more to be said and, with muttered thanks, de Wolfe stalked away, tight-lipped in his disappointment. The damned woman was not only twenty-five miles away but now had a new husband, so that chapter in his life was closed for good. He had chanced to meet Brigit Godfin at a fair two years ago, when he had come here with his partner Hugh de Relaga to buy breeding sheep. She was a dark, attractive woman of thirty-two, recently widowed from a cloth merchant in Sidmouth. He was soon sharing her bed and although his visits from Exeter were difficult to arrange, except at infrequent intervals, he had managed to keep the affair going until he took up the coroner's appointment. Since then, pressure of work and his increasing involvement with Nesta had caused him to neglect Brigit – he had not seen her for more than six months. Now she had found other fish to fry and he could draw a line under what had been a pleasant, if desultory affair.

He marched back to the Anchor, dropped back on to the bench he had left and glared at Gwyn as if daring him to enquire where he had been.

'Another couple of quarts, then it's time to sleep,' he muttered. 'We must be on the road to Exeter first thing in the morning.'

CHAPTER FIVE

*In which Crowner John takes his wife
to a banquet*

On the way back to the city next day, Odin cast a
shoe and de Wolfe spent the rest of the morning
with Andrew the farrier, restoring the big warhorse
to working condition, before he reluctantly crossed the
lane to his house.

The midday meal was silent as usual, with Matilda
sulking over her husband's absence the previous night.
As they sat at each end of the long table in their hall,
the two yards between them might as well have been two
miles, for all the social intercourse that took place.

His head bent over Mary's mutton stew and fresh
bread, John pondered the events in Sidmouth and was
thankful that Matilda was unaware of this amorous
fiasco. She had mocked him unmercifully when she
learned of his rift with Nesta and had long sneered
at his ill-concealed fondness for his youthful sweetheart
in Dawlish, so he was greatly relieved to know that the
Brigit Godfin episode had been entirely outside her
knowledge.

The thought of Dawlish crept into his mind now,
as he turned over the diminishing choices in his love-
life. With Brigit gone and Nesta apparently resolute in
her rejection of him, the beautiful Hilda was his only
remaining option. The thought of her warmed him, her

glorious blonde hair and her lissom body flooding into his mind as they had with increasing frequency over the past few weeks.

He had been deprived of her company for too long, he decided. His last attempt to call at Dawlish had been frustrated by an unexpected corpse in the River Teign. He determined to pay an early visit to his mother, sister and brother at the family manor at Stoke-in-Teignhead, the road to which passed through Dawlish. It only required Hilda's elderly husband, Thorgils, to be away on his boat – preferably as far away as St Malo – for John's plotting to come to delightful fruition in the arms of the fair young wife.

With these devious thoughts in his mind, he stole a covert glance at his wife as she chewed grimly, trying to gauge the depth of her current displeasure.

They had to go to this damned banquet that evening, he thought despondently, which would be even harder to endure if she was in a really caustic mood.

He decided to try to lighten the atmosphere, if only for his own sake. However, his favourable comments about the meal were met with disdain, because Matilda disliked Mary and nothing the maid did ever found favour in her eyes. She suspected that there was something going on between the serving woman and her husband – correctly, as it happened, although it was now in the past, for Mary was more attached to her employment than her employer, fond though she was of him.

His next attempt at conversation was more successful, as the subject was her brother and the imminent arrival of the royal judges. 'I must go up to Rougemont this afternoon and talk to Richard about the arrangements for the Eyre next week. We have not yet heard who the Justices will be.'

'I trust they will be men of stature, not just common

clerks like those who came as Commissioners of Assize last time,' she snapped.

'They will be senior men, as this is a General Eyre, not just an Assize,' he replied, pandering to her incorrigible snobbishness. The prospect of some noble barons or a bishop coming to the city perked up her interest.

'I never understood all these different courts,' she whined. 'Why are there eminent men of the king's court at some and only snivelling clerks at others?'

De Wolfe grinned to himself at her derogatory description of some learned Commissioners, though it was true that some were but very able clerks, administrators from the Exchequer or Chancery. To humour her, he launched into an explanation. 'In the old days, anyone seeking justice from the king, first had to find him. That meant journeying either to Winchester, London or even Normandy in the hope of catching him at his court – or else chasing around the countryside after him, as he paraded around the shires, fighting, hunting or just battening on his barons for lodging.'

He swallowed a piece of fat mutton, before continuing. 'Then old King Henry, a great one for law-making, decided this wasn't good enough and demanded that members of his court should go around regularly to each county and hear the Pleas of the Crown, cases that were not dealt with by the local courts.'

Matilda paused in her chewing to glare at him. 'But that doesn't explain why sometimes we get barons and bishops here, but more often a pack of London clerks – "men raised from the dust", as my brother calls them.'

John got up and filled her pewter cup with more wine, thinking that a little gracious behaviour on his part might mellow her in time for the evening. He topped up his own and sat down again, ready to explain a little more. 'The justices who are coming next week are also holding a General Eyre, so they will be the most senior men. As well as hearing royal pleas in serious cases, they look into the whole administration of the county, which is why your brother is so flustered and uneasy.'

For the sake of avoiding a tantrum, he did not pursue this subject, thinking it wiser to avoid antagonising his wife with hints at Richard's dishonesty.

'The General Eyre comes but seldom these days – it has to call at every county in England, but trundles around so slowly that years pass between visitations,' he added.

'So what are the other courts? We get visits more often than that,' she demanded truculently.

'Those are the ones you complain are held by clerks,' he replied, trying to keep the sarcasm from his voice. 'Again, they are supposed to take place every quarter, but the Commissioners have never reached Exeter more than twice a year, if that. As the Justices in Eyre come so seldom, these lesser courts are meant to clear up the royal pleas at much more frequent intervals. That's why they're called, "Gaol Delivery", to try those who have been incarcerated, to save expense and reduce the number escaping.'

The lesson over, Matilda reverted to her main interest in the matter. 'Well, I just hope that we get some notables here next week. Exeter is such a backwater. When you became coroner, I had hopes that your connections with the King and the Chief Justiciar would get you preferment. Then, maybe, we could move to somewhere more civilised, like Winchester.'

God forbid, thought de Wolfe. Devon was his birthplace and his home; the last thing he wanted was to end up near a royal court, with all the intrigue and manoeuvring for social advancement that that would mean.

The meal ended and de Wolfe, satisfied that Matilda was talking to him in a moderately agreeable way, waited for her to go up to the solar for her afternoon slumber. Then he walked up to Rougemont. Gwyn had gone to St Sidwell's to see his family, after his night spent away from their hut, but Thomas was in the chamber above the gatehouse, making copies of documents of presentment for the Justices next week.

De Wolfe sat at the other end of the trestle from his peculiar but industrious clerk and spent an hour silently mouthing Latin phrases from the parchments left for him by his tutor at the cathedral.

After a while, he became aware that his were not the only lips moving in the silence. Peering up from below his beetling brows, he watched Thomas covertly. The clerk's pen had stopped and he was staring blindly through the window slit at the sky. He was having some silent conversation with unseen beings and from the scowl on his face and the occasional grimace that showed his yellowed teeth, he seemed to be directing some silent diatribe at an invisible audience.

The coroner was becoming increasingly concerned for his assistant's sanity. Although Thomas had always been a miserable companion, it was only since he had learned that there was little hope of him being received back into the Church that he had become so morose. De Wolfe threw down his parchment and cleared his throat loudly, the sign that he was about to launch into some possibly embarrassing topic.

'How goes it with you now, Thomas?' he asked, rather fiercely. 'Are you in better spirits these days?'

Startled, the former priest looked up, his beaky face showing surprise at such an unexpectedly personal question from his revered master. 'I am fairly well, Crowner,' he stammered, 'though never can I be happy again while I am excluded from the company of my fellows in Holy Orders. But I have to live from day to day, as the Almighty indicated not long ago.' When, in a paroxysm of despair, he had tried to kill himself a month or so ago, his uncle, the Archdeacon, had cleverly convinced Thomas that his failure was a miraculous sign that he was meant to live for some greater purpose. He still hoped that, some day, his ejection from Holy Orders for an alleged indecent assault on a girl pupil at the cathedral school in Winchester would be reversed – although his uncle held little hope that this would come about for a very long time, if ever.

'Are you living well enough – your bed and board, I mean?' continued the coroner gruffly. He paid his clerk twopence a day and knew that he had a free mattress in a servant's hut in one of the houses in Canon's Row.

'I am well enough provided for in my bodily needs, thanks to you and my uncle, sir. It is rather my soul that needs the nourishment of belonging in the House of God.' Suddenly he scowled at some inner thought. 'There are those who persecute me and should be punished. False witnesses ruined my life, yet there seems no sign from God that they will be humbled,' he added darkly.

'I can't help you there, Thomas. I did my best with the Archdeacon, but you know what he said. You must contain yourself in patience, I'm afraid. Meanwhile, you are very valuable to me, both as an excellent clerk and an invaluable fount of knowledge.'

At this extraordinarily rare compliment Thomas's pale features pinked with pleasure. It was all the more precious coming from this stern, gaunt man of whom he was half afraid. Thomas respected him with almost dog-like devotion, being grateful for John having given him a job – and indeed the means to stay alive at a time when he was destitute.

They went back to their work for a while, but de Wolfe's attention span for Latin texts was very limited and soon he threw down the parchments and took himself off to the castle keep. The hall was a hive of activity, and many of the tables, which were usually in use for eating, drinking or gaming, were occupied by the sheriff's and burgesses' clerks, all busily writing or shuffling parchments. Harassed-looking stewards, bailiffs and more clerks were hurrying around with sheaves of documents, all intent on trying to get the county's affairs in order before the eagle eyes of the Justices in Eyre arrived next week.

When de Wolfe marched into the sheriff's chamber, the scene was even more frantic. De Revelle was almost submerged under a pile of bound parchments and three clerks were jostling at his shoulder to place more sheets in front of him, jabbering their insistence that their problem was the most urgent. When he saw John come in, he yelled before the coroner could open his mouth, 'Not now, John, please! I am going mad with these fellows battening on me every hour of the day. God curse these laws that send visitations from London to make our lives a misery! I hope all your affairs are in better order than mine.'

For once, de Wolfe felt almost sorry for his brother-in-law, but the realisation that de Revelle was spending most of his energy in trying to cover up the signs of his corruption hardened his heart. 'Your dear sister wants to know who the justices will be next week. Tell me, if you know, and I'll leave you in peace.'

De Revelle's pointed beard jutted up at him. 'There are four this time,' he snapped petulantly. 'Sir Peter Peverel, that over-rich baron from Middlesex, and Serlo de Vallibus, a senior Chancery clerk.'

'You said four?'

'Gervase de Bosco, an archdeacon from Gloucester, and someone with local connections, Sir Walter de Ralegh.'

From the sheriff's tone, de Wolfe was not sure if the

last name was welcome to him or not. A baron with Devon connections might know too much about de Revelle's scheming for the sheriff's comfort. 'I suppose two will hear the civil pleas and the others the criminal,' he observed.

The sheriff's narrow face puckered with disgust. 'And all four of the bloody men will make a nuisance of themselves by poking their noses into our affairs!'

The clerks were shaking parchments at him again and John left his brother-in-law to their urgent ministrations. Outside in the hall, he met Ralph Morin, who had just been giving orders to Sergeant Gabriel about escort arrangements for the king's judges. The castle constable was a massive man, with the blue eyes and forked beard of his Norse ancestors, only a few generations removed from their Norman descendants. He had been directly appointed by the King, as Exeter Castle had been a Crown possession ever since it was built by William the Bastard.

Now Morin took de Wolfe's arm and steered him to a vacant spot on a nearby bench. He yelled at a passing servant to bring them some ale, and when the pots arrived, he raised his in salute to the coroner.

'This place is a mad-house this week. Thank Christ these Justices don't come more often than every few years.'

'Are they staying in Rougement?'

'No damned fear! They like their comfort too much to be stuck in this draughty hole – no wonder de Revelle's wife refuses to live here with him.'

'So where are you putting them – in the New Inn?' This was the largest hostelry in Exeter, in the high street between Martin's Lane and the East Gate.

'It belongs to the cathedral Chapter, so they'll make a few shillings out of lodging the judges and their acolytes,' said Ralph sarcastically. 'Last time, the bishop put them up in his palace, but I hear he found it too expensive to provide free bed and board for them all.'

They talked together for a while, each comfortable in the company of another professional soldier, both familiar with the campaigns in France and Outremer. Morin had some fairly recent news of Coeur de Lion's exploits against the hated Philip of France and de Wolfe responded with tales he had heard about the endless wrestling between the Marcher Lords and the Welsh princes.

After an hour's pleasant gossip and another few jars of ale, the coroner reluctantly decided that he had better make tracks for home, to avoid the evil eye from Matilda, if he was late in preparing for the Guild feast that evening.

'Are you attending this damned performance in the Guildhall tonight?' he demanded, as he rose to leave the keep.

Morin shook his head. 'Rough soldiers like me are rarely invited. The burgesses are glad enough of my men-at-arms when something goes wrong, but otherwise they look down their noses at me – thanks be to Christ!'

With a grin and a friendly clap of the shoulder, the two friends parted and John made his way slowly back to Martin's Lane.

Two banquets in a week was a form of torture to John de Wolfe, akin to the *peine forte et dure* that was applied to reluctant witnesses or to those who refused to accept trial by battle.

He sat sullenly near the end of the top table in the smoky Guildhall, a new stone building in the centre of High Street, gazing down the other trestles that ran in three rows down the length of the chamber. The gabble of conversation and tipsy laughter drowned out the efforts of three musicians who were trying to entertain the crowd from a small gallery above John's head. At about three hours before midnight, the meal was well advanced and the first courses lay in disarray on the scrubbed tables all around. Servants were struggling through the narrow gaps between the trestles to pick up the remnants of bread trenchers, soggy with gravy, to give to the beggars who clamoured outside the doors. Wooden and pewter platters held chicken and goose carcasses, while bones and scraps of meat were scattered over the tables. Hunks of bread, dishes of butter, cream and slabs of cheese vied with the ragged skeletons of fish as the most prominent debris of the lavish meal. All this was lubricated with spilt ale, cider and wine from an assortment of cups, goblets and horns that were standing on the boards or grasped in unsteady hands.

In the centre of the top table sat the Master of the Guild of Tanners, a hearty, florid burgess who was already quite drunk. On either side of him were his two Wardens, themselves flanked by lesser officials. On the other side of the table from de Wolfe, the wives sat together, including Matilda, who was happily exchanging gossip and scandal with her cronies. The only consolation for the antisocial coroner was that his friend Hugh de Relaga was next to him, a guest favoured both as a Portreeve of the city and a Guild Master in his own right. On John's other side, at the extreme end of the table, was another guest, a Warden from the Company of Silversmiths, whose sole object seemed to be to get as much food and drink into himself as humanly possible.

The tipsy Master had just made a speech, welcoming his guests and extolling the virtues of his Guild in only slightly slurred tones, before sitting down heavily to devote the rest of the evening to getting even more drunk.

'I suppose you have to endure many of these bloody

charades?' growled John to his friend Hugh. There was
little fear of anyone taking offence at his sentiments, as
the noise of clashing platters, shouting servants and a
rising crescendo of babbling voices made any conversation inaudible beyond a foot or two.

'I've got used to them over the years. Quite a lot of
business is conducted at these affairs, most of it while
pissing in the yard, where at least you can hear yourself
think.' The cheerful Portreeve, resplendent in purple
silk and a fur-trimmed mantle of green velvet, tore off
the leg of a roast duck lying on the table and began
to gnaw it with every appearance of satisfaction at the
evening's fare.

A serving man came around behind them, laying new
trenchers of thick bread on the table, one between two
diners. John absently reached out with his dagger and
pulled a large slice of pink flesh from a salmon carcass
lying on a pewter plate nearby and dumped it with
the neatness of long practice on their trencher. 'Try
some of this, Hugh. They say that fish strengthens your
brain, so maybe you can make even more money for us
tomorrow.'

They began to talk about their wool-exporting part-
nership, which had shown good returns since the last
shearing season. 'We still have a few hundred bales
stored down at the quayside, John. Our agent in St
Malo has had a firm offer at a good price.' The rotund
burgess frowned as he laid a piece of fish on a fresh
crust. 'That reminds me. Tomorrow I must make some
new arrangements about shipping them out.'

'What's the problem?' asked de Wolfe.

'We usually get Thorgils to move our goods to Brittany
but I hear that his vessel was badly damaged in a storm
last week. It'll be a month on the beach at Dawlish
for repairs, so he won't be taking wool anywhere for
a while.'

The Portreeve was unaware of John's liaison with Thorgils's wife, so had no idea of the frustration that de Wolfe felt at this bad news. The coroner said nothing, but he cursed silently at this second blow to his love-life within the space of a day. With old Thorgils beached at home, there was no way he could enjoy the delicious company of his young wife.

De Relaga had turned now to the guild treasurer on his other side to respond to some chatter about the extortionate increase in journeymen's wages and John felt no inclination to strike up a conversation with the inarticulate silversmith who was still gorging himself on his other side. He refilled his goblet with wine imported from Rouen and sat drinking moodily, half watching the antics of a troupe of jugglers who were performing as best they could with drunken revellers falling against them and servants thrusting irritably past them with jugs and plates.

He craned his neck to see how Matilda was faring. She seemed to be in her element, filled with good food and drink and engrossed in loud conversation with the other guests, both next to her and at the top end of two of the spur tables. In such company, he saw that she was a different woman from the surly malcontent he knew at home – she was gesturing animatedly and smiling and smirking with the pompous merchants and priests around her.

John drew back with a long sigh, feeling sorry for himself at the prospect of enforced celibacy for the foreseeable future and applied himself with grim determination to serious drinking, even though he knew he would suffer for it in the morning.

While the festivities went on in the Guildhall, the parish priest at the church of St Mary the Less, known to everyone as 'St Mary Steps', was preparing for Matins, the first Office of the new day, which began at midnight. The numerous churches scattered all over Exeter did not keep to the strict regime of the nine daily services that were celebrated in the cathedral. The number varied according to the diligence of each incumbent.

At St Mary Steps, at the bottom of Stepcote Hill near the West Gate, the attendance at a Thursday midnight service was likely to be sparse. Although many of those who lived within the few hundred paces served by the church would come on a Sunday, Adam of Dol knew that only a handful of the most devout would appear in the middle of a week-night. No one would come to Prime at dawn, so Adam had given up any pretence at public devotions then, reserving his efforts for High Mass in mid-morning and Vespers in the afternoon.

He was a stocky man of medium height, thick-necked and red-faced, his high colour tending to deepen rapidly when his short temper was aroused. This evening, as the May light was fading, he moved about his church with short, jerky steps, as if he was always in a hurry, though the tempo of life at St Mary's was hardly demanding.

The building was slightly larger than All-Hallows-on-the-Wall, its near neighbour just along the road. The rectangular nave was quite high and the end facing the road had a new stumpy tower with two bells. Originally wood, it had been rebuilt in stone about fifty years previously, with a bequest from the wealthy owner of a fulling mill on Exe Island, just the other side of the city wall; the man had wished to ensure the welfare of his immortal soul with such generosity.

Dedicated to St Mary, as were three other Exeter churches, it took its nickname from the cross-steps that traversed Stepcote Hill alongside the church, which was so steep as to need shallow terracing to prevent man and beast from falling flat on their faces. Though better endowed than All-Hallows, it was not a wealthy establishment and Father Adam remained disappointed that this was all that had been allotted to a priest of his talents.

At forty-two, his ambition to become a canon had stagnated, but he had insufficient insight to realise that his own abrasive nature was the main stumbling-block to his advancement. As he strutted around his domain, adjusting the embroidered altar-cloth and pointlessly moving the brass candlesticks half an inch, he irritated himself – as he did several times a day – by rehearsing his life history and bemoaning the cruelties of fate that had held him back.

Born in Brittany, under the shadow of St Samson's great church, he was the second son of a second son of a noble of Dol. When Adam was a child his father had crossed the water to Devon and with family help, had become a substantial land-owner near Totnes. With an elder brother, Adam had had little inheritance to look forward to, so he had been packed off at an early age to the abbey school in Bath and followed the expected route into Holy Orders. At sixteen, he moved to Wells and although it had long lost its bishop in favour of Bath, there were still canons there and eventually he became a secondary, then a vicar. He had hoped to stay in Wells and eventually obtain a prebend, which would elevate him to the rank of canon, but his short temper and argumentative nature caused him to fall out with both members of the Chapter and many of his fellows. At twenty-seven, he cast the dust of Wells from his feet and moved to Exeter as a vicar-choral, with the same ambition to obtain a prebend.

Once again, the pattern was repeated, and although he stayed in the cathedral precinct for half a decade, his imperious manner won him few friends and he was repeatedly disappointed in his hopes to become a canon-elect. Finally, the Archdeacon of Exeter, a predecessor of John de Alençon, took him aside and whispered a few home truths, but offered him the solace of a living at St Mary Steps where he would at least be his own man.

He had accepted reluctantly, and there he had stayed, a disgruntled priest convinced he was cut out for higher office, an attitude he shared with Matilda's hero, the priest of St Olave's. Adam still had a modest income from a share in his father's estate at Totnes and, with some money saved from that, he had purchased a richly embroidered alb and chasuble, which he kept locked in a chest in his lodgings behind the church, ready for the time when he would become an archdeacon or even a bishop.

Since his days in Wells, he had acquired a reputation as an impassioned preacher, and his fiery sermons were one reason for the respectable attendance at his church on Sundays: many of his flock enjoyed being thrilled and temporarily frightened by his graphic description of the horrors of hell that awaited them unless they trod in the paths of righteousness. He was under no illusions about the ephemeral nature of his threats and knew that most of his parishioners had forgotten them by the time they reached home for dinner or the tavern for their ale. But his outbursts were a welcome safety valve for his own frustrations and he enjoyed the reactions of his audience to the lurid pictures he drew of tortures in Hades – the groans, the blanched faces and even a dead faint from the more susceptible matrons.

Now as he replaced the stumps of candle on the altar with new ones, he was already working on the horrors for his sermon on the coming Sabbath. This week he rather fancied tearing out tongues with barbed hooks and seizing nipples in red-hot pincers. These ideas gave him a sexual frisson, and he knew that before long he would have to make another journey to Bristol or

Salisbury, ostensibly a pilgrimage but really to visit a brothel. Some of his priestly colleagues in Exeter were quite open about their mistresses or their whoring, but something had always inhibited Adam from fouling his own nest.

As the years went by, his mind divided increasingly between his crusade to warn his flock of the perils of hell-fire that awaited them if they sinned – and the sins he himself enjoyed, both with harlots and the vicarious thrills of increasingly perverted imaginings of the reward Satan had in store for those who failed to heed their priest's warnings.

He stood back from the altar and crossed himself, checking that the new candles were straight in their holders. Wax candles were expensive and the rest of the church was lit by cheap tallow dips, pieces of cord floating in a dish of ox-fat. He took the remnants of the altar candles home to use in his small room where he read his religious books until the small hours.

He turned from the altar to the body of the church, and surveyed the empty nave in the dim flickering light. This was where his flock would stand on Sunday for him to harangue them about their horrific sojourn in eternity. There were no seats, apart from stone benches around the walls for the old and infirm.

Below the window slits some old tapestries depicted saints and scenes from the scriptures, but his pride and joy were the new wall-paintings alongside the chancel-arch and on the west wall. He had paid to have parts of the rough masonry plastered and then had begun to paint lurid scenes from the Fiery Pit. Horned devils with tridents, cloven-hoofed goblins, loathsome serpents and misshapen ogres inflicted every imaginable torment on screaming wretches – among whom naked females seemed to predominate. He had recently discovered in himself a hitherto unsuspected artistic talent. Within the last couple of months, he had filled the plastered areas with these diabolical murals and had only one space left to fill, on the right of the chancel arch, which he had already started upon. Space was becoming so short that he had begun to add smaller figures and faces to the existing murals, so that some were a writhing mass of miniature agonised sinners and their tormenting imps.

For a few moments he contemplated his dimly visible masterpieces, seeming to draw a little consolation from their threatening message, then picked up his mantle from the floor and went out into the street. Father Adam slammed the door behind him, then toiled in the dark up the terraces of Stepcote Hill to his dwelling and his frugal supper.

It was midnight, and though the feast in the Guildhall continued, the participants were thinning out. Some had drunk so much that they were either vomiting in the backyard or had been helped home by their servants or angry wives. A few senior priests, including a couple of cathedral canons, had left to attend Matins, but plenty of revellers remained. Some were singing, some fighting and others lying peacefully asleep across the wreckage of the meal on the trestle boards. The county coroner had consumed a great deal of ale and wine, but his hard head had resisted their effects – although he knew that the morning might tell a different story.

He sat slumped glumly in his black clothing, shoulders hunched, looking melancholy and dejected, waiting for Matilda to finish gossiping amongst the wives at the other end of the table. His friend Hugh de Relaga had tottered out unsteadily some time ago, claiming he was going to empty his bladder, and had not returned. De Wolfe suspected that his servant had waylaid him outside and wisely decided that the best place for the Portreeve was home and bed.

The candles on the tables and in the wall sconces had burned low and the light was dim, but John's eye was caught by a familiar figure standing inside the draught screens that sheltered the main door at the far end of the hall. It was difficult to miss the shambling giant with a tangle of unruly hair on his head and face. Gwyn was beckoning with a hand the size of a ham, his gestures carrying more than a hint of urgency.

With an almost guilty look towards Matilda, de Wolfe stood up and squeezed behind the now slumbering silversmith, then threaded his way to meet Gwyn at the bottom of the hall. To de Wolfe's surprise, old Edwin, the one-eyed potman from the Bush, was standing behind his officer. 'Looks like we've got another, Crowner!' Gwyn raised his voice above the babble in the hall.

'What's he doing here?' demanded John, fearful that something had happened to Nesta.

'He came and sought me out, just after the bell for Matins,' explained Gwyn. 'I was in the Bush earlier and mentioned to Edwin that I was going on to the Ship Inn in Rack Lane, where he found me.'

As usual, Gwyn was spinning out his yarn, but de Wolfe turned impatiently to the tavern servant. 'What's all this about? Is your mistress in trouble?'

Edwin, an old sack draped about his thin shoulders, shook his head. 'Not as such, Cap'n, but she's mortal upset, so I slipped away and found Gwyn here. I reckon the sight of you might ease her mind a great deal.'

De Wolfe fumed at this pair, who would never come to the point. 'Hell's teeth, damn you both, what's happened?'

Gwyn sensed that his master was about to explode and hurriedly explained. 'Another corpse, Crowner.

Girl this time, strangled in the backyard of the Bush. And your Nesta found her.'

'She tripped over the body, in fact,' added Edwin, rolling his one good eye ghoulishly. 'Outside the brew-shed she was. The mistress come upon her when she went out to stir the mash.'

De Wolfe glared at them, and waited for them to add the most obvious piece of information.

'A whore, it was,' rumbled Gwyn. 'That new fancy piece with the red wig – Joanna of London they call her.'

De Wolfe's mind was fixed on Nesta's distress, rather than the murder of a harlot. He glanced back up the hall, to see that the knot of gossiping wives was at last breaking up. They were on their feet, still talking, but raising their mantles to their shoulders and arranging their head-rails and wimples. For a moment he stood irresolute. Though the Guildhall was but a few yards from Martin's Lane, there was no way that he could leave his wife to walk home alone. Hugh de Relaga, who might have chaperoned her if he had been sober, had left, and although John was not much concerned for Matilda's safety on a hundred-pace journey to their house, she would never let him hear the end of it if he abandoned her – especially when she discovered that it was to rush to the aid of his ex-mistress.

'You go back to the Bush now and wait for me. Tell Nesta I'll be there as soon as I've escorted my wife to our door – hardly a few minutes, with luck.' He pushed them towards the screens, then loped towards the other end of the top table, pushing servants, diners and drunks out of his way in his hurry to reach his wife.

As he came up to the four ladies, who were still shrugging their gowns and cloaks into position, he gabbled, 'I am called out to a killing, lady. I have to go without delay, so I will see you home straight away.' He grabbed Matilda's arm and, with a jerky bow towards her friends, hauled her unceremoniously towards the doors.

At first she was too astonished to protest, but soon found her voice and berated him for his rudeness all the way to the corner of Martin's Lane. He managed to fob off her questions about the reason for urgency, except to claim that it was foul murder 'somewhere in the lower town', though he knew full well that by morning the exact location of the corpse would be known to the whole of Exeter, and that he would get the length of Matilda's tongue when she discovered she had been hustled out so that he could rush off to his 'Welsh whore'.

However, that was trouble stored for the future and within minutes he had delivered his wife to her maid and hurried off across the cathedral Close, almost running in his haste to get to Idle Lane.

CHAPTER SIX

In which Crowner John deals with a harlot

De Wolfe hurried across the wasteground to the side gate of the tavern, which opened directly into the large backyard.

Gwyn was waiting for him inside the gate, which was the only entrance through a line of rough but sturdy palings that marked off the land belonging to the inn. The light was poor, but the moon and a pitch-brand stuck over the back door, in defiance of the curfew regulations, gave enough light for those who wanted to empty their bladders against the fence. As he arrived, Edwin came out with a horn lantern, which though feeble, threw a pool of light over a small area.

'Where's your mistress?' de Wolfe demanded harshly.

'Inside. She had a sit-down and cup of brandy-wine to settle her nerves, then went up to her bed. She had a terrible shock, Cap'n.'

'Want to see the cadaver first?' asked Gwyn pointedly.

De Wolfe gave one of his ambiguous grunts. He was more concerned with Nesta, but decided that he must salve his official conscience by delaying another minute or two. The potman held up his lantern and limped up the yard. It was almost square, about twenty-five paces each way. The brew-shed was the largest hut, facing the cookhouse and the privy, which were too close together for good health. Against the end fence was an open stable, a fowl-house and a pigsty, all set in a patch of grassless mud that, fortunately, was now fairly dry.

A murmur of voices came from the back door of the tavern and, turning, John dimly saw a cluster of curious onlookers. Gwyn followed his gaze. 'They were all over the damn place when I came, but I chased them back and threatened them with amercement if they set foot up here again,' he boomed, as they reached the crudely boarded hut where the ale was brewed.

'There she is, Cap'n!' croaked Edwin, almost as if he owned the corpse. He held up his lamp and de Wolfe saw a still form lying on the hard earth. The woman's head was almost touching the planks of the brew-house door, and she was flat on her back, with her legs crossed at the ankles. Her right arm was outstretched and just beyond her fingers was a pottery wine-cup, tipped on its side. The striped hood of her cloak was still in place, almost concealing her red wig. Its front edge was across her forehead, but the rest of her face and neck were exposed to the pale moon and the flickering lantern.

'This time it's a strangling,' said Gwyn, unnecessarily, for it was obvious that a white band was cutting tightly into her throat, a loose end lying across her chest. The cloak had fallen open and her crumpled silk kirtle was visible all the way down to her ankles.

It was hard to tell the colour in that light, but John thought that the cloak was purple and the gown a bright red. 'Put that light down close to her face,' commanded the coroner. Even his anxiety about Nesta had been temporarily dampened by his professional interest in the mode of death.

'No doubt she's been throttled,' repeated his officer. 'Her face is dark and swollen.'

The boldly handsome face of the prostitute was

reddish-purple in the light from the lantern. Her tongue protruded slightly from between the carmined lips and a dribble of frothy saliva issued from one corner. De Wolfe placed the back of his hand against her cheek. 'Still warm, she's not been dead long.' He picked up one of her outflung hands and dropped it again. 'Not a trace of stiffness, either.'

'She weren't here an hour before the Matins bell, Crowner,' offered Edwin. 'I came out for a new cask then. The mistress found her a few minutes before the bell so it must have been done between them times.'

De Wolfe rocked back on his heels alongside the body. A strangled whore was no great novelty, usually related to a dispute over payment or because the girl had taunted the client for his pathetic performance. In the great scheme of things, this was not a serious crime.

Yet when he looked up at Gwyn, he had a foreboding of greater problems to come. The man was looking at him with a sly grin that John had come to know only too well over the past twenty years.

'Well, what is it? Out with it, damn you!' he barked.

His henchman continued to leer at John in his infuriating way. 'Lift up the cowl, Crowner, and you'll see.'

Suspiciously, John turned back to the dead girl and pushed back her hood. He stared at her forehead, then beckoned impatiently to Edwin to hold the lantern closer. 'There's some marks on her skin – looks like soot or lamp-black across her temples.'

Gwyn nodded. 'It's surely writing. I can't read a bloody word, but I know letters when I see them.'

De Wolfe grabbed the lamp from the potman and held it almost touching the woman's face, in an effort to make out what the marks were. They were certainly letters of the Latin alphabet, but the edge of the hood had smudged them. Desperately, he tried to recall all his lessons and managed to make out that it was a long word beginning with R, but he could not decipher the rest. He stood up quickly and yelled urgently at the crowd still loitering near the back entrance to the inn. 'Is there anyone among you who can read? A priest or a merchant's clerk?' It was asking a lot to find someone literate among the late-night drinkers in a city tavern, but John was afraid that the writing on the girl's face would smudge off before it could be read, as it seemed only to be made with a finger soiled with soot from a fire-pit.

'Shall I go and find our miserable clerk?' suggested Gwyn.

De Wolfe was about to agree when there was a minor commotion at the inn door and a figure was pushed forward. When he came hesitantly up the yard, John could see it was a youth in the sober garments of a secondary, one of the junior acolytes from the cathedral. These young men assisted their vicars and canons, as a stepping stone to priesthood, which could only be achieved after the age of twenty-five. 'Sir, they say you need someone who can read,' he said reluctantly. John nodded brusquely and beckoned him forward. The lad recoiled when he saw a corpse garbed in the well-known uniform of a whore, but he steeled himself to crouch down alongside the coroner.

'Can you tell me what that says?' demanded de Wolfe. He held the lantern as close as he could to the woman's forehead, while the secondary peered at the smudged markings.

'It reads ... a strange word ...' He hesitated, and formed sounds with his lips. 'It says "revelation", Crowner. Just that one word, revelation.'

'You are quite sure?'

'I am certain what the word is, sir, though what it signifies, I have no idea.' De Wolfe grunted his thanks and the aspiring priest scurried away, to be treated to a quart of reviving ale by his friends in the tavern.

Gwyn looked down knowingly at his master. 'Is this another like the Jew?' he asked, with a hint of morbid satisfaction in his tone.

The coroner shrugged and hauled himself to his feet. 'It may well be. We must consult Thomas, our oracle, for he is most likely to have the answer.'

The urgency of dealing with Nesta flooded back to him and he pointed at the corpse. 'Send for the constables or Gabriel to move her to where we can examine her later – anywhere out of sight of our friend the innkeeper.'

'It's a long way to haul a body to the castle from here,' objected the Cornishman. 'What about carrying her to St Nicholas's Priory, where we took that dead lady, Adele de Courcy, a while back?'

De Wolfe agreed impatiently – at the moment, he didn't care if they carried her to Dartmoor, as long as she was removed and he could get to see Nesta. 'Don't go there yourself, Gwyn. Seize all these idle drinkers and impound them for a jury tomorrow. Find out if they know anything about this strumpet, if she was in the inn tonight and who was with her. You know what to do. And bring that wine-cup – for all we know, it might have been drugged. Then find that God-forsaken clerk of ours!' he added as a parting shot.

The coroner strode to the inn door and pushed his way in through the gawking throng, with Edwin limping after him clutching the lantern. 'She's up in her garret, Cap'n,' he wheezed, as they entered the odorous drinking chamber that filled the ground floor. It was almost empty: many patrons had slunk away when they knew that a crime had been committed, anxious to avoid any contact with the law and its possible effect on their person or their purse. The only ones whose curiosity had got the better of their caution were those in the yard behind.

John made straight for the wide ladder that led to the upper floor, and climbed its treads with a feeling of nostalgia for the many times that he had ascended them with Nesta. He reached the loft, its peaked roof lost in the darkness. A few lodgers snored on their pallets, those who were too tired or too drunk to have joined the curious crowd in the yard. The only light came dimly from a corner, where a small room was partitioned off for the landlady's own use. It had no ceiling and the dim light of a tallow dip reflected off the hazel withies that supported the thatch above. He picked his way through the straw mattresses that lay on the floor to the little room, Edwin and his lantern having diplomatically stayed downstairs. John tapped softly on the door and called her name.

'Who's there? What do you want?' The voice sounded more weary than distressed.

'It's John. I came to see if you were in need of anything. I have dealt with . . . with what was in the yard.'

There was a pause, then the bar across the inside of the door was lifted and the wooden latch raised. A face appeared, a taper held high alongside it to throw light upon his face. 'It really is you, John!' Nesta sounded genuinely surprised.

He grinned lopsidedly, in spite of the tenseness of the moment. 'It really is, Nesta – not some evil spirit.'

She opened the door wider and stood before him, still in her working gown and linen apron. They stared at each other as if meeting for the first time, her eyes wide in her oval face. Even in the gloom, he could see the rich red of her hair and the fullness of her lips. 'Can I come in?' he asked.

A moment later she was in his arms, sobbing with relief – though he was not sure if the relief was from the shock of falling over a throttled corpse or at being reunited with him. He pulled her gently to the bed and sat her alongside him, his arm around her shoulders in an almost fatherly embrace. 'I've missed you sorely, Nesta. Are you going to send me packing again?'

She shook her head and gulped back tears. After the hard life she had led, Nesta was rarely given to visible emotion, but now many weeks of loneliness and remorse leaked away in muffled sobs. The inarticulate John also felt an unaccustomed lump rise in his throat, which he attempted to clear with his usual grunts and spasmodic squeezes of her shoulders.

'Am I welcome back again, dear woman?' He didn't know whether he meant in her inn, her heart or her bed.

She nodded vigorously and then, with a snort of anger at her weakness, sniffed back her tears and wiped her eyes with the hem of her apron. 'It was horrible, John. Although she was a whore, she didn't deserve to die like that. And why in my bailey?'

'Murder is a hazard of her trade, Nesta.' But even as he said it, he remembered the sooty writing on the woman's brow and knew that this was no common killing. However, did not want to talk about the pursuit of justice. 'I have been foolish these past months, Nesta. I should not have let you keep me at arm's length.'

'I've missed you more than I can say, John. It has been the most miserable time of my life – certainly since Meredydd died.'

Her husband had been a Welsh archer, a friend of de Wolfe. When Meredydd had given up fighting, he had settled down as landlord of the Bush, but soon a fever had carried him off and John had helped his widow pay his debts and carry on with the tavern. An innocent friendship had blossomed into affection and passion.

'But nothing has changed, John. I love you dearly, yet the future holds little for us,' she said, with infinite sadness.

De Wolfe had just regained what he had lost for months and was in no mood to surrender it. 'We can go on as we did before, Nesta!' he exclaimed vehemently. 'Why should we forfeit even a moment of the pleasure we get from each other's company? And I don't only mean *here.*' He bumped up and down on the mattress to illustrate his point.

'Everyone knows about us, John, even Matilda.' But she was fighting a rearguard action and she spoke with no real conviction in her voice.

'I don't give a damn what people think. Almost every man I know has a woman or two tucked away – and usually not one he cherishes, as I cherish you.'

She burrowed closer to him. 'But what if I become with child, John? It's a wonder it hasn't happened already.'

'And what if you did?' he bellowed recklessly. 'I would honour and support it and be glad to give it the name Fitz-Wolfe. There's no shame in becoming a father. Even the bloody sheriff has at least two bastards that I know of, and no one points a finger at him.'

Nesta wanted to be convinced and stifled her protests, though she knew that stormy passages lay ahead. 'Let us see how it goes, then, *cariad,*' she murmured, in the Welsh they always used when together. They held each other tightly for a few minutes, but de Wolfe was aware of noises coming through the thatch from the yard below. Then he heard Gwyn yelling orders at whoever had arrived to move the murdered woman's body out. There was a crash as the gate was thrown back on its hinges.

The commotion was like a douche of cold water over the pair.

'I've seen dead bodies before, John, but to fall over one in my own yard . . .'

He gave Nesta's shoulders squeeze, but felt a restless urge to go down to see what was happening. 'Was the woman in the inn tonight? I saw her flaunting herself here a few days ago,' he said.

Nesta nodded, her face rubbing against his tunic. 'She has been here a few times lately. I don't encourage whores, but if I had them all thrown out, I'd lose the trade of the men, especially those merchants and travellers who lodge here and want a woman. But I never let them use the loft – not like that fat swine in the Saracen.' It was a low-class tavern not far away on Stepcote Hill, run by Willem the Fleming, notorious for harbouring cutpurses and harlots.

'But was this Joanna here tonight?'

'I saw her earlier on, drinking with a couple of strangers. She was plying her trade with them, and when she vanished, I assumed she had gone off to serve them in some doorway or under a bush.'

'When would that have been?

'Oh, God knows, John. I'm too busy to watch the comings and goings of the local whores. I would think it was a couple of hours before midnight.'

'Edwin says the corpse wasn't there an hour before that time – and you stumbled across it at about the time of the Matins bell?'

'Yes – so she must have gone elsewhere from here, not straight out to her death. I've no idea who the men she was with might have been. They weren't regular customers – nor were they staying here the night. I've only three or four lodging.' She jerked a thumb towards the door, from beyond which came a stuttering snore.

'What do you know about the girl? Where did she stay?'

Nesta frowned a little. 'John, you're getting too official already. Am I going to lose you again within minutes of finding you?'

He hugged her close, knowing how carefully he must tread in the future. 'But I have to protect you, my loved one. If that was some stray madman in your yard, he might have attacked you, rather than the whore.' He omitted to mention the bizarre matter of the inscribed forehead, which was likely to mean that this had been no random killing.

'And another thing. You're the First Finder. I will have to have you at the inquest in the morning.'

She smiled up at him impishly, a welcome return of her old nature. 'And will you amerce me two marks if you find I failed to raise the hue and cry, Sir Crowner?'

It took the staid de Wolfe a second to realise that she was teasing him. 'You did raise it, for those men in the inn were on the scene at once. That's as good a hue and cry as I need.' He stood up and placed his long fingers on her shoulders. 'I'll not sacrifice you for the law again, woman of mine! But I will have to see to this business now, for both our sakes.'

She stood up with him and threw her arms around his waist, her head coming only to the level of his collarbones. 'I'll give you but a few hours, Keeper of the Pleas of the Crown!' she mocked. 'If you desert me until after breakfast, never darken these doors again.' She stood on tip-toe and raised her face to be kissed.

John went out in a haze of joy, almost falling down the steep ladder as his feet trod air.

St Nicholas's Priory was a small establishment of Benedictines, a dependency of Battle Abbey, the mother church that had been set up in Sussex to commemorate the Conqueror's great victory over Harold and his Saxons. It stood in a lane on the outer edge of the dismal area of Bretayne, not far from St Olave's on Fore Street, which in turn belonged to St Nicholas's.

It was a single building set in a small plot of land and housed half a score of monks under a sour-natured prior. They kept a couple of beds for the local sick and a storeroom that not infrequently doubled as a mortuary, for there was a high death rate in that squalid part of the city.

The two town constables, one of them the Saxon Osric, had been called to the Bush from their patrol. As usual, they had been attempting to enforce the curfew and catch those who had failed to damp down their fires. The curfew – the *couvre-feu* – demanded that all open fires had to be either extinguished or banked down each night, though it was a rule observed more in the breach than in reality. Aided by a couple of the Bush's patrons they had carried away the cadaver on a hurdle pulled from behind the tower's pig-pen. By the time John arrived at St Nicholas's, they had already negotiated with the prior to place the body in his storeroom and it now lay on three planks, supported by trestles, ready for his inspection.

The last time he had seen a woman's corpse in this room, he had enlisted the services of the formidable Dame Madge from the nunnery at Polsloe, two miles away. But in the early hours of the morning, with all the city gates firmly barred, it was impossible to bring her to help him examine Joanna of London. Without the aid of a chaperone, he decided to tread cautiously and confine his investigations to the upper part of the body, at least until the nun could be called next day.

After Matins and Lauds, the surly prior had gone back to bed until Prime at dawn, leaving a sleepy monk to lean against the door-post of the mortuary and keep an eye on the coroner. The other town constable had gone about his business, but the skinny

Osric stayed to help. Just as de Wolfe was about to approach the corpse, he heard Gwyn's heavy tread in the lane outside. The Cornishman came through the priory gate with Thomas de Peyne in tow. 'Found the little knave wandering the Close. He wasn't on his bed after all.'

'I couldn't sleep – I went for a walk to clear my head, that's all,' protested the clerk. 'Do you expect me to crouch in my lodging all night, just in case you want me?'

Ignoring their bickering, the coroner beckoned them into the storeroom, where a couple of candles, remnants from the altar in the priory chapel, threw a flickering light over the body. 'Thomas, come and look at these marks, before they are rubbed away for ever.' He grabbed the ex-priest's hunched shoulder and dragged him to the head of the bier. 'What do make of that? A young secondary at the Bush claimed that it spelled a word.'

Thomas peered closer, the hunt for truth overcoming his revulsion at the proximity of a dead woman. His thin lips moved as he tried to trace out the smudged marks, which even to de Wolfe's illiterate eyes were less clear now than when he had first seen them. 'It's hard to make out . . . A couple of letters are gone. What did that other fellow claim he saw?'

'He said it read "revelation".'

Thomas scanned the marks again. 'Ah! Now you tell me that I can fill in the blurred parts. It is indeed "Revelation".'

'And what the hell might that mean, written on the brow of a whore?' demanded Gwyn.

'A whore, you say?' Further light dawned on the clerk's face. 'Of course, St John the Divine! This is another message – like the one we saw with the old Jew, Crowner.'

De Wolfe sighed. 'Come on, Thomas, explain yourself. What's St John to do with marks daubed in lampblack? Do you mean this comes from the fourth Gospel?'

Thomas frowned at his ignorance. 'No, no! The same disciple, but a different book of the New Testament. He also wrote the very last one of the whole Vulgate – the Revelation of St John the Divine, the most obscure and mystical of them all.'

'You're right there, little toad,' growled Gwyn rudely. 'It's totally obscure to me. But what's this to do with a throttled drab?'

Thomas closed his eyes, not in disgust at his companions' Philistine failings but as an aid to searching his memory. 'Let me see – yes, I have the words! Not literally, but those that seem so relevant to these circumstances. Just look at the colours of her clothing.'

De Wolfe ground his teeth: Thomas was becoming as long-winded as Gwyn. 'God's guts, man – spit it out, will you?'

The clerk pointed at the dead woman's temples. 'Towards the end of the Book of Revelation, John describes a woman dressed in purple and scarlet, with a cup in her hand filled with the abominations of her fornication. And on her forehead was written "Mother of whores and every obscenity on earth".'

There was a silence, in which they all looked at the gaudy colours of Joanna's clothing, the wine cup left alongside her and the writing on her forehead.

'Whoever's doing this, he certainly knows his Bible,' muttered de Wolfe. He looked sharply at Thomas. 'Is every priest able to recognise these passages from the scriptures as well as you?' His tone was almost accusatory.

'I told you last time, Crowner, many priests can hardly read. Whoever is doing this must have had a good education.'

'Do you mean it would be a canon or an archdeacon?' demanded Gwyn.

The clerk shook his head. 'Far from it. Some canons are as ignorant as their bottlers. I suspect some are even totally uncaring about their faith, perhaps even unbelievers.' His face darkened as some inner thought erupted. 'And some are evil men, who think nothing of taking away a man's soul.'

De Wolfe had more urgent problems than Thomas's soul. 'Has he left a message this time, as he did with the moneylender?'

They began to search the body, but were hampered in that none of the men wanted to undress her, although in life she had earned her living by exposing her body to men. The removal of her hooded mantle was as far as they went, which at least gave them access to her head and neck. The gaudy wig, made of some bright orange-red tow, was awry, revealing her short brown hair beneath. The ligature around her neck was made of silk and when Gwyn unwrapped it, they saw it was a thin stocking, looped twice around her slender throat and tied in a double knot at the side. It had cut into her neck, leaving a deep groove from the pressure.

'It was done during life, no doubt of that,' growled the coroner, pointing at the two edges of the groove. 'The upper edge has a line of blood spots along it and above that, the skin is purple and swollen, whereas it is pale and clear below.'

'Why should you think otherwise, Crowner?' asked Thomas, with his unfailing curiosity, even for the macabre.

'Because I have seen ligatures around the already dead – and this one has a head injury, just like the Jew.'

De Wolfe, who had been supporting the head while Gwyn unwrapped the stocking, showed the palm of his hand, which was covered in sticky blood. 'The back of her head was violently struck – this time with force enough to crack the skull in spite of her wig. I can feel pieces of bone grating together under the hair and skin.' He wiped his hand on the crumpled silk stocking. 'We have a killer who seems to stick to his methods – first a blow to the head to silence the victim, then another means of causing their death.'

He stood back and gazed at the pathetically still harlot. For the first time, he noticed that an ominous bloodstain was spreading through her gown over the area of her lower belly and upper thighs. The significance was all too obvious, but still the men shied away from the intimate probing that would be necessary to determine exactly what had happened.

'We need a wise woman's help here,' de Wolfe muttered gruffly. 'Gwyn, make sure that a message gets to Polsloe soon after dawn to get that midwife nun over here.'

Gwyn nodded, then, anxious to change the subject, said 'No sign of any written message, though?'

'The written message was on her temple, Crowner,' pointed out Thomas, sensibly. 'It seems clear enough to me.'

John nodded reluctantly. 'I suppose you're right. There's little else we can do here, now – we know who she was, how she died and that it was by the same crazy hand that killed Aaron.' He led them outside, and Osric pulled the door shut.

'Can we do any more tonight?' asked Gwyn. 'It must be halfway to dawn now.'

De Wolfe remembered Nesta's threat about breakfast, but he also had Matilda to contend with. He was back on the old knife-edge of weaving a safe path between them.

'If you have the names of those who were at the Bush,

we can leave it until early morning. The Saracen will be our first call, to get that evil swine Willem to the inquest, if this girl was working mainly out of his lousy ale-house.' He trudged away, leaving Thomas to find his pallet in the Close and Gwyn to bed down in the castle gatehouse, while he himself went home to make his peace with Matilda as best he could – although he knew that when she discovered his new case was centred around the Bush, she would make his life hell.

ChAPTER SEVEN

In which Crowner John eats a hearty breakfast

It was not long before Sir John de Wolfe, warrior and Crusader, again showed his yellow streak when it came to facing up to women. Matilda was sound asleep when he eased himself quietly into the solar and even more quietly on to his side of the wide mattress. He was up before dawn and slid out before she awoke, putting off the evil hour when he must tell her about the body in the Bush.

Mary was also up and about, getting the cooking fire going, but he refused her offer of food and took himself off to Idle Lane just as it was getting light. The Bush was already in full swing, with the lodgers breaking their fast and some early traders calling in for food and ale.

Nesta looked sleepy but was full of smiles, and John's morbid fears that she might have had second thoughts about their reconciliation were unfounded. 'I came before breakfast, as you demanded, woman,' he said, with mock ferocity. She gave a swift kiss and sat him down at his favourite table, behind a wattle screen near the empty fireplace. She hurried away, yelling for her two maidservants, and within minutes a wide pewter platter, heaped with thick slices of bacon, three griddled eggs and leeks fried in mutton fat, was put before him even though it was Friday and a fish day in the eyes of the Church. A wooden bowl filled with boiled oatmeal followed, swimming in milk and honey, and a quart of best ale completed his meal. Nesta sat opposite him, chin in hand, daring him not to eat every morsel.

'This is fit to break the fast of a Gwyn, not a John!' he complained happily, tucking in with a will, determined to swallow every scrap to please her, even if it killed him.

Between mouthfuls, he told her of the discoveries at St Nicholas and brought her up to date on the similarity of this case with the death of the Jewish moneylender. He knew that Nesta would keep his confidences – and also that, like Thomas de Peyne, she was an invaluable source of information, for little happened in Exeter, and for miles around, that was not gossiped about in the Bush, which was one of the city's busiest taverns.

'So you feel it must be a priest?' she asked, wide-eyed at the macabre story.

'With that knowledge of the scriptures and the ability to write, it can hardly be anyone else. Only someone like Thomas would be able to pick such appropriate texts.'

There was a sudden awkward pause, as both realised what he had just suggested. Nesta laughed, a short embarrassed laugh. 'Of course, that's nonsense. Anyway, he would have been with you each time.'

There was another short silence.

'He wasn't, in fact. But it's still damn ridiculous – although he has been acting strangely since he tried to kill himself.'

They both made a conscious effort to throw the foolish thought from their minds.

'What's the next thing, then?' she asked. 'Put every priest in Exeter to the *peine forte et dure*?'

'That would please Gwyn, I'm sure. No, I'll have to seek out those clerics who are known to be a bit strange and put some pressure on them.'

The landlady made a rude noise, indicating her derision. 'You've got little chance of that, Sir Crowner! The Bishop will have you excommunicated if you start pestering his troops – Benefit of Clergy and all that.'

'He can waive that right if he is so persuaded, just as he has agreed we may have jurisdiction in the cathedral precinct over any crime of violence there.'

Nesta sniffed disdainfully – she was tiring of all this talk of the law, when she just had her lover back again. But it was too early in the day for passion and when John had finished his massive breakfast, he felt more like slumping back against the wattle screen than investigating a murder. As always, his sense of duty triumphed. This was just as well, because the inn door flew open and his officer stormed in. When he saw his master with Nesta, Gwyn's craggy face broke into a radiant smile, his blue eyes dancing above the ginger foliage on his face. He adored the Welsh woman and his mortification when they had split up was only equalled by his present delight at the healing of the wound.

Nesta, who was familiar with his gargantuan appetite, offered him food, but he had already eaten at a stall on the way down from Rougemont. He would have succumbed to the mildest persuasion to have another meal, but de Wolfe hauled him away. 'To the Saracen, man! We have a day's work before us. There are hangings to attend as well. Where's that bloody clerk of ours? He knows how many swing today.' He left the Bush with a promise to Nesta that he would return later and trudged off with Gwyn to the tavern where Joanna was said to have had her base. The Saracen was at the top of Stepcote Hill, between Idle Lane and St Mary Steps, a couple of minutes' walk from the Bush. It was a similar building, though lower in the roof. Its walls were dirty pink, washed with white lime coloured with ox-blood. Over the door was a crude painting of a man with a turban, holding a scimitar, though de Wolfe decided that the artist could never have been nearer the Holy Land than Exmouth.

'Have you set up the inquest at St Nicholas?' he asked Gwyn, as they approached the inn.

'Yes, the jury will be there at the ninth hour – the prior was not pleased, the miserable old sod.'

They stepped aside to let a donkey pass them, heavily laden with bales of wool going to the fulling mills, its hoofs slipping on the cobbles of the steep lane. When it had passed, they were opposite the inn door and John ducked inside. The stench, even at that early hour, was ten times stronger than the Bush, which Nesta kept cleaner than any other ale-house in Exeter. The Saracen was indeed a foul den. The four maids were all prostitutes, paying Willem the Fleming half their fee for the privilege of picking up their customers between serving ale and cider. Many of his patrons were thieves and coiners and much of the business transacted there was the disposal of stolen goods.

When they went in the landlord was at the back of the room, throwing a thin layer of mouldy rushes on top of the filthy ones that were already strewn over the floor. They looked as if they had not been changed since old King Henry died, for they were dotted with scraps of food, dog droppings and assorted rubbish. Here and there they moved, as a rat foraged among them.

When he saw his visitors the Fleming dropped his bundle. The arrival of law officers always meant trouble and his flabby features signalled his suspicion and displeasure. 'The bloody crowner, no less!' he grated, his foreign accent still strong even after twenty years in Devon. 'What in hell do you want this time?'

He was as big as Gwyn, but fat rather than muscular. His jowls hung over the collar of his grimy smock and the long leather apron bulged over his belly.

'You have been harbouring a girl known as Joanna of London?' snapped de Wolfe.

'Harbouring? What d'you mean, harbouring?' The small eyes glittered over a sneering mouth. 'An inn is open to anyone who wishes to enter. The law demands it.'

John sighed, he had no inclination to bandy words with this fat bastard.

'Don't waste my time, Willem. She was a whore who worked out of your ale-house, we all know that. I'm not interested in the way you run your business, I just want to know about this Joanna.'

The little eyes narrowed. 'If it's the crowner that's asking, then she must be dead, eh?'

'Yes – and you've lost your cut from her earnings. The girl's been murdered. I want to know where she lived, when you last saw her and who she was with.'

The inn-keeper roared with laughter. 'Would you like to know her grandmother's maiden name while you're at it? She slept here sometimes, yes – when she wasn't in some man's bed elsewhere. But where she went and who with – Holy Mary, she was whore! A dozen different men on a good day.'

It was the answer de Wolfe had expected, but he felt he had to go through the motions. 'She slept here sometimes, though?'

'Up in the loft. She usually had money and paid for a twopenny pallet. As she was a regular, so to speak, I let her stay in one that has a screen at the side – though I suspect she usually crept out to service the other lodgers at a penny a time.'

'Did she have any belongings?'

'She left a bundle alongside her mattress. Clothes, I suppose.'

The coroner demanded to see them and, grumbling under his breath, Willem reluctantly led them up a flight of wooden steps to the floor above. It was similar to that in the Bush, only smaller and dirtier. A row of verminous straw-filled mattresses lay on the floor. At each end was a vertical screen of woven reeds, which gave some slight privacy to the mattress behind it.

'When did she come here?'

'About two months ago. Said she had had to run from London, as she had stabbed her keeper, who was beating her for holding back some money. Sounded like the truth, for once.'

John looked behind the screen and saw a bundle tied up in a scarf, lying on the bed. Ignoring the fleas that hopped on the sacking cover of the pallet, he untied it and, in the dim light under the thatch, looked cursorily at two gaudy dresses, a gauze shift, some stockings that matched the one that had been around her neck and a cloth bag containing a dirty hairbrush and a tiny pot of rouge.

'No money, I see. There was nothing on her body, either.'

Willem sneered again. 'A girl like that would be too wise to leave a ha'penny lying here. It would be stolen within two minutes. She'll have stashed her funds in a hole somewhere. Harlots never carry it on their person – most of their customers would cut their throat for the price of a drink. Maybe that's what happened, anyway. Why are you bothering about a dead strumpet?'

De Wolfe ignored him and clambered back down the steps. At the door, he had one last question. 'When did you last see this Joanna?'

The Fleming scowled at him. 'I don't mark the comings and goings of every whore who uses this place. She was around sometime yesterday, as far as I recall. In the morning, I think.'

They left the Saracen with some relief, Gwyn scratching vigorously after having added to the colony of fleas that normally lived in his clothing. As they loped up Smythen

Street, past the clanging of the forges to where St John's Row turned through to Fore Street, Gwyn vented his opinion of the Saracen and Willem the Fleming, his description coloured by a string of oaths.

'But, for once, I think he has no involvement in this,' grunted de Wolfe. 'The business with the Biblical quotations makes this a more sinister affair than just the casual croaking of a harlot.'

They passed St John's church and crossed the main street then turned again into the narrow lanes at the top of Bretayne to reach St Nicholas's, squelching through a rivulet of sewage that ran down the middle of the alley and pushing aside goats and a pig. Inside the gate, the compound around the monastic building was well kept, compared to the squalor outside. A cobbled area lay around the walls and outside was a garden where the monks grew vegetables and herbs. A few fruit trees around the boundary fence were well into leaf.

A score of men hung around the door to the mortuary, watched suspiciously by two monks set there by the prior to prevent them stealing anything. Thomas was there too, looking as unhappy as ever, his lips making silent conversation with some invisible being.

'Let's get on with this, there's hangings to be attended afterwards,' snapped the coroner, going to the store-room door and flinging it open. He heard the lane gate scrape open and turned back to see Nesta coming in, with one of her serving-maids in attendance. As the discoverer of the body, she was obliged to be present at the inquest and had covered herself for the occasion with a decorously dull-green cloak with a hood that covered her linen coif and burnished copper hair. Old Edwin limped gallantly behind them, grasping a knobbly staff in his fist, to guard them through this disreputable part of the city.

Gwyn marshalled the jury to each side of the door,

like a dog with a flock of sheep. They were all last night's drinkers from the Bush, with the two constables at each end. A handful of old men and goodwives from the nearby hovels came in to listen at the back – a dead whore was a welcome diversion from the sordid routine of life in Bretayne.

Gwyn gabbled his usual royal command to open the inquest and Thomas squatted on a keg just inside the storeroom, with his parchment and pens on a piece of board across his knees. John stood in the open doorway to conduct the proceedings and, after a quick preamble, asked Nesta to step forward. With a dead-pan face, he asked her to identify herself, then went on to question her. She answered demurely, with downcast eyes, and although almost everyone there knew that she was the coroner's mistress, not an eyebrow lifted and not a smirk passed across a face. 'Lady, can you put a name to the deceased from your own knowledge – and were you the First Finder?'

Nesta said softly but clearly that the woman was known as Joanna of London and that she had frequented her hostelry a number of times, even though prostitutes were not encouraged there. She had last seen her in the Bush late last night, then described how she had gone out to her brew-house some time before midnight to attend to her latest batch of mash. She had taken a horn lantern, but had tripped over something in the shadows and almost fallen. It was then that she had seen the dead girl lying on her back. She had screamed and run to the back door of the inn, where Edwin was coming out to investigate, followed by several of the patrons.

'And was a Hue and Cry made straight away?' demanded de Wolfe, with deliberate sternness.

'It was indeed! Some of the men rushed around the yard to make sure no one was lurking there – they looked in the kitchen, the privy, the brew-house and even the pig-sty. Others ran out of the gate and searched the wasteground in Idle Lane and went as far as Priest Street, Stepcote Hill and Smythen Street. But they found nothing suspicious, so they called Osric, the constable, then sent Edwin up to the castle, where he found Gwyn of Polruan.'

The coroner had one last question, which he had genuinely forgotten to ask Nesta back at the Bush. 'There was a drinking cup near the dead girl's hand. Do you know where it may have come from?'

The landlady shook her head. 'Gwyn showed it to me last night, but it's not one from the Bush. Mine come from a different potter.'

De Wolfe thanked her gravely and Nesta stepped back to stand with her maid. Then a succession of jurors was called, those who had been involved in chasing around the streets of Exeter in the middle of the night. They all told the same story, confirmed by Osric and his fellow constable when they gave their evidence.

As with the inquest on Aaron, John felt no obligation to mention the writing and the strange circumstances, so there was little else to be said. The jurors had to view the corpse, so they paraded through the storeroom, where Gwyn showed them the stocking that had been around Joanna's neck, then pointed out the strangulation groove on her skin and the bloody wound on the back of her head.

Outside again, de Wolfe concluded the proceedings in short order. 'The dead woman is Joanna, a whore reputed to be from London, as her striped hood would confirm. She lodged at the Saracen, but they know nothing of her movements last night. As she is a woman, there is no need to present Englishry, which would be impossible, anyway, as she is a stranger. The cause of death is clear. She was struck on the head to relieve her of her wits, a blow that broke her cranium and which alone would have killed her within hours. But before she died she was throttled with one of her own stockings – a spare one, as she was wearing two, but it matches some that were found with her chattels at the Saracen. Dame Madge from Polsloe Priory has earlier this morning examined the girl on my behalf and found certain injuries of a depraved and licentious nature, which need not be described to you in any detail. It seems likely that they were inflicted immediately after death.'

He paused to glower around the half-circle of uneasy jurors.

'So the verdict is yours, but I am sure you will find that her death was murder against the King's peace, by person or persons as yet unknown.'

There was no disputing de Wolfe's direction, and minutes later, the jury was streaming through the gate, heading back to the Bush for a few reviving quarts of ale.

Only a few yards away from the scene of the inquest, stood another of Exeter's plethora of churches. Indeed, the thirsty jurors had to pass St Olave's on their way back the Bush, though at that moment, praising the Lord was not on the minds of the few that happened to notice the incumbent standing at the door, which opened directly on to Fore Street.

Julian Fulk was fleetingly curious about the group of men who emerged from the lane, but he had other things to concern him. He was chronically anxious about his future and this had generated a slow anger that burned constantly and never left him. Although on the surface, he appeared amiable to the point of obsequious affability, this was a façade over the seething discontent beneath. To the members of his congregation, like

Matilda, he was an urbane, unctuous priest, full of the social graces that attracted many of the more prominent wives of burgesses and officials like Sir John de Wolfe. They came to St Olave's even when their dwellings were distant from his church.

Though formal parish boundaries were a thing of the future in Exeter, most people went to the nearest of about twenty-seven city churches, some only a few steps from their front doors. But Julian Fulk appealed to – and cultivated – those who, like himself, wanted social advancement. Though he was unaware of it, he had much in common with Adam of Dol of St Mary Steps, who also desired to be a canon and was as bitterly resentful that no such elevation seemed to be contemplated by the powers in the cathedral precinct.

Fulk turned away as the men disappeared from Fore Street and went inside his little church. Another oblong stone box, it was the cleanest of them all and, though bare of any decoration, its floor had fresh rushes strewn about and the shutters on the high windows were freshly painted. The altar table was covered with a lace-edged linen cloth, personally worked by the wife of one of the guild masters. The cross was filigreed silver donated by another guild, and before it was a pot containing fresh flowers, an unusual sight in an urban church.

But all of this was ashes in Father Julian's mouth, though none of his gushing lady parishioners would have guessed it. He sat down on the unused bishop's chair at the side of the altar to rest his bulk, for he was the shape of a barrel and perspired copiously at the slightest exertion. His moon-shaped face was pink, virtually the same colour as his almost bald head – he had only a rim of sandy hair from ear to ear. Nerves caused him to chew his flabby lower lip as he sat in his empty church, waiting for the few worshippers to arrive for his mid-morning Mass.

When the ladies came, he would smile and bob his head, for there were seldom men on a week-day. Julian Fulk would appear the soul of affability, especially to those he thought had husbands who might have influence with the ecclesiastical hierarchy. Fulk knew that it was the gossip around dining tables in Canon's Row and the guildsmen's houses that made or broke reputations, and where preferment was assisted or frustrated with a nudge and wink.

As he pondered beside his altar, he once again cursed the fact that St Olave's was different from all the other city churches, in that it belonged to St Nicholas Priory and its living was controlled by the Abbot of Battle, far away in Sussex. He had never even visited Battle and never met the Abbot, so he was at a double disadvantage in angling to be a canon-elect; the Bishop and Archdeacon here had no responsibility for his curacy of St Olave's. Even that madman down at St Mary Steps had a better chance of promotion, for at least he was within the fold of Exeter.

Julian Fulk had got the living here almost by accident and had regretted it ever since. He was the son of a canon of Winchester and had been educated at the school there, some years earlier than Thomas de Peyne but he had been in the cathedral as a vicar-choral when Thomas was teaching juniors. His father had died suddenly and any chance of paternal influence had died with him, given the intense competition in Winchester between an excess of senior vicars. At a guest-night dinner in the Bishop's palace, he had chanced to sit next to a monk who was Precentor at Battle – and Fulk, disillusioned with Winchester, was offered the living of St Olave's. Without appreciating the insignificance of the church and the grave disadvantage of being outside the pale of Exeter's episcopal establishment, he had moved and stagnated ever since. The impasse had become like a cancer, eating away at his soul and monopolising his every thought, but unlike Adam of Dol, he masked his resentment with a falsely benign face. Yet he knew that, like a cooking pot with a jammed lid, the pressure inside him was building.

De Wolfe had intended to go up to Rougemont after the hangings, to tell the sheriff about the second murder, but de Revelle spared him the trouble by attending the executions himself.

To be more accurate, he came to attend one of them, for the frantic activity to get everything ready for the Justices was mortgaging his time, if he was to conceal every irregularity in the accounts and records. However, he could not deny himself the pleasure of seeing Gocius de Vado swing that morning, after all the trouble the damned man had caused.

Gocius was a freeman who lived near de Revelle's manor at Tiverton and had successfully fought the sheriff's efforts to claim a hide of land from him through an attempted distortion of a land charter going back to the Domesday Commissioners. De Vado had even petitioned the King over the dispute and received a favourable judgement from Hubert Walter. De Revelle swore vindictively to get even with him and, using an *agent provocateur* and several bribed false witnesses, had his enemy convicted in his own shire court of receiving stolen property to a value of ten marks, far above the legal minimum of twelve pence for a felony and thus a capital offence. De Wolfe had not been involved, as no death, robbery or violence had taken place, but when he heard ale-house gossip on the matter, he strongly suspected some underhand dealing by his brother-in-law.

On this Friday morning, the coroner, followed by his officer and clerk, went out of the South Gate and up

Magdalen Street on foot – it was not worth the trouble of saddling up three steeds for a half-mile journey. Though it was called a street, the way to the gallows became a country road, once beyond the huts and ramshackle dwellings that had sprung up outside the walls. These were not villages, like St Sidwell's beyond the East Gate where Gwyn lived, but the overflow of the city. Due to its burgeoning prosperity, Exeter had expanded rapidly and the old walls could no longer house all those who worked there.

The coroner's party walked with scores of others who were going to the hanging tree, either for entertainment or to see off a relative or acquaintance on their journey into eternity. Old men, too aged to work, and mothers with small children to entertain formed the bulk of the crowd, while hawkers with trays of pies and pasties, trinkets and lucky charms made up the rest. There were a few beggars too and even a hooded leper, forbidden to enter the city from the hospital outside the East Gate, but hoping for a few coins in his wooden bowl from those rash enough to brave the warning of his wooden rattle.

Magdalene Street, where Aaron had just been buried in the tiny Jewish cemetery, became the King's highway to Honiton, and thence far away to Salisbury, Southampton, Winchester and even London. But today four men would never get beyond the first half mile, as their journey through life was to end abruptly at the gallows at the road-side.

Hanging was an accepted part of everyday life, preferred by many miscreants to mutilation, blinding or castration, which William the Bastard had favoured when he took over England. The Conqueror preferred these methods because the maimed victims remained in the community as a grim example to other potential wrongdoers. But conviction for a felony usually ended in a hanging, and all the executed person's land and chattels were confiscated. It was not only the Crown that benefited: the power of life and death also resided in the manor and burgess courts when forfeited goods went to the lord or the town council. At this time, England hanged a greater proportion of its inhabitants than any other country in Christendom.

John de Wolfe had no quarrel with this state of affairs – in fact, it never crossed his mind. He was concerned with injustice, but if a man or woman had been sentenced to death in a legitimate court, then like almost every other man in the kingdom, he accepted that death was the proper remedy. His thoughts were on his own problems, not those of the condemned – how to manage the still-delicate relationship with Nesta and Matilda's wrath when she became aware of it. The two latest murders nagged at his mind, with the knowledge that a warped killer was at large within the city.

As he loped along, Gwyn broke into his reveries. 'What's going on up there, then?'

De Wolfe lifted his head and saw a knot of people around a horseman, grouped at the edge of the road level with the gallows. Even at this distance, the angry gesticulations of the rider marked some extremely bad temper.

'It's the sheriff – and Ralph Morin and Gabriel,' exclaimed the sharp-eyed Cornishman. 'They seem to be arguing about the death cart.'

Alongside the group, with a few men-at-arms as escort, was an open wagon with large solid wheels, a patient ox between its shafts. Standing inside, their wrists bound to the front rail, were two men and a woman, their heads drooping in terminal hopelessness.

'There should have been four this morning,' bleated Thomas, who was almost running to keep up with them.

As they covered the last hundred paces, de Wolfe looked to his left at the hanging tree. It consisted of a massive beam twelve feet off the ground, supported at each end by stout posts buried in the earth. Today it indeed had four rope nooses dangling from it.

'You'll answer for this, you incompetent fools,' de Revelle ranted, the objects of his rage being Osric, the constable, and another man who John recognised as one of the gaolers from the city prison in the towers of the South Gate.

'Easy, Richard, you'll give yourself apoplexy,' he advised, as he came up to the sheriff's big black horse. John looked across at Ralph Morin and Gabriel, the sergeant of the guard, but got only a deadpan look from the latter and a covert wink from Morin.

'What's the problem?'

The red-faced sheriff launched into a repetition of his tirade. 'One of the felons has escaped, the very one I came to see dispatched! The fools – or, more likely, corrupt knaves – in the South Gate allowed him to vanish last night.'

'Would that be de Vado, the one to whom you lost that land suit?' asked John with straight-faced innocence.

De Revelle's colour heightened even more and he glared around the faces of the other men, daring them to show even the vestige of a grin.

'It was de Vado, yes. The man who was found with God knows how much stolen loot in his house.'

'Prisoners vanish all the time,' said de Wolfe, reasonably. 'The city couldn't afford to keep all of them in food for months on end, even if there was room in that stinking tower.' He almost added that Richard had never shown any interest in escapees before, but thought it best not to inflame him even more. Many prisoners, especially those in the town gaol, never came to trial or execution, almost always because their relatives or friends bribed the gaolers to let them run for sanctuary in the nearest church or melt away into the countryside to become outlaws. Others just slipped away to another part of England or even abroad, until they could slink back to their homes unobserved.

It was only the sheriff's chagrin at being done out of seeing Gocius de Vado perform the dance of death this morning, that had prompted his condemnation of gaol-breaking. He tried to include his men at the castle in the blame, but Ralph Morin was having none of it.

'Nothing to do with us, sheriff,' he snapped. 'The city gaol belongs to the council and the Portreeves. I'm only responsible for Rougemont. Though we all know that Stigand is not above forgetting to lock a door, if the price is right!'

De Revelle wheeled his horse around, still glowering at his disappointment ... He was about to kick his stallion into a trot, to go back to the city gate, when John reached up to grip one of the reins.

'Wait a moment, Richard. I have to talk to you.'

'I'm in no mood for gossip, John. I have a legion of pestilent clerks clamouring for my attention before this damned Eyre.'

'You'll listen to this – for the Justices certainly will.'

The mention of the royal visitors sharpened the sheriff's attention. His sharp face stared down, the pointed beard bristled with impatience.

'What is it now? Another dead moneylender?'

'No, a dead whore – but slain by the same priestly hand.'

De Revelle's forehead creased in puzzlement. 'How d'you know that? And who was she?'

De Wolfe explained the circumstances quickly, knowing that it was difficult to hold the sheriff's attention if he had more pressing affairs – especially ones which might affect his purse. But this time the sheriff was intrigued. 'Joanna of London, you say? A handsome harlot with the striped clothing?'

'That's the one – and with flame-coloured hair.'

'Her hair's not flame-coloured all over!' sneered Richard, unable to resist a cynical quip. John wondered how he knew so much about a tavern drab, though being aware of the sheriff's nocturnal diversions, he could make a good guess.

'We have to do something about this – and quickly,' he said. 'The Justices, especially Walter de Ralegh, are sharp men and they'll be aware of the latest scandals in the city before they get their boots off. They'll want some explanations, mainly from you.'

For once de Revelle agreed with his sister's husband. 'What do you suggest? If it's a damned cleric, then the Church should be involved. Your bosom friend the Archdeacon is responsible for parish priests, why not ask him?'

'I'm seeing him today, but we must get a few more wise heads together to see if we can draw up a list of possible madmen.'

De Revelle shook the rein free of John's fingers, and as he rode off he jerked a thumb towards Thomas de Peyne, who was setting out his pen and ink on a nearby tree-stump. 'There's one for the top of your list,' he called back over his shoulder.

CHAPTER EIGHT

In which Crowner John visits the Archdeacon

The three routine hangings passed off without incident, and even the sobs and screams of the close relatives were relatively muted, compared with the hysterical scuffles that often occurred. The small crowd watched impassively, until the moment when the ropes tightened around the helpless necks, when a chorus of 'oohs' and 'aahhs' and a few jeers were mingled with the wailing of the families. The woman, who had stabbed her husband when she could no longer stand his endless drunken assaults on her, was turned off first, as a measure of compassion so that she would not have to see the agonal jerks and spasms of the other felons.

Sometimes, varying with the habits of the hangman, the felons were pushed off a ladder propped against the beam, but today the cart was in use. Three times it was driven under the gallows beam and a rope dropped over the victim's neck by the executioner, a part-time butcher from the Shambles. The victim was stood on a board placed high across the back end of the side rails and the butcher smacked the ox's rump. Well used to the procedure, the burly animal plodded forward sufficiently for the cart to move out from under the condemned, who fell into space and began the macabre jerking and twitching which was usually mercifully shortened by a distraught relative running out and dragging desperately on the legs.

John de Wolfe watched all this impassively, then dictated the details of name and domicile to Thomas, who wrote them on his parchment roll, along with a record of the worldly goods, if any, that were forfeit to the Crown.

When the show was over, the crowd set off for home, leaving the bodies to hang for the prescribed time until dusk. The distraught relatives waited beneath to claim them for burial, as none were to be gibbeted, an added disgrace for heinous crimes like treason, where the corpses were locked in an iron cage and hung up for weeks or months for the crows to pick the decaying remnants to pieces.

De Wolfe and Gwyn walked back to the South Gate, Thomas following behind, muttering and crossing himself at frequent intervals. The coroner's footsteps became slower as they entered the cathedral Close and the inevitable confrontation with Matilda became imminent. Thomas wandered off to his lodging in Canon's Row and Gwyn, sensing John's morbid preoccupation, murmured some excuse then peeled off outside St Martin's Church and vanished up the back lane in search of the nearest ale-house.

With leaden feet, de Wolfe walked on to the nemesis of his front door, not sparing a glance for the cleric who stood in the entrance of the little church opposite.

Though de Wolfe did not notice him, Edwin of Frome took note of the coroner's comings and goings. His church was rarely busy and he had plenty of time to lurk just inside the door and watch all who went by, speculating on their business.

The parish priest of St Martin's was unusual in that he was a Saxon. Though the distinction between Norman and Saxon was becoming blurred, many on both sides still took it seriously. The difference in appearance of some pure-bred men and women of either race was still striking and their names proclaimed the persisting schism.

Edwin of Frome had the classic appearance of a Saxon. He was tall, fair-skinned, and his hair was almost yellow, though all that remained of it was a thick rim running around between his shaven crown and shaven neck. He had been born in Somerset thirty-five years ago, a great-grandson of one of the few Saxons to keep their land after the invasion.

At seven, he had been dispatched to the school of Bath Abbey where he had known Adam of Dol. Perhaps that was why they had the same fire-and-brimstone style of preaching, though Edwin was more restrained than the ranting priest of St Mary Steps. Although he had a large chip on his shoulder about his Saxon blood, he had none of the resentment of Julian Fulk or Adam concerning his lack of advancement in the Church. He was content with his modest living in the little chapel of St Martin and was realistic enough to know that, in a solidly Norman enclave like the hierarchy of Exeter Cathedral, he was lucky to have risen as far as he had. Edwin's discontent led in a different direction: he had an obsessional interest in the scriptures. Although every priest should revere, study and love the Bible, his devotion to it was abnormal by any standard.

He was well lettered, though not over-endowed with high intelligence. Edwin believed that every word, every syllable of the Vulgate was God's own utterance, and could neither understand nor accept that all his fellow men, even many priests, did not feel the same way. He knew virtually every word of his own tattered copy by heart and several times had been mortified – and almost driven into madness – to discover that other copies were not identical with his. The logical part of his mind accepted that translations might vary from the original Greek and also that the scribes, who had laboriously written each copy, occasionally made mistakes which were then perpetuated and added to, by further scriveners down the line.

But then his tunnel-vision mentality spawned an agitated concern as to whether *his* copy was the true Word of God or whether the different version was – and as there were many different versions, which of them were true and which false? Though he spoke good Norman French and Latin, his preferred tongue was his native Middle English – so when he had realised that there were also many vernacular versions of the Scriptures, as well as the Latin Vulgate, the far worse variations of text in these almost drove him insane! The issue came to dominate his life, and robust sermons that he delivered to his meagre congregation, inevitably slid towards the iniquity of men who allowed the Word of God to be perverted by false Gospels.

Soon his small flock began to tire of the theme and he lost more of his congregation to the numerous other churches, of which there were three around the Close alone.

Edwin had sporadic insight into his own condition and knew that he was getting worse. For his own safety, he now rarely strayed off the route between his church and his room in Priest Street: he often felt an almost irresistible urge to confront people in the street and demand to know whether they believed every word of the Holy Book. Some weeks ago, he had encountered a mendicant monk, preaching to a knot of curious loungers in the Serge Market. The unfortunate lecturer happened to quote a passage from the Acts of the Apostles, just as Edwin was passing – but according to Edwin's version, he misquoted three words. In a flash, the Saxon priest had the monk by the throat and was wrestling him to the ground, screaming that he must be the anti-Christ, for misleading honest folk. The hugely entertained bystanders dragged him off the bemused preacher and shoved him on his way.

A vicar-choral had seen the extraordinary encounter, which duly came to the ears of the Archdeacon, who gave Edwin a stern warning. He expected that more severe censure would come sooner or later and added this to the burden he carried of being a Saxon in a Norman world.

All these thoughts churned in his head as he turned from his door and stared blankly at the interior of his little church.

The midday meal was as unpleasant as John had expected. A stony silence prevailed for the first half and Matilda, dressed in funeral black, ate stolidly without raising her eyes from her bowl and platter. His gruff attempts at conversation were ignored, but he knew from long experience that this was the quiet before the storm. Even Brutus knew that something was amiss, as he lay quietly before the empty hearth, the white showing in the corner of one eye, as it swivelled cautiously towards his master. Mary came in and out almost on tiptoe and her surreptitious wink from behind Matilda's chair did little to cheer him.

De Wolfe had little appetite, but for the sake of appearances, he sucked at the Friday fish stew and champed on boiled turnip ringed with onions fried in butter. When the maid cleared the debris of the meal and brought in thick slices of bread and a slab of crusted cheese, John knew that the dam was about to burst and tried to forestall it. 'There's been another strange murder,' he said, 'and again the culprit must be a priest.'

Matilda's face rose slowly, framed by the white linen coverchief and wimple around her neck. 'Strange? Yes –

strange that it should happen outside the Bush Inn.' The words were snapped out of a mouth as unforgiving as a rat-trap.

'It was a whore from London,' he went on doggedly.

'So, two whores in that tavern. I've no doubt that now your investigations will take you there frequently.'

From there, the dialogue followed a familiar pattern, all downhill. As Matilda became angrier, she became more vociferous and her voice rose steadily in pitch and volume. De Wolfe's temper rose too, and within minutes they were yelling at each other, intriguing those folk in Martin's Lane who passed the ill-fitting window shutters.

The quarrel ended in its usual fashion: de Wolfe stood up and threw over his stool with a crash. 'I'll not stay here to be endlessly insulted by you, you miserable old harridan!' he bellowed. 'I went to the Bush to see a murdered corpse, as is my duty – a duty you encouraged me to undertake. But if you are set on turning it into a scandal, then I may as well fulfil your accusations, for I've nothing to gain by denying it!'

With a face like stone, he stalked to the hall door and slammed it behind him, leaving Matilda at the table, red-faced but unrepentant. In the vestibule where the yard passage opened behind the heavy street door, he found Mary waiting with his short cloak already in her hand.

'I guessed you would be wanting this very soon,' she whispered, with a knowing glint in her eye.

He slung it over his shoulders and pulled the top corner through the pewter ring on his right shoulder. 'She'll not speak to me for days after this,' he muttered. 'At least that's some consolation.'

As he opened the iron-bound door and disappeared into the lane, Mary shook her head in despair. 'What's to become of you, Black John?' she murmured.

*   *   *

There was no hesitation in de Wolfe's step this time as he approached the Bush. With long, determined strides, he hurried down Idle Lane and pushed his way into the tap-room, which today was more crowded than usual. He stared around almost aggressively, until his eyes were used to the gloom and the smoke – Edwin had lit a fire in the hearth, as the day was cooler now. The back door opened and Nesta bustled through, bearing a tray with bowls and trenchers from the kitchen-shed. He barged across the big room towards her, pushing aside other drinkers. The landlady had just put the food before some travellers at a table near the potman's row of kegs when she felt two lean hands gripping her waist. 'Upstairs – now!' came a gruff command.

Twisting round, she saw de Wolfe hovering over her, his dark eyes boring into hers. 'I'm busy, John,' she protested half-heartedly. 'Look at them, they're all thirsty or starving!'

'I've been starving these two months, Nesta,' he said in Welsh, and pulled her to the broad ladder.

With a few token protests, the landlady allowed herself to be propelled up the steps, the coroner's hands still on her waist. He was oblivious to the sudden quiet in the room, the turned heads and curious eyes that followed them.

Above, the loft was deserted and seconds later, they were in her cubicle, with the bar dropped into its sockets behind the door. John's hand slid from her waist to lie around her shoulders and he pulled her to him as if he would crush her body into his, rib against rib. He pulled off her linen helmet and buried his face in the loosened cascade of auburn hair that escaped, until her face turned up to find his lips. With a groan of pleasure, he lifted Nesta off her feet and fell with her on to the wide French bed. For long minutes, he did nothing but press her to him and smother her face with kisses.

Then, as if by some silent signal that reached them at the same instant, they began to pull at the fastenings of each other's clothing.

A few minutes later, in the room below, Griswold the Carter, one of the Bush's most regular patrons, rapped on a corner table with the base of his quart pot, made an urgent gesture to the rest of the room and hissed for quiet, holding a hand to his ear in an exaggerated gesture. In the sudden silence, a score of men heard, faintly but distinctly, the rhythmic thumping of a bed-head against one of the thick supporting posts that came down from above through the ceiling.

Grins and chortles erupted among them and ale pots were raised all round. 'To the crowner, God save him – the lucky bastard!'

John de Alençon had heard of the killing of a whore from the Saracen, but was mortified to hear from his friend that another Biblical reference had been found on the body. 'You are sure that these marks on the brow did say what you claim – this is not some delusion of that poor nephew of mine?'

De Wolfe shook his head. 'It was not only Thomas – the secondary who saw them first was of the same opinion.'

The Archdeacon, sitting at his table in Canon Row, sighed resignedly. He fingered the wooden cross hanging around his neck, seeking consolation from it. 'At least this ogre has an apt quotation for each situation,' he murmured wryly. 'That dreaded part of the Book of Revelation is St John at his most pessimistic and threatening. I've read it a hundred times and still don't understand it.'

'The quotation may be apt for the situation – but this devil also makes the scene apt for the quotation,' countered de Wolfe.

'In what way?'

'With Aaron, he overturned the table in the room, to fit the Gospel story. It wasn't part of the assault. And with the woman last night, he left a cup near her hand, to fit the written version, for I'm sure she wouldn't have been drinking wine in the dark backyard of the Bush.'

De Alençon considered this for a moment, his lean face frowning with concern. 'So our man seems fond of play-acting, too? But it doesn't help us in discovering who he is.'

The coroner sipped the wine his friend had provided, an excellent ruby imported from Rouen. 'We urgently need the names of any priests whose nature is strange.'

'It may not be a priest in the strict sense, John. There are many in minor orders in the city – and unordained monks, many of whom are well lettered.'

'Not many of those – a few at St Nicholas and at the hospitals of St John and St Alexis. But I'm lumping all men of God together, those who can write and who know their Scriptures.'

'It has to be someone within the city, you say?'

De Wolfe nodded. 'Both killings were in the middle of the night, long after curfew. Unless he came into the city during the day and stayed overnight, the gates would have kept him out.'

De Alençon toyed with his wine-cup and sighed. 'We need the advice of those who have been much longer in Exeter than I. Some of the older canons have been here almost a lifetime and know every cleric within the walls. We must take this to Chapter.' He promised to consult some of his fellow canons, especially the Precentor and Treasurer and invited the coroner to attend the Chapter House after the regular meeting next day. 'Probably they will insist on the sheriff being present as well,' said de Alençon, wryly. Both he and de Wolfe were politically on the opposite side from de Revelle, the Precentor and even the Bishop himself, when it came to partiality between King Richard and Prince John. Hopefully, prayed the Archdeacon, this antipathy would not stretch to a murder investigation.

As he was leaving the priest's Spartan room, de Wolfe returned to something that both the sheriff and the Archdeacon had raised. 'Richard de Revelle keeps goading me with the thought that my own clerk might be involved. Surely you cannot believe that your nephew might be the culprit?'

De Alençon put a hand on John's shoulder. 'I trust to God that such a thing cannot seriously be entertained. Yet he certainly has the learning and writing skills – and he has been acting and speaking in an increasingly strange manner lately. But no doubt you can exclude him on other grounds. Where was he at the material times? And is that feeble waif capable of killing two healthy persons?'

John gave one of his ambiguous grunts. 'Both were struck on the head, probably an unexpected blow. Any girl or even a strong child could have done that. And, no, I have no idea where Thomas was at the times of both killings – though that applies to almost all the citizens of Exeter, yourself included.'

The couple of hours before Vespers were free for most parish priests to do as they wished. The more earnest often visited the sick or read their Vulgate, others drank and slept or did their washing. Today Ralph de Capra used the time to leave his church in Bretayne and trudge dispiritedly along inside the city wall to St Mary Steps to call upon his nearest priestly neighbour, Adam of Dol.

De Capra had been wont to do this frequently, though

of late his attendances at confession had become irregular: his problem was growing increasingly acute. Every priest took another as his confessor, though Adam did not disclose his own transgressions to de Capra.

When he entered the cool nave, he found Adam up a ladder, busily working on one of his lurid wall paintings. He appeared to be adding another small head to the confused tangle of faces suffering the agonies of the Inferno. Adam was not at pains to hide his irritation at the interruption, but eventually came down grudgingly to give his colleague a brusque greeting. As they stood face to face, the contrast between the two was marked: Adam was large, pugnacious and dominant, his colleague thin, diffident and dismal.

'I wish to make confession, Father,' murmured Ralph.

The other priest glared at him. 'Again? It was but a fortnight since you were here last. Is it the same trouble, hey?'

Abashed by his reception, de Capra dropped his eyes to stare at his feet. Adam's response was hardly encouraging to a penitent seeking absolution.

'I need to speak to someone about it. I'll not take up much of your time.'

Impatiently Adam banged down his tray of paints on the stone bench at the side of the nave and rubbed his hands on the grubby cassock he kept for his artistic labours. 'Very well, but I must finish that head before Vespers.'

He marched away to the tiny sacristy that opened off the chancel and came out with his second-best stole, a faded length of brocade that he draped around his neck, where it clashed incongruously with the paint-stained robe. Standing on the step between the nave and the small chancel, he rapidly made the Sign of the Cross in the air, with a vigour more appropriate to slashing with a sword. 'Right, let's get on with it,' he commanded testily.

De Capra knelt on the hard flagstones before him. He bowed his head and clasped his hands over his waist. 'Forgive me, Father, for I have sinned,' he said, then began a low, incoherent mumbling that soon ended in sobs.

'Speak up, man! And lift your head, I can't hear a word you say.'

De Capra's head rose slowly, to reveal two tears trickling down his distraught face. 'My soul tells me I must make confession, yet my mind denies that there is any God to whom I can confess!' he blurted out.

Adam of Dol glowered down at him, his face darkening with his ever-ready anger. 'Then you should listen to that soul, wretch, before you lose it altogether,' he snapped. 'Take a grip on yourself, man! You're an ordained priest, you've been brought up in the faith, you've been trained in the ways of the Church! How can you not believe in all that you have been professing these past years?'

Ralph stared upwards beseechingly, seeking some understanding in the furious red face glaring down at him.

'I spend my life trying to believe. I win the fight for an hour, then the doubts creep back in. Where is God? Why does He not give us signs? Why does He allow cruelty, pain, misery, poverty, warfare? All we know of Him is relayed by the mouths of men or their writings in the Vulgate. Where is God Himself?'

Momentarily, Adam softened at the agonised and impassioned words of de Capra. He reached out a hand and laid it on the other's head, until he noticed the skin ailment and rapidly withdrew his fingers. 'Ralph, we all have had our doubts at some stage. Thankfully, mine came when I was but a young secondary in Wells and lasted half a day, no more. For proof of God's presence, you must accept the learning and assurances of the thousands of greater men than us over hundreds of years. And look about you, where did the world come from? Did it make itself? You can see God in the trees and hills and bodies of your fellow men.'

To Ralph, this began to sound like a catechism learned by rote, rather than Adam's inner conviction. 'I have tried all that, a dozen times a day! But the doubts creep back. How can I minister to my flock, give them the sacraments and preach to them of heaven and God's forgiveness, when deep down I don't believe any of it?'

At this, the priest of St Mary Steps lost his temper again. 'Forget heaven and forgiveness! You want to beware of hell and everlasting damnation! Satan has invaded your soul and is working your destruction. That is what you should be preaching to your congregation, not milk-and-water promises about the afterlife. Neither they nor you will have anything after death, except eternal damnation and torture unless you root out Lucifer without delay!' Red in the face, he advanced down the steps and de Capra stumbled to his feet to retreat before him. Prodding the man's chest with a fleshy finger, Adam drove him back down the nave, ranting the same advice as he went. 'Pray every hour of every day, de Capra. Keep the fires of hell in the forefront of your mind! Strengthen your own resolve by telling your flock of the mortal dangers of their sinning.'

De Capra backed away rapidly, nodding his agreement as a sop to the other man's fiery temper, which seemed in danger of giving him apoplexy. 'I will try, Father, I will try, believe me,' he stammered, as he sought his escape. Turning to seek the door, he twisted into a halfbowing, half-running shamble to get away from the priest who was now more accuser than confessor.

'It were better that you died soon, even by fire or water, if you can achieve a state of grace, than linger on in sin and spend eternity in Satan's hellfire.' Adam shouted after him.

The words echoed in de Capra's ears as he hurried, sobbing, along the road, in a far worse state of mind than when he had gone to find help and absolution.

De Wolfe spent the rest of the afternoon going over many of the coroner's rolls that were to be presented to the Justices in Eyre the following week. Thomas had been working indefatigably to complete extra copies and was reading out lists of names and verdicts to his master in the upper room of the gatehouse. Gwyn, bored by the proceedings, had gone to the guardroom below for a gossip and a jar of cider with Gabriel. He came back with the news that a welcoming cavalcade was being organised for Monday to meet the judicial procession as it came along the road from Honiton. 'You are expected to be on it, of course,' he concluded, 'not us lesser fish, but Ralph Morin, the Portreeves and the archdeacons. Some of the other burgesses, the guild masters and a few canons will be there too. Gabriel has to organise a score of men-at-arms as escort, he says.'

As coroner, John had expected to be among those who formed a reception party for the Justices in Eyre, but this seemed too much. 'Damned mummery, I call it,' he growled. 'We only went as far as the West Gate to receive the Chief Justiciar when he came last year, not go flouncing halfway to Dorchester to meet a handful of working judges. It's that bloody sheriff, trying to impress them so that they don't notice his embezzlements – a wonder he doesn't have a troupe of musicians and tumblers prancing in front of us!'

Gwyn grinned and Thomas went back to his pen and parchment. De Wolfe pulled out the scrap of parchment they had found on Aaron's body and scowled at it for a long moment, as if he could read some secret message among the marks. Thomas had carefully spelled out each word, so that with the rudimentary knowledge he had acquired about the alphabet, John could now follow the sense of the biblical text. His lips slowly and silently re-formed the words, but he was still no wiser as to the author. Impatiently, he dropped it on to the table.

'Thomas, look at that writing again, will you?'

The clerk put down his quill obediently and leaned across the trestle to pick up the text.

'I know I've asked you this before but d'you think there's any prospect of matching it with the writer's hand?'

The pinched, sad face stared at it for a moment. Then the bright, bird-like eyes swivelled to the coroner. 'I suspect he has thought of that himself, Crowner, and deliberately disguised his penmanship.' He held up the torn scrap so that it faced his master and pointed out the words with a thin forefinger. 'See? The letters slope mainly backwards. Some scribes write like that, but they are constant in their leaning. These vary from word to word – some are even upright and, in a couple of places, he has forgotten himself and they angle slightly forward.'

Gwyn, interested in spite of his professed disdain of clerks and literacy, ambled across to look over Thomas's head at the parchment. 'The bottom of all those marks are not on the same level, not straight, like the way you do them,' he observed.

'That's another sign that the writer is disguising them. He might have done this with his left hand, instead of the usual right.'

John grunted at these expert opinions. He had pre-viously – and secretly – compared the writing with Thomas's own hand on the many documents in the office and, to his relief, had found them totally unlike. Yet now his clerk was proving that there were ways of disguising the style of a person's script – but surely that in itself must be an indication that Thomas could not have written it. Or was it some double bluff?

'So you think it's useless trying to match this with anyone we might suspect?' he asked.

'I see no chance of success, Crowner. The colour of the ink is ordinary black and the parchment might have been torn from anywhere.'

That reminded de Wolfe of Matilda's comments: 'My wife pointed out that the text is copied from a Vulgate. He could have torn out the appropriate page instead to avoid any risk of his handwriting being recognised.'

Thomas shuddered and crossed himself at the thought of such desecration, both religious and literary. 'Even a murderous priest would baulk at defacing his Bible! And, of course, if the book was later found with the significant pages missing, it would be disaster for him,' he added shrewdly.

De Wolfe made a few more throat noises as he considered the seemingly hopeless task before him. 'You'd better come with me to this Chapter meeting in the cathedral tomorrow, in case I need any advice about texts or gospels and the like. Late in the morning, after Terce, right?'

Thomas almost smiled at the prospect of being admitted to the daily meeting of the canons, when cathedral business was discussed. Anything that got him into a religious building and among priests was balm to his injured soul.

While the little clerk was savouring the prospect of infiltrating the cathedral establishment, John de Wolfe had more secular prospects on his mind. He stood up and buckled on his heavy leather belt, with his long dagger at the back. 'I've had enough of this place. I'm going to give my old hound a bit of exercise.'

As he left, Gwyn had a fair notion of where Brutus would be within the next hour.

As if to make up for lost time, John spent another energetic hour in the little cubicle in the loft of the Bush Inn, until Nesta declared that not only her strength but her business would wither away if she stayed any longer. She left him on the big bed while she made herself respectable then climbed down to supervise the cook-maid and the two serving-girls, as the early-evening clientele often wanted food to go with their ale and cider.

After de Wolfe's two Herculean efforts that day, she decided he needed a substantial meal to replenish his strength and by the time he ambled down the ladder a thick trencher, dripping with gravy, was ready for him at his favourite table near the hearth. A large boiled pig's knuckle sat in the centre and a platter of cabbage, onions and turnip lay next to it. A small loaf, complete with a pewter pot of butter, rounded off the meal, which de Wolfe washed down with a quart of rough, turbid cider.

Nesta was bustling about, trying to conceal the radiance of a woman well satisfied with the day's events. Her rounded figure was shown off by her tight-waisted green kirtle, laced down the back; her linen apron emphasised, rather than concealed, her prominent bosom. John looked up frequently from his meal to watch her joke with the regular customers, her heart-shaped face and high forehead perfectly balanced by the small, turned-up nose and smiling lips.

Even the memory of Hilda, beyond his reach in Dawlish, faded when he looked at Nesta, and he scowled at the thought that he might be in love. He cursed himself for a middle-aged fool – how could a hardened, cynical old campaigner, married for too many years to a cold, unloving battleaxe like Matilda, feel like a callow youth? If he wasn't careful, he would be writing poetry next and bringing her flowers!

He tried to tell himself that it was the prospect of two sessions each day in the French bed that made him so happy, but glance across the room at the sweet-natured woman who had an easy word for everyone and no guile or spite to dispense, told him he wanted to be with her always, bed or no bed.

Feeling at peace with the world, he dropped his stripped knuckle-bone on to the rushes under the table, where Brutus was patiently waiting for it.

ChAPTER NINE

In which Crowner John goes to St Mary Arches

Next morning, de Wolfe felt as if time was replaying itself from the previous Tuesday, as a thunderous knocking on the front door woke him soon after dawn. This time he was alone on the wide pallet in the solar: the evening before Matilda had announced to Mary that after her devotions in St Olave's she would spend the night with her cousin in Fore Street – an abdication for which John was profoundly thankful.

Mary had answered the door before he could struggle into his tunic and shoes and get down the stairs from the solar. When he reached the vestibule, he found that, instead of the expected Gwyn, the callers were Gabriel from the castle, with Osric the constable lurking behind him. Bleary-eyed from sleep and his heavy night at the Bush, the coroner waited for the sergeant to explain himself.

'We've got another, Crowner! At least, we think we have.'

John glowered at him as he pushed his brain into full working order. With his black locks tousled from bed, and a week's growth of dark stubble on his cadaverous face, he looked even more menacing than usual. 'Got what? And where's Gwyn?' he demanded sourly.

'Hasn't appeared yet – he was probably on the ale at

St Sidwell's last night,' replied Gabriel. 'A dead priest is what we've got. At St Mary Arches.'

De Wolfe sat down heavily on the vestibule bench, where he usually changed his footwear. 'A priest? Murdered?'

The lanky Osric chimed in nervously, 'Gabriel thinks so – but I wonder if he didn't kill himself, in remorse for the other slayings.'

De Wolfe glared up at them. 'Well, which is it? A murder or a *felo de se*?'

The sergeant of the guard threw the town constable a withering look. 'God's bones, man of course it's a bloody murder!' He appealed to de Wolfe: 'Come and look for yourself, Crowner.'

John pulled on a pair of boots and threw his worn wolfskin over his shoulders. As they opened the big oak door, he snapped a request to his maid-servant, who was standing in the entrance to the passageway: 'Mary, slip down to Canons' Row and tell Thomas to get himself up to St Mary Arches as quick as he can. If Gabriel's right, we might need his reading and biblical skills.'

A few minutes later, after pushing through the early morning crowd of traders and their customers that thronged the narrow high street, Osric and the sergeant led the coroner up a lane that turned off Fore Street just before St Olave's. A few yards up on the right was the church that gave the narrow street its name. St Mary Arches was bigger and wealthier than many of its fellows in Exeter, as although Bretayne was but a few hundred yards away, it lay in a district of craftsmen and merchants. Even so, it was still a simple, rectangular building, albeit in new stone with a sturdy tower at the street end. A handful of people clustered around the open twin doors, kept out of the church by the other constable, Theobald, who was as fat as Osric was stringy.

The three men hurried up the steps and went through a round Norman arch into an empty nave. High clerestory window openings gave a good light, revealing walls painted with scenes from the scriptures, though not of the hell-fire variety depicted down at St Mary Steps. At the other end, another round arch led into a short chancel, two steps up from the paved floor of the nave. A large gilded wooden cross stood above a carved rood screen and, beyond, the altar, of solid Dartmoor slate, was covered with a lacy white cloth. Paintings of Christ and the church's patron saint, Mary, hung on each side of the altar, which boasted a silver cross and candlesticks.

The only thing that disturbed the symmetry was a body sprawled across the chancel steps. The legs pointed towards the altar, the arms were outspread and the head tilted down, the shaven tonsure gleaming in the morning light.

'There he is, Crowner, just as the first parishioner attending for Prime found him,' said Gabriel, his voice echoing in the empty nave.

Taking the lead now, de Wolfe hurried up the church, his boots slapping on the sandstone floor. A few yards from the chancel steps, he stopped abruptly. 'What the hell is his face in?' he exclaimed irreverently.

'That's why I reckon he drowned hisself,' claimed Osric.

As he moved up to the body, de Wolfe saw that the priest, dressed in a white linen alb, lay with his face in a shallow copper pan, which sat on the floor below the lower step. Stooping down, he could see that it was half full of a red fluid, which looked like diluted blood, submerging his mouth and nose.

'If it's a suicide, he was damned clever to have hit himself on the head first.' snapped Gabriel, scowling at the city constable.

Following the sergeant's pointing finger, de Wolfe saw that towards the back of the head, in the thick brown hair that surrounded the shaven patch, was a mat of drying blood.

'Could that blood in the dish have drained from that?' quavered Osric, his suicide theory demolished.

De Wolfe dipped a finger in the pan and held it to his nose. 'It's not blood, it's wine!' He got to his feet and stood with his hands on his hips, hunched over the bizarre scene. 'Drowned in wine, by Christ! This surely has to be unique!'

Gabriel looked at him. 'Can you drown in a pan? There's no more than a couple of quarts in that.'

'Why not? We were built to breathe air, not Anjou red or whatever it is! If the nose and mouth are covered, that's good enough.' De Wolfe turned and looked back down the nave, to where a clutch of curious faces was peering in, past Theobald, the rotund constable. 'Do we know who he is? Which man found him?'

Osric yelled to his colleague, oblivious of the sacred surroundings, and Theobald marched an elderly man down towards them. He was well dressed in a good serge tunic, over which was draped a dark red velvet cloak. A tight-fitting leather helmet was tied with tapes under his chin. His large grey moustache failed to hide the anxious look on his lined face. 'Crowner,' he said, 'we met briefly at one of those guild banquets a month or so past, though you'll hardly remember me. I am William de Stanlinche, a silversmith from this street.' He tried to avert his eyes from the corpse on the steps.

'Who is this unfortunate cleric?' grated de Wolfe.

'Our deputy priest, poor Arnulf de Mowbray. I can hardly believe that this is happening, Crowner.' The silversmith seemed distraught at the loss of his vicar.

'And you found him this morning?'

'I was first here, almost an hour ago. I come to Prime

several times a week before I go to my workshop. He was lying there, just as you see him. I touched his head and hand to make sure he was dead and he was cold. Then I ran to knock at all the doors in the lane, as we must, and someone went off to find the constable.'

'Do we know when he was last seen alive?'

William de Stanlinche nodded and pointed quaveringly at the crowd gawping at the door. 'Several of them were at Matins at midnight. Arnulf held the service for about the usual half-hour.'

'Why did you say "deputy" priest?'

William turned his back on the corpse and spoke with apparent relief about something different.

'Father Simon Hoxtone is our regular priest, but he's been laid low with phthisis these past nine months – sick unto death, I fear. We have had several priests sent here in his place, mostly vicars loaned from the cathedral. The last was Arnulf, who came about three months ago.'

Something in his voice made John suspicious. 'Was there something about him I should know?'

The elderly man shuffled awkwardly. 'He was not a great success, Crowner. I fear he had a great partiality for ale and wine. Sometimes he was incapable of holding the Mass or even taking confession, because of his disability.'

He hesitated, and John knew there was something more. 'Was it only the drink?' he demanded.

William cleared his throat uneasily. 'I'm afraid he was seen more than once with loose women when he was in his cups. Some parishioners were outraged, especially some of the wives. It was reported to the Archdeacon, and some other cleric was to have taken his place as soon as they found someone more suitable.' He paused and gave an embarrassed cough. 'De Mowbray seems to have been shunted from place to place, as every position he held soon became untenable.'

John gave one of his throat rumbles. Arnulf de Mowbray was obviously a burden to every church that was saddled with him, but he could hardly imagine John de Alençon ridding himself of even such a troublesome priest in such a drastic fashion as this!

He dismissed William with a curt word of thanks and told Osric to hold any others outside who had been present at Matins or who had come to attend Prime. He was just going to curse Gwyn for not being on hand, when his lumbering officer burst through the church entrance with Thomas de Peyne in tow. Pushing aside the crowd at the door, he ambled down the nave with the clerk trying to keep up with him.

'I went up to Rougemont when the gates opened, but they told me you were down here with Gabriel,' he boomed, oblivious of his surroundings. When he reached the group at the chancel steps, he stared with interest at the dead priest. 'Got another, have we? Who's it this time?'

The sergeant gave him a quick summary while Thomas bobbed his knee to the altar, then began crossing himself spasmodically beside the corpse, muttering to himself.

'Never heard of the Eucharist wine being dispensed in a wash-bowl before!' chortled Gwyn irreverently, earning a poisonous glance from the devout Thomas.

De Wolfe ignored his officer's sacrilege and dropped to a crouch to look again more closely at the head of the corpse. 'I wonder what was used to strike him? Like the other two, there's no pattern of any particular weapon.'

Gwyn bent over and prodded the bloody pad at the back of the man's head. 'Must have been something round or flat, as the skin is split in a star-shape. Could have been almost anything.'

De Wolfe gazed at what he could see of the face above the few inches of wine in the copper pan. 'His features are reddened, but he's tipped downwards, across these steps, so the blood would sink there anyway. We'd better get him up, I suppose.'

He rose to his feet and motioned to Gwyn to lift the dead man on to his back. Just as the Cornishman took a grip beneath the armpits, the coroner suddenly stopped him with a gesture. 'Wait! What's this on the stone alongside him?'

Gwyn released his hold and looked to where de Wolfe was pointing, at the lower step, which was almost obscured by the corpse's shoulder. He saw an irregular disc of dried wax, about half the size of his palm. 'There's some marks scratched on it,' he grunted.

De Wolfe touched the yellowish-grey plaque. 'Dried candle-wax. It has some letters on it and a strange outline.'

'Looks like a little snake, with a head and tail. It's even got an eye and a forked tongue,' observed Gwyn.

Thomas was too small to see past the two large men hovering over the cadaver, but his master moved aside and beckoned him forward. 'Thomas, d'you think these four marks are letters? The first looks like a P, but I can't make out the others.'

Gingerly, trying not to get his face too near the body, the squeamish clerk squinted at the dried pool of grease. He saw that letters had been crudely scratched into it with something sharp, like a pin. 'They must have been done when the wax was still soft, for the lines have melted a little, making it hard to read,' he murmured.

'Maybe, but that's certainly a serpent,' snapped John impatiently. 'What do you say the letters are?'

Thomas's long nose moved a little nearer to the chancel steps. 'They seem to be P-R-O-V, as far as I can make out,' he said uncertainly.

'What in hell's name does that mean?' growled Gwyn.

Thomas stepped back from the body thankfully and stood thinking for a moment, looking woebegone in his threadbare black gown, tied around the waist with a grubby white cord.

'Given the two previous biblical messages on the Jew and the woman, it surely can mean only one thing.'

'Which is what?' barked the coroner, exasperated by his long-winded assistants.

'The other two were from the Gospels, but this must be the Old Testament. "P-R-O-V" must refer to the Book of Proverbs.'

'And what does that tell us?'

The clerk looked sheepish, as his much-vaunted scholarship was, for once, found wanting. 'The Old Testament is very large, Crowner. I know almost every word of the new books of Christ, but there are few priests, even great scholars, who can recollect every part of the Old Testament. I will have to refresh my memory.'

Gwyn gave a loud guffaw, which echoed throughout the empty church. 'Caught you out at last, have we, Thomas-Know-It-All! I thought you had this religion business at your fingertips.'

The clerk looked angry. 'I only have the Vulgate for the Gospels in my bag here. I will have to find the full Bible to study Proverbs.'

Sergeant Gabriel made an obvious suggestion. 'This is a church, surely they'll have one here?'

'Not by any means. Some parish priests can't even read and many poor churches can't afford the Vulgate of St Jerome,' retorted Thomas cynically. 'St Mary Arches is a cut above many, though, so perhaps they will. I'll try the aumbry.'

He looked around the building and limped off to a small door in the north wall of the chancel, bowing and making the Sign of the Cross repeatedly as he

cut across in front of the altar. There was a large
locker or cupboard behind the oaken door, built into
the thickness of the wall, where the priests kept their
service books and where the materials for the Sacred
Host were stored. The others watched while Thomas
rooted about on the shelves, crossing himself repeatedly
as his hands passed near the chrismatory for holy oil
and the pyx for the reserved bread. Then he backed
out and reverently closed the door, holding a heavy
leatherbound book. After a low obeisance to the altar,
he crossed to the south side of the chancel and sat in
the centre of the sedilia, a trio of wooden seats for the
priest and his helpers. As he carefully turned the pages,
John lost patience with watching him and motioned to
Gwyn to lift the body from the steps. 'Haul him away
from this wax. I want to lever it off the stones without
damaging it.'

His officer picked up the dead priest like a baby and
stepped down to the floor of the nave. Red wine dripped
from the nose and chin, staining the flagstones. Then
Gwyn turned him over and laid him flat on his back
below the steps.

Meanwhile, John had carefully slid the edge of his
dagger under the plaque of candle-grease and popped
it up intact. He opened the pouch on his belt, wrapped
the wax in the ragged sheet of parchment that had been
left on Aaron's body and put them away. 'Now let's have
a proper look at him,' he grunted.

'Are we taking him to St Nicholas's?' queried Gwyn,
doubtfully. 'That miserable prior won't take kindly to
us using his store as a mortuary again.'

'This is a priest, so we'll have to abide by what
the clerics want done with the cadaver. I'll get the
Archdeacon up here straight away.' De Wolfe called to
Osric and told him to go to the cathedral and tell John
de Alençon what had happened. Then John turned his

attention to the corpse. There was nothing obvious to be seen, apart from the wetness and the reddish suffusion of the face. The lips and cheeks were violet, and a dribble of froth came from the mouth.

'His phlegm is pinkish,' observed Gwyn.

'It's no wonder, as he's been breathing in good red communion wine,' replied de Wolfe. 'Let's look at his neck and hands.'

There was nothing untoward to be seen there and the coroner rocked back on his heels alongside the body. 'We can hardly undress him here, in front of the altar of his own church,' he said. The priest wore his alb, a long robe of whitish-cream linen, with long sleeves, embroidered around the neck and hem. The coroner shied away from hauling it up to his neck to examine his chest and belly. 'We'll leave it until the cathedral settles him somewhere more private,' he decided, getting to his feet.

In the chancel, Thomas de Peyne also rose and came to the steps, the Vulgate in his hands. For a moment, John thought that the little clerk was about to read a passage to the congregation, but Thomas said, 'I've found it, Crowner. Once again, it's most apt for the circumstances.'

De Wolfe and Gwyn stood silently side by side under the chancel arch as Thomas began reading. 'I'll just translate the general sense of bits of the later part of Solomon's Book of Proverbs, for it's scattered over a page or two.' The clerk was in his element and his own troubles were forgotten for the moment as he stood in the church with the Book of Books in his hands.

'Just get on with it, man' grated his master, breaking the spell.

Thomas cleared his throat and slowly turned the Latin script into Middle English.

' "Who has redness of the eyes? They that tarry long

at the wine. Look not upon the wine when it is red for it bites like a serpent and stings like an adder."'

He turned back a page. 'Here it says, "Oh, my son, take my advice and stay away from whores, for they form a deep and narrow grave."' Thomas closed the book. 'There's more advice about staying on the path of righteousness, but the principal message is to avoid strong drink and loose women.'

De Wolfe stroked the black stubble on his chin. 'The serpent and the adder certainly fit the little sketch on the wax. This fellow, whoever he is, undoubtedly knows his way about the scriptures.'

As Thomas limped back across the chancel to replace the book, Gwyn stated the obvious once more. 'It has to be a priest. No one else would carry on like this.'

John nodded in agreement. 'The sooner we get the cathedral heads together over this, the more chance we have of getting somewhere – for, I must admit, I have not the faintest idea where to start.'

'And the deaths are starting to come more quickly,' observed Gwyn. 'Where does this bloody madman intend to stop, I wonder?'

The daily Chapter was to be held late in the morning, but before that, the coroner had another meeting with Exeter's archdeacon, John de Alençon. The senior priest had already met de Wolfe earlier at St Mary Arches, when he had hurried around after being summoned by the constable Osric.

The ascetic cleric had been greatly distressed to see the body lying in the nave and had himself shriven it and given absolution, with Thomas de Peyne acting as his self-appointed assistant.

Soon a trio of other canons arrived, having heard the news on the episcopal grapevine, followed by a gaggle of vicars, secondaries and priests of other parishes. Soon the church had more people in it than it did at an average service and de Wolfe began to despair of performing his legal obligations. 'Priest or no priest, there must be an inquest,' he muttered, in the Archdeacon's ear.

'But not here and now, John,' replied his friend. 'The body must be taken down to the cathedral. There is a small chamber off the cloisters that is used as a mortuary when required.' He looked around at the people milling in the nave. 'This place must be brought to order – devotions here must be resumed as soon as possible. I'll get one of the vicars to take charge – he was to be appointed here very shortly anyway, in place of this poor wretch.'

Leaving Gwyn to supervise the removal of the corpse, the two Johns made their way down to the great cathedral church of St Peter and St Mary, Thomas tagging along unobtrusively behind. The Archdeacon led the way to the Chapter House, a square wooden building just outside the south tower of the cathedral. The ground floor was the daily meeting place of the canons, where current church business was debated, everything from the order of services and choral matters, to finance and the disciplining of errant priests.

The Chapter was run by the senior canons, and although the bishop was a member, he had no direct control over the business, his remit being the whole diocese of Devon and Cornwall, rather than the cathedral itself – though in practice, his will and word were never challenged. Inside the room contained a quadrangle of benches, with a wooden lectern in the centre for the reading of the scriptures. In one corner, an open wooden staircase rose to the floor above, which was the 'Exchequer', the scriptorium and library of the cathedral. It was old, cramped and outdated, and plans were afoot to build a bigger Chapter House in stone, once the bishop had confirmed the gift of part of his adjacent palace garden.

'Come upstairs, we can talk there awhile, before Chapter begins,' invited de Alençon, leading the others up to the Exchequer. It was a musty chamber, with a number of high desks and stools. There were shuttered window openings in each wall, between which were shelves carrying scores of parchment and a few books, some chained to the sloping reading boards below the shelves.

Two priests were working laboriously on the diocesan accounts at a couple of the desks and another was reading at a desk. The Archdeacon crossed to a corner furthest from them, and motioned de Wolfe to a stool and took another facing him. The coroner's clerk melted into the shadows behind his uncle, determined not to be left out of anything even remotely ecclesiastical.

'This is a tragic state of affairs, John,' began de Alençon. 'I have sent a message to the Bishop, who says he will receive us later today to discuss this matter. Thank God he is in Exeter for once, because of the arrival of the Justices.'

De Wolfe perched on his high stool like some great hunched crow, his mantle hanging from his shoulders like a pair of folded wings. 'The culprit has to be one of your priests, John. He must be stopped quickly, for he seems to have developed a taste for killing. Unless we find him, I doubt this will be the last tragedy.'

The canon anxiously fingered the wooden cross hanging around his neck. His thin face was furrowed with concern and he passed his other hand through his wiry hair in a gesture of despair. 'But how can we trap such a madman – for crazy he must be?'

'Crazy and cunning, it seems. Have you no idea who among your flock of clerics might be deranged enough to act like this?'

De Alençon gave a heavy sigh. 'I have not the slightest notion, my friend.'

'But you must know every priest in Exeter, if not the whole of Devon,' said de Wolfe, impatiently. 'Surely you can narrow down our search to those who are in some way unbalanced in their minds?'

The troubled archdeacon rubbed his forehead in anguish. 'Some of these matters involve the confessional, John. That is inviolate, even in murder.'

'I'm not asking you to reveal any detail, only to help me list those priests you consider worthy of investigation. Ones who have some marked peculiarity of character.'

John de Alençon cast around for some means of assuaging his conscience. 'Well, naturally the number from whom I personally have heard confessions is very small – all priests have their allotted confessor and the ones that I have taken are few. What I have heard of some priests has come from my administrative role as archdeacon, aided by common cathedral gossip!'

De Wolfe managed to conceal his impatience. His old friend was sometimes as long-winded as Gwyn. 'So, can you name a few, John? I must get started soon – this series of killings cannot be kept from the king's Justices next week. They will not look kindly upon a community that cannot protect its citizens from one of it own priests!'

The Archdeacon nodded, convinced by the coroner's appeal to the public good and the possible censure of his monarch's judges, for like John de Wolfe, John de Alençon was devoted to Richard the Lionheart.

'There are certainly some odd characters among our clerics, John. For example, Adam of Dol, down at St Mary Steps, has a most ferocious notion of Christianity – but apart from that, he seems sane enough. Peter de Clancy at St Lawrence is eccentric in that he shouts every word of the services, instead of speaking or chanting, but that is a far cry from being a multiple murderer.'

De Wolfe felt that this was not getting him very far in his quest. 'Do you know every priest here?' he asked.

'I know their names, certainly, and I have probably met every one, too. But I cannot claim an intimate knowledge of each. As I said, every priest has his own confessor – even the Bishop – and they would be more acquainted with the nature of their charge. But that brings us back to the sacred trust of the confession and you cannot expect to get far along that road.'

The coroner scowled. 'Is confession so inviolate that it conceals a killer and puts others of God's flock at risk?'

De Alençon turned up his hands in a gesture of supplication. 'All depends upon the person confessing. If his confessor advises or pleads with him that such a dire sin must be brought into the open, then the subject may disclose it outwith the religious confession. But that would be extraordinarily rare – who is going to put their head voluntarily into the hangman's noose?'

There was a heavy silence.

'So how are we to proceed?' asked de Wolfe.

'Take this matter to the Chapter, when it assembles below. There are many there who know different priests better than I. They can at least offer some suggestions as to who to interrogate – if the bishop allows, of course.'

De Wolfe bristled. 'The Bishop allows? He may be able to divert accused clerics from the secular courts to his own, but he cannot stop me asking questions of anyone I choose, priest or not.'

The Archdeacon smiled wryly. 'You may find that Henry Marshal has powers you had not guessed at. But let us meet that problem when it comes.' He sighed. 'Meanwhile, the urgent task is to place this affair before the members of Chapter. Now that one of our own brethren has fallen victim, you should find that the Church will stir itself to take action.'

As if to underline his words, John heard the shuffle of feet and the murmur of many voices below, as the canons and their vicars began to assemble for the short service before their daily meeting. De Alençon rose to his feet, but motioned to John to stay where he was.

'We have some chants to sing and prayers to say first, then there will be the usual daily business. When that is done, I will send up for you to join us to discuss this sad affair.'

He gathered his black robe about him and set off for the steps in the corner of the library. Thomas moved towards his master and whispered urgently into his ear, causing de Wolfe to call after the Archdeacon, 'Thomas has a caution for us, John.'

The senior canon stopped and came back to the pair.

'What has that fertile mind of yours thrown up now, nephew?'

The coroner answered for him: 'He points out sensibly that for all we know the culprit may be a member of your Chapter.'

The clerk, looking slightly shamefaced, crossed himself hurriedly, as if insuring himself against his uncle's displeasure at what he was about to say. 'Whoever is leaving these messages must be well versed in the Vulgate, sir. Perhaps someone quite senior in the priesthood is responsible, for it is a matter of regret that many parish priests are unlikely to have that degree of learning.'

De Wolfe agreed. 'When we had that problem over treasure in Dunsford church a few months back, it was your canons who helped – especially Jordan de Brent, the curator of this very scriptorium.'

'Not that my master is accusing *him* of anything, Uncle,' gabbled Thomas hastily, touching his head, heart and shoulders rapidly as if warding off the very thought.

De Alençon bobbed his head in understanding. 'You think that if the miscreant is among us, he might profit by learning of our efforts to unmask him?'

'Yes. We will discuss any possible candidates openly, but if it comes to devising stratagems to catch him, we must guard our tongues. Even if the fellow is not within the Chapter, I'm sure that the famed gossip of the cathedral Close would soon spread the message far and wide.'

The Archdeacon patted John's shoulder. 'I think I have the answer to that – I'll call you down shortly.'

De Wolfe sat in a reverie for the next half-hour, while Thomas wandered off and became engrossed in a thick volume of theology chained to a nearby shelf. From below, came the harmonious chanting of the vicars-choral and some choristers, then the mutter of prayers, followed by a series of voices, the content of which was inaudible upstairs.

As he waited, John wondered what life with Matilda was going to be like for the next few days. Long experience had taught him that when he offended her, she was at first enraged, then ignored him for a day or two. This usually thawed into a period of sarcastic comments about his infidelity, before she returned to her normal state of sulky instability, where any incautious remark tipped her back into fury.

He suspected that, later today, when she returned from staying with her widowed cousin she would act as if he was invisible, keeping out of his way either in her solar or at church. But de Wolfe also knew that as the judges were arriving next week, she would recover rapidly to take up invitations to dine with the great and good.

Then his musing turned to more pleasant things, his delight at the reconciliation with Nesta. The greyness of the past weeks had lifted and he looked forward to his visits to the Bush like a child with a new toy. He hardly dare admit to himself that he loved her, his self-image of an ageing warrior too world-weary and cynical to indulge in such adolescent fancies. But being with her and enjoying her open nature and affectionate manner, lifted his spirit like nothing else could. Even their coupling in the big bed – glorious though it was – was no longer the main attraction at the Bush Inn.

He never wished Matilda dead – in truth, the thought had never crossed his mind – but he hoped that one day her religious mania would lead her to its logical end and she would enter a nunnery. He was not sure if that was enough to annul the marriage that neither of them had wanted – he must tactfully sound out his friend the Archdeacon one day. Sometimes, he even contemplated throwing up this life in Exeter and running away with Nesta – maybe back to Wales, where she would feel at home and where he had many friends.

Suddenly his musing was interrupted by a change in the muffled sounds from below. The chanting ended and a young chorister came far enough up the steps to summon him down to the meeting. With Thomas slinking unobtrusively behind, John descended into the hall, with a score of faces upturned towards him. The vicars and other minor orders had gone, leaving almost the full complement of Exeter's twenty-four canons to offer their advice.

John de Alençon stood at the lectern in the centre, with the Precentor, Treasurer and two other senior canons seated behind him. The other double rank of benches formed a square around the chamber, filled with black-cloaked priests, an occasional flash of white surplice showing underneath. The Archdeacon invited the coroner to sit opposite the lectern, and as he did so, Thomas rapidly slid behind him. The sonorous voice of de Alençon began the proceedings.

'Brothers in God, you are all well aware of the reason for this unusual extension of our session. Regretfully, our brother Arnulf now lies before the altar of St Paul in the cathedral, done to death by someone of evil intent who, even more regrettably, may also be a priest.'

A buzz of concern whispered about the Chapter House, as although everyone knew of de Mowbray's death, the actual circumstances were not yet common knowledge. De Alençon held up his hand for silence.

'Though the crime occurred in a church and to a man in Holy Orders, it was outwith the confines of the cathedral precinct. In any event, our Lord Bishop is well known to have delegated his ecclesiastical jurisdiction in cases of violent crime to the secular authorities – though if the culprit truly is a priest, then he will decide whether or not the Church will deal with him.'

He paused and looked around the silently attentive throng. 'The purpose of this meeting is to see if Chapter can assist the king's sheriff and coroner in discovering the identity of this madman. This cruel and blasphemous death seems to be one of a series committed by the same perpetrator, who is well versed in Holy Scripture.' He went on to outline the circumstances of the three deaths, with emphasis on the biblical quotations. After more shocked murmuring had subsided, he beckoned to the coroner and stepped aside for him to take his place at the lectern.

De Wolfe's tall figure stooped over it, a hand braced on each edge. He scowled around the expectant faces, feeling almost as if he was about to deliver a sermon. 'There is no doubt that the man who committed these foul deeds is indeed one of you, in that he must be in Holy Orders,' he began, his voice echoing harshly in that bare chamber. 'Moreover, he must be a priest within these city walls. My inquests on these crimes against the King's Peace have revealed nothing to put a name to the killer, so the sheriff and I need your help to bring him to justice – and, indeed, to prevent further tragedies.'

He gazed around the chamber as if trying to spot the villain by the sheer intensity of his gaze.

'We need to be told of any of your colleagues, either in the cathedral or in the city churches, who might be so unbalanced in their minds as to be capable of these awful acts.'

There was a silence as each member of Chapter looked covertly at his neighbours, as if expecting to see the mark of Cain on their brows. Then de Wolfe stepped aside from the lectern and the Archdeacon took his place again. 'If there is any brother who wishes to speak, let him do so now.'

Once more, a wave of murmuring swept along the benches, heads going together and eyes shifting this way and that, but no one volunteered anything. De Alençon repeated his exhortation and eventually an older canon stood up from his place in the front row. He was Simon Lund, a corpulent man with fleshy lips, drooped on one side from a slight stroke. 'I presume that, with this request, you are not inviting us to break the sanctity of the confessional, Archdeacon?' he brayed, rather indistinctly. 'Not that I have anything useful to divulge myself,' he added hastily.

John de Alençon shook his head decisively. 'Indeed not, Simon. That remains inviolate, as always. But no one should be inhibited from adding names to a list of priests whose habits and preferences may make them worthy of some enquiries. We are not seeking accusations, only some leads as to who might merit investigation.'

This was followed by another silence and the Archdeacon became impatient. 'I appreciate that it might be difficult for you to speak frankly on such a sensitive issue at such short notice and in such a public fashion. So let me say that the Precentor, the Treasurer, the King's coroner and I will form a small group which you may approach confidentially at any time. We will be meeting with the Lord Bishop later today to discuss this matter further and hope that before then some of you will feel able to offer us some suggestions.'

He stood down from the lectern and the meeting broke up, with groups of canons animatedly discussing the drama, which had brought some welcome excitement into their otherwise humdrum routine.

The two Johns walked out into the May sunshine, and moved out of the crowd's earshot.

'I gave them no idea of what steps we were likely to take in this matter, John,' said de Alençon with a wry smile. 'Mainly because I have no idea what can be done. Let's hope that some will provide a few clues as to the more unbalanced of our clerical community before we meet the bishop this afternoon.'

The coroner grunted, he was not hopeful that anything useful would come out of his friend's appeal to his colleagues. De Alençon noted his silence. 'Give me until this afternoon, John,' he said. 'I will speak with the other canons and see what we come up with. I think I will ask our archivist, Jordan de Brent, to join the Precentor and Treasurer when we go to meet Bishop Marshal. Jordan has the best knowledge of the other churches in Exeter and is an astute, wily old fellow.'

All the members of Chapter were rapidly vanishing in search of their midday meal and the thought of food was suddenly attractive to the coroner. With a final exhortation to his priestly friend to think hard about renegade clerks, he decided to abandon any thought of returning to Martin's Lane and set off in happy expectation for the Bush, leaving the forlorn figure of his clerk standing in the doorway of the Chapter House, his lips still moving in silent conversation with himself.

CHAPTER TEN

In which Crowner John meets the Bishop

De Wolfe's visit that day to the tavern in Idle Lane was more gustatory than amorous. With a meeting at the Bishop's Palace in mid-afternoon, as well as an increase in the Bush's business with the imminent arrival in the city of the Justices in Eyre, there was no time for dalliance in the big French bed. However, he was more than content to be back in favour with his mistress and settled happily for a large bowl of onion soup, boiled salmon, half a loaf and cheese, all washed down with a brew of ale that exceeded even Nesta's usual excellence.

The auburn-haired Welshwoman came to sit with him in between harassing her serving maids and potman. She had recovered now from the shock of tripping over the corpse of Joanna of London and was eager to hear details of the latest bizarre slaying in St Mary Arches, word of which had flashed all over the city. When John had described the weird event, Nesta astutely seized on one aspect that he had not so far considered. 'I wonder why these killings have started now?' she pondered. 'They seem to be getting more frequent. Is he going to kill every day?'

'I hope to God not, though we cannot prevent it until we get some clue as to who is responsible,' he said fervently. 'But what you say is interesting, my love.

The man must have been here in Exeter for some time so why did they start now? No new priests have arrived lately, according to John de Alençon, apart from Brother Rufus, the castle chaplain.'

'The only thing that is soon to happen is the arrival of the judges,' she mused. 'Could that be connected in any way?'

De Wolfe broke the last chunk of bread in half and used his dagger to hack a thick slice of hard cheese to go with it. 'Perhaps he's trying to point out that his type of justice is better than that of the country,' he grunted. 'Though his victims so far have been offenders against the scriptures, rather than against the King's Peace.'

Nesta picked up a jug of ale and slid along the bench to refill his pot. John took the opportunity to slip an arm around her waist and knead her breast gently through her green gown. In the shelter of the wattle screen that backed on to his table, she gave him a quick peck on his stubbly cheek. 'Can you come down tonight, John? Since I've got you back, I want you more than ever,' she whispered into his ear.

He gave one of the lopsided grins that lit up his usually grim features and dropped his hand to caress her smooth bottom. 'I'm so out of favour with Matilda that she'll not care where I am until next week, when she'll be desperate to get invited to these bloody banquets that I'll have to attend. So I'll be down here, bonny woman, as long as our resident murderer doesn't get up to his tricks again tonight.'

A crash from the other side of the room as a quart pot hit the floor and a babble of abuse from one of the maids, abruptly took Nesta away to pacify the girl and to throw out a drunken customer. John looked around to see if his help was needed, but the landlady was well in control, jabbing at the staggering patron with the handle of a broom, urging him out with a stream of invective in mixed English and Welsh. As soon as the door slammed behind the bemused drunk, she propped the besom against the wall and calmly walked back to John, accompanied by a chorus of laughing approval from the other customers.

'Damned fool, he shouldn't drink so much in the middle of the day if he can't hold it,' she observed equably, sitting down again alongside John. He looked at her admiringly. This really was a woman to be treasured, he thought happily, regretting even more the months that had been wasted when they were at odds with each other.

'Will this meeting today with the priests be of any use?' she asked, taking a drink from his clay tankard.

'I doubt it. They stick together like horse droppings, each guarding the others' backs against the unordained,' he answered cynically. 'But we need the consent of Henry Marshal to question his precious priests.'

'Do you think the Archdeacon's plea for information will yield up anything?'

John shrugged. 'Maybe a couple of clerks will use the chance to vent their spite on the brother they hate most. It will be a good opportunity for old scores to be settled, denouncing a colleague as a pervert or rogue. We need some names, that's for sure, but whether any we get are anything other than the victims of petty spite and jealousy remains to be seen.'

'Who's going with you to see the Bishop, then?' Nesta's curiosity seemed unbounded.

'De Alençon, of course, and my old friend the Treasurer.' He scowled at the lump of cheese in his hand, thinking of the other men he disliked.

'Then there's the bloody Precentor, together with my damned brother-in-law, who won't be able to resist fawning over Henry Marshal.'

Both the sheriff and Precentor Thomas de Boterellis had been involved with the Bishop in the last abortive attempt by Prince John to seize power from the Lionheart during his absence abroad. As fervent supporters of the King, the three Johns – the coroner, the Archdeacon and John of Exeter, the cathedral Treasurer – were at permanent odds with the others and regarded them with suspicion. However, in this matter of multiple murders, de Wolfe had to admit that politics was unlikely to cause dissent between them.

As he finished his meal, a distant bell sounded for afternoon Vespers, so he knew he still had some time before the meeting to be held immediately after Compline, the last of the canonical hours. He began to think about the room upstairs, but at that moment Nesta dashed away again to settle some new shouting match between one of the serving-girls and a customer. Then the door opened and the light was momentarily blocked by the huge frame of Gwyn of Polruan, who ambled in and sat himself down opposite his master.

The coroner glared at him suspiciously. 'Don't tell me there's been another killing?'

Gwyn shrugged off his cracked leather jerkin, dropped it on to the floor rushes and signalled to Edwin for a pot of ale. 'No, Crowner – just an assault in the Crown tavern up at Eastgate. A cutpurse tried it on with a pig-herder from Clyst St George and got his skull cracked for his trouble.'

'Will he die?'

'I doubt it – the skin's not breached and he was already getting his wits back when I left. The pig-herder was dragged up to Rougemont by a constable for Stigand to lodge in his cells, though he was pretty indignant about being arrested for whacking the thief who tried to rob him.'

'Do I need to see this fellow now?'

'No, after the meeting at the palace will be soon enough.' The Cornishman smacked his lips at the arrival of a quart jug of ale. 'Everyone's sympathies are with the pigman, so you can probably let him go home.'

In such a case, de Wolfe usually felt inclined to commit the injured man to the care of the assailant, as the latter had a vested interest in keeping the victim alive to avoid a murder charge.

Nesta came back and punched Gwyn's shoulder affectionately as she sat down. Gwyn beamed at them like some benevolent uncle, delighted that his master and the Welsh woman had made up their differences.

'Has he told you all the news, *cariad*?' he asked, using the language that the three always spoke when together.

'Yes, we're all on the look-out for a malignant priest now – though whether he has two heads and horns, John hasn't yet confirmed.'

For once, her light-hearted manner failed to strike a similar response from the Cornishman. 'Talking of strange priests, I'm getting increasingly worried about our Thomas,' he said soberly. 'I fear he may do something rash, like trying to jump off the cathedral roof again.'

Nesta, who pitied the scrawny clerk as she would a stray dog, was instantly concerned. 'He looked sadder than ever when I last saw him. Is there something new about his low spirits?'

'The fellow mutters to himself all the time and he's even stopped insulting me, so there must be something radically wrong with him,' said Gwyn. He sucked down almost a pint of Nesta's best ale before continuing. 'And I heard a couple of comments among those damned vicars when I was waiting for you outside St Mary Arches today – they were saying that the crowner should look nearest to home for a wayward priest. And that's not the first time I've heard the name Thomas de Peyne mentioned in that direction, God blast them!'

Nesta protested vehemently at the idea that the clerk could be involved. 'The poor man is too frail to be the killer, anyway,' she concluded, nudging de Wolfe to prompt him into joining their denials.

'Of course the little turd has nothing to do with it,' he agreed, 'but that won't stop tongues wagging, especially those of certain persons who would delight in using any means to discredit or discomfort me.' He crumbled some bread absently between his long fingers. 'The awkward fact remains that Thomas was out of sight during each of the three occasions when the deaths occurred – and it takes little strength to crack an unsuspecting victim on the head with a rock.'

'And he, above all people, knows the Gospel inside out,' added Gwyn, reluctantly acting as devil's advocate.

However, Nesta was robust in Thomas's defence. 'What nonsense you talk, both of you!' she snapped. 'He's a sad, disillusioned young man who deserves our help and sympathy, not stupid remarks like that, which could do him even more harm if they were overheard.'

Chastened, the coroner and his officer mumbled some excuses, but privately both felt a niggle of concern deep in their minds.

Later that afternoon a line of priests and their juniors straggled out of the cathedral after Compline and went their various ways, free of any more services until the midnight Matins. As arranged, de Wolfe met the Archdeacon and his colleagues outside the Chapter House, where the sheriff was already deep in conversation with his crony the Precentor. The latter was responsible for the order of services, the music and much of the other ecclesiastical rigmarole that de Wolfe found so tedious. The other canons were John of Exeter, the Treasurer and Jordan de Brent, the library archivist.

John de Alençon led the way through an arched gate into the grounds of the Bishop's Palace, set on the south side of the cathedral. This time, Thomas de Peyne was unable to infiltrate the meeting, much to his chagrin.

The palace was a two-storeyed building of a stone that matched the massive cathedral that overshadowed it. Apart from the several chambers that housed the prelate, there were guest rooms for visiting dignitaries, which might range from other senior churchmen to the monarch. The place was underused, as Henry Marshal was rarely in residence, preferring to live in one of his many manors dotted around England when he was not dabbling in state affairs in Winchester or London. His brother was William, the Marshal of England, who, after Hubert Walter, was probably the most powerful statesman and soldier in the land. He had already served two kings faithfully and perhaps would serve another, if Prince John's fortunes improved.

As the deputation filed into the audience chamber on the ground floor, the Bishop of Devon and Cornwall was already seated in a large high-backed chair on a podium at one end of the room. The other churchmen filed past him, bending their knee to kiss his ring. Richard de Revelle followed suit with an obsequious flourish and an even deeper bow, with de Wolfe bringing up a reluctant rear. Grudgingly, he bobbed his head and knee and brought his face near to Henry Marshal's hand without actually touching the ring with his lips. He disliked these sycophantic gestures, but was obliged to go through the motions, albeit with an ill grace.

Servants had placed a row of stools in front of the Bishop's dais and after paying homage to their prelate, the six men sat awkwardly before him, like pupils in a classroom. Henry Marshal, who was clothed in a sombre cassock of dark red, had a sallow young priest at his shoulder, presumably his personal chaplain. The Bishop had an unusually long face, his clean-shaven jaw adding to the smooth sweep of his features. A fringe of grey hair peeped from under his skull-cap and a large silver cross hung from a chain around his neck. He opened the meeting without any preamble, his mellow voice directed at the Archdeacon.

'Brother John, you appear to have the most profound involvement with this sorry affair, so please begin.'

De Alençon stood to outline the circumstances of the death of the priest at St Mary Arches. Then he related the details of the earlier killings, emphasising the common factors. 'So the intimate knowledge of appropriate texts from the Bible – and the ability to write – can only mean that the culprit is an educated man, inevitably one in Holy Orders,' he concluded.

Bishop Henry digested the facts for a moment, his chin cupped in a hand gloved in soft leather. His grey eyes scanned the row of men before him and stopped at the sheriff. 'Sir Richard, how do you think we can assist you?'

De Wolfe suppressed a snort of derision: de Revelle had taken not the slightest interest until a priest was killed, giving him the chance to parade his importance before the Bishop, a potentially powerful political force if and when the Lionheart's brother took the throne.

'I fear more killings of the same pattern, my lord, unless we find the miscreant very soon,' he brayed sententiously, as if the matter occupied all his waking hours. 'If indeed it is a clerk in Orders, then we urgently need to know whom we should interrogate.'

De Wolfe wondered who the 'we' might be and charitably hoped that the sheriff included the coroner in the description.

Henry Marshal's brow furrowed. 'I must admit that my duties, both in such a large diocese and especially elsewhere in England and Normandy, have given me little time to know all my labourers in the vineyard of this city. My canons and their assistants will have a far more intimate knowledge of them.'

De Revelle's foxy face slid into an obsequious smile. 'Your Grace's heavy burden is well known to us all, but your assent to my using the wide knowledge of your senior priests would be of inestimable value.'

The coroner, who sat next to his slimy brother-in-law, felt like ramming his elbow violently into Richard's ribs, but managed to control himself as the Bishop spoke again. 'We most certainly will do all we can to bring this killer to book. If it is a priest, then only his speedy apprehension can help reduce the shame it brings upon the ministry of Christ in this diocese.' He ran his piercing gaze along the row of canons, sitting like magpies on a branch. 'Let us see what suggestions each of you can offer. I think you have all had time to seek other opinions among your fellow prebendaries and your vicars?' His eye stopped at Thomas de Boterellis, a podgy man with a pale waxy-complexioned face and small piggy eyes. 'Precentor, have you any suggestions?'

De Boterellis was a favourite of Henry Marshal and he launched into an opinion with no hesitation. 'My Lord Bishop, among our devout and hard-working brothers, there are a few who have somewhat strange personalities. I hesitate to name them, but in these urgent circumstances, some enquiries seem justified.'

For the Virgin's sake, get on with it, you crawler, thought de Wolfe savagely.

Thankfully, the Bishop expressed the same sentiment, if more politely, and de Boterellis hauled a small sheet of parchment from his pouch and consulted it.

'There is Ralph de Capra, the incumbent of All-Hallows-on-the-Wall, who is a strange man, to say the least! He is solitary, even in a calling where many are withdrawn and not given to socialising. He does his job, but his flock complain that he is unapproachable and aloof. He seems to spend much of his time staring into space, talking to himself, and appears to be getting worse by the week.'

John thought that was also a fair description of Thomas de Peyne, but listened as the Precentor continued. 'My brother John de Alençon can confirm this, I know, as he has had parishioners petition him on the matter.'

'Is there nothing more specific, Precentor?' asked the Bishop. 'Being surly or disinterested is hardly suspicion of homicide.'

De Boterellis turned up his hands in a gesture of resignation. 'I agree, my Lord, but we are grasping at straws, suggesting any man who varies from the norm. Another might be Henry de Feugères of St Petroc, who is well known to have a flaring temper when crossed. Two weeks ago, it seems he was involved in a brawl with one of his flock over some minor dispute about money.'

'But these well-planned crimes seem at odds with such eruptions of anger, however reprehensible they may be.'

'Indeed, Bishop, but again I say we are stabbing in the dark, if that is not too crude a phrase in the circumstances.'

'So far we have not had a stabbing, thanks be to God,' commented Henry Marshal wryly, seemingly determined to have the last word.

He turned to John de Alençon. 'What about you, Archdeacon?'

The gaunt priest rose again to speak. 'I concur with

the Precentor's choice, but have several other suggestions. The incumbent of St Mary Steps, Adam of Dol,
is also a peculiar person. He proclaims and preaches
an extreme version of hell-fire and damnation, which
terrifies some of his flock, though I admit he attracts a
large congregation.'

'There is nothing wrong with reminding people of the
penalties of sin,' objected Thomas de Boterellis, anxious
to claim the high moral ground before his bishop.

'Certainly, but with Adam it has become an obsession.
One has only to look at the murals he has painted on the
walls of his nave to appreciate that he has a very morbid
view indeed of life and death.'

John of Exeter, the cathedral Treasurer, broke in to
offer support to the Archdeacon. He was an amiable-
looking man, rather florid of face and with a shock of
curly brown hair. 'I have had several complaints from
residents at the lower end of town about Adam's style
of curacy. Of course, we should always keep the wages of
sin before our congregations, but with him punishment
and retribution seem to be the only issues in his religious
teachings.'

Henry Marshal, who had also received communi-
cations about the situation at St Mary Steps, let the
matter pass for now. 'You said you had several suggestions, Archdeacon?'

'Yes, my Lord, I also feel uneasy about Walter le Bai,
who is a vicar to our brother Canon Hugh de Wilton.
He is older than many others of that rank in the clergy,
probably because he has not been given preferment
on account of his fondness for wine and ale. He has
been absent from many of his duties and the canon
informs me that he is seriously considering discharging
him from his service.'

'Does being a drunkard have any relevance to multiple murder?' asked the Bishop, rather testily.

'Not in itself, my Lord – but it seems that Walter le Bai is taking this prospect of discharge badly and when in his cups has been heard to utter threats against Canon de Wilton and indeed the diocesan powers generally.'

In turn, the remaining prebendaries offered their suggestions. John of Exeter rose again to point out Edwin of Frome, the priest of St Martins. 'As we all know, Edwin is one of the few Saxons to have the cure of souls in this city and I am afraid that he feels this distinction adversely. He fails to blend well with his fellow priests and, perhaps from some unjustified conviction of persecution, has been heard to utter disparaging remarks about we Norman conquerors, even to the point of suggesting that another Saxon rebellion might be a good thing.'

There were contemptuous snorts and cluckings from the Precentor and the sheriff at this, but the Treasurer was undaunted. 'Of course we know it is nonsense, but Edwin slides these ideas into his preaching. As it happens, the congregation at St Martin's is small, but it points to a man who has other matters than the care of his parishioners in his mind, which divert him from his true vocation. He also has an obsession, like Adam of Dol – only Edwin's is the literal accuracy of the Vulgate, which thesis he rams down the throat of almost everyone he meets.'

The Bishop nodded, though his face showed he thought little of Edwin of Frome as a murderer.

'Finally you, Jordan. What have you unearthed from your rolls and manuscripts?' His attempt at jocularity fell flat.

Canon de Brent lumbered to his feet. 'I would point out that there is one priest in Exeter whose living is not in the gift of this diocese. Along with the priory of St Nicholas, St Olave's is a daughter establishment of Battle Abbey. I know that its incumbent, Julian Fulk, is another disappointed man – indeed, an embittered man. He thought himself ready for far higher things than curator of a small church in the city. He has been to the archives several times, searching for all the details of the exclusion of St Olave's from the general run of Church affairs in Exeter – our own copy of the Exon Domesday Book, kept here in this building, even mentions it as "Battle Church", granted personally by King William.'

He caught the Bishop's cold eye and realised he had wandered too far into his passion for history. He returned hastily to his story. 'On those occasions, he has waxed angrily to me – indeed, once working himself up to a frenzy – about the iniquity of the Church authorities in denying him the high status to which he feels his education and character entitle him.'

He sat down again and the Bishop spent another moment or two musing on their suggestions, before passing his opinion.

'It seems to me that the grounds for suspecting any of these men of crimes of violence are sparse indeed. It is true that, like any profession or calling, there will be a proportion of drunkards, libertines, disgruntled and disaffected men among our brethren, but from what you have just told me, I see no realistic suspicion of the sin of Cain among them.' He paused and looked directly at the coroner and then the sheriff. 'But we must do all we can to support our law officers, so I have no hesitation in consenting to whatever questioning they think fit. The royal judges are due here in a day or two, and let us hope that some resolution of this unhappy affair can be found before then. It would be a sad reflection on our city and county if the Justices in Eyre discovered a series of unsolved murders on their doorstep.'

He made as if to rise from his chair and the chaplain jerked forward to help him – but Henry Marshal sank back on to his red velvet cushion to make one last appeal. 'Are we certain that there is no more to be said? Is there any last-minute thought in the minds of any of you?'

There was a short silent pause, then Thomas de Boterellis got to his feet again, with a show of reluctance. 'My Lord Bishop, your final appeal causes me to speak again, for previously some embarrassment concerning the crowner here kept my tongue still.' He half turned to give John de Wolfe a false smile of apology. 'But it has to be said, no matter what offence I might give. You asked for names of priests whose behaviour might lead to suspicion. Perhaps we should cast our net a little wider to include former priests, those who have been ejected by our Mother Church for scandalous behaviour.'

There was a dead silence, as everyone knew what was coming.

'It is no secret that the clerk to the coroner falls into that category and not only has a shameful history of indecent assault but since then is well known both to have attempted the mortal sin of self-destruction and for acting in a most abnormal manner. As reported to me by junior clerks who share his company in the cathedral precinct, he constantly mutters to himself and is in an unstable frame of mind, almost as if he is possessed by some unclean spirit.'

John de Wolfe hauled himself up to counter this blatant antagonism to himself, using his servant as the means. The only problem was that the Precentor was telling the bald truth, but John felt honour bound to defend his clerk.

'Your Grace, it is true that Thomas de Peyne has suffered much recently, in that his deepest desire to be reinstated into Holy Orders has been peremptorily rejected. It is not relevant here to record that he claims his original ejection was ill-founded – but there is no possibility at all that he is involved in these crimes. Indeed, it has been his expertise in Latin and scripture that speedily explained the cryptic messages left by this cunning murderer.'

As he sat down, the Bishop turned his stern gaze upon de Wolfe. 'That's as may be, Sir John – but can you swear that he was within your sight at the time of every one of these deaths?'

There was another profound silence, during which de Wolfe realised that this was a trap, primed by the Precentor, who must have told the Bishop previously that Thomas had no alibi for any of the killings.

'If you cannot so prove, Crowner, then I see no reason to exclude your clerk from the list of potential suspects. What is good for the parish priests of this city must also be good for your servant.'

At this he rose and swept away rapidly to a door behind the platform, leaving his audience to rise and bow after his departing figure.

CHAPTER ELEVEN

In which Crowner John goes to church

That Saturday evening was surprisingly peaceful for de Wolfe, as Matilda was again visiting her cousin in the town – more from a desire to ignore him, he suspected, than from any feeling of familial affection. He spent his time in the Bush, some of it eating, drinking and yarning with some of the locals – the rest upstairs in Nesta's closet. He was tempted to risk spending the whole night there but caution got the better of him and by midnight he wound his way unsteadily back to Martin's Lane. He undressed in the dark and crept on to his side of the wide palliasse, thankful that the loud snores from his wife removed the need for attempted explanations and the inevitable recriminations.

In the morning, he was not so fortunate: when he awoke, Matilda was sitting bolt upright. Her head was swathed in a cloth that concealed wooden pegs put there by the rabbit-toothed Lucille, intended to torture her hair into the ringlets alleged to be the latest fashion in France. Her husband was reminded of a turbaned Saracen warrior, the impression reinforced by the fierce look on her face.

However, after the usual sarcastic jousting, her manner moderated a little and John, reading the signs from years of practice, knew she wanted news of his meeting with the Bishop, who to Matilda was only a finger's breadth below the Almighty Himself.

He avoided any reference to Thomas de Peyne, whom she hated like hemlock, because he was, as she thought, a renegade and perverted priest. However, he unwisely forgot also to censor the reference to Julian Fulk as one of the suspects. To his wife, the priest of St Olave's was but a shade less saintly than the Bishop and she took umbrage at the slur on his character. De Wolfe lay patiently under the sheepskins, waiting for this latest squall to blow over. It subsided quite rapidly and he correctly guessed the reason.

'When you were at the Bishop's Palace, did you learn anything of the festivities laid on for the royal Justices this week?' she demanded.

'There will be a feast on Tuesday, given by Henry Marshal in their honour.'

'We will be invited, of course?' It was an aggressive statement rather than a question.

'I have little doubt of that, wife, though I am not in the Bishop's best favour, these days.'

'That's because you're a fool, John de Wolfe. Why you antagonise persons of stature and influence, I cannot imagine.'

Her condemnation was of necessity muted: she knew that Henry Marshal trod the same dangerous political path as her brother, whose reputation, and possibly his neck, depended upon her husband's forbearance in proclaiming his treachery. 'And what of the burgesses – and the castle? What are they putting on?'

'The Portreeves are entertaining them next Thursday – and your brother will have them at Rougemont on the following Saturday. No doubt we will be there, as your dear brother could hardly disappoint you,' he added sarcastically.

The prospect of three grand occasions in one week

mollified Matilda and diverted her into concern for which gowns, wimples and mantles to wear. Thankful for the distraction, de Wolfe crept out of bed and dressed. Under her cold gaze, he took a bone comb from a wall ledge and dragged it perfunctorily through his tangled black hair, then with his boots in his hand, he opened the solar door and padded down the stairs. He had had his weekly wash and shave the day before, so went straight to Mary's kitchen-hut to eat the oat porridge, salt bacon, butter-fried eggs and fresh bread that she put before him.

'And what mischief is the king's crowner up to today?' she asked, with blunt affection.

'Chasing around after these bloody priests, I suppose,' he growled, washing his food down with murky cider. 'It's Sunday, so at least they should all be at their duties. Though what good it is likely to do, I can't imagine. No assassin as clever as this one is going to break down and confess to us. And we can't even drag them to Stigand's dungeon for a little persuasion, as the Bishop has made it clear that he's doing us a favour by even letting us talk to them.'

'I suppose Gwyn will be with you – but what about Thomas?

De Wolfe champed down a slice of bread running with egg yolk before replying. 'That's a difficult one, given that my enemies have deliberately thrown suspicion upon him. But I need him, he has such a knowledge of the Church and the scriptures that he might spot some slip of the tongue that would be lost on myself or Gwyn. Yes, he must come with us and be damned to the consequences!' he ended with a snarl.

When he had finished eating, he pulled on the boots that Mary had just cleaned and marched off to the vestibule, telling the disappointed Brutus to stay behind.

It was a fine May morning, the yard and the street were dry, so John decided to leave his wolfskin on its peg. He looked at his broadsword, but decided that he was unlikely to have to fight any of the Exeter priests and settled for his dagger.

As the coroner stepped out into the lane, the cathedral bells were ringing for the Matins and Lauds of Our Lady, which preceded Prime, the first major service of the day. Apart from the more devout going to worship, the streets were quiet so early on a Sunday, and within a few minutes he had walked through the pale sunshine to the castle gatehouse. Gwyn had come into the city from St Sidwells as soon as the East Gate was opened after curfew and was waiting for him in the guardroom. His master told him the plan for the day, then added, 'Last night, I told our little fellow to be at All-Hallows by Prime. If we are going to see these priests, I thought we may as well start furthest away and work back up the hill.'

As they walked down through the outer ward of Rougement, redolent with the smoke from fire-pits and the aroma of cooking from the huts of soldiers' families and camp-followers, Gwyn echoed Mary's concerns by raising the problem of Thomas's presence. 'Are we wise to have him at these interrogations, Crowner? I know he's perfectly innocent, poor little sod,' he added hastily, 'but can it be held against us, if we have an alleged suspect as part of the inquisition?'

'We need his knowledge, Gwyn,' said de Wolfe wearily. 'How is he, d'you think? Is his mind still unstrung?'

The officer shrugged his huge shoulders. 'He still mumbles to himself all the time – and when he thinks I'm not watching him, I sometimes see tears running down his face. Thomas is in the depths of despair and I see no way of shaking him out of it, other than making him a priest again.'

There was no answer to this and they trudged on in silence until they reached the bottom of Fore Street and turned right by the West Gate, inside the wall.

'We'll call there next,' said de Wolfe, jerking a thumb over his shoulder at St Mary Steps, behind them at the bottom of Stepcote Hill.

Ahead, he could see their clerk, standing forlornly outside the small church built into the city wall. His shabby black cassock, which reached his ankles, emphasised the slight hump over his left shoulder, weighed down by the strap of his bag of writing materials. He was oblivious of their presence, staring at the open church door, from which the final phrases of the Mass could be heard, chanted in a reedy voice by the priest they had come to interview.

As they came up behind Thomas, they heard a ragged response from the small congregation inside and as the last muttered 'Amens' were heard, Thomas joined in, crossing himself repeatedly as he stood in the dusty street.

He became aware of his master and Gwyn just as the first of the score or so parishioners came out of the simple building, most of them poorly dressed inhabitants of Bretayne.

'Just the right moment, Thomas,' said de Wolfe, with a brusqueness that tried to conceal his concern for his clerk. 'The devotions are over, so he'll be free. Do you know this fellow at all?'

Thomas pulled himself together with an effort. 'Ralph de Capra? Yes, I've met him, Crowner. A strange man – like me, I think he is tired of life. He is a local fellow, his father was a silversmith who put Ralph to the priesthood as he was a poor specimen, with a hare-lip and some ailment of the skin.'

'Why has the cathedral pointed a finger at him, then?' asked Gwyn.

'Only because he was said to be surly and unapproachable, not the ideal qualities for a parish priest,' replied John, advancing towards the steps that led into the church.

Inside, the last of the few worshippers had left and the bare nave was silent. Gwyn followed with his usual reluctance to enter any religious premises but contrarily, Thomas bobbed his knees and crossed himself as enthusiastically as if he was entering St Peter's in Rome.

De Wolfe peered around until his eyes adjusted to the gloom. He saw a figure up at the altar, pulling a white surplice up over his head, leaving a long black tunic similar to that worn by Thomas. As they made their way towards him, de Capra swung around, the discarded vestment dangling from his hand. He stared at them, then his gaze focused on John. 'You are the crowner, sir. What brings you here?'

'We are seeking the killer of three victims in the city this week. I need to ask you some questions.'

'Why me? Why have you come here?' The hare-lip slightly distorted his speech, which was high-pitched and querulous. He looked annoyed and apprehensive, so the coroner decided to temper his own tone, to avoid antagonising the priest.

'The Bishop has given us leave to make enquiries among priests in various parts of the city, to see if any clues can be gained as to the identity of the killer. I'm sure everyone in Exeter knows by now that the perpetrator must be literate and have a sound knowledge of the scriptures.'

De Capra's tense features relaxed a little. 'I had heard something of the kind, though I do not indulge in common gossip. But I cannot help you, I know nothing of these tragedies.'

Gwyn moved to stand at the priest's shoulder, as if

his great bulk might intimidate the man into some indiscretion.

'Did you know any of the victims?' he boomed, almost into Ralph's ear.

'Of course I knew Arnulf de Mowbray, he was a fellow priest – though he was likely not to have been one for much longer, when the Consistory Court caught up with him.' The sarcastic tone was quickly replaced by anger. 'But why should you think I knew anything of a Jewish money-lender and a painted whore, eh?'

For several more minutes, the interchange continued in the same vein, with de Capra indignantly responding to questions concerning his whereabouts at the periods in which the murders took place. He knew nothing, he was always at his church or at his lodging in Priest Street. There was no one to vouch for this, but why should there be? He was a celibate priest! Agitated and outraged, he stalked up and down the chancel step, waving his arms, the surplice flapping like a battle flag. 'I resent you pestering me like this, sir! I am charged with the care of my flock in this part of the city, God-forsaken area that it is, and I do my best to try to teach them about goodness and sin, the saints and martyrs, the Holy Virgin, the Blessed Son and God himself – if He exists.'

With this peculiar finale, he turned his back on them, dropped to his knees before the altar and burst into tears. Thomas involuntarily went to him and laid a consoling hand on his bent shoulder, whispering some calming words into his ear. As always, strong emotion embarrassed de Wolfe, who preferred to clash swords with a man rather than see him cry. Rolling his eyes at Gwyn in despair, he accepted that there was nothing useful to be got from the priest and waited impatiently until his clerk had coaxed the man back to his feet. Then he beckoned to Thomas and muttered into his ear. The clerk nodded, fumbled in his bag and produced a quill, an ink-bottle and a torn scrap of parchment pinned to a small square of thick leather for a support.

'Father Ralph, we need a short note from you, for the records,' lied John. 'Just a few words to include with my inquest roll, to say that you have no knowledge of any of the circumstances of these deaths.'

Suspiciously and with bad grace, Ralph de Capra sniffed back his tears and went to the stone ledge that ran around the nave for the aged and infirm to rest on during services. He sat down, and when Thomas proffered the writing materials, irritably scratched a few sentences. De Wolfe noticed that he wrote with his left hand. When he had finished, he thrust the leather back at the clerk. 'Is that all you want of me? I trust you will leave me in peace now.'

De Wolfe grunted some words of thanks and led his team out into the street, leaving the incumbent to glare after them.

'That was no great victory for us,' snorted Gwyn in disgust, as they walked back towards the West Gate. 'I suspect that's the kind of reception we'll get from them all.'

The coroner was not so despondent – he had expected nothing more. 'This is just the start. We need to get a feel for these priests one by one. Probably none of the names given to us is our man, but someone might let fall something useful.'

Gwyn looked less optimistic. 'The only way we'll find this bastard is by catching him red-handed or discovering an eye-witness.'

Thomas was pattering along behind the two long-striding men and now his voice piped up. 'His script is nothing like the handwriting on the note left with the moneylender.'

They stopped and he showed them the pieces of

parchment. Even though neither could read the words, it was obvious that the script was totally different.

'He did that with his left hand,' observed de Wolfe.

Thomas lifted his humped shoulder in a gesture of indifference. 'That means nothing – if he is truly left-handed, he could have disguised his script by using his right. The note found on the Jew is much less regular than the usual quality of writing, so it was almost certainly disguised.'

Gwyn looked at the coroner. 'Then we're wasting our time trying to compare it with our suspect's hand,' he complained.

Thomas shook his head. The challenge of this hunt had lifted his spirits somewhat, by distracting him from his own problems for a while.

'There might just be some particular thing that gives it away. Even if a man tries hard to disguise his writing, the way he makes some stroke or line may unconsciously be repeated.'

They were approaching the next church now. St Mary Steps stood behind the West Gate, at the foot of the hill leading towards the Saracen Inn and the Bush. When they entered, there was no sign of the priest. Gwyn and de Wolfe stood in the nave, gazing with astonishment at the lurid murals painted along the high walls, some not yet completed and partly obscured by sacking draped from nails in the roof-beams. Thomas scuttled off to the sacristy to see if Adam of Dol was lurking there.

'What sort of priest wants these hell-fire pictures in his church?' murmured John, gazing at the graphic illustrations of sinners being disembowelled and tormented by devils with tridents. Some female victims were suffering agonising indignities that seemed grossly out of place in a house of worship.

'Must be a madman, Crowner. Do you think we might have found him already?' asked Gwyn, scowling at the sadistic promises of the after-life for those who failed to tread the straight and narrow path of righteousness.

There was a slam behind them and they turned to see a thick-set priest dropping the hasp of the big door to the street. He strode towards them, his long robe swishing across the bare flagstones, the expression on his ruddy face anything but welcoming. Short-necked and bull-chested, he was an aggressive-looking man of middle age, his brown hair cut strangely into a thick circular shelf below his shaven tonsure.

'I know who you are – and what you want!' he shouted, still yards away.

Gwyn sighed. 'Is this bloody man going to behave himself or am I going to have to break his neck?' he growled under his breath.

Adam of Dol marched up to them and stood with his fists aggressively planted on his hips. 'I've heard what went on in Chapter yesterday! You've come to persecute any priest who doesn't fit in with the milk-sop notions of those gutless canons down in the cathedral Close!' Almost purple in the face now, he swept Thomas aside with his brawny arm and advanced so that his fleshy nose was within a hand's breadth of de Wolfe's chin. 'Well, you will leave my church now, d'you hear? I've nothing to say to you, except to tell you that, alone in this God-forsaken city, I have the courage to tell the people the truth about the wages of sin!'

John looked back calmly at the irate priest, holding up a hand to restrain Gwyn from the violence that he could see building up in his officer.

'I care nothing for your religious beliefs or methods, priest. I am here as an officer of King Richard, to uphold his peace through the office of coroner.' He paused and looked intently into Adam's protuberent eyes, which reminded John of an angry bull surrounded by baiting dogs.

'I can take it, I trust, that whatever your views on theology, you revere the name of your king, as well as that of your God?' He had hoped that this invitation to reject treason would cool the man's temper, but Adam seemed impervious to such an approach.

'All you law men – crowners, sheriffs and those pompous asses of judges who come tomorrow – are misled by Satan!' he snarled. 'Your efforts at punishing the evildoer are futile. The only way is to convince the weak-minded people of this world that sin leads to eternal damnation!'

The coroner sighed, resigning himself to another wasted visit. Men like this were deaf to argument, steeped in obsession and unwavering in their delusions, but he had to try to make some progress. 'Where were you last night, after Matins?' he snapped.

'In my bed, gathering strength for the never-ending battle against the legions of Lucifer! And alone, not with a wench or a young boy, like some of the vermin who call themselves priests!' screeched Adam, a dribble of froth appearing at the corner of his mouth.

De Wolfe tried to pursue his questions, asking about the other nights on which a killing had occurred, but it was in vain. The burly priest became more and more agitated and abusive, almost dancing with rage and throwing his arms about. One of his fists swung back against Thomas as the little man was getting out his pen and ink for another sample of writing. The bottle flew across the nave and smashed on the floor, a spray of ink blackening the flagstones. The clerk screeched in fright, though he was not hurt, but Gwyn, ever-protective of his feeble friend, gave a roar of anger, grabbed the priest by the collar of his robe and shook him.

Though physically no match for the huge Cornishman, the raging Adam promptly smashed his fist into Gwyn's prominent belly and a full-scale brawl erupted before the chancel steps. As the two men rolled about on the cold stones, Thomas was jumping up and down in horror at this desecration of God's house, crossing himself frantically and squeaking at his master to do something to stop the blasphemy.

Groaning with frustration at the way the interview had turned out, John yelled at the two men and gave them a few random kicks, but to no avail. Looking around, he saw a large stone ewer against the foot of the chancel arch, for replenishing the holy water in the piscina. He picked it up and threw the contents over the heads of the combatants, like dousing a pair of dogs fighting in the street.

The two men fell apart, spluttering at the impact of the cold fluid, while Thomas looked on aghast, for once bereft of his twittering protests at the enormity of this sacrilegious misuse of holy water.

Gwyn sat up on the flagstones, his red hair plastered to his face, and laughed uproariously. 'I'll be purified for at least month after that lot, Crowner!' he crowed, climbing to his feet and dragging the priest up with him.

Where Adam had been puce with rage, he was now white with anger, and shaking as if he was about to explode. With water dribbling down his face and neck, he held up an arm and pointed his forefinger at the door. 'Get out, damn you! I shall pray tonight that you roast in hell for all eternity!'

De Wolfe ignored him and turned to the clerk. 'Thomas, it is pointless to try to get this man to write for us. It occurs to me that there must surely be parish records of some sort, so look now in the sacristy for your samples of writing.'

Reluctantly, Thomas made a wide circle around the gibbering priest and tiptoed towards the small door where books might be kept along with vestments and the materials for the Host.

Adam of Dol screamed in protest and began to follow

the clerk, who scuttled away with squeaks of terror –
but Gwyn grabbed the priest again and this time held
him fast in an armlock around his neck until Thomas
reappeared. With an almost imperceptible shake of his
head, the clerk gave the three men a wide berth and
hurried towards the door.

'Leave him be, Gwyn,' commanded the coroner, signalling his officer to release the almost apoplectic cleric.
'Priest, you have resisted the lawful enquiries of the
King's officers – and even assaulted one,' he said sternly.
'We are here with the full permission of the Bishop,
who has authority over you and every other priest in the
diocese, so spare me your righteous indignation! I will
be back if necessary – with the sheriff's men-at-arms, if
I so decide. You are an intolerant, violent man, Adam
of Dol, and I advise you to watch your step.'

With this admonition, he stalked to the door and left,
followed by Gwyn, who covertly raised two fingers at the
furious priest, the derisory gesture of archers who had
evaded having their bow-string fingers amputated by the
enemy.

The next on the list was Julian Fulk at St Olave's, both
priest and church all too well known to de Wolfe. It was
his own church, in the sense that on the infrequent
occasions that he attended any place of worship, it was
to St Olave's that he was dragged by Matilda. Unlike his
officer, he had no strong views on religion. He believed
in God, Jesus Christ and all the pantheon of saints and
prophets that had been accepted as part of everyday life
since childhood. When it did happen to cross his mind,
he found the rituals and ceremonies of the Church
curiously redundant. What had embroidered vestments,
tinkling bells, swinging incense-burners, droning chants
and wealthy bishops to do with a humble carpenter who
lived a millennium ago in a barren land far away? But

the panoply of organised religion was so familiar that he lost no sleep over this paradox – he had spent two years fighting to try to eject the Saracen heathen from Palestine, without any real conviction that this was a Holy Crusade. It was just another campaign, in which he had followed his king and fought whatever enemies were put in front of him.

None of this bothered him now as he led the way into the small church, named after the first Christian king of Norway. It was between services and the incumbent was busy at the aumbry, a wooden locker on the north wall of the chancel for storing the paraphernalia of the Mass. Julian Fulk was a fat middle-aged man. His head was bald and shiny, his face round and smooth, with a waxy complexion. To de Wolfe, the man's smile was benign, until he looked at the cold, blue eyes, which gave the lie to the man's amiability.

This smile was turned on as the trio advanced across the floor to where Fulk was placing the cruet, a vessel for the communion wine, alongside the pyx, which held the bread for the Host. He closed the lid of the aumbry and turned to them.

'The word spreads, rapidly, Sir John. I am well aware of why you pay me the honour of a visit.' There was a slightly mocking tone to his words.

'We are working our way through the more prominent parish priests, Father,' said the coroner, bending the truth a little.

Fulk's fixed smile stayed in place. 'Thank you, Crowner, but I also know the names on your list and why they were chosen. We are the trouble-makers, as far as the Chapter House and the Palace are concerned.'

De Wolfe marvelled at the accuracy of the underground signal system in the city, but made no attempt to contradict the priest. 'Is there any aid you can give us? Anything that might help us make this city a safer place? The last victim, after all, was one of your own brethren.'

Julian Fulk spent ten minutes being overtly helpful, but his information amounted to nothing. He knew of no fellow priest whom he could even suspect of harming a fly, he said. The only chink in his amiable armour appeared when the coroner brought the questions round to the cathedral clergy. Fulk's smile slipped a fraction and he was caustic about the worth of some of the upper ranks of the hierarchy in the Close – but hastened to add that none could be imagined as party to any evil works.

Hoping to provoke him to some indiscretion, de Wolfe led him on to the difference in status between St Olave's and other city churches, which induced strong words about the lack of preferment that outsiders could expect in the biased organisation of this diocese. But none of this had any relevance to the coroner's quest and soon he tired of the bland replies. 'Could we see your church records?' he asked innocently, implying that this was a matter of mere personal interest.

Father Julian's smile became positively sardonic. 'You want to compare my ability with the quill with your murderous note, no doubt?' he said, with barbed directness. He went to his aumbry again, for there was no sacristy in the tiny building, took out a heavy book bound between wooden boards and laid it on the lid. 'This is for the eyes of your clerk, no doubt,' he said, with a sly dig at John's inability to read it himself. Thomas had no need to pull out the note left at the Jew's death scene, as by now he knew by heart every stroke of the pen.

A few seconds' looking at entries of births and marriages was enough for him to be able to tell the coroner later that, as with Adam of Dol's records, he could match up nothing between the disguised script and the writing in the book.

There was no more to be gained so they took their leave of the priest of St Olave's, who seemed mildly amused. No doubt he would delight in telling Matilda about the visit, which was why John had been keen not to upset the man too much, for it would undoubtedly rebound upon him via his wife. After leaving the church, he took the opportunity to go down to the Bush for some more breakfast and to see Nesta. Gwyn was naturally enthusiastic about the prospect of food and drink, and only Thomas saw little merit in calling at a tavern at the ninth hour of a Sunday morning. However, he sat quietly at the end of the table, taking a bowl of meat broth that Nesta pressed on him, with her usual concern for the morose little clerk.

John and Gwyn ate bread and cheese and drank ale while they discussed their lack of success.

'Ralph de Capra was strange and indignant – and Adam of Dol mad and just plain bloody violent,' observed Gwyn, after de Wolfe had outlined their activities to Nesta, who hovered over the table, avid for their news.

'At least we now have a better method of comparing their penmanship,' grunted John. 'I should have thought of the church registers before this. It means they don't get a chance to alter their writing style further, if that was in their mind.'

'Will all of them keep such records?' asked Nesta.

John raised his eyebrows at Thomas, to get his expert opinion.

'All those who can write,' answered the clerk. 'The town priests are mostly literate, or they wouldn't have been given the living. The ignorant ones are shunted out into the countryside.'

'But does every church keep these books?' she persisted.

'In some degree, yes. Many never keep full lists

of everything, but they have to record baptisms and marriages. Burials come to the cathedral ground, of course.'

'As long as each of these suspect priests has written only a few lines somewhere, that's good enough for our purposes – though almost certainly the killer's writing will have been heavily disguised. We have only the one note left with the money-lender to compare with the registers,' said John.

Nesta topped up their pots from a jug of her best ale. 'Why do you have to do all this work?' she pouted. 'I thought it was the responsibility of the sheriff and his merry men to enforce the law in Devon.'

De Wolfe snorted in derision. 'Dear Richard says he is too busy with the arrival of the justices tomorrow to be diverted by mere multiple murders. And he says that all of his men at the castle are preparing for the ceremonial escort that he hopes will impress them enough to take tales of his prowess back to Winchester and London.' He took a long drink and wiped his mouth on his hand. 'Anyway, I prefer to do this my way, however futile it seems. I'll have three inquests with unresolved verdicts and the only way these will be settled is by finding the bastard responsible.'

Gwyn ran fingers through his unruly hair. 'What are we to do next, Crowner? There are another five on the cathedral list, but I'll wager none of them gives us anything worthwhile, other than a punch in the belly.' He grinned at the memory of the fracas in St Mary Steps, which he had quite enjoyed. Since he had finished campaigning at de Wolfe's side, a good scuffle rarely came his way.

The coroner rose reluctantly to his feet. 'Carry on with the rest, I suppose. Thomas has the list from the Archdeacon. The fellow in St Petroc is the nearest, so let's go there.'

For the next few hours, they walked the city, visiting the other priests whose names had been suggested by the canons. As it was Sunday, they had to wait for some to finish their devotions before they could waylay them.

The result was just as Gwyn had gloomily suggested: all they met with was hostility, annoyance and indignation. Late in the morning, they climbed the gatehouse stairs to the upper chamber to take some liquid refreshment before going off for their noonday meal. De Wolfe slumped behind his trestle table, with Thomas perched on a stool at one end, while Gwyn sat on his favourite window-ledge. The clerk refused any drink, but the other two supped cider from the stone jar in the corner.

'So, we're none the wiser, Crowner,' grumbled his officer. 'That Robert Cheever was the least obnoxious – too drunk to care what we wanted with him.' The incumbent of St Petroc was undoubtedly an enthusiastic drinker.

'I would like it to have been that oily swine Fulk,' muttered de Wolfe. 'I've had to suffer several years of his prancing and preaching when my wife drags me to St Olave's. But I can hardly arrest him for being pompous.'

They went over the other futile interviews, including that with Ranulph Burnell at Holy Trinity near the South Gate, who was alleged, on rather tenuous gossip, to have a liking for small boys. Peter Tyler at St Bartholomew's on the edge of Bretayne was a rather sad individual who openly lived in sin with a woman who looked old enough to be his mother, but he displayed no homicidal tendencies.

De Wolfe was already familiar with his neighbour Edwin of Frome at St Martin's, but given the nature of his peculiarity, the coroner doubted that either a Jew or a whore had provoked him to murder by disputing the true origin of the Scriptures. Peter de Clancy at St Lawrence, towards the East Gate, was the priest who shouted every word of the Mass and his sermons, but used a normal voice when they interrogated him and showed not a trace of any other idiosyncrasy, apart from resentment at their presence. This also applied to Henry de Feugères at St Paul's in Goldsmith Street, known far and wide for his violent temper. He was extremely annoyed at their visit and, like Adam of Dol, shouted and raved at the indignity. But de Wolfe felt that these manifestations were of no help at all in eliminating or strengthening any suspicions about any of the priests.

'What about this one we couldn't find – Walter le Bai?' asked Gwyn.

'He was the only one who isn't a parish priest,' ruminated the coroner. 'A useless vicar to one of the prebendaries – who was it? Hugh de Wilton?'

The Cornishman nodded and kicked the leg of Thomas's stool. 'We'll have to send the ferret here into the cathedral precinct to flush him out like a rabbit.'

'He lives down in Priest Street with most of the others,' replied Thomas dully. He had relapsed into his sombre mood again, after the excitements of the morning.

'Well, dig him out later today and send him up to us. You can tell him that it's on the orders of the Bishop – that's not too far from the truth.'

There was another hiatus in the conversation: Gwyn was sucking at his cider-pot and Thomas stared glumly at the bare boards of the table, his lips moving in some silent monologue.

'D'you have any feeling about any of this morning's rascals?' asked Gwyn, when he came up for air.

De Wolfe shook his head slowly. 'None of them took my fancy as a killer. But whoever he is, he's a cunning devil, not likely to make a slip easily. All we got from that lot was bluster and outrage, a good enough cover for any guilty manner.' He turned to his clerk. 'You say there was nothing in their writing to give you any cause for suspicion?'

Thomas pulled himself back to reality from whatever scenario had been playing within his head and shook his head. 'The script on that note was heavily disguised, master. Nothing in the registers or on de Capra's note matched in any way.'

'So what now, Crowner?' asked Gwyn.

'There's little we can do, other than watch and wait.'

As it turned out, they had not long to wait.

CHAPTER TWELVE

In which Crowner John goes to the well

De Wolfe went back to his tall, narrow house for another silent meal with Matilda. He knew that she would not be overtly objectionable until after the Justices's banqueting sessions, but she was still surly, in spite of his attempts to regale her with details of his priestly interviews. He was careful to censor these, making no mention of the rumpus in St Mary Steps or of the nature of his conversation with her hero Julian Fulk. Her only questions were whether he had yet had official invitations to the celebrations at the Bishop's Palace and the castle. When he had to admit that he had forgotten to make any enquiries about them, she fell into a glowering sulk.

Long experience of Matilda's moods ensured that his appetite did not suffer and he did full justice to Mary's spit-roasted duck with leeks and cabbage, followed by oats boiled in milk with a piece of honeycomb to sweeten it. Washed down with a pewter mugful of watered Anjou wine, he rose from the table as soon as he could and went across to the stables to visit Odin. The previous day his great destrier had suffered a kick on the hind-leg from another horse on the pasture at Bull Mead, just outside the walls.

'It's no problem, Crowner,' Andrew the farrier reassured him. 'I've bathed the cut with witch-hazel and covered it with goose-grease. He'll be fine in a day or two.'

Unlike the previous month when de Wolfe had spent half his days in the saddle – to the detriment of his love-life – there had been few distant cases lately, especially now that the north of the county was covered by the newly appointed coroner in Barnstaple.

'I'll have to take him out when he's fit – the old horse's joints will be rusting up from disuse,' he told Andrew, a wiry young man with an uncanny rapport with horses. They stood talking about the stallion and the farrier suggested de Wolfe take him hunting, though the lumbering warhorse was not really suitable for dashing through the forest after deer or boar.

As they stood in amiable idleness, a large figure came around the corner of Martin's Lane from the high street. For once it was not the coroner's officer, but the portly frame of Brother Rufus, the castle chaplain. He hurried up to them, puffing and red-faced, the twisted cords of his girdle flying from his waist. 'Sir John, I met your man Gwyn running down Castle Hill and he asked me to fetch you quickly as I was coming this way.'

'What's the urgency, Brother? Did he say?'

'He had one of the burgess's constables with him, that thin Saxon. Your man said there was another body. He claimed you'd know what he meant.'

Yes, John knew what Gwyn meant, and a cold prickling spread across the back of his neck. 'Where were they going?' he snapped.

'Across the high street and into the lane that goes towards that little almshouse and hospital – St John's, I think it is.'

Leaving the farrier holding Odin's bridle, de Wolfe marched off and within seconds had vanished around the corner into the high street. He loped along towards

Eastgate, thrusting aside the few Sunday afternoon drifters that got in his way. The Benedictine hurried after him unbidden, almost keeping up with him. Although he was heavily built, much of Rufus's bulk was muscle rather than fat.

A few hundred paces along the main street, John turned right to dive into Raden Lane, which led to the little priory and hospital of St John. This north-east quadrant of the city was relatively affluent, and most of the houses there were owned by burgesses and merchants. Many had a garden behind high walls and it was outside one of these that the coroner saw Gwyn, waving his arms to attract attention.

'We've got another body, Crowner!' bellowed his officer, as his master came near. A few curious heads were already poking out of nearby doors and a couple of urchins were dodging Gwyn's slaps as they tried to see past him through the garden gate. Even before he asked for details, de Wolfe stopped to look at the place. The solid two-storey house of new stone had a round arch over the central front door, with shuttered windows on each side and on the upper floor. The roof was of slate slabs and a chest-high stone wall ran in a rectangle around the sides and back, with a narrow lane on each side separating the house from its neighbours.

The coroner glared at Gwyn, daring him to spin out the story. 'Well, tell me the worst!'

'Osric called me – I was in the guardroom playing dice after dinner.' He hurriedly continued, before de Wolfe could berate him for his usual irrelevancies. 'This house belongs to William Fitz-William, a burgess of the Cordwainers' Guild.'

'I know who lives here, damn it! What's happened?

For once, Gwyn was brutally brief. 'He's dead. Dropped into the well.'

'Dropped? How do you know? He could just have fallen in.'

'He's lived here for years, so why should he now fall down his own well? And the water can't be very deep so he could have stood up, not drowned.'

'He might have hit his head on the way down.' The coroner was sceptical about Gwyn's intuitions, but the officer was stubborn in his opinion. 'I just feel it in my water, Crowner. Something isn't right.'

'Let's have a look, then. Why are you so sure it's another murder?'

IIis officer pulled worriedly at his shaggy red moustache. 'There's something strange about this household. Judge for yourself.'

As he stood aside to let de Wolfe though the gate, which stood at the side of the house, Brother Rufus came panting up, closely followed by Thomas de Peyne, who had been sent down from the castle by Sergeant Gabriel.

'Can I come with you?' asked the monk. 'If there's something related to the scriptures, maybe I can assist young Thomas here.'

The coroner nodded his assent and his clerk scowled behind Rufus's back, but they all trooped through the gate, which Gwyn shut firmly in the faces of the gathering onlookers.

De Wolfe saw a large yard with the usual huts for kitchen, privy and wash-house, as well as a small stable at the back, beside a vegetable patch. In the centre, between the house and the thatched wooden kitchen, was a well, with a knee-high circular stone wall. A leather bucket with a length of thin rope lay on the ground alongside, at the feet of Osric, the lanky Saxon constable. Sitting on the wall, slumped in a posture of despair, was a lad of about ten and alongside him was an older boy, probably thirteen or fourteen, whose hand rested on the younger one's shoulder as if to comfort him.

The constable beckoned urgently. 'Over here, Crowner. Take a look down the well first.'

John strode across the yard and peered down the shaft. About ten feet below ground level the surface of the water was broken by the buttocks and thighs of a man. The visible part of the body was clothed in a red tunic with a wide embroidered pattern on the hem.

The coroner stood back and looked at the top rim of the stone wall. He waved at the young boy to get off, so that he could see the whole circumference. 'Fresh scratches here,' he grunted to Gwyn, pointing. The others followed his finger and saw three irregular lines running roughly parallel to the inner edge of the shaft, a few inches apart. He turned at last to look at the boys, whom he had so far ignored. 'Who are they?'

Osric took it upon himself to explain. 'These are the two servants of William Fitz-William. This one is Edward,' he said, tapping the elder on the shoulder, 'And that's Harry.'

De Wolfe stared at the lads, who seemed cowed and speechless in the presence of these large strangers. 'Young for servants, are they not?' he barked.

'Fitz-William has a cook as well, but he lives elsewhere and comes in only during the day. These two look after his other needs.'

The constable's tone made John aware that this might be no ordinary household, but he concentrated on the immediate situation. 'So, what's the story?' Before Osric could start explaining, the coroner swung round to Gwyn. 'Better find some way of getting him up from there. I presume this is William Fitz-William down the well?'

The elder boy spoke for the first time, in a dull

subdued voice. 'It is, sir. That's the master's tunic, with that embroidery on it.'

As Gwyn picked up the rope from the bucket and went to the edge of the well to ponder the best way of recovering the corpse, Osric continued his interrupted tale. 'The lads sleep in the house, in a closet under the staircase. They say they heard their master come home late last night from some Guild meeting and go up to his bedroom as usual. This morning, they were up at dawn to light the cook-shed fire and begin preparing William's breakfast.'

'He always wants it soon after the sixth hour, when we hear the church bells for Prime,' cut in Harry. His cherubic face was deathly white and he was shivering.

The constable took up the tale again. 'Fitz-William failed to appear in his hall for the meal and after a time, Edward here went up to knock on his bedroom door.'

'There was no answer, so I looked in and he wasn't there, and the bed hadn't been slept in.' The older boy was blond and would be handsome when he grew, but he had the same pallid, pinched expression as the other lad, with wary, anxious eyes.

'So what did you do, if your master was missing?' demanded de Wolfe.

Edward shrugged. 'He never likes us prying into his business, sir. He can get very angry with us.' His eyes strayed to Harry's, and de Wolfe noticed some mutual signal seemed to pass between them.

'If this happened early in the morning, why did it take until this afternoon to discover him?' Brother Rufus entered the questioning.

'We didn't need water until then,' explained Edward, hesitantly. 'I had filled the big jar in the kitchen last night and only went to the well about an hour ago as I had to carry a few buckets for the young plants in the vegetable patch.' His voice went up a few tones. 'It was then that I saw him. I almost hit him with the bucket, but pulled back on the rope in time.'

Though both boys looked scared, de Wolfe could see no signs of sorrow for the sudden death of their lord – he suspected that it was not a matter of particular regret to them.

Gwyn had worked out a way to retrieve the master shoemaker from his pit. 'Someone will have to go down and pass this rope under his shoulders.'

He looked speculatively at the elder boy, but de Wolfe shook his head. 'You can't ask him to handle his master's corpse. I'll go, you take the strain.'

Osric vetoed this. 'You are too big a man, Crowner, and Gwyn is even bigger. I'm thin and light so I'll do it.'

Gwyn untied the bucket and wrapped the line twice around his middle, then threw the free end down the well. The skinny constable tucked his tunic up into his belt, revealing his nakedness underneath, apart from his thigh-length woollen hose. He climbed nimbly down the rope, his feet against the inside wall, Gwyn's bulk taking the strain.

'It's not deep,' said Edward reassuringly. 'Only a couple of feet, since this dry weather.' He seemed to have become more confident since these strange men had not treated him unkindly.

Osric lowered his feet into the water and sank well above the knees, his feet squeezing down into soft mud at the bottom. Quickly, he bent over the corpse and passed the rope under an armpit and across the chest. He tied it firmly between the shoulder-blades, then signalled to the ring of faces above.

Gwyn stepped on to the rim of the well, one foot each side and hauled straight up, with the burly monk leaning out to keep the line in the centre to avoid the body scraping against the rough stones of the shaft.

With a squelch and a splash, it left the water and,

almost at once, Osric gave a yell. 'There's a damned great stone hanging around his neck!'

With Gwyn straining every sinew to hoist Fitz-William up, there was no chance to pause for an investigation. Grunting and cursing breathlessly, he hauled the body level with the parapet, and Rufus and John reached out to pull it in to the side and roll it over on to the ground. Red in the face, Gwyn stepped down and threw a look of triumph at his master. 'What did I tell you, Crowner?'

Still unconvinced, de Wolfe gave one of his grunts. 'Could be a suicide – we've both seen folk tie a weight to themselves to make sure.'

Gwyn snorted his derision as he untied the rope from both himself and the corpse. He threw the end back down the well to rescue Osric, who nimbly scaled the shaft with Rufus taking the strain at the top.

When they were all together again, they turned to the body, which lay crumpled, face down, in the yard. The two boys stood at a distance with Thomas de Peyne, Edward with his arm still around Harry's shoulders, as if protecting him against the world as they watched with horrified fascination.

'Turn him over, Gwyn. Let's make sure it is Fitz-William.'

As soon as de Wolfe saw the face, discoloured though it was, he knew that this was the master shoemaker, for he had seen him about the town and at various Guild functions. Of middle age, he had fair hair cut short on his neck and a sparse beard and moustache.

'He's pretty blue in the face. Is that cord strangling him?' asked the chaplain, pointing at a thin line wrapped around his neck.

De Wolfe bent down and put a finger between the cord and the skin. 'No, it's loose – the blueness is because he was face down for many hours, the blood sinks that way.'

'No wonder he was face down with that damned great weight hanging around his neck.' Gwyn lifted a crudely circular stone from Fitz-William's chest. It was about a foot across and had a hole chiseled in the centre, through which the cord passed to suspend it from his neck.

'That's the top half of a hand quern, surely?' exclaimed the monk.

The Cornishman slid the twine loop over the dead man's head and stood up with the stone in his hands. He hefted it to gauge its weight then passed it to the coroner. 'A good many pounds, that. It would certainly drop him head first under the water and keep him there.'

De Wolfe grinned lopsidedly at his officer, as he well knew what was in his mind. 'Go on then, Gwyn. Perform your usual trick.'

The ginger giant dropped to his knees and placed the palms of his hands on the corpse's chest and pressed hard. A gush of froth, tinged pink, erupted from Fitz-William's nostrils and lips. Gwyn looked up, a satisfied smile on his face. 'Drowned, no doubt about it. He was certainly alive when he went down the shaft.'

'So why did he let someone hang a quern around his neck?' demanded Rufus, to whom coroner's enquiries were a novelty.

'Perhaps for the same reason that the priest at St Mary Arches let someone push his face into a bowl of communion wine. Have a look, Gwyn.'

Still on his knees, the officer ran his big fingers over the sodden hair of the deceased and almost immediately found what they expected. 'Swollen at the back – and I can feel a cut, with the bone crackling underneath. No blood, as the water has soaked it off.' He stood up and wiped his fingers on his tattered tunic. 'Exactly the same as the others. A hefty whack on the head from behind.'

Thomas, who had kept his distance while they prodded the corpse, left the two lads to come across to them. With a rather furtive glance at the boys, he pointed to the quern, which John still held. 'That's part of a hand-mill for corn, isn't it?' he asked.

'Yes, a woman's mill for the cook-house. It sits on another flat stone and she pours grain through the hole, then turns it round with her hands.'

'Then I know what it means here – the scriptures again,' said the clerk.

Before he had a chance to explain, Brother Rufus beat him to it. 'Yes, Crowner, it's obvious. The Gospels say, "Who so shall offend one of these little ones, it were better for him that a millstone be hanged about his neck and he were drowned in the depths of the sea."' He jerked his head significantly in the direction of the two boys.

Thomas glared at the chaplain, outraged that he had stolen his thunder in front of his master. It was *his* task to interpret for Sir John, not this fat stranger! But worse was to come for the little clerk, as Rufus leaned over to look more closely at the quern. 'Now that it's drying, there are marks appearing – there!' He pointed to some small scratches on the top surface, which appeared as fresh as those on the parapet of the well.

De Wolfe looked at them, but could make no sense of them.

'Turn it round – they're upside down this way,' commanded the monk. 'Now, see there – they read MT, MK and LK. That can only mean Matthew, Mark and Luke, the Gospels that record those particular words of Jesus Christ.'

'Yes, St John doesn't mention it,' snapped Thomas, but he was too late, the monk had already stolen his glory.

The four men looked at each other then rather covertly at the two boys, who still stood together, watching them warily.

'Is there no one else in the house?' asked John.

'No one. Fitz-William's wife died in childbed years ago,' answered Osric. 'The lads work in the cordwainer's shop during the day and wait upon the master when they return home. They were orphans, it seems, whom he brought here from a priory near Dorchester a couple of years ago.'

John rubbed his black stubble reflectively. 'Then for their own sakes they had better be looked after in another priory here. St John's is but a few yards away and they have almshouses and few orphans, as well as their hospital. I know Brother Saulf, who runs the infirmary. I'm sure he will take them in, at least for the time being.'

He lowered his voice to avoid the boys hearing him. 'If this millstone business is what we think it means, then some delicate questioning is needed – but not at the moment.'

Together with the nearby hospital of St Alexis, founded by a wealthy city merchant a quarter of a century earlier, the priory of St John cared for most of the sick in Exeter. A mile or so away, the nuns at Polsloe Priory specialised in childbirth and women's ailments. For the destitute, the aged sick and the beggars, St Alexis was the main refuge, but abandoned or orphaned children usually found a home in a priory or monastery, where they were often brought up to enter the Church.

Brother Saulf, a tall, wiry Saxon, administered the infirmary at St John's and had helped the coroner on several occasions, the last when Thomas de Peyne had injured himself in his abortive suicide attempt. He sat now with the coroner, Gwyn and Thomas in a small room inside the porch of the priory. Brother Rufus had taken himself off to his little chapel in Rougemont and Osric had gone about his business, which included informing the two Portreeves that the city had just lost one of its burgesses.

The two boys had been delivered to the priory an hour before, and Saulf had settled them down in the refectory until it had been decided what was to be done with them. 'They are apprentices of a sort, though Harry is very young,' he explained to de Wolfe. 'I had a long talk with them and they would like to continue at Fitz-William's shop, to get themselves a trade for the future.'

'Will the business survive his death?' asked John.

'No doubt of it. He has a partner with an equal share. They have half a dozen craftsmen making shoes in Curre Street,* as well as the shop in High Street. The lads can carry on there and come back here to sleep until some better arrangement can be made. Maybe eventually the partner can accommodate them at the workplace.' He gazed candidly at de Wolfe. 'I think it best if they stayed here for some time, where they can feel safe and not be preyed upon as they were before.'

De Wolfe nodded, understanding. 'You think it's true then, that they were maltreated by Fitz-William?'

'They admitted it to me, softly and reluctantly. He had brought them from Dorchester because they would not be known in the city.'

John had difficulty in suppressing the outrage he felt at two lonely boys being preyed upon by a pedcrast like Fitz-William. 'Osric said he had heard rumours about Fitz-William from men in his shop, but there was no proof. He thinks the boys were too cowed to mention anything outside that damned house.'

'Our killer obviously knew the truth of it,' grunted

* *Now Gandy Street*

Gwyn. 'For once, I feel he's done the world a service in getting rid of that bastard.'

'It should have been through the process of the law, though I agree that dangling from a rope was too good for Fitz-William,' snapped the coroner.

Saulf brought them back to practicalities. 'What are we to do with the corpse?' he asked. 'It lies in our little mortuary now, but with this weather warming up it won't last long.'

'I'll hold my usual fruitless inquest in the morning, then he can be buried. Osric is finding out whether he has relatives hereabouts. If not, his damned Guild will have to pay for his funeral.'

'It seems wrong to give such a man a decent plot in the cathedral Close,' growled Gwyn. 'He should be left to hang in a gibbet cage until he rots!'

'We can't bring a corpse to trial, so he can never be judged guilty.'

'Don't worry, he'll be judged and sentenced by Almighty God,' promised Brother Saulf, whose voice confirmed his absolute faith in heavenly justice.

'I wonder what He will make of his killer, though?' mused de Wolfe.

A modest cavalcade set out from the South Gate shortly after noon on the next day, to meet the King's Justices and escort them into the city. Ralph Morin, the constable of Rougemont, was in the lead, with a dozen men-at-arms behind him. As Richard de Revelle was eager to make the best impression, they were all in full battle array, even though there had been no fighting in Devon for decades.

Morin made an imposing figure on a big black stallion, his massive frame draped in a long hauberk of chain-mail, each link laboriously shined with fine sand to get rid of the rust. In a round iron helmet with a prominent nose-guard, the huge, bearded man resembled his Norse ancestors. Like the men behind him, he had a huge sword dangling at his waist, hung from the leather baldric over his shoulder, and his left arm was thrust through the loop of a kite-shaped shield. As they trotted proudly through the streets, the older Saxons and Celts they thrust aside had a brief but unpleasant reminder that these were still the invaders who had come with the Conqueror to dispossess them of their land and their heritage.

Behind the military vanguard came the less belligerent-looking members of the procession. The sheriff was first, as the King's representative in the county. Dressed in a dandified outfit of gold-trimmed green, he rode alongside Thomas de Boterellis, who had been told by the Bishop to represent him. Behind him was John de Alençon, appearing for the clergy of the city. His riding companion was Sir John de Wolfe, who as the county coroner ranked immediately behind the sheriff in the pecking order of law officers. Then came the two Portreeves, Henry Rifford and Hugh de Relaga, the latter outshining even de Revelle in a peacock-blue surcoat and feathered cap. The tail-end of the line of horses carried some clerks from the castle and court, as well as a pair of Guild Masters, the whole entourage protected at the rear by Sergeant Gabriel and another six soldiers, also attired in hauberk and helmet.

As they jogged along, harnesses jingling, the horses' hoofs threw up clouds of dust from the main road. De Wolfe was dressed in his usual black tunic and grey breeches, and was feeling warm under his short wolfskin cape. Unlike most of the others, who wore a variety of headgear, he was bare-headed and his thick jet hair bounced over his collar as Odin steadily thumped his great feet on the track.

As they passed the public execution site on Magdalen

Street, free from business on a Monday, the Archdeacon waved at the sinister shape of the empty gallows. 'Any chance of finding a customer for that, John?'

De Wolfe had told him earlier of the latest killing and its now familiar biblical signature. 'We have no idea at all. I had hoped that he would make some slip that would help us find him, but there's been nothing.'

'The royal judges are not going to be pleased, sitting in a town with a clutch of unsolved murders,' the Archdeacon said, with a hint of grim satisfaction as he nodded towards the sheriff.

'That's why he's looking so agitated today,' replied John with a wolfish grin. 'He has a cartload of problems already – the Dartmoor tinners want to get rid of him as their Warden, the Justices know of his leaning towards Prince John, his accounting for the county "farm" is more than suspect, and now he has four unsolved homicides perpetrated by a city priest.'

The 'farm' to which he referred was the total annual tax revenue for Devonshire. It was fixed each year by the King and his ministers, and the sheriff had to ensure its collection from the people, then deliver it in person twice a year to the royal treasury in Winchester. If he could screw more out of the population than the agreed amount he could keep the excess – which was why so many candidates, including barons and bishops, competed fiercely, with bribes and inducements, whenever a sheriff's post fell vacant. Some nobles even managed to be sheriff of two or more counties at the same time!

The cavalacade trotted on for a few more miles along the road towards Honiton, the first town to the east. The countryside was pleasant in the late spring sunshine, primroses and bluebells still abundant. The trees were now in full leaf and white scented mayflower was scattered on the thorn bushes. They passed ox-carts, donkeys, flocks of sheep, squealing pigs and all the usual traffic until eventually, the castle constable spotted a distant cloud of red dust. One of the men-at-arms behind him blew a blast on his horn to signal that the judicial party was in sight. A few minutes later, the two processions met and pulled off into a clearing beneath the trees to make the formal greetings and assemble themselves for the march to Exeter. The sheriff of Somerset had provided a dozen soldiers as an escort from Taunton; they now turned round and made for home. Horses and ponies milled around as the arrivals moved among the Exeter party for the formal arm-grippings and hand-shakings.

De Wolfe knew one of them fairly well – Sir Walter de Ralegh was originally a Devon man – but the others were strangers to him. De Ralegh was an older man in his sixties and had known John's father. He was a hard-faced individual, his features looking as if they been hacked out of granite with a blunt chisel, but he had a reputation for honesty and was a staunch supporter of King Richard. He introduced de Wolfe to the second judge, Sir Peter Peverel, a wealthy land-owner from Middlesex, who had manors all over eastern England. Peverel reminded de Wolfe of Hugh de Relaga, in that he dressed extravagantly and expensively. A rather stout, dapper man, the coroner felt disinclined to trust him too far, though that was perhaps an unfair judgement on such short acquaintance.

The third was Scrlo de Vallibus, a senior clerk from the Chancery. He was a thin, silent man of about forty, with a high forehead and a sparse rim of beard around his sallow face. He wore a plain oatmeal tunic under a brown cotte, which matched the colour of the handsome palfrey he rode.

The last Justice, dressed in cleric's garb, was deep in conversation with the Precentor, and de Wolfe sidled up to de Alençon while he waited to introduce himself. 'Do you know this priest, John?' he asked quietly, inclining his head towards the newcomer. Gervase de Bosco was a small, wiry fellow wearing the black robe of an Augustinian canon. Like Thomas de Peyne, he rode side-saddle, though on a better mare than Thomas's dismal pony.

'He is my counterpart in Gloucester, though when he has any time for any episcopal duties, heaven alone knows! He's always off indulging in politics or sitting in judgement.'

'Is he a fair-minded man?'

'I've heard nothing to the contrary. He's no lover of the Prince, so that's something in his favour.'

When the greetings were finished, they set off on the hour's ride back to Exeter, the newcomers pairing off with the locals in the procession. They were followed by the dozen court clerks and servants who had accompanied the justices and a few more were way behind with the two wagons that hauled their personal belongings and documents. The carts were slower than the horses and part of Ralph Morin's contingent stayed with them as escort.

De Wolfe rode with Walter de Ralegh, and the two Devon-bred men found they had plenty of mutual acquaintances and local topics to make easy conversation.

'How is this new crowner's business going, de Wolfe?' said de Ralegh suddenly.

'The sheriff doesn't like it, but that was part of the reason for Hubert Walter setting it up,' answered de Wolfe wryly.

De Ralegh's face cracked into a smile. 'You're taking business away from his courts into ours, I hear,' he cackled. 'Keep up the good work. These bloody sheriffs need bringing to heel – especially this one.' He dropped his voice, though de Revelle was many yards ahead, gabbling to Peter Peverel, who the sheriff had rapidly identified as the one with most clout at court.

'I hear you have some murderous problems in the city?'

De Ralegh's abrupt change of subject caught John by surprise. He had no idea that news of the Gospel killer had spread so rapidly outside Devon, but seeing no reason to conceal or minimise the situation, he gave a detailed account of the four deaths.

'And the last one was only yesterday, you say? God's bones, what's the sheriff doing about it?'

'Very little, I'm afraid. He's been too concerned with your visit to bother his head with a triviality like multiple murder! He's left it to me to worry about.'

The justice shook his head in dismay, but what de Wolfe had said was true. After yesterday's killing of William Fitz-William, he had gone up to Rougemont to inform the sheriff of yet another murder, but all de Revelle had said was 'Just get on with seeking the villain, John – that sort of challenge is right up your stret, I know,' as he scanned a roll of parchment.

'I'm the coroner, not the law-enforcement system of Devonshire!' de Wolfe had muttered irritably.

'If you need more help, take some men-at-arms. Ralph Morin will see to it,' the sheriff had said, with a dismissive wave. 'You enjoy ferreting out details, so leave me to deal with the important job of running the county,' he added condescendingly.

De Wolfe knew only too well that de Revelle would be happy enough to take any credit for unmasking the serial killer, but was unwilling to burden himself with any effort to achieve it.

When the party reached the city, the judges were lodged in the New Inn at the upper end of the high street, the only one with separate chambers upstairs to accommodate them. Their servants were housed in Rougemont and the court clerks were distributed among the spare beds in the vicars' lodgings in the cathedral Close and Priest Street.

John was tempted to go down to the Bush, but thought he had better put in an appearance at home for diplomacy's sake: Matilda would be winding herself up for the first of the banquets the following evening. As he had anticipated, she was moderately civil and sat opposite him near the empty hearth, sharing a stone bottle of wine. At times like this, John had glimpses of what it must be like to have an amiable wife and a settled home-life, and resolved yet again to try to heal the breach between them. He knew deep down, though, that her abrasive nature and his quick temper were incompatible with the pleasant, ordered existence that some couples seemed to enjoy, but he resolved to keep her sweet for as long as possible this week.

Matilda insisted that he recount every detail of the Justices' arrival and their entourage, especially what they were wearing. He invented most of it to keep her content, but his account of Peter Peverel's gaudy fashions was not far from the truth.

He followed up with details of yesterday's murder, which also grabbed her attention, especially as the victim had been one of the city's commercial worthies. Through her familiarity with the town gossip, relayed through her cronies at St Olave's, she was even able to confirm her husband's suspicions about William Fitz-William's perverted tendencies with young boys. Many of the women she met at her devotions were the wives of other burgesses and craftsmen and the lifestyle of Fitz-William since his wife's death had caused tongues to wag.

'So why didn't someone do something to save the boys from such evil?' de Wolfe grunted, aware that he was on dangerous ground by criticising her and her friends.

'And what could we have done?' she snapped. 'Send

the constable or the sheriff – or you, for that matter –
to his house to ask him if he was committing the sin of
Sodom?'

'Maybe a priest might have been able to turn his heart
– or, at least, try to aid the boys. Would your priest Julian
Fulk have known of these rumours?'

Matilda stared at him suspiciously. 'Why do you ask?
I heard that you had been to see him. Have you been
pestering that good man with useless questions?'

'We're just asking prominent priests in the city for any
help they might be able to suggest,' de Wolfe replied
diplomatically.

'Well, you can forget Father Julian,' she said acidly.
'If he knew anything useful, he would have come to you
or his archdeacon.'

De Wolfe let the subject drop, and after their early-
evening meal, he decided to go up to his chamber in
the castle to see Gwyn before he left for St Sidwell's
ahead of the gates closing at dusk. It was also useful as
an excuse for his intended foray down to see Nesta at
the Bush.

As he climbed the last few steps of the steep winding
stair in the gatehouse, he heard snuffling noises and
Gwyn's deep tones. Pushing through the sackcloth curtain over the doorway, he came across a curious sight.
The big Cornishman was leaning over Thomas, with his
arm around his humped shoulders, pulling him against
the rough leather of his worn jerkin. As John entered,
he grinned sheepishly, embarrassed that his master had
caught him comforting the little clerk. For Thomas,
when he jerked his face from Gwyn's large chest, showed
unmistakable signs of misery, his eyes moist and his lips
quivering. He sniffed and wiped his face with the back
of his hand, before scurrying across to his usual stool
at the end of the table.

'What's going on?' demanded de Wolfe, speaking

gruffly to cover his own discomfort at seeing grown men display emotion – especially Gwyn of Polruan, who was normally about as sensitive as a stone wall.

'It's those swine down at the Close. They've thrown him out of his lodgings.'

John looked across at his clerk, who was giving an impersonation of a hunted rabbit. 'Come on, tell me all about it,' he commanded.

In a small voice choked with emotion, Thomas spilled out the sad story. 'Two of the vicars and a secondary complained to the canon that they objected to having me – a suspected criminal – in their house. All I have is but a pallet in the servants' corridor in Canon Simon's dwelling, but the whispers about this killer have driven me out.'

De Wolfe dropped on to his own stool and thumped the table. 'Who's been spreading these malicious rumours?' he grated. 'I'll go down to the Archdeacon and stop this outrage.'

Thomas half rose in terror. 'No, Crowner! I don't want my uncle involved any further in my troubles. I don't think the canon himself wanted to throw me out, but I suspect the vicars were put up to it by someone above them.'

'And that would be that bloody Precentor, no doubt!' growled Gwyn.

'When the real murderer is caught, all this will blow over and I can go back,' said Thomas, with a marked lack of conviction. 'But I couldn't return there now, with this hanging over me.'

De Wolfe looked across at Gwyn and knew that the evil worm burrowing in his mind was also in his officer's. Though they stoutly defended their clerk against any outsiders, a tiny voice kept whispering that Thomas had no alibi for any of the killings, he was unusually well versed in the scriptures, could use a pen as well as any man in Devon, and undoubtedly was in a disturbed frame of mind.

Guiltily, the coroner shook off these unwelcome thoughts to come to grips with the present problem. 'We must find you somewhere to sleep until this foolishness is past. Let's go down to the Bush and I'll have words with Nesta.'

With Gwyn muttering imprecations under his breath against all priests, from the Pope downwards – and being uncharacteristically gentle with Thomas – they trooped out and made for Idle Lane.

CHAPTER THIRTEEN

In which Crowner John attends a house fire

As the trio were walking through the town on that pleasant May evening, a pair of priests had their heads together in their lodgings in Priest Street. They were not normally friendly and rarely said more than a civil good-day to each other, but circumstances had driven them closer.

Many of the narrow houses in the street were divided into rooms for the lesser ranks of the clergy. This evening, Edwin of Frome, the Saxon priest from St Martin's, had met Henry de Feugères of St Paul's on the doorstep as they returned for their supper and a few hours' sleep before Matins. The incumbent of St Paul's stood aside for the other to enter and, with a casualness that was too good to be true, offered an invitation to the other: 'Father Edwin, have you a moment to spare? Perhaps a cup of wine in my chamber?'

Startled by this unusual gesture, the morose priest from St Martin's nodded and followed the other down the gloomy passage to a room at the back, which had a shuttered window that looked into the yard behind. The house had two floors with six rooms for resident clerics, plus a common refectory and cubby-holes for three servants. As usual, the kitchen, privy and wash-shed were outside in the yard.

Edwin pushed aside the heavy leather flap that closed

his doorway and led his guest into a room that contained some good furniture, including a raised bed, an oak table and several leather-backed chairs. There were two cupboards on the walls and, apart from a small crucifix on the wall, there was little to show that it was a priest's cell. Henry de Feugères went to one of the cupboards and took down a stone bottle and a couple of pewter cups. Pouring a drink for them both, he waved Edwin to a chair and sat himself on the other side of the table.

'Unfortunately, we have something in common,' he began, looking keenly at the sad features of the other priest.

Edwin nodded, knowing exactly what he meant. 'Both favoured by a visit from the crowner as a result of being branded a misfit by those in the cathedral precinct,' he muttered bitterly.

'At least we are not alone, Brother,' said the burlier priest, with an irony that was not lost on the Saxon. 'Gossip has it that half a dozen have had the episcopal finger pointed at them.'

They drank the red wine in silence for a moment. Then Edwin spoke. 'It is an outrage, but we Saxons have suffered such persecution for the last hundred years and more. I have no doubt that that is the reason for my name being on this shameful list.'

It was an invitation for Father Henry to hazard a guess at why he was included in the Bishop's black list, but he was more circumspect. 'I can think of no excuse for such an insult in my case!' he blustered, 'except that my face does not fit in the exclusive clique that the canons run down at the cathedral there.' He failed to mention his reputation for unreasonable rages, which exceeded in violence those Edwin visited upon perverters of the Vulgate. They sipped their wine silently, each brooding on his problems.

'What can we do about this slight on our characters?' demanded Edwin. 'It's pointless petitioning the Archdeacon or the Bishop, for it's they who have caused this in the first place.'

'If we raise too much dust, we'll get posted to an outlandish chapel on Bodmin Moor or some such remote place,' agreed Henry de Feugères.

'Then what about a letter to the Archbishop?' suggested the Saxon.

The priest of St Paul's snorted. 'Hubert Walter is more a soldier and politician than a priest – God knows why the King appointed him to the See of Canterbury. We'd get nothing from him, except a reference back to Henry Marshal – and we'd end up on Bodmin Moor just the same.'

Another sullen silence ensued while their minds roved over the limited possibilities, until Edwin of Frome spoke again. 'Then what about the Justices? They're in the city now and although one is another canon, the other is a cleric from Chancery, Serlo de Vallibus. Maybe he can do something.'

'We certainly want our names cleared,' declared de Feugères, slamming his fist on the table, his temper always simmering near the surface. 'Everyone now knows they sent John de Wolfe to interrogate us. I've seen my own parishioners staring at me and whispering. One child even threw a mud pie at me this morning – I smacked his arse roundly for his trouble.'

The Saxon looked dubious. 'What we need is for the real killer to be caught. That's the only way these sneers will abate. But if you think petitioning the Justices in Eyre might help, we can do it – there's little to lose, after all. We'll go along to the court tomorrow and waylay this Chancery clerk.'

The priest of St Paul's had a distant look in his eyes. 'Something you just said, Edwin. About the real killer being caught. That would indeed be the best way to lift this burden from our shoulders.'

'But we have no idea who that might be,' objected the Saxon.

'The gossip is that the coroner's clerk is the most likely candidate. I'm not concerned about whether he is or not, but giving the sheriff or the Justices a name would take the pressure off us.'

'Unless the killer struck again afterwards,' said the still dubious Edwin.

De Feugères downed the rest of his wine and refilled their mugs. 'It's better than nothing. I'm damned if I want law officers pestering me every few days, trying to get me to confess to something I didn't do.' He gave a quick, shrewd glance across at the other priest. 'I certainly know that I'm not the culprit. I presume that also applies to you?'

Edwin of Frome looked shocked. 'Of course not! How could such a thought even cross your mind? Because I'm a Saxon, I suppose, dedicated to slaying the invaders of my country.'

De Feugères held his temper in check and held up a placating hand. 'Let's keep to the problem of accusing this Thomas de Peyne, who may well be the true killer, anyway. We can't name him as such openly, because the fact that we are suspected ourselves would make our testimony worthless.'

'So we must betray him anonymously?'

De Feugère nodded. 'The easiest way would be with an unsigned note. We could get some urchin to deliver it for a halfpenny, I could get one of the servants to find one in the street well away from here, so that it could never be traced back to us.'

Edwin looked dubious. 'Deliver it to whom? It's no good sending it to the coroner who investigated us, he would never accept a threat to his own clerk.'

The irascible de Feugères struggled to control his impatience with the stupid fellow opposite – no wonder a handful of Norman invaders were able to defeat millions of his race within a few months.

'Of course not. Send it to the sheriff – there's no love lost between them. De Revelle would be delighted with such a suggestion.'

'Will you write it or shall I? The script needs to be disguised, just as I understand that the note left at that Jew's murder was deliberately obscured.'

'Then you pen it and I'll have it delivered,' said de Feugères. 'Maybe we can think of something else on another day to reinforce suspicion against de Peyne. As my patron St Paul wrote to the Corinthians, "*in the mouth of two or three witnesses, shall everything be established*".'

This final cleverness was a mistake on Henry's part, as Edwin's obsession took fire like flame across dry heathland.

'You misquote, sir!' he yelled. 'The true word of God is "*shall every word be established*".'

It took de Feugères a full ten minutes to assuage Edwin's outrage and get down to composing their mischevious note.

As the priests were plotting over their wine, de Wolfe and his companions were only a few hundred paces away in the Bush, telling Nesta Thomas's tale of woe.

'Of course you must stay here, Thomas. I'll give you a corner upstairs – there's a spare straw pallet hanging across the rafters. No doubt Edwin and the girls can find you some victuals – you eat hardly enough to keep a mouse alive.'

'I've twopence a day from the crowner, lady,' said the clerk anxiously. 'Will that do for now?'

John grinned at him. 'I think I can persuade the landlady here to accept that, so don't fret, young fellow.

Just do your tasks, get your body and your mind sound again and all will turn out well.'

This was a long speech for the taciturn coroner and Nesta beamed at him, her eyes, for some reason, filling with tears. 'You just go down to the Close and get your belongings. Bring them back here and I'll tell Sarah to show you where you can sleep.'

Thomas grabbed her hand and, with a quick bob of his head, kissed it. Then he crossed himself jerkily and, his pinched face working with emotion, ran off to collect his meagre possessions from the canon's house. All he owned was his scribe's bag, a spare under-shirt and hose and a couple of books.

Gwyn hauled himself from the table where they sat and, with a tact unusual for him, said that he would go with Thomas to his lodging in case he was set upon by spiteful vicars. His real motive was to leave his master alone with Nesta, as he recognised the look in the crowner's eye.

Gwyn was hardly out of the door before John slid his arm around Nesta's shoulders and was whispering in her ear, his eyes rolling suggestively towards the floorboards above. 'Let's slip upstairs so that you can show me where poor Thomas will be lodged – and then maybe we can rest awhile in your room before we come down again.'

She dug him hard in the ribs with her elbow, but slid off the bench with no sign of reluctance and pulled the white linen coif from her head to let her dark auburn hair cascade over her shoulders. 'You'd better be quick then, Sir Crowner – it's but a short walk for him from here to the Close and back!'

As it happened, Gwyn returned before Thomas. He had called at the Crown tavern on the way back to give his master long enough to inspect the upper regions of the inn. He found the coroner sitting decorously in his usual seat, with a jug of best ale and a satisfied expression on his long face. Nesta sat complacently by his side.

'The little fellow has gone off to reclaim one of his precious books, which he loaned to some secondary, lodging in Goldsmith Street. He says he'll be back to claim his bed within the hour.'

'It's a disgrace the way they treat that poor man.' Nesta was still indignant at the heartless eviction of Thomas. 'It wasn't much they gave him, and then to get him thrown out on some trumped-up excuse like that!'

'The Precentor sees it as yet another way to goad me, I'm afraid,' grunted de Wolfe, 'so poor Thomas suffers on my account. De Boterellis knows of my hold over the sheriff because of the Prince John affair and attacks me out of spite on his behalf.'

Nesta signalled to the old potman to refill their mugs. 'Are you no nearer discovering the madman responsible for these killings?' she asked. 'Until you do, Thomas will be for ever under a cloud.'

John shook his head glumly. 'Whoever it is is too clever for us so far. I thought that with the drowning of William Fitz-William, we might have a chance, but nothing came of it.'

The Welshwoman's pretty round face screwed up into a scowl at the mention of the dead merchant. 'There's been so much gossip about that evil man and those poor boys that it's a wonder something like that hasn't happened before. His treatment of them was no secret in the town, but the lads had no one to speak or act for them. So much for the caring nature of the parish priests – it's a wonder a few more of them haven't been murdered like that Arnulf de Mowbray.'

De Wolfe reflected that Nesta was always one to help the afflicted and the neglected.

'Have you questioned all the priests that your friend the Archdeacon suggested?' she demanded.

'We have indeed – and much good it did us,' he replied glumly. 'They either told us to go to hell, or played dumb, or looked shocked that we should even think they were not perfect angels.'

Gwyn sucked down some ale and squeezed the dregs from his huge moustache. 'We've not seen Walter le Bai yet. He's a skivvy to one of the canons, isn't he?'

'He assists Hugh de Wilton, according to the Archdeacon, but they are both out of the city until tomorrow. If they have been away for a couple of days, that clears him anyway, as Fitz-William was killed during that time.'

They sat talking for another hour, with Nesta jumping up at intervals to speak to a favoured customer or to sort out some problem with Edwin or the serving girls. As well as being a popular ale-house, the Bush provided the best tavern food in Exeter and offered the cleanest lodging for travellers. Nesta's hard work and her pride in keeping a decent house had amply repaid de Wolfe's help in the desperately difficult days after her husband's death.

The May evening was sinking towards dusk and reluctantly John had to think about leaving the comfortable company of his friends for the frosty atmosphere of Martin's Lane. 'Are you heading for the gate before curfew tonight?' he asked Gwyn, as they hauled themselves to their feet.

A rueful grin spread over the hairy officer's ruddy face. 'I'd better go home once in a while, Crowner, though one of the wife's sisters is staying to have yet another baby and I'll probably have to sleep with the dog.'

John knew that Gwyn lived in a one-roomed hut at St Sidwell's, with two young sons and a huge hound – but he also knew that they were as happy a family as could be found anywhere in the county.

There was still no sign of Thomas returning, but Nesta had promised to give him a meal and lay him a mattress in the roof space above, so the coroner gave her a last hug and a peck on the cheek then followed Gwyn out into the twilit city. They walked in companionable silence up through the lanes towards Carfoix, the central crossing of the main streets. Though it was still dry, clouds had rolled in to make the evening seem darker. Suddenly Gwyn noticed a faint glimmer above the roof-tops. 'Is all that good drink affecting my eyes, or can I see a red glow up ahead?'

De Wolfe, whose mind had been on Nesta's fair face and body, looked up. Between two steeply pitched roofs on the corner of the high street, he could just make out a pulsating redness, then a few rising sparks. In every city, where most of the buildings were still made of timber, fire was the ever-present fear. Few boroughs had escaped being burned to the ground over the years, many of them repeatedly.

'It's towards St Keryan's, I reckon,' bellowed Gwyn, and began a lumbering run across Carfoix to reach the street that led to the North Gate. The small church he had named was almost halfway to the gate on the right-hand side, but it was soon clear that the fire was in a side-street that turned off before it. Other townspeople were running in the same direction, partly from curiosity and partly from dread of a widespread conflagration.

'It's here in Waterbeer Street!' called Gwyn, as he skidded round the first corner into the lane that ran parallel with High Street to join Goldsmith Street. About four houses up from the turning, on the opposite side of the alley, smoke and flame were pouring from behind the upper storey of a house. Luckily, it was half-timbered rather than just wood, with stone walls on the ground floor and plastered cob between a timber framework on the upper part. It was roofed with split stone, rather than thatch or wooden shingle, which again delayed the flames taking hold.

De Wolfe ran close behind the galloping Cornishman until they halted before the closed front door. A score of neighbours and gawking sightseers were clustered there, shouting and gabbling, but with no apparent plan of action.

'Is anyone inside?' roared de Wolfe above the clamour of voices and the crackle of flames from the back. He knew that most of the houses in Waterbeer Street were let as lodgings and several were known to be brothels, so the occupants tended to be a shifting population.

Gwyn pushed at the stout oaken door, but it was barred from inside.

'Around to the yard!' snapped John.

The house, typically tall and narrow, was very close to its neighbours on either side, but on the right there was a passage wide enough for a person or a handcart to get through. They pounded down it, ignoring a shower of sparks that a gust of wind sent at them. A handful of people stood at the back, including Theobald, one of the town constables. Also, to John's surprise, the robust figure of Brother Rufus was there in his black robe, gazing up like the others at the upper floor.

'It's the bloody steps that are burning!' yelled Gwyn. Like John's own house, a substantial wooden staircase rose from the yard to a balcony that gave access to the two solar rooms at first-storey level. It was burning briskly, and the flames were spreading across the part of the balcony supported on beams projecting from the house wall. Someone up there was screaming, regularly and repetitively. It was a woman's voice, but no one could be seen on the balcony.

As no one on the ground seemed keen to launch

a rescue, de Wolfe jabbed Gwyn in the back and ran across to stand under the end of the balcony that was not on fire. A pair of thick posts ran up from the ground to take its weight, braced by a series of cross-beams.

'Here's a ready-made ladder! You go round and see if you can batter in that front door, while I shin up this way.'

Reluctant to leave his master to the more dangerous job, Gwyn hesitated, but a steely look in de Wolfe's eye made him shrug and lumber back down the passageway. They had been in many tighter corners than this over the years and, with a little thrill at a rerun of their old adventures, he felt sure that the coroner could look after himself.

By now, de Wolfe was climbing the cross-braces, ignoring the twittering protests of Theobald, who had run across as soon as he had seen what the coroner was doing. De Wolfe yelled at him to stay where he was. 'No need for extra weight on this thing – the damned lot will fall down once the fire spreads a bit more,' he yelled.

Once on the slatted planks of the balcony, the fire and smoke were almost overpowering, but thankfully the breeze blew them away from him. The screaming was still coming from behind the nearest of the two doors that opened off the platform. Without hesitation, de Wolfe raised his foot and crashed his boot against it near where the inside latch would be. The flimsy fixing gave way, the door flew open with a bang and the screaming stopped. He dodged a wave of flame as the wind momentarily changed direction, and dived for cover into the room. Though it was dark inside, the reflection of the flames outside gave enough flickering light for him to see two frightened occupants – a sight that almost felled him with surprise!

Cowering against the wall, alongside a disordered bed, was a young woman clutching a crumpled blanket around her, which failed to hide the fact that she was naked beneath it. On the other side of the bed, frantically pulling on a pair of long woollen hose, was Sir Richard de Revelle, the King's sheriff for the county of Devon.

The room was filling with a strangely scented smoke through the open door. A quick glance backwards showed that the fire was creeping rapidly along the boards of the balcony and had almost reached the threshold.

'We've got to get out fast!' snapped de Wolfe, putting aside his astonishment in the urgency of the moment.

'I can't go out there,' hissed de Revelle, frantically. 'not with her and those people watching down below!' By now he had pulled his tunic over his head and grabbed his shoes.

For a split second, de Wolfe exulted that his brother-in-law was, once again, in a tight corner, but the vision of Matilda rose up in his mind's eye and he knew he had to do something fast to save her shame, if not her brother's.

In the further corner of the room was a curtain-covered doorway. He sped across and pushed his head through the opening. Beyond was a small passage leading to the room opposite. In the dim light, he could just see a pair of hinges and a ring set in the floor. When he pulled it open, he found he was looking down into a similar passage behind the front door. Thunderous blows told him that Gwyn was busy forcing it open. There was no ladder in place, but this was no time for such luxuries.

He dodged back into the upper room and pulled Richard to the trap-door. 'Drop down there and hide somewhere. When Gwyn gets the front door open, slip outside and pretend you've just arrived to investigate the fire.'

The desperate sheriff swung down, his hands gripping the edge then dropped. The fall was too low to cause him any damage. Dropping the trap and rushing back into the bedroom, John unceremoniously grabbed the woman, who had started to scream again. He slapped a hand over her mouth and wrapped a sheepskin from the bed-coverings over her blanket. 'Come on, my girl! Out of the door and keep going!'

He bundled the terrified wench on to the balcony, then pushed her to the right, a wayward pulse of flame singeing the curly wool of the sheepskin, as they ran the few steps to the further end. He hoisted her over the rail on to the upper cross-member, and a dozen faces gaped up at them from below as the girl felt with her bare feet for the lower bars. Halfway down, both sheepskin and blanket fell off her and the bemused audience gaped as she scrambled stark naked the rest of the way to the ground. The constable threw the fallen coverings back over her shoulders and led her across the yard, away from the fire, as de Wolfe shinned more expertly down from the balcony.

Several onlookers had found leather buckets and large pottery jars, which they filled from the well in the yard and threw on to the fire – to no avail, for with a crash and an explosion of sparks, the burning balcony collapsed as the supports burnt through. This removed the danger of igniting the whole house and brought the flaming timbers down within reach of the water carriers.

Meanwhile, John had hurried over to Theobald and the girl, who were huddled against the wall of the next house. He saw that she was moderately attractive and under the smuts on her face, her lips and cheeks were reddened with rouge. It was time for urgent action if he was to save the sheriff from shame and dishonour. 'Are you from the Saracen, girl?' he asked, in a low voice.

She nodded. 'Then say nothing to anyone, d'you hear? Nothing as to who was with you. Do you understand?'

The tone of his voice penetrated her shock and she nodded again, her teeth chattering with delayed terror. John turned to the constable. 'Take her back to the Saracen straight away and see that she speaks to no one – especially the landlord, Willem the Fleming. Stay with her, get her some clothes and drink. I'll come down to talk to her within the hour.'

Mystified, but obedient to the coroner's commands, the constable led the young harlot away, swathed in a blanket. After a quick glance to see that the fire was now no longer a threat to the house or its neighbours, de Wolfe hurried round to the front, where a large crowd was now thronging the narrow street. He found Gwyn blocking the doorway.

'What in hell's name is going on, Crowner?' he growled. 'I found the sheriff lurking inside. How did he get there?'

De Wolfe groaned – things were getting out of hand. 'Let me past, I'll speak to him. Say nothing to anyone outside.'

Inside the dark passageway, he found de Revelle skulking inside the doorway to one of the lower rooms, which appeared to be vacant lodgings.

'I told you to slip into the street and look as if you'd just arrived!' he hissed, in exasperation.

'That hairy monster that attends you refused to let me out until he'd spoken to you,' spat de Revelle, as ungrateful as ever, even after John had once again saved his reputation and possibly his life.

The coroner looked his brother-in-law up and down in the gloom. 'Are you respectable now? If so, we will pretend to examine these rooms together, then go out as if we have been companions here all along.' For a few moments, they strode about – thankfully, the sparsely furnished rooms were empty of their transient lodgers and fornicating couples. In the meantime Gwyn had understood the subterfuge, and was pushing back the curious crowd loudly demanding that they make way for the coroner and the sheriff. When they came out of the door behind him, John hissed again into Richard's ear. 'Just drift away now, back to Rougemont and say nothing. I'm off to see that girl and make sure of her silence. You'd better pray hard that none of this comes out. And there's probably no need to tell your confessor – Brother Rufus is in the backyard!'

He walked up the lane with de Revelle until they were past the crowd, then left him and came back to Gwyn. 'Let's get round to the yard again.'

As they hurried down the side passage, his officer broached a matter that had concerned de Wolfe.

'Did you notice that smell, Crowner? I can still get a whiff of it even now. It reminds me of that Greek fire that was used in the battle at Acre.'

In the yard, the flames were dying under endless buckets of water from the well, but hissing steam was rising from the blackened wreckage of the balcony. An aromatic pungency hung in the air and both John and his officer sniffed deeply.

'It's naphtha, that's what that smell is!' said a deep voice behind them. The burly chaplain from the castle was sniffing at his fingertips. 'I pulled away some of the timber for them to throw water on it and now my hands are stinking of it. They used to use it in flares when I was a chaplain with William Marshal's troops.'

De Wolfe nodded at this confirmation of Gwyn's identification.

'So that means the fire was set deliberately,' he said. 'Those stout timbers wouldn't have caught fire just from a flint and tinder or the light from a candle. Someone has lit a block of naphtha against them.'

The three men stared at each other, trying to make sense of this arson.

'Why try to burn down a lodging house in a mean street like this?' asked the priest.

De Wolfe studied his face for any sign of duplicity or sarcasm, but saw none. Yet he wondered if the monk, Richard de Revelle's chaplain and confessor, had known of his master's clandestine presence in the house that night.

Gwyn had wandered over to where the neighbours were still pouring water over the sizzling wreckage. There were two shuttered window openings on the ground floor and John saw his officer bend to stare at something on the stone sill of the one furthest from the fire. After a moment's close scrutiny, Gwyn turned and beckoned to the coroner. 'Does this mean anything? It looks like writing'

De Wolfe stooped alongside him and Gwyn pointed out a series of fresh scratches in the soft limestone of the window surround. Though shallow, they were clean and distinct, looking as if they had been made with the point of a knife, like the letters on the millstone in Fitz-William's well.

A growing unease pervaded John's mind and he cursed that Thomas was not here to offer his usual expertise. 'It's writing surely enough, but I can't read it.'

'Let me see, then,' came a voice from behind and there was the ubiquitous Brother Rufus. Somewhat reluctantly, Gwyn moved aside for him and the heavily built priest peered short-sightedly at the sill.

'Is it another Biblical quotation?' demanded de Wolfe impatiently. If it was, their killer had radically changed his *modus operandi.*

'It is indeed, this time from the Epistle of St Paul to the Romans.'

'And what does it say, for Christ's sake?'

'It was for Christ's sake, Crowner. But I fear that our scribe has a warped sense of religious faith, for this one is hardly appropriate to an attempt at murder.' De Wolfe felt like murdering the monk himself, as he seemed as long-winded as Gwyn in getting to the point. But before he could bellow his frustration, the chaplain continued. 'It reads, "Vengeance is mine – heap coals of fire on his head."'

'That seems apt enough in the circumstances – though it doesn't tell us why it was done and against whom.' De Wolfe choked back the fact that the occupants had included a corrupt sheriff, an appropriate target for a self-appointed avenging angel.

Gwyn, insensitive to the careful path his master had to tread, stated the obvious in a loud voice: 'But there was another bloody harlot there, Crowner! Our killer has done for one already, so he must be having a crusade against loose women.'

De Wolfe reflected that the identity of the girl who had climbed naked down from the balcony must surely have been known to half the men who saw her in the yard, but as long as the sheriff's presence was kept secret, no harm was done.

'Why did you say that the quotation is not right for a murder?' growled Gwyn, who did not take to any priests, apart from Thomas.

'To the best of my recollection, the full sense of that passage from Romans is that "Vengeance is mine; I will repay, saith the Lord,"' answered Rufus. 'But it goes on to tell us ordinary mortals not to take the law into our own hands, as the Almighty is quite capable of doing his own work when it comes to retribution.'

'What about these "coals of fire"?' demanded John. 'They seem to fit this scene.' He waved his hand at the glowing embers and the clouds of smoke still wafting around the yard.

The monk smiled knowingly. 'But Paul said, "If thine enemy hungers, feed him, and if he thirsts, give him drink – for in doing so, you shall heap coals of fire on his head." This is hardly such an act of kindness, trying to burn him to death.'

De Wolfe noticed that Rufus said 'him' even though only a girl had been seen escaping from the house – but perhaps he had been referring to the 'enemy' in the scriptures. However, he had a gut feeling that the nosy priest knew that Richard de Revelle had been inside. 'How came you to be in this yard so quickly tonight?' he snapped.

Brother Rufus looked at him guilelessly. 'I was on my way back to Rougemont from the cathedral, to prepare for Matins in my little chapel. I saw the flames and, being curious, followed these other good men in case I could be of some assistance.'

Waterbeer Street was by no means on a direct route from cathedral to castle and the coroner told him so. The affable monk took no offence at this oblique expression of suspicion. 'You'll remember that I have lately come from Bristol and previously had no knowledge of Exeter. So I make a point of varying my path each day, to build up my familiarity with the city.' The man seemed to have an answer for everything.

De Wolfe turned to Gwyn. 'Stay here until you have questioned as many people as you can about the start of the fire. Catch some in the street before they leave – and talk to the neighbours. See if they remember any strangers loitering about. Then find the owners and other residents of this place – if there are any who stay longer than it takes to drop their breeches!' He dipped his hands into a nearby bucket of water and rinsed the soot off them.

'You've got more on your cheeks, and your hair is singed at the front,' said Gwyn.

As de Wolfe sluiced water over his face, he gave more orders to his officer. 'Find Thomas and get him up here to check on those words under the window.' He looked sideways at the priest. 'I mean no slight on your biblical prowess, Brother, but I have to hold an inquest on all fires in the city, even when there's no corpse, so my own clerk needs to record any evidence.'

He rubbed his face dry with the sleeve of his tunic. 'Now I'm going down to the Saracen to see that girl, and then I'm off to Rougemont to talk to the sheriff. He'll not be pleased that this has happened on the very night the King's Justices are here.'

After he had been to the Saracen, de Wolfe barged into the sheriff's chamber unannounced. He found de Revelle slumped morosely behind his table, a large goblet of wine in his hand, for once ignoring the profusion of parchments spread before him. He had already washed the smuts from his face and hair and was swathed in a plum-coloured velvet house-gown. He raised his head slowly to the coroner, a scowl on his petulant face. 'Come to crow over me again, I suppose?'

John grinned at him, though it was more of a leer. 'How you enjoy yourself at night is none of my business – unless it involves plotting against the King whom you represent in this county.'

The sheriff tried to counter this veiled threat with haughty bluster. 'You are in no position to preach about morals! It's common knowledge that you have been betraying my sister for years with that woman from the inn – and God knows how many others.'

De Wolfe kept his grin in place. 'But, Richard, I don't pick up painted whores and have to flee almost bare-arsed from burning buildings in full view of our worthy citizens.'

The sheriff seemed to sag in his chair, his attempt at defiance crumpling. 'I need a woman now and then! My wife is never here and a man has natural desires. You should know that above all people.'

The frosty Lady de Revelle kept away from Rougemont and her husband as much as she could, though she would have to put in an appearance at the feasting this week.

'I've just come from the Saracen, where I had a few words with your paramour,' announced John, planting himself in a folding chair opposite the sheriff.

De Revelle drunk the rest of his wine and banged down the pewter cup. 'I never even got my money's worth, damn it! We'd hardly got started when that fire began.' He stared wildly at the coroner. 'What the hell is going on, John? Was that sheer coincidence?'

De Wolfe shook his head slowly. 'You're not going to like this – and neither are the royal judges, if they get to hear of it.'

With his brother-in-law becoming more incredulous as he went on, John related their findings in the backyard at Waterbeer Street: that naphtha had been used in a deliberate arson attack and an ambiguous Biblical text had been scrawled at the scene, reduced Richard to a state of furious agitation.

'Why should this murderous swine want to kill me? And what is that damned nonsense about vengeance and coals of fire?' He jumped up and shakily poured more wine, without offering any to his saviour.

De Wolfe watched him stalk about the room, his fair hair and beard spiky from its recent wetting, his small head sticking out of the long red gown like a globe atop a tournament tent. 'There's plenty of folk who'd be happy to see you dead or shamed,' he said. 'You send men to the gallows every other week from your shire court, and their families might want vengeance. Even the tinners have threatened violence to get rid of you as Lord Warden of the Stannaries.' He paused. 'To say nothing of those who despise you for your adherence to Prince John.'

Richard's face flushed with anger and shame. 'But if what you say is true about this poxy message scratched on the window-ledge, this is the same man who's been killing sodomites, whores and Jews. What's that to do with me?'

'He seems to have a private crusade against evildoers – and that includes you!' answered de Wolfe, with some relish. 'At least you are unique.'

'What the hell d'you mean by that?' snarled the sheriff.

'You're his first failure – thanks to Gwyn and myself!'

De Revelle muttered something under his breath, which sounded far removed from an expression of gratitude, but he sat down and seemed to remember his duty as a host: he poured some wine for his brother-in-law. 'Is any of this going to come out?' he mumbled anxiously.

'The fact of the fire is already common knowledge, and as for the rescue of the girl, a dozen men saw that – much to their delight.'

'You say you've spoken to her?

'Just now, at the Saracen. She was more frightened of my threats of retribution if she talked about you than she was at the shock of almost being burned alive like a witch.' He took a deep swallow of the good red wine. 'And I promised her that you will send her a purse of silver, to make sure that she stays silent.'

The tight-fisted sheriff scowled again, but managed to hold his tongue.

'As far as I can make out, no one has realised that

you were in the house with her – except the would-be assassin, of course. I can't believe he would go to those lengths just to dispose of another common harlot.'

'He did so before, with that red-headed strumpet,' the sheriff objected.

'I suspect he's choosing to punish one example of each sin,' said John. 'If he intends eliminating every prostitute in Exeter, he'll be working full-time until Christ Mass! Anyway, that text from the Gospels fitted you better than the girl, with its talk of vengeance.'

'Vengeance for what?'

'There's plenty to choose from, Richard. Sheriffs are the least popular people in the land. Maybe your good wife hired an assassin?'

De Revelle groaned. 'I hope by all the saints in heaven that she never gets to hear of this! She will be here by noon tomorrow.' The chill prospect of his wife's acid tongue caused him to think of his sister. 'And Matilda? What about her? Does she have to know?'

This was one score that de Wolfe was not going to let pass. When he had caught out her brother in his attempted treachery last year, Matilda had pleaded with him to save the sheriff from disgrace and perhaps even execution. He had agreed, and in return gained several months' respite from her domineering abuse. Now he had the chance to build up a little more credit, by telling her how he had saved her brother from both cremation and ridicule.

'There can be no secrets between husband and wife, Richard,' he said, with a straight face but with under-lying glee. The sheriff groaned and pleaded for his silence, but John cut across his words. 'There are more important things at the moment. How did that new chaplain of yours happen to be around Waterbeer Street at the wrong time? Could he have known you were in the house?'

De Revelle's eyes widened. 'Was he there? He didn't see me, did he? He's an inquisitive bastard. I don't know why William the Marshal sent such an unsuitable fellow to us. It must have been some arrangement with his brother, Bishop Henry.' Then a further thought struck him. 'A priest . . . well lettered, knows the Gospels. John, do you think . . . ?'

De Wolfe knew well enough what the sheriff meant, for the same idea had cropped up in his own mind, but there was no real evidence for incriminating the genial Franciscan.

'But it can't be him. He's from Bristol and knows almost no one in these parts,' went on de Revelle. 'Though he may have followed me down from the castle out of sheer curiosity.' He shook his head. 'No, I can't believe it was Rufus. What about that other priest, though?'

De Wolfe stared at him. 'What other priest?'

'Your damned clerk, that twisted little runt with the evil eye. Where was he when all this was happening tonight?'

He said this with a return of his old spitefulness and John was incensed, not only because of the slight against Thomas but because he had no answer. He had no idea where Thomas de Peyne had been that evening, after he left the Bush to fetch his belongings. 'He's well accounted for,' he lied brusquely, but vowed to check this as soon as he next had Thomas and Gwyn together.

A crafty look came into his brother-in-law's eye. He moved across to his littered table and produced a small leaf of parchment from under a ledger. 'This was delivered to me today, John. I know you have no understanding of letters, but I'm sure you'll accept it when I read it out. You can have it checked by someone else later.'

De Wolfe glowered suspiciously at him, ignoring the

slur on his literacy as he nodded brusquely for the sheriff to continue.

'It reads as follows. "I saw the short clerk who scribes for the crowner running away from the house of the cordwainer, soon after the Matin bells on the night he was slain." So what about that, Crowner?' The triumph in his voice was evident.

'Very good, Richard. Did you write it yourself?'

De Revelle leered back at his brother-in-law. 'You can't shrug it off so easily. It was handed to your friend Sergeant Gabriel, no less, by some street child who was given a coin by some nameless man in the town.'

'Great evidence, sheriff! Unsigned, uncorroborated, unproven – and who could have seen my clerk or anyone else in the city in the pitch darkness of midnight?'

'I don't care about that. The very fact that someone has sent this note strengthens the suspicions against your clerk. The finger is pointing, John.'

Though inwardly he felt more concerned than he dared show, de Wolfe again dismissed the message with an airy nonchalance. 'God forbid that we should take any notice of some mischief-maker who can use a pen and ink. In fact, this almost certainly points to a literate priest – and there is a whole clutch of those who are aggravated by being named by the cathedral as suspects.' He slammed his palm hard on to the table in front of the sheriff. 'I should worry more about the Justices in Eyre, if I were you. They may well hear of the fire and even the fact that our resident Exeter murderer left his trademark behind once again. Of course, your part in this must never come to light – unless you do something stupid.'

He drank the rest of his wine and left for the gate-house, leaving a chastened de Revelle behind him.

It was past midnight when de Wolfe reached home, but

for once he cared nothing for his lateness or for the noise he made when he clumped up the solar steps and dropped his boots with a thump on the bedroom floor. Tonight, he cared little for Matilda's scowling face at the disturbance he caused, as he usually tiptoed in stockinged feet to escape her withering tongue. A single rush light burned in a dish of water on the floor, giving enough light for him to see her sitting up in bed, her hair confined in twisted wires and parchment scraps, to be wrestled into ringlets by Lucille for the banquet next evening.

As soon as he dropped on to the edge of the bed to pull off his hose, he went on the attack. 'I have disturbing and distressing news for you, wife,' he began, and launched into a full and accurate version of the evening's events, sparing her no details of her brother's dishonourable part in the affair. Matilda listened in frozen disbelief as he finished his catalogue of Richard's misdemeanours. 'All he was concerned with, was his own escape and the concealment of his presence there,' he concluded.

Matilda was still bolt upright in bed, her back against the wall. Her face was grim and, although he waited for her denials of everything he had said and a diatribe about his wanting further to discredit her brother, she said nothing. She knew that what he had told her must be the truth. Matilda was not blind to the weakness of men when it came to women, but the shame he had narrowly escaped that night would weigh heavily on her for a long time to come. John could imagine the verbal lashing that her brother would get from Matilda in the very near future.

'Will this melancholy tale become common knowledge, John?' were the only words she could find. There was ineffable sadness in her voice and suddenly her husband abandoned any trace of satisfaction in possessing this weapon against her. His voice softened as he said,

'I promised you before that I would protect him as best I can and I will keep my word – short of him becoming involved in any more acts of treason. This affair tonight was conduct unbecoming a senior law officer, but carnal weakness is a lesser offence than seditious leanings against the King.'

He took this opportunity to hint that amorous exploits were of little consequence, compared to the important activities in life. Matilda, for all her many failings, was an intelligent woman and the message was not lost on her.

A simple 'Thank you, John,' was her uncharacteristically short response, as she heaved herself down under the blanket and turned away from him.

He stripped off the rest of his clothes and slipped into his side of the bed. As they lay there, one on each edge, he listened uneasily to her muffled sobs as she cried herself to sleep over her repeatedly fallen idol, Richard de Revelle. Once again, his emotions were confused. She was his wife and would be until death – or until she took herself to a nunnery: his iron sense of duty would keep them bound together in this loveless union. Yet he would never allow her to be harmed and – except when he was in a temper – he had no wish to see her unhappy. At times like this, when she cried into her pillow, he felt guilt, shame, and almost tenderness for the woman who had shared his life for sixteen years. But he knew that in the morning, she would be grim old Matilda once more, throwing his feeble attempts at companionship back in his face and driving him down to the Bush, where humour, love and understanding would start the cycle of his emotions turning full circle once again.

CHAPTER FOURTEEN

In which Crowner John goes to court

Early next morning, the King's Justices attended Mass at the cathedral, and the Bishop himself officiated, which was rare indeed. It was an official event, the preliminary to the opening of the Eyre and, like it or not, all the law officers and their hangers-on had to attend.

All the canons who were not away from the city were there, as were the sheriff, coroner, constable, Portreeves, many burgesses, clerks, and a bevy of lesser officials and priests. When the service was over, the leading participants paraded solemnly through the city streets to Rougemont. They were escorted by a troop of Ralph Morin's men-at-arms, led by Sergeant Gabriel, who, to the accompaniment of raucous blasts on their war-horns, pushed aside the curious onlookers to make way for the austere quartet of Justices and their acolytes.

At the castle, an attempt had been made to make the barn-like Shire Hall more presentable for this important session, which would last well over a week. Banners and tapestries had been draped at each end, and along the walls a line of shields sported freshly painted armorial bearings of the Devon barons. Another dais had been erected at the other end, so that two sets of proceedings could be held simultaneously: the two pairs of Justices had to work at the same time to get through all the cases. More trestle tables had been brought in for the clerks, and towards the front of the platforms, several large chairs borrowed from the keep and from various burgesses, provided seating for the judges and senior officials.

In the body of the hall and spilling outside into the inner ward of Rougemont, a mass of people milled around. They were mainly jurors, called from the many Hundreds of the county, with witnesses, petitioners, appealers and their families, all trying to get what passed for justice. As the session wore on, relays of soldiers brought bedraggled prisoners from the cells under the keep and the two constables, aided by some hired thugs, escorted more miscreants from the larger burgesses' gaol in the towers of the South Gate.

The aloof Sir Peter Peverel sat with Gervase de Bosco, the archdeacon from Gloucester. They dealt mainly with civil proceedings, mostly disputes about land and boundaries, matters of inheritance and claims from widows on their late husbands' property. Sir Walter de Ralegh took the Chancery clerk, Serlo de Vallibus, with him to the other end of the hall, where most of their labours concerned felony, outlawry, suspicious deaths and the seedier side of Devonshire life.

The sheriff and the coroner were obliged to stay at the court the whole time, unless pressing business took them elsewhere. De Wolfe had to justify his title, Keeper of the King's Pleas, by presenting the numerous cases with which he had dealt and Thomas de Peyne found he had no time for miserable reflection.

Though de Wolfe had attended an Eyre before, this was the first since he had become coroner. Somewhat bemused by the frenetic activity, he had little time to speak to either Gwyn or Thomas. The latter was almost panting with exertion as he ran around with plea rolls and Gwyn was doing sterling service in delivering and collecting parchments from various benches, at the direction of John or his clerk.

After a couple of hours, the Justices, well used to their routine, called a halt for refreshment and the strangely subdued sheriff escorted them across to his chambers in the keep for wine and pastries. As he left, he gestured for John to accompany them, but the coroner wanted to use the lull to speak to his assistants.

'Gwyn, did you learn anything from the crowd in the street last night?'

'Nothing worthwhile – no one seemed to know who was lurking inside.'

'Did anyone see anything suspicious?'

Gwyn scratched his crotch vigorously as an aid to memory. 'One young lad said he thought he saw someone in a black mantle coming out of the side passage a few minutes before the fire was spotted, but he might have been romancing – though another old fellow also claims he saw a tall figure with a hood standing in the entrance to the passage alongside the house, but he spoilt it by saying that men are always slipping in and out of there, the place being partly used as a bawdy house.'

De Wolfe turned to the silent clerk. 'What about you, Thomas? Did you get the mattress in the Bush?'

'I did indeed, master. God bless you for your kindness – and that of Mistress Nesta, who fed me too.'

'We needed you last night, but Brother Rufus took over your task of deciphering that text.'

An expression of mortification crept over the little man's face. 'Forgive me, Crowner. I was trying to find a secondary who had borrowed my precious book of the sayings of St Augustine. He was not in the Close and I had to search Priest Street to find him.'

Uneasily, de Wolfe thought that although this was an

excuse that might be true, it was impossible to prove or deny.

'I found Thomas at the Bush and dragged him back to Waterbeer Street to check those scratches,' declared Gwyn.

The clerk bobbed his head in solemn agreement. 'That castle chaplain was quite right – the text was from Paul to the Romans, though the words were used out of context. I suppose the writer needed to twist them to suit the circumstances.'

'Do you read anything into them?' demanded John.

'The coals-of-fire part is obvious, naming the means he used to try to kill the—'

Afraid that Thomas might blurt out the sheriff's name in public, John jabbed a finger to his lips. 'What about the vengeance part?'

Thomas shrugged. 'It can only mean that this was revenge for some evil act. But God alone knows what that might have been.' He jerkily made the Sign of the Cross as he uttered the words.

At that moment the justices returned and carried on trying cases until late morning, when they broke for their midday dinner.

All manner of events were looked into by the keen-eared Justices, mainly with a view to squeezing money out of the population for the royal treasury. Many of these events involved deaths, both homicidal, accidental and suicidal, though the mortal sin of *felo de se* was relatively uncommon. It was in these cases that de Wolfe was constantly involved, reporting on his investigations, with the invaluable help of Thomas's precious parchment rolls.

They rushed through the hearings at breakneck speed, though de Wolfe was impressed by the fairness of most judgements, even though the penalties on conviction were harsh. Many cases were dismissed from lack of evidence, and quite a number of prisoners and men under attachment fines were released, to the noisy delight of their families.

A few lawyers attended the more affluent defendants, though their efforts were mainly concerned with the civil arguments, where the fees and pickings were greater than with those accused of crimes, who were usually poor or destitute. John was glad when the half-day break was called and this time had no hesitation in joining the judges for food and drink in the hall of the castle, provided somewhat reluctantly by the sheriff out of his own purse. He sat on the main table, reserved for the Justices and law officers, finding himself next to Serlo de Vallibus, the Chancery clerk. Many low-born but able men, such as de Vallibus, rose to positions of power in the government of England and being appointed as a Justice of Eyre was a significant stepping-stone to such prominence. Opposite was the gruff Walter de Ralegh, with Richard de Revelle alongside him, and further down the table the two other judges sat with the Portreeves and senior churchmen, who had come to listen to the morning's proceedings.

After they had attacked their bowls of stew and trenchers loaded with meat, they began to gossip. The notorious Exeter grapevine had been busy already, as de Ralegh's first words confirmed: 'Now, de Revelle, tell us more about these remarkable murders you have had in the city. We had heard of them in Somerset, but I gather you have had more since then.'

This was the last topic that the sheriff wanted to discuss, but he had little choice. He tried to make light of the killings and dismiss them as just another facet of urban life, but de Ralegh would have none of it. 'Come, Sheriff, it's a poor state of affairs to have a string of unsolved slaughters within your walls at the very time that the Eyre of Assize is visiting.

Puts a rather poor complexion on your stewardship here, eh?'

This was just what de Revelle had feared so he tried to shift the onus on to the coroner: 'De Wolfe here can tell you about them. He's the investigator – not that he's had much success, poor fellow.'

De Wolfe scowled at his brother-in-law and flashed him a warning glance, given the fragile state of his credit.

'Crowner, bring us up to date. I heard that even last night there was trouble that was likely to have been the work of this Grim Reaper.'

This was Serlo, whose sibilant voice seemed always to carry a veiled threat. John wondered how he had got to hear of the arson attack so quickly and concluded that his clerks must be professional spies.

Somewhat reluctantly, de Wolfe summarised the story of the four murders and the arson attack, carefully leaving out the slightest hint of the involvement of the sheriff.

'So this madman seems to have a grudge against whores, if one was also in that burning house,' commented de Ralegh. John was happy to let him think so and went on to describe the biblical references that made it certain that the culprit was a priest.

Walter, who seemed the dominant member of the judicial quartet, was impatient about the city's inability to catch the killer.

'If he's a cleric, surely you can catch the swine?' de Ralegh barked. 'Interrogate every one, put any likely suspects to the torture until you get a confession.'

Further down the table heads turned, especially those of the senior cathedral canons, the Archdeacon and Precentor. The look on their faces told what they thought of de Ralegh's robust solution.

Serlo de Vallibus had a more realistic notion of the

situation. 'Walter, that would be difficult. I gather there are more than a hundred religious men of various rank in this city. Almost all come under the jurisdiction and protection of the Lord Bishop – the cathedral precinct is not even within the purview of the secular law. The clergy cannot be coerced – the Pope himself would be enraged if it came to his ears.'

De Ralegh, a former soldier with a fiery reputation, snorted at this but held his tongue. However, Sir Peter Peverel, listening across the table, took up the criticism of the law officers. 'It seems incredible that in a walled city such as this, with the gates closed at night and constables walking the streets, that a killer can strike repeatedly and with apparent impunity.'

Stung by these criticisms of his wardship, de Revelle launched into an exaggerated account of the investigations and hinted that lack of co-operation on the part of the cathedral authorities was part of the reason for their failure. This provoked an angry response from Thomas de Boterellis and soon a first-class argument had broken out along the table. It petered out after everyone had declaimed their pet theories and impractical solutions. Much to de Wolfe's dismay, Serlo de Vallibus had the last word: 'I also hear that a favoured candidate for these crimes is your own clerk, de Wolfe. A most unsavoury and unstable person, ejected from the Church, but well versed in the scriptures and adeptly literate. Neither has he any alibi for each of these evil events, so I am told.'

Red with annoyance, John almost shouted his denials and ended with a final declaration of Thomas's innocence: 'I would stake my own life on it. And remember, he was the very one who deciphered the biblical clues in almost every case.'

De Vallibus smiled his icy smile. 'And that might be the best sign of his cunning, Crowner.'

*   *   *

When the afternoon session began, de Wolfe was still smarting as the Justices' criticisms of their hunt for the murderer and their accusations against Thomas de Peyne. He glowered throughout the long proceedings, making his many presentations with a thunderous face. After an hour or so, there was a diversion: Sergeant Gabriel pushed his way through the throng to report that a man had been knifed in a brawl down on the quayside. Unable to leave the Shire Hall himself, he sent Gwyn to investigate.

The cases came and went, men shuffled and jostled as the juries of the various Hundreds were called to account. De Wolfe had to listen to an endless catalogue of rural dramas that had occured over the past ten months. The requisite twelve jurors of Teignbridge Hundred reported that Adam le Pale took refuge in the church after robbing a traveller and then abjured the realm.

Budleigh Hundred produced only nine jurors and the missing three were 'put in mercy' by the judges to the tune of two marks each.

The sergeant of Plympton Hundred reported the washing up of a tun of wine on the beach, worth six shillings and eight-pence, but as the barrel was only half full when viewed by the coroner, they were amerced five shillings.

The cases went on and on – drownings, crushing by carts, rapes, murdrum fines, sentences of death, arguments over fences, declarations of outlawry, claims on land by ancient tenure and the finding of treasure trove were the endless grist to the legal mill. John was quite bemused by the early evening when the court adjourned, though one case remained in his memory. The jurors of Axminster Hundred presented that William de Pisswelle was suspect because he ate, drank and dressed expensively, yet they did not know where his money came from, but suspected that he stole pigs. They were unable to support their accusation with any evidence of William's wrongdoing, so the Justices dismissed the case and fined the jurors ten shillings for malice!

With this example of good sense in his mind, de Wolfe made his way home where, as he had anticipated, Matilda was in a ferment of excitement and anxiety about the banquet in the Bishop's Palace that evening. He was banished to Mary's kitchen-hut in the yard while his wife and Lucille fussed over her kirtle, apparently requiring the dining table to spread it out and run a heated smoothing iron over the skirt.

There was no meal at home that night, in anticipation of lavish episcopal victuals, but Mary had made some honey-filled pastry cups and, with a cold leg of chicken, de Wolfe staved off the pangs of hunger. As he washed down the food with a quart of cider, Mary sat with him at the kitchen table, while he told her of the scenes in the Shire Hall that day. When he indignantly mentioned the Justices' comments about Thomas, she nodded sadly. 'It's all over the town already,' she said. 'At the bread stall, I heard a man telling Will Baker that the crowner's clerk was about to be arrested and hanged – stupid fool!'

She looked up anxiously at her master for, like Nesta, she had a soft spot for the ex-priest. 'There's no chance that he—'

Mary failed to get the words out, but John banged his pot on the table, his anger covering his own concern. 'Of course not, woman! Can you see that poor wretch as a multiple killer? He faints if he as much as cuts his own finger!'

Outside there was a babble of voices and crunching of feet as Matilda and her maid came through the side passage, holding the precious gown between them. De Wolfe jumped up, feeling guilty without knowing why he should, in time to see them climbing the steps to the solar, where no doubt Lucille would lever her mistress into the dress then start the laborious business of arranging her hair – a process that always invoked a stream of invective from Matilda. As they vanished into the upper room and slammed the door, John slunk back into the kitchen-hut to finish his drink.

'I'll give them half an hour, then I'd better go up and get into my best tunic.' He rubbed a hand over his chin. 'I'll run a comb through my hair to please her, but I don't need a wash, do I, Mary?'

She examined his face critically, then planted a swift kiss on his dark-shadowed cheek. 'You'll last until next Saturday, Sir Crowner – though don't go kissing any girls or your stubble will rip their faces!'

Eventually he braved the two women upstairs to collect his best clothes from the chest in the solar and went down to the hall to put them on, where Mary gave him the clean linen shirt that was his only undergarment. Against Matilda's desire for more flamboyant dress, he put on a grey tunic that reached below his knees, a wide belt of black leather with a Moorish silver buckle, black woollen hose and a pair of ankle-length soft boots, with only modestly pointed toes. The evening was warm enough for him to dispense with a mantle or pelisse, but he pulled on an armless surcoat of a darker grey and was ready to go.

However, familiar with Matilda's dilatory ways, he sat down again by his empty hearth and fondled Brutus's ears while he pondered his current problems, foremost of which was the apparent invincibility of the man he had come to think of as the Gospel killer. Linked to that was a nagging worry over Thomas – his continuing depression and the insidious rumours about his involvement in the murders. His hound seemed to share in his worries for, with a sigh, he laid his head on his master's thigh, giving him a soulful look of sympathy and a streak of frothy saliva on his best tunic.

De Wolfe's ruminations were ended by the grand entry of his wife, with Lucille running behind to make adjustments to the new kirtle of green silk. Though Matilda could never have been beautiful, if she had lost her perpetual expression of sullen ill-temper, she might have been handsome. In her fine clothes, with bell-shaped sleeves sweeping the floor and a white satin gorget pinned under the snowy coverchief that framed her face, she looked every inch a Norman lady. De Wolfe sometimes felt that only her love of finery kept her from entering a nunnery and wondered whether the latest bitterness and shame over her brother's behaviour might tip the balance in favour of her taking the veil.

Lucille had her mistress's mantle across her arm and now helped her drape the scarlet velvet across her broad back and secure it with a round gold brooch on the front of the right shoulder.

'Are you ready, husband?' grated Matilda, eyeing his dull outfit with distaste. Feeling like a crow alongside a peacock, he escorted her back through the screen around the door into the vestibule, where he took his wide-brimmed black hat from a peg and held the front door open for her.

With Lucille and Mary – who detested each other – watching from the doorway, the couple set off on the short walk into the cathedral Close and around the west front to the palace entrance. De Wolfe sensed the conflict within his wife, as she tried to balance the pleasure and anticipation of such a welcome social event with the anger she felt at her brother's foolishness.

Other guests were converging on the gateway into Henry Marshal's garden and John cynically observed the intensity with which each wife studied another's raiment with a mixture of admiration, criticism and jealousy. Within the garden, along the paved way that led to the porch, two lines of cathedral choristers stood in cassock and surplice, singing the guests into the palace, with descanted chants, which to John's totally tone-deaf ears, sounded like dirges.

Inside, the dining hall was bright with candles, adding to the spring evening light coming through the high clerestory windows. Two rows of tables ran up the hall to join a cross table at the top, which had the Bishop's chair in the centre. The chamber was not nearly as large as the hall in the castle keep so the much sought-after invitations had been limited. Though they were not awarded the honour of seats at the upper table, Matilda was mollified by being placed with her husband at the top of one of the long trestles, with her brother and the icy Lady Eleanor in equivalent places on the other spur. A manservant took her cloak and Matilda made sure that he hung it carefully in an alcove in the wall behind.

When all the guests had filled the long tables, a door opened behind the Bishop's chair and a cathedral proctor entered with his silver staff, which he banged peremptorily on the table. Everyone lumbered to their feet as the Lord Bishop of Devon and Cornwall entered and took his place before his high-backed chair. He wore a caped tunic of dark purple, with a silver cross hanging on his breast from a chain around his shoulders. His head was covered with a close-fitting black coif, tied under his chin. Behind him the important guests filed in, the four Justices, two of the four archdeacons in the diocese, then the Precentor and Treasurer.

The proctor banged his staff again and the Precentor began a long grace in Latin, which to John, whose calves were being cut into by the edge of the bench behind him, seemed to go on for ever. Eventually they reached the muttered 'Amen' and with much scraping of stools and benches, the guests subsided with relief, ready to eat as much of the Bishop's provisions as they could manage. A small army of servants appeared and trenchers of bread were placed on the scrubbed boards. As a modern luxury, there were also pewter platters, and wooden bowls and horn spoons were placed before each guest to supplement the daggers of the men, whose duty it was to serve the neighbouring ladies. As there were a considerable number of celibate priests, many of the pairs were male, but they still gave each other the courtesy of serving one another.

Wine, ale and mead appeared, and then a succession of dishes, and de Wolfe, though no sycophantic admirer of the Church, had to admit that Henry Marshal had not stinted in his hospitality that evening. There was duck, goose, heron and pheasant in abundance, venison and other red meat, fish of all kinds, from salmon to herring, then capon, rabbit, hare and boar, with a wide variety of herbed and scented sauces. Afterwards, sweet puddings, cakes and bowls of raisins and nuts were accompanied by a second relay of wines from Anjou and Rouen and sweeter ones from the South of France. When most of the serious business of eating had been accomplished, there was time for chatter and the endless supply of wine jugs aided the flow of conversation.

De Wolfe was opposite Walter de Ralegh, Peter Peverel, and his old friend, Archdeacon John de Alençon seated on the top trestle. They began an animated conversation about the cases of that day's session, the successes and failures of King Richard against Philip of France and, inevitably, the mysterious killer of Exeter City.

Matilda, now confident that her new gown and mantle were at least the equal of any other in the hall – and undoubtedly better than those of her arch-rival sister-in-law, Lady Eleanor de Revelle – sat back content. She had eaten twice as much as her husband, who had worked hard to keep their trencher filled. Now she drank Henry Marshal's best wine with smug appreciation and looked about the chamber to make sure that her lady rivals were aware of her prime position in the table hierarchy.

She was particularly pleased that John was relatively sociable tonight and glowed with reflected pride to see her own husband, a senior law officer, publicly engrossed in conversation with two of the King's Justices, as well as senior churchmen. If only she could coax him to do this more often and curry favour with the top Guild-Masters and burgesses, then her life would be more tolerable.

Then her gaze moved to the next table and fell upon her brother. Immediately her euphoria faded: the man who had been her idol since childhood, now the sheriff of the whole county, had recently proved he had feet of clay. She had no political preferences of her own – indeed, she was ignorant of much that went on in the rest of England – but it was humiliating to discover that he had not only allied himself to a traitor, but to a traitor who had failed. Now the fool had almost ruined himself again in lusting after a strumpet. Though she detested Eleanor, mainly because she came from a far higher-born family than the de Revelles, she almost felt a twinge of sympathy for her at being married to a man who picked losing causes and cavorted with whores in back-street brothels. Though she was well aware that her own husband was constantly unfaithful, at least to the best of her knowledge he never paid for his fornication – and he certainly never let himself be caught in such humiliating situations as the burning stew in Waterbeer Street.

A sudden drop in the level of babble meant that the Bishop was rising to make his formal speech of welcome to the King's Justices. As de Wolfe listened to the dry tones and humourless platitudes of the leader of God's ministry in this part of England, he thought of Henry Marshal's own political partialities. A supporter of Prince John, he had sailed close to the wind of treachery more than once – and de Wolfe suspected that, if the conditions were right, he might do so again, allying himself with other malcontents like de Revelle in an uprising against Richard the Lionheart. To stand there and welcome the King's undoubtedly loyal judges, as if he himself was an equally dedicated champion of Coeur de Lion seemed the height of hypocrisy.

Once he had sat down, Walter de Ralegh made a short and rather gruff reply of thanks for the Bishop's remarks and for his lavish hospitality. When that was over, the Bishop rose to give a final blessing, then bowed in farewell to his special guests and glided out through the door, attended by his proctor and confessor.

As soon as he had vanished, the hubbub of talk and laughter rose to new levels as the crowd made sure that all the Bishop's wine jugs and ale pitchers would go back empty to the kitchens. Having exhausted politics, the talk around de Wolfe gravitated back to the series of killings and de Ralegh, made pugnacious by drink, became more critical of the city's law enforcement.

'That damn sheriff over there needs to get a better grip on things,' he bellowed. 'He seems to leave it all to you, de Wolfe – and you've not made much progress, by the look of it!'

The Archdeacon attempted to come to his friend's rescue. 'This is not a village, Sir Walter, where everyone knows everyone else's business and where the frank-pledge system keeps a tight rein on all men.'

'What's the difference?' demanded de Ralegh.

'In the countryside, the culprit is known instantly – he usually runs away or is caught within minutes. But in a city of almost five thousand souls like Exeter, there are hundreds of merchants, travellers, pilgrims, sailors and other itinerants. It's a permanently shifting population. If someone hides around the corner of a lane at night and robs, kills or rapes the first person who passes, how can he be found if there are no witnesses?'

Walter de Ralegh would have none of this. 'We're not talking about casual thuggery! Some mad priest is methodically acting as God, dispensing what he sees as justice where the law fails to act. That's the work of a clever brain, not some footpad hiding around a corner.'

John intervened to pay back de Alençon's support. 'But it makes it no easier to detect – the opposite, in fact, for, as you say, this person has a clever mind.'

Serlo, the Chancery judge, leaned across from further along the top table. 'I hear you've tried matching these messages against the writings of certain priests in the city, to see if their hand corresponds?'

'We have indeed, but my clerk, who has a considerable facility with literary matters, assures us that the writing was deliberately disguised.'

Serlo smiled his secret smile. 'Well, perhaps it was in his own interests to say that, if he himself is the perpetrator.'

The Archdeacon bristled at this further indictment of his nephew. 'Not so, sir! The same opinion was given by our cathedral archivist, Canon Jordan de Brent, who spends his life with manuscripts and scribes.'

The discussion went back and forth, getting nowhere, with the Justices sticking to their opinion that the coroner's clerk was the most likely candidate for the killings. With the Bishop retired, the party gradually wound down, hastened by the servants who finally stopped replenishing the wine and ale. The guests began to drift away and de Wolfe signalled to a servant for Matilda's cloak. He was thankful that this time there had been no sign of Gwyn signalling urgently from the doorway to tell him of some new death – and glad that, so far, the Gospel killer seemed to have taken a night's rest.

Matilda made the best of the remaining minutes to parade herself around her other matronly acquaintances, taking care to grip John's arm to emphasise her ownership of the King's coroner, even though everyone in the city was well aware of his identity and status. At last he prised her away from the final farewells to her friends and rivals and they passed under the pitch flares along the garden path.

Matilda had studiously ignored her brother and his wife all evening, but at the gate they came across the de Revelles as they bade goodnight to Henry Rifford, one of the city's Portreeves. Forced to acknowledge them, Matilda muttered a frosty greeting to Richard, and turned her back on him to falsely admire Lady Eleanor's mantle. Then she jerked John onwards towards Martin's Lane.

Relieved that the night had gone without incident, de Wolfe loped silently alongside her, his weary body and tired mind welcoming the thought of even their loveless bed in the solar – but envying his clerk, sleeping in the loft of the Bush within a few feet of his beloved Nesta.

CHAPTER FIFTEEN

In which Crowner John suffers great distress

When de Wolfe slid out of bed before dawn next day Matilda was still sound asleep. He dressed and had boiled bacon, eggs and bread in Mary's kitchen-hut before setting off alone to the bottom of the town. He wanted to stir up the priests who were on the cathedral's suspect list, to see if any allowed their guard to slip. He also hoped, rather forlornly, that he might find some clue as to who had sent the anonymous note to the sheriff. It must surely be one of the suspected priests, he thought. The court began at the eighth hour and he had to be back at Rougemont by then, so early morning was the only opportunity for him to make such visits.

He hurried down to the West Gate, which was just opening to admit the flood of dawn traders, then turned towards All-Hallows and found that an early Mass, de Capra's version of Prime, was just finishing. He waited for the dozen parishioners to leave, then walked into the barren church. A figure was on its knees before the altar, still wearing a creased surplice over his cassock, with a threadbare stole around his neck and a maniple over his arm.

Ralph de Capra was muttering to himself, but as soon as he heard de Wolfe's footsteps behind him, he jumped to his feet. 'You again, Crowner! Why don't you leave me be? I've nothing to tell you.' His face was haggard and suffused, the defect in his upper lip looking like a white scar against the flushed face.

'Did you write an unsigned letter to the sheriff, falsely accusing my clerk of being at the scene of a killing the other night?'

De Wolfe had neither the time nor the inclination to be circumspect, and he wanted to provoke the priest as much as possible. Even as de Capra was hotly denying it, he followed up with a barrage of questions and accusations about his movements during the past few nights. Prodding the man in the chest with his forefinger, he drove him back down the nave, hoping that the confusion and resentment he was generating might cause him to drop some unguarded statement.

However, the priest frustrated the coroner's tactics by screaming suddenly and, dropping his surplice on the floor, turned to rush towards his simple altar. Throwing his arms across the cloth, each side of the Cross, he hung across its front and began to wail and gabble. He was largely incoherent, but de Wolfe picked out some words. He seemed to be making a desperate plea for forgiveness for 'his great sin'.

'What sin is that, Ralph?' he asked loudly, as he came to stand behind the man. 'Is it the sin of murder? Did you kill the Jew, the whore and the merchant?'

The priest slid down the front of the altar and squatted in a crumpled heap on the floor below the Cross. 'Let me be, Crowner,' he whimpered. 'My sin is greater than ten thousand murders. It is the sin of rejecting God Almighty, for which I will surely roast in hell.'

De Wolfe failed to get any further response from him and, feeling compassion, embarrassment and frustration, abandoned the attempt and left the little church.

He had even less satisfaction at his next call: at St Mary Steps there was no sign of Adam of Dol, either in the church or at his dwelling around the corner.

At St Olave's, further up on his route back to the castle, John found Julian Fulk on his knees at the chancel step, deep in silent prayer. On hearing someone enter, he crossed himself and rose to his feet, but his smile of welcome faded when he saw the coroner.

John knew that shock tactics would be wasted on an urbane, calculating person like Fulk, so he asked his questions in measured terms. As he expected, the moon-faced priest answered him coldly but civilly, denying any knowledge of the note sent to de Revelle and flatly rejecting any notion that he had been skulking in the midnight streets of the city. 'I realise that you have your obligations as a law officer, Sir John,' he said levelly, 'but it really is a waste of your time and mine for you to come here repeatedly asking me questions, the answers to which are self-evident. No, I am not the avenging killer of Exeter, I do not know who it might be, and I appear to have no information that could possibly help you. Now, is that sufficient for you to leave me in peace to attend to my own duties – which includes ministering to my congregation, among which your good wife and, indeed, yourself are numbered?'

Though de Wolfe had a thick skin, he felt put in his place by this reasoned statement and, partly spurred by the fear that Fulk would complain to Matilda, he muttered some platitudes and left Julian Fulk to his prayers.

In the Shire Hall that morning de Wolfe found the same mixture of cases, with the same organised confusion of milling people, harassed clerks and clumsy soldiers shunting prisoners in and out. At least the whole of that week would have to be devoted to the Eyre of Assize, dealing with a great backlog of civil cases, plus current criminal matters and 'Gaol Delivery', meant to flush out the chronically overcrowded jails in the city. Many of these long-term prisoners never made it to trial, as they had either escaped, bribed their way out, died of gaol fever or been fatally abused by their fellow evildoers in the stinking cells.

The second part of the judges' visit, the General Eyre, which looked into the administration of the county, was not due to begin until the following week, so Richard de Revelle had a few more days in which to cook his accounts, and to fret about the vigilance with which the four Justices would probe his management of Devon on behalf of the King.

Meanwhile, de Wolfe was called frequently to present new matters, which came from the mass of parchment rolls that Thomas de Peyne produced from a wooden box at the back of the dais, with Walter de Ralegh and Serlo de Vallibus officiating from their chairs at the front. John had a stool at the end of one of the clerk's tables, to be near Thomas's store of documents. When required, he grabbed a roll from his clerk and marched over to stand alongside the Justices and recite a summary of the case, with which Thomas had primed him a few minutes earlier. Being unable to read what was on the roll made it difficult, but if any clarification of the matter was needed, he thrust the parchment at Serlo and let him pick out what he wanted.

At the other end of the court, his more literate brother-in-law was carrying out much the same function as himself with the other two judges, though their cases were slower and more complex, dealing with land, inheritance, marriage contracts and arguments about freemen and villeins. The morning wore on until a break was called at noon, when the four Justices went back to the New Inn for their meal. This was no more than a few hundred yards from Rougemont, and de Wolfe walked with them, flanked by Sergeant Gabriel and the four men-at-arms that Ralph Morin had assigned as an escort whenever the King's men were abroad in the streets. He left them at the door of the inn and went on to Martin's Lane to have his own meal with Matilda. She was still relatively benign after the previous night's banquet – and with the prospect of another at the castle the following evening.

He managed to hold her attention with an account of the more colourful of the morning's cases, until near the end of the meal when there was a dramatic interruption. The outer door crashed open, then the inner one to the hall burst open and someone almost fell inside, behind the screens that kept the winter draughts at bay. A wild figure appeared and Matilda leapt to her feet to shriek her protests at such an unseemly intrusion, for it was the despised Gwyn, the usual harbinger of bad news. For once, he was not cowed by her outburst, as the news he had for his master was too urgent.

'Crowner, one of the Justices has been attacked! And there was another Bible message and they've arrested Thomas for it!' he yelled, his arms flailing like the sails of a windmill.

Ignoring Matilda's commands for the dishevelled man to get out of her hall, John hurried across, seized Gwyn's arm and hustled him out into the vestibule and then into the lane. 'Calm down, man. Tell me what's happened.'

Gwyn tugged at the coroner's sleeve, urging him towards the high street and the New Inn. 'You told Thomas to take the rolls for some of this afternoon's cases down to Serlo de Vallibus, so that he could look at them before they were presented.'

'I know that – two of the killings are false allegations, I suspect,' John said. They were hurrying around the corner into the main street.

'One of Gabriel's men came racing up to the gate-house just now, yelling that an attempt had been made on the life of de Vallibus. He went off to find the sheriff, and I ran like hell down to the New Inn.'

They were trotting now, thrusting aside townsfolk who were standing at stalls or looking into the shop fronts of traders.

'When I got there, Thomas had been grabbed by the guards, apparently on Sir Peter Peverel's orders, and marched away to the castle.'

The inn was now a few yards away, and Gwyn had just enough time to finish telling the little he knew. 'Alan Spere, the landlord, let me through and pointed up the stairs. I dashed up and saw the three other Justices clustered round de Vallibus, who was lying on his pallet, groaning. Then Peverel recognised me and began shouting that I was another of them, whatever that meant. Walter de Ralegh pulled me out of the room and told me to go for you, saying that Thomas had attacked Serlo and left a Gospel message, proving he was the killer.'

Bewildered and incredulous, John reached the doorway of the New Inn just ahead of his officer and skidded into the short passage and up the stairs. Ahead was a narrow stairway with open treads, divided into short two flights with a small landing halfway. At the top, stood one of the men-at-arms and as John thundered up the stairs, he looked uncertain whether or not to challenge him, but John brushed him aside impatiently and Gwyn followed up with a shove that sent the soldier staggering against the wooden wall. A planked door on the left was open and a babble of voices came from inside. As de Wolfe barged in, five heads turned towards him.

'Here he is, the King's damned crowner!' brayed Peter Peverel, 'Now perhaps he'll see reason about his evil little clerk.'

The others in the room were the three judges, Richard de Revelle and Ralph Morin, with Serlo de Vallibus groaning on his blanket. The left side of his head was partly covered by a damp cloth, whose centre was pink with watery blood.

Gwyn hovered in the doorway, behind his master, who took in the scene at a glance, then fixed Walter de Ralegh with his dark eyes. 'What happened?' he said shortly, his incisive manner quelling the ferment of talk.

De Revelle answered for the Justices: 'Your accursed clerk attacked our noble judge, that's what happened. And left a trademark that denounces him as this killer.'

The sheriff gloated over the situation, for at last he was giving his brother-in-law grief, instead of receiving it from him.

'Who saw de Peyne strike the blow?' snapped John, glaring about him, as whatever had been said, he refused to believe it.

'Come on, de Wolfe, just accept what you're told,' bellowed de Ralegh. 'The little swine was seen to come into the inn as bold as brass. He went upstairs and then ran out as if the devil was after him, but the man-at-arms grabbed him as he was going out of the door.'

'Why did he hold him?' grated John.

'Because at that moment, Serlo here staggered out of this room and called for help – then fell down the stairs,' cut in Peter Peverel, with almost malicious glee.

'I asked if anyone saw him attack de Vallibus,' de Wolfe repeated. 'I sent him here with a bundle of rolls, as arranged.' He looked quickly around the chamber. 'There they are, on that chest.' Four or five rolls of parchment lay on an oak box, and a couple had fallen on to the floor.

'He must have taken the opportunity to try to kill Serlo,' boomed Gervase de Bosco, the one Justice who so far had stayed silent.

'Mary, Mother of God, why should he do that?' burst out de Wolfe, desperately trying keep the alleged truth at arm's length.

'Because of this – some warped notion of justice.'

De Ralegh held out a torn scrap of parchment, which even in the turmoil reminded de Wolfe of the message left at the scene of the Jewish moneylender's death. There was writing on it, but he handed it back straight away. 'What does it say?'

Archdeacon Gervase took the fragment, which was about the size of his hand. 'It's a quotation from the Gospel of St Matthew, though virtually the same one is in St Luke.'

De Wolfe felt a sudden intense sadness that it was not Thomas who was explaining this to him. The last time, Brother Rufus had translated the clue, but now it was a portly archdeacon from Gloucester.

'Tell me again what it says,' demanded Walter de Ralegh.

Gervase held out the vellum at arm's length better to see the penned words. ' "Judge not, that ye be not judged," ' he intoned.

Suddenly a voice came from the bed, wavering yet clear. 'The full quotation goes on, "For with what judgement ye judge, ye shall be judged. And with what measure ye mete, it shall be measured to you again." '

They all turned to look down at the bed, where the previously inert Serlo now appeared wide awake. Before they could speak, he continued, 'Luke adds, "Condemn not and ye shall not be condemned", but I'm unaware why someone should have taken such a dislike to the many judgements I must have handed down since I became a King's Justice.'

The others now crowded around him, solicitously asking after his welfare, offering the services of an apothecary or to take him to St John's infirmary nearby.

Serlo shook his head, which made him wince, then struggled to a sitting position on the bed. 'My head is hard, I'll survive, thank you.' He touched his scalp gingerly. 'But I think I'll not sit in court for the rest of the day.'

The others jabbered protests at the idea of his return- ing to the Shire Hall, and the sheriff was almost bursting with the desire to smooth over this dangerous fiasco, although he still delighted in John's discomfiture. 'Did you actually see that it was this evil clerk who tried to kill you?' he demanded. 'I have him in chains already and will hang him as soon as possible.'

'You'll do nothing of the sort, damn you,' yelled de Wolfe. 'He'll have a fair trial and, if guilty, be condemned on good evidence, not at your whim.'

Walter de Ralegh, whose large size and dominating presence always made him the leading figure in any group, held up his hands. 'Wait, wait! Of course the fellow will be tried – though a confession would ease the process.'

'He'll confess, I'll guarantee that!' snarled the sheriff. 'I have a gaoler who, though he is an imbecile, is a genius at extracting confessions.'

De Ralegh ignored this and spoke again to Serlo, who was now hunched on the mattress, holding his head in both hands. 'What happened, de Vallibus? Can you help us?'

Unable to shake his head because of the throbbing pain in his cranium, the Chancery clerk murmured his reply: 'I remember nothing after sitting on this bed for a short sleep after our meal. The next thing I recollect is tumbling down those damned stairs. I must have staggered out of the room after receiving this blow and lost my footing at the top.'

'You remember nothing about my clerk being here?' demanded de Wolfe eagerly.

'Nothing at all. But those rolls of yours were not there before I lost my senses.'

Richard de Revelle gave a triumphant cry. 'Ha! There is the proof. De Peyne comes with them as an excuse, de Vallibus is attacked, the clerk runs away and is caught by the guard. The complete story!'

The coroner glimpsed the landlord hovering anxiously outside the door. 'Alan Spere, are these stairs the only way up to these chambers?'

The normally jovial host was as white as sheet, wondering whether it was a capital offence for a King's Justice to be attacked on his premises. 'No, Crowner, the passage goes past the other five rooms then down at the back into the stabling yard.'

'Was there a guard there?' the coroner demanded of the silent Ralph Morin.

The castle constable was glad of the chance to deflate the sheriff, for whom he had the same lack of regard as de Wolfe. 'No. The escort was a mark of respect rather than a necessity.'

John shrugged and held up his hands in a Gallic gesture. 'So whoever made this cowardly attack on Justice Serlo might have come into the yard from the lane alongside the inn and up the back stairs – for the man-at-arms at the front saw no one.'

'He saw this bastard de Peyne, that's who he saw!' objected Peter, Peverel, who sided with the sheriff's prejudices. The party was already dividing into two factions: those who were ready to hang Thomas out of hand and those who had a more open mind.

'This is getting us nowhere, unless de Vallibus's memory returns,' said de Ralegh reasonably.

'And we need to hear what my clerk has to say on the matter,' snapped de Wolfe.

Ralph Morin agreed to send a soldier to St John's to fetch Brother Saulf to attend to Serlo's head and prescribe some salve, while the other three Justices returned to the court to carry on the afternoon session. With a couple of extra men-at-arms guarding them, the sheriff, constable and coroner walked behind them to the inner ward and the Shire Hall. De Wolfe kept silent during the five-minute walk, ignoring the smirk of triumph that lurked on the sheriff's face.

When they reached the wide entrance to the Shire Hall, de Wolfe stopped. 'I'm going to see Thomas first,' he announced.

'The fellow is in my custody, I'll not have you interfering,' retorted de Revelle, rejoicing in this unexpected return of his supremacy.

'Go to the devil, Richard! A coroner is empowered – indeed, obliged – to investigate all serious crimes in his jurisdiction. Not only murders, but also assaults. So I am going to investigate this one, whether you like it or not.'

The sheriff became red in face and began to huff and puff about his absolute powers in the county.

'Talk all you like, Sheriff, I'm going to the undercroft to see him now.'

As he stalked off, de Revelle hissed after him, 'You dare to interfere or try to engineer his release and I'll have the full force of the Justices on you. They're not taking kindly to one of their own number being half killed, so don't expect any aid from *them*!' With that, he turned on his elegant heel and strode into the Shire Hall.

About an hour later on this tumultuous Wednesday afternoon, another drama was being played out in the lower part of Exeter. A small crowd, which increased by the minute, had gathered in the narrow street between the West Gate and the church of All-Hallows-on-the-Wall. A cluster of street traders, porters, good-wives, children and beggars were pointing and gesticulating at a figure parading agitatedly along the narrow walkway that topped the city wall, twenty feet above the street. He was barefoot and dressed in a shapeless, ragged garment of what looked at that distance to be of sacking. In his hand, he grasped a rough wooden cross made of two thin sticks tied together.

'Is it an absconder from sanctuary?' asked one onlooker of her neighbour, for the figure's garb was that of someone abjuring the realm after seeking refuge in a church.

The crowd was soon joined by Osric, attracted by the rising hubbub in the street. Shielding his eyes from the afternoon sun, the constable stared up and asked the nearest man, a crippled pedlar with a tray of dusty pies hung around his neck, 'Who is it up there? And what's he think he's doing?'

'Gone raving mad, whoever it is,' answered the pedlar, exposing broken, yellowed teeth as he squinted up at the top of the wall.

Osric watched for a moment, uncertain as to what to do. He was responsible for keeping order in the streets of Exeter, but it was hard to decide whether a man prancing about on the city wall, shaking his cross at the sky, was a hazard to the citizens. The fellow seemed to be chanting and wailing alternately, his face upturned towards the heavens, as he capered about. Suddenly, he turned and faced the crowd below, teetering on the edge of the parapet as if gathering the courage to jump. The crowd fell silent at his dangerous pose, then voices began to shout: 'It's the priest! It's Ralph de Capra – it's the father from All-Hallows!'

Now that he faced them, they could see that de Capra's face had a wild, haunted look, and his head was plastered with wet ashes.

'I'd better get up there to fetch him down,' muttered

the constable, and made for a flight of steps built into the back of the wall, almost against the pine end of the little church.

Before he could reach the bottom stair, there was a pounding of feet behind him and he was pushed aside. Adam of Dol was climbing up ahead of him to the parapet. He was well known to Osric as the priest of St Mary Steps, just along the street. He had heard the tumult of the crowd as he came out of his church and had hurried down the lane to see what was amiss.

Hoisting up his black cassock in both hands, the cleric mounted the steps surprisingly fast for such a burly man. At the top, he turned right and, followed by the constable, slowed down as he approached the wild figure of the All-Hallows priest as he rocked on his bare toes at the very edge of the stone precipice.

'Ralph! Ralph, come to me, good man!'

De Capra stared vacantly at his brother priest, then turned and began running away along the battlement walk towards his own church, which came straight out of the wall, the stone-tiled roof sloping up just below the parapet, a small bell-arch level with the walkway.

Seemingly afraid that Ralph was going to go beyond the church and throw himself off to certain injury and perhaps death, the priest of St Mary Steps put on a burst of speed and threw himself at de Capra. The pair overbalanced and fell off the parapet – but only a couple of feet down on to the church roof. De Capra struggled, yelling and wailing, but the burly Adam held him with ease as Osric stepped down carefully on to the roof. Between them, they hauled Ralph back to the city wall, conscious of the ominous cracking of thin stone tiles under their feet.

By now several other spectators had climbed the steps and were staring open-mouthed at the unexpected entertainment, but Adam of Dol roared at them and waved them away furiously. Then he glared at Osric and told him to clear off too: this was a matter between men of God. The constable retreated a few yards, but felt it his duty to stay within earshot: he crouched at the top of the steps, down which the banished townsfolk were retreating.

'What are you thinking of, you foolish man?' bellowed Adam at his colleague, his tone as abrasive as when he had yelled at the onlookers. 'Why the sackcloth and ashes? The devil is fighting for your soul, Ralph, and you must resist him!'

Osric felt this was hardly the way to pacify a deranged man on the point of committing suicide, but he had no intention of clashing with the pugnacious priest, whose reputation for anger was legendary.

Ralph de Capra sagged into submission, his struggles ceasing. His face was gaunt under the streaks of grey ash that had run down from his hair and his hollow-eyed expression was one of abject misery. 'I have sinned, Adam, sinned most grievously,' the constable heard him say. 'There is no hope for me, either in this world or the next – if there is a next, which I often doubt.'

His fellow priest shook him angrily by the shoulders. 'You must fight back, man! Faith has to be earned. I have said time and again that the great horned devil never sleeps. He waits for such doubts to weaken your armour. And throwing yourself from this wall is no answer – you'd probably break a leg rather than your neck. Preach hell-fire, Ralph! Keep it in the forefront of your mind that failure means eternal agony in the great furnace below. Be like me – never let your flock forget that the wages of sin are not death but unceasing torture until and beyond the end of time. That way you will keep Lucifer at bay.'

With that, Father Adam hauled his brother priest back along the parapet towards the steps, still cursing the powers of darkness. Osric wisely retreated before them, determined to tell the coroner what he had heard.

John had returned reluctantly to the court but without Thomas to guide him it was far more difficult: he had to borrow one of the junior clerks of Assize to help him with his rolls, and put up with smirks and knowing glances from the sheriff. The scowls of the Justices, especially Peter Peverel, boded ill for Thomas's future.

His visit to the cells under the keep had been brief and unhelpful. The obese gaoler, Stigand, had tried to prevent him and Gwyn entering Thomas's cell, until Gwyn pinned him against the wall by his throat and threatened to tear out his tongue by the roots.

Poor Thomas sat in a pathetic heap on the dirty straw inside the almost dark cell. He had been vomiting with fright into the battered bucket that was the only furniture, apart from the slate slab of a bed. All de Wolfe could get out of him was a flat denial of any wrongdoing. He had gone to the New Inn as ordered, taken the bundle of rolls upstairs past the guard on the door, whom he recognised from the gatehouse duty at Rougemont. The door to de Vallibus's room was open – Thomas had known it from a visit with rolls the evening before – and when he had gone in he had found the Justice groaning on the floor, with a bloody wound on his head. Serlo was just conscious but incoherent. In panic, Thomas had rushed to knock on the other doors upstairs, but found the rooms either locked or empty. Then he heard a crash and saw that de Vallibus had crawled out of the room and fallen down the upper flight of stairs to the half-landing. Even more frantic by now, Thomas had pounded down to the ground floor, looking for help, and run straight into the arms of the soldier, who grabbed him: he had just seen the judge crash on to the landing above. The pandemonium that followed led to the little ex-priest being hauled off to the cells in Rougemont without the chance to explain anything.

'You saw no one else upstairs?' demanded de Wolfe, and Thomas's denial was his only other contribution to a sterile investigation.

Now the coroner waited impatiently for the court session to end so that he could try to do something more for his clerk. But as the raucous trumpets signalled the end of the day's cases and the three judges solemnly paraded out, Richard de Revelle sidled up to him, a supercilious sneer on his face. 'John, the justices have decided to be present tonight at the interrogation of that rat-like servant of yours. A confession will be drawn from him and they will bring him before them tomorrow morning, for that superfluous trial you're so keen to have. Then we can have him hanged by afternoon.' With that he hurried after the judges before John could think of a forceful enough protest.

Gwyn had overheard the sheriff's gloating message and his already worried face became even more disconsolate. 'Is there nothing we can do, Crowner? They'll hang the poor sod, just to prove their point.' Though he had endlessly teased Thomas, the amiable Cornishman was protective towards the little man and the prospect of him being executed was too much to contemplate. For a moment de Wolfe stood in the doorway of the court, brooding and chewing his lip. Then he drew himself up and loped off towards the gatehouse, beckoning Gwyn to follow. 'I must talk to his uncle. The Archdeacon is the most honest and sensible man I know, as well as being Thomas's relative. Let's see what he has to say.'

At this slack period in the episcopal day, John de Alençon was usually at home and they found him in his austere room, reading a treatise on Eusebius of

Caesaria. When he heard of his nephew's arrest, he groaned. 'Thomas, Thomas! He's been nothing but trouble to his family since he was born! Yet none of it was his doing, I'm sure.'

De Wolfe was blunt in his summary of the situation. 'They're keen to hang him, no doubt of that. These rumours have been going around for days, started by de Revelle and that malicious colleague of yours, Thomas de Boterellis.'

'What can we do about saving him?' asked the Archdeacon, his lean face etched with concern.

'We have to get him out of Rougemont. Tonight they'll torture him to get a confession – and knowing Thomas's lack of courage, he'll give it in the first half-minute. Then they'll hang him, unless we can plead Benefit of Clergy.'

John de Alençon's face fell. 'But he's no longer a priest! When he was unfrocked, he lost the privilege of being tried by a consistory court.'

'I thought that proving he could read and write was sufficient,' objected de Wolfe.

The Archdeacon hesitated, deep doubt showing on his face. 'I agree that this is a popular notion, as virtually everyone who is literate is in Holy Orders. But it's not a definition that can be relied on, especially when you have the King's Justices, a sheriff and a Precentor eager to deny it.'

'It's his only hope, short of Gwyn and I storming the castle' growled John. 'If the Bishop threw his weight behind the idea, then surely it would succeed?'

The Archdeacon looked dubious. 'You know quite well that he has no love for you, especially since you crushed de Revelle.'

However, after John had argued and pleaded with him for several minutes, de Alençon agreed to go to his bishop and seek to have Thomas de Peyne transferred to the custody of the cathedral proctors, instead of being incarcerated in Rougemont.

'It's desperately urgent,' pressed the coroner. 'Within a couple of hours, he may have his limbs broken or burned unless we can prevent it.'

With this awful prospect drilling into his mind, the Archdeacon rose and threw his long black cloak around his shoulders, though the early-evening air was mild. 'I'll go straight away – thank God the bishop's still in the city. But don't have too high hopes of this, John – you may still have to storm Stigand's prison.'

Uneasily, de Wolfe and his henchman went to the Bush for food and ale and to wait for news from Henry Marshal. Thankfully, de Wolfe knew that Matilda was on some charitable visit with her friends to one of the city's almshouses, so he felt no obligation to return for the evening meal. In Idle Lane, the prospect of what might soon befall the little clerk extinguished any humour or passion, and although they ate heartily the coroner and Gwyn were subdued and anxious. To break the glum silences, Nesta retailed some of the day's gossip. 'We had a strange tale brought by Alfred Fuller from Frog Lane. It seems that the priest of All-Hallows went crazy this afternoon.'

'Which All-Hallows?' demanded John, his interest aroused.

There were two All-Hallows churches, one in Goldsmith Street, the other near the West Gate, about which he had a special concern.

'Oh, on-the-Wall – for it seems he tried to jump from it.'

'You mean Ralph de Capra?'

'That's the one – apparently he was in sackcloth and ashes and raving about his great sin.'

Nesta stopped abruptly, her hand to her mouth.

'He was one of those you were investigating, wasn't he?'

De Wolfe nodded grimly. 'I saw him this very morning. Now he's gone mad, you say.' He stood up, feeling suddenly old and weary. 'Is that all you know about it?' John would have known more, but Osric the constable had not yet encountered him to give him his eye-witness version.

Nesta beckoned urgently across the tavern. 'It was Edwin who had the tale – you know he's the nosiest man in the city. Edwin!' she cried.

The old potman came limping across the floor, his dead eye horribly white in his lined face. At his mistress's prompting, he told what he knew of the incident in Bretayne. 'The priest from St Mary Steps got him down, they say. Then took him away back to his lodging. Adam of Dol lives behind his church, not down in Priest Street like most of them.'

'What was it all about?' asked Nesta, but Edwin shrugged.

De Wolfe got up and paced restlessly before the empty hearth. 'I must talk to those two priests again – perhaps I stirred up something when I questioned de Capra this morning.'

'But he couldn't have been the one who attacked de Vallibus, could he?' objected Gwyn. 'Not if all this fuss happened down in Bretayne at almost the same time.'

'We don't know how much time there was between. Maybe he had visited Serlo and the experience turned him off his head.' He put an arm around Nesta's shoulders and gave her a quick hug. 'But I can't risk going down there now, with poor Thomas facing *peine forte et dure* at any moment. I hope by the Holy Virgin that the Archdeacon has had some influence with the Bishop.'

With Nesta looking after them anxiously, the coroner

and his officer hurried out into Idle Lane and made for the castle.

The Moors almshouses were just outside the city, near the half-completed new bridge over the Exe. The short row of dwellings for the poor, built some years earlier by the benefaction of a wealthy fulling-mill owner, was supported by donations from city merchants and some of the churches. This evening, a dozen good ladies of St Olave's, accompanied by their priest Julian Fulk, were making their monthly pilgrimage with gifts of food, clothing and money. Prominent among them was Matilda de Wolfe, playing Lady Bountiful with a large pie made by Mary, some cast-off clothing and a purse of coins extracted from her husband.

The hard-faced harridan who was the warden had lined up the inmates for inspection and the ladies of St Olave's paraded past the aged crones, the cripples and the despised unmarried mothers, doling out their gifts. Later, they sat in the narrow hall of the building to share the food they had brought, but they occupied separate trestles and did their best not to mingle with the destitute.

Julian Fulk tried to be his usual unctuous self, though it was difficult as he had a lot on his mind. Dressed in a new black tunic, flapping round his ankles, his head was covered in a tight coif, on top of which was a floppy beret of black velvet. Matilda made sure that she sat next to him at the table, with her back to the toothless hags and the anaemic drabs who dragged out their wretched existence in this place.

'You were not at the Bishop's banquet last night?' she asked sweetly, knowing that no parish priest would have had even the smell of an invitation, but it gave her an opportunity to describe her husband's eminence and the exact position on the tables that they had occupied.

Of course Fulk knew who her husband was and, in fact, his preoccupation tonight was due to the coroner. The repeated visits that de Wolfe had made to him over the murders had done nothing to help his reputation, at a time when he was bursting every sinew to improve his standing in the Church. Being on the suspect list for multiple murders did nothing for his dreams of advancement.

As Matilda's prattle washed over him, Fulk contemplated his limited options – he must try to see the Bishop again, while he was still in Exeter, and he must also make the arduous journey to Sussex, to see the Abbot of Battle. One way or the other, he must get away from these maddeningly dull people who were holding back his career in the Holy Ministry. Could no one recognise his theological prowess, his mastery of the liturgy, his God-given understanding of the scriptures? Was he condemned to waste his talents in a tiny chapel in a mediocre city at the far end of England, when he had the makings of a bishop – or even an archbishop? He must do something soon, for desperate situations require desperate solutions

That evening, Thomas de Peyne, chains on his wrists and ankles, was half led, half dragged through the gate in the iron grille that divided the undercroft of the castle keep. The grotesque gaoler, Stigand, pulled him along by the manacles, with a soldier walking rather shamefacedly behind – this wretched prisoner was hardly likely to put up a fight.

Stigand hauled the clerk across the damp earth of the forbidding basement towards the group of men waiting silently for him. Three of the Justices were there, as well as the sheriff, the constable, the coroner and a priest. The latter was the castle chaplain, Brother Rufus, his usual affability muted this evening. De Wolfe had had to banish Gwyn from Rougemont, afraid that his outrage at the arrest of his little friend might provoke him into some rash act, such as a hopeless rescue attempt. Now he glanced repeatedly towards the steps coming down from the inner ward, desperately hoping for some sign that de Alençon's plea to Bishop Marshal had been successful.

The gaoler dragged the clerk before the row of brooding men and stood aside, his bloated face grinning with anticipation as he poked at a brazier in which branding irons glowed.

Richard de Revelle opened the proceedings. 'A confession would make it easier for all of us, fellow. We are busy men, as you know from your own work, when you are not murdering honest folk.'

De Peyne stood in the mud, his narrow shoulders drooping, the left more than the right, which accentuated the hump on his back. Though he had been incarcerated for only a few hours, his shabby black tunic was already badly stained, with pieces of filthy straw clinging to it. His lank hair hung over his high forehead and his mournful eyes stared fearfully from behind it. He mumbled something in reply to the sheriff's words.

'What was that? Speak up, damn you!' snapped Sir Peter Peverel, muffled in a brown cloak against the cold of the dank undercroft, where the outside air never seemed to penetrate.

'I said I have done nothing wrong, sir, so what can I confess?'

The sheriff stamped his foot in annoyance. 'Stop wasting our time, I say. You were caught running away from the scene of your cowardly attack on Serlo de Vallibus.'

Thomas mumbled, 'I was going to get help,' but Walter de Ralegh interrupted, 'De Peyne, you have been

under suspicion for some time. This merely confirms
your guilt.'

'The only suspicion he was under came from malicious gossip!' cut in de Wolfe angrily. 'There has not
been a shred of proof against this man – only mischievous tittle-tattle.'

Peverel seemed determined to blacken Thomas's
chances. 'Not gossip, Coroner. As a former priest – and
one with a grudge against the world, so I understand – he
can read, write and has a good knowledge of the Vulgate.
That narrows down the field a hundredfold in this city.'

'And he cannot account for his movements on any
of the occasions when these outrages occurred,' brayed
the sheriff triumphantly.

'Can any of us account for our movements at all those
times?' demanded the coroner. 'Though I know where
you were on one occasion, Richard.' This was an oblique
threat to the sheriff, but he knew it was insufficient to
help Thomas. Desperately, he looked again towards the
bright square of the entrance, hoping against hope that
relief would arrive. De Ralegh began to lose patience
and started to shout at the prisoner. 'If your lips are
sealed by malice, there are ways to open them! As a
servant of the Crowner, you must know better than most
how confessions can be obtained. See sense, man, and
speak now!'

Thomas's response was to fall to his knees in a rattle
of chains and burst into tears. 'I am innocent!' he
screamed. 'Master, save me!'

This was no prayer, but a direct plea to John de
Wolfe, who stood impotent, swinging between intense
anger and deep sorrow. 'This is intolerable!' he shouted.
'There is no evidence whatsoever to link this man
with the crimes. Let a jury decide tomorrow! What
use is there in torturing a false confession from this
poor soul?'

At this, de Revelle rounded on his brother-in-law. 'You should not be here, John. As this creature's master, you can have no balanced view of how things really are. You should leave well alone!'

Archdeacon de Bosco had been silent until now, but looked uneasy at the prospect of a fellow priest, albeit one dishonourably discharged from the Church, being subjected to *peine forte et dure* like a common felon. The procedure to extract confessions varied, but should have been performed by placing increasing weights of iron on the chest of the victim, lying flat on his back, until he either spoke or expired. However, the practice had been widened to include many forms of torture, some sadistically ingenious.

'Perhaps it should be left to the court tomorrow, brothers,' said the Archdeacon tentatively.

'You are biased because the man was once in Holy Orders,' retorted Peverel nastily. 'But he's not now, so that can no longer be an issue.'

De Ralegh walked over to the clerk and hoisted him to his feet by grabbing a handful of his hair. 'Tell us why you did it, wretch!' he bellowed. 'All those deaths, were you trying to play God, eh? Is not the King's justice enough to punish evildoers that you have to take the law into your own hands?'

Outraged at seeing the puny clerk mishandled, de Wolfe stepped forward and seemed ready to strike de Ralegh, a move which would have had disastrous consequences, given that he was a Justice of the King. Almost casually, the bulky figure of Brother Rufus stepped sideways in front of him and pressed him back, giving enough time for de Wolfe's passion to subside.

Then, providentially, a cry came from the entrance arch, which distracted them from the mounting tension. 'Stop! I have orders from the Bishop.'

It was John de Alençon, looking more haggard even

than usual as he stumbled across the uneven floor towards them.

'Is he granting Benefit of Clergy?' De Wolfe asked eagerly.

'Not as such, no,' panted the Archdeacon. 'Bishop Marshal declines to refer the matter to the Consistory Court, as he rightly points out that my nephew is no longer an ordained priest. But he takes great exception to a former man of the cloth being put to the torture for a confession and forbids you to proceed.'

The sheriff looked as if he was going to object, then thought of his relationship with the Bishop and decided not to risk damaging it for the sake of a fleeting victory over the coroner. He kept silent, but Walter de Ralegh and Peter Peverel felt no such inhibitions. They protested strongly that even the head of the Church in this diocese had no power over a secular court, especially the will of the King's Justices. However, Archdeacon de Bosco came down firmly on the side of the Church, as this confirmed his own recent misgivings.

They argued for a few minutes, while the dishevelled Thomas, red-eyed and forlorn, looked from face to face seeking any crumb of hope.

Richard de Revelle settled the matter. 'Our Lord Bishop in his wisdom has made no attempt to take the judgement into the hands of the Church so, confession or not, we can proceed with the trial tomorrow morning – and I suspect there is little doubt of the outcome, so any bickering tonight is hardly worth the effort.'

Tired, irritated and in need of their evening meal, the others agreed grudgingly and Thomas was dragged back to his foetid cell by a disappointed Stigand. The others dispersed, most of them confident that the murderous clerk would be swinging at the end of a rope within a day or two.

* * *

De Wolfe spent a miserable night worrying about Thomas's fate. Though he was grateful for John de Alençon's intercession with the Bishop as far as the forced confession was concerned, he had little hope that the Eyre of Assize would acquit him in the morning. As he had told a depressed Gwyn and a tearful Nesta, when they had sat discussing the crisis in the Bush that evening, it was the attack on de Vallibus, one of their own number, that was likely to seal the clerk's fate.

Nesta clutched de Wolfe's arm and rested her head against his shoulder for comfort. 'They mustn't hang the poor fellow, he wouldn't hurt a fly, let alone kill a string of people,' she sobbed. 'He's had nothing but trouble and misery all his life, being afflicted in his back and his leg and his eye, then being falsely accused of rape and thrown out of his beloved Church.'

'Maybe he'll be glad to leave this earth,' said de Wolfe, mournfully. 'He tried to go the other month, when he jumped from the cathedral roof.'

'Is there nothing more we can do for him?' demanded Gwyn, his great red moustache drooping as low as his own spirits.

'There is so little time,' answered John. 'If the sentence goes against him tomorrow, as surely it must, they'll demand a hanging next day – and I'll wager all the Justices will turn out to watch it.'

'Can you not petition the King or the Justiciar or someone?' wailed Nesta.

'The Lionheart is in France, God knows where Hubert Walter is, but it would take a week or more to reach him and another to get back here. It's hopeless, even if they would listen to a plea for clemency.'

'The only miracle that would save him would be another Gospel killing before he's hanged,' said Nesta sadly. 'And though we've had a string of attacks these past few days, the swine who's doing them will now no doubt lie low, just to avoid obliging us.'

When he came home to Martin's Lane, de Wolfe went straight to bed, despondent about the morrow. Though Matilda was still awake, he could not bring himself to tell her what had happened, as she was likely to crow over the disaster that had befallen Thomas. After a restless night, when sleep came only fitfully between bouts of anxious worry, de Wolfe reluctantly made his way up to the castle. Before the court began its session, he made a last attempt to influence Richard de Revelle, even threatening to revoke his promise to keep quiet about his involvement in the brothel fire, but the sheriff called his bluff: 'You gave me your word, John, that you would stay silent. As a knight, you know you will disgrace yourself if you go back on that – and it would be futile, as you undoubtedly know.'

Then John tried to talk the judges into a more reasonable attitude. Indeed, Gervase de Bosco was not pressing for a conviction and Serlo de Vallibus, even though he was the injured party, honestly admitted that he had no recollection of Thomas being his assailant. But the other two were adamant and, with a heavy heart, de Wolfe sat in a corner of the dais when the case was called halfway through the morning. Once again, he had ordered Gwyn to stay out of the castle and even managed to get Sergeant Gabriel to stay with him at an ale-house, to make sure that he did nothing foolish.

Twelve jurors representing the city of Exeter were already empanelled for other cases and were dragooned into hearing this interposed indictment.

The proceedings were short and predictable.

Thomas de Peyne was led into the Shire Hall in chains, amid hisses, shouts of abuse and a few vegetables hurled from the crowd. Bedraggled and pathetic, he stood with his head bowed before Walter de Ralegh and the other judges. A clerk – one he knew well – read out the charges of murder. The sheriff made an abrasive speech, detailing each foul homicide and laid them all at Thomas's door, as well as the arson in Waterbeer Lane and the assault on Serlo de Vallibus.

Both Peverel and de Ralegh weighed in with their own vituperative opinions about a literate ex-priest, haranguing the bemused jurors about Thomas's proficiency in writing and expert knowledge of the scriptures. They ended with an embellished account of the attack on de Vallibus that sounded as if they themselves had witnessed the whole incident.

At the end of this, there was no opportunity for any defence to be offered, apart from a harsh invitation for the accused to speak up – which Thomas ignored, continuing to stare at the earthen floor. De Wolfe had pleaded with the Justices to be allowed to speak in his clerk's defence, but they had vetoed this on the grounds that he had no right to do so and, furthermore, was obviously highly prejudiced – an argument which he cynically thought was sheer hypocrisy, coming from a pair who had decided on guilt well before the case came before them.

The jury were then virtually commanded to return a verdict of guilty, which they did without hesitation. De Ralegh, as the senior justice, then snarled a sentence of death and commanded that this be carried out next day. Without looking up, Thomas meekly followed two men-at-arms back to the prison in the undercroft and the whole sad episode was over.

For the rest of the day, de Wolfe went about his duties as if he was in a nightmare. He would liked to have saddled up Odin and gone alone into the countryside, to be away from everyone and suffer his resentment and anger in solitude. But he was required in the court as if nothing had happened, for without his presentment of the cases in which he was involved none could be dealt with. The clerk who tried to carry out Thomas's functions with the rolls was a shadow of the little man's efficiency and his clumsy efforts only reminded de Wolfe the more of what he had lost.

By the time of the midday meal, Matilda had heard of the conviction and John expected her to rub his nose in it, but to his surprise she was muted in her comments and he soon sensed that she realised this was a topic so sensitive that she might get the worst of it if she crossed him. Instead, almost as if she was trying to divert his troubled mind from such a painful subject, she launched into some gossip about her favourite topic: the clergy of Exeter.

'Our priest at St Olave's is to leave! He saw the Bishop last evening, so it is said, and tomorrow he is to journey to Sussex to see his Abbot.'

John managed to drag his attention to her words, as Fulk was one of those who had been fingered by the cathedral as a potential malcontent. Was the fact that he was suddenly leaving in any way significant, he wondered?

'What brought that on?' he asked his wife.

'I can't imagine. At the alms-giving yesterday he said nothing about it. I thought he might have mentioned something to me, as one of the staunchest members of his congregation.' She sniffed in disapproval of the priest's attitude and John sensed that her infatuation had begun to evaporate.

'When I talked to him the other day, he seemed discontented to be at a small church like St Olave's,' de Wolfe mused. 'He seemed to think he was destined for greater things.'

For once, Matilda agreed with him. 'He's a clever and able man, wasted in a small chapel like that –

especially as he could get no advancement in the diocese.'

The coroner was not interested in Julian Fulk's ambitions, but Matilda's next remark was of more interest. 'That was a strange business with the priests down at All-Hallows and St Mary Steps. They say that Ralph de Capra has gone completely mad now and is locked in the infirmary of St Nicholas.'

De Wolfe looked up from his bread and cheese. 'I thought that hell-fire merchant, Adam of Dol had taken him under his wing?'

'He had, but it seems that de Capra ran away and tried to drown himself in the river. They fished him out and took him to the monks at St Nicholas for his own safety.'

Though it was difficult for John to shake off the depressed torpor that enveloped him, he decided that he had better talk to those three priests again. He was convinced that the true killer was still somewhere in the city, so the search must go on. When he found the culprit, at least he could throw it in the faces of the sheriff and the Justices – though much good that would do his poor clerk.

In the afternoon, he returned to the Shire Hall and tried to concentrate on the cases, to keep himself from dwelling on Thomas's fate.

Near the end of the session Gwyn turned up, surprising de Wolfe by being sober. The Cornishman looked a decade older than he had when de Wolfe had last seen him. Gabriel was behind him and gave a covert shrug towards the coroner, as if to convey that he could do nothing with Gwyn in his present depressed mood. They remained behind when the court emptied, sitting in forlorn silence among the bare tables and benches.

'It is useless appealing again to those men,' growled

de Wolfe. 'They say that once a jury has pronounced a verdict, they are powerless to alter it.'

'Bloody hypocrites – that jury would have said whatever their lordships decreed,' snarled Gwyn.

De Wolfe uncoiled himself wearily from his stool and stepped down on to the floor of the court. 'I'm going across to see Thomas now. Are you coming?'

His officer shook his head. 'I'll go later – when I've gathered the courage to face him.'

When John descended the few steps into the undercroft, Stigand made no attempt to obstruct him and sullenly waddled across to open the gate into the cells with a clinking bunch of keys. Inside was a short passage with a series of cells on either side and the gaoler opened the first door to admit the coroner.

Almost fearfully, de Wolfe squelched through the blackened, wet straw to stand over his clerk, who sat motionless on the edge of the slate slab. A lion in battle, willing to face any adversary with a sword or lance, de Wolfe cringed in any situation such as this: emotion and compassion confused him. Yet when Thomas looked up, it was almost as if the little ex-priest was the one who was ready to give comfort to him, rather than the reverse. He wore a beatific smile and seemed quite at ease. 'Don't fret, master, this is what was ordained by our Creator. At least I can't make a mess of being hanged tomorrow – my cloak is hardly likely to get hooked on the gallows-tree as it did on the cathedral wall.'

His calmness and his attempts at humour almost broke John and only by coughing and choking could he keep his emotions in check.

They spoke together for some time, though Thomas did most of the talking. He told his master of his childhood and his long, lonely schooling in Winchester, of the death of his mother from the same phthisis that had crippled his own back and hip, and of the good days when he had taught at his old school, until his downfall over the girl, who had trapped him into making an innocent advance then alleged that he had ravished her. He told de Wolfe that there was nothing he wanted as his uncle the Archdeacon had already brought him his precious Vulgate. He clasped it in his hands as he spoke. Eventually, there was nothing left to say and, with a promise to see him again on the fateful morrow, John left with a heavy heart, telling Thomas that Gwyn had promised to visit him later that evening.

As he trudged home, he wondered if his officer had some notion of a last-minute rescue. Part of him hoped Gwyn would make some attempt, but common sense told him it would be a futile, disastrous act. The gaol was inside a locked compound, itself in the undercroft, guarded by the gaoler and often a man-at-arms too. The inner ward was impregnable, with a guardroom and sentries always on duty at the gatehouse. The whole castle – indeed, the whole city – knew of Thomas's conviction, and no trickery or brute force on Gwyn's part could get them both out of Rougemont then through the city gates. If they did, both would immediately be outlawed, legitimate prey to anyone who wished to kill them and claim a bounty for their heads. And Gwyn had a wife and sons to support, so even the affection he had for the little clerk was surely not worth that sacrifice.

It was early evening and he went home for a subdued meal with Matilda, who again was unusually docile, stealing puzzled glances at him from under her heavy brows as she sensed his distress. Although they spent most of their life together in mutual antagonism, when serious matters oppressed them, they were somehow drawn together, albeit temporarily. When John had broken his leg in combat some months previously, Matilda had nursed him with a fierce solicitude, and when she had suffered acute distress over her brother's misdeeds, he had pledged and delivered his absolute support.

After the meal he paced the hall restlessly, then announced that he was going to talk to Adam of Dol and possibly the unhinged Ralph de Capra, if he could get into the sickroom of St Nicholas Priory. He also wanted to talk yet again to Julian Fulk about his sudden desire to leave Exeter, but knowing of Matilda's interest in that particular priest, he avoided mentioning his intention.

The sun was going down as he reached St Mary Steps. The church was deserted once again, so he went round to the living quarters. The incumbent lived in a small house tacked on to the back wall of the church, its door opening on to the terraced cobbles of the hill. It was little more than a single room, with a box-like bed forming one wall. A lean-to shed at the other side provided space for cooking, which was done by an old man who also cleaned the church and rang the bell for devotions.

De Wolfe rapped on the upper half of the split door, which opened to reveal the truculent features of Father Adam. 'What do you want, Crowner?'

'To speak to you about de Capra.'

'What business is it of yours? You've caused enough trouble as it is.'

De Wolfe took no umbrage at his manner, accepting that this strange man was incapable of civility. 'As coroner, I have a duty to inquire into unlawful events. And it seems Ralph de Capra has twice attempted to kill himself, which is a *felo de se.*'

'So what are you going to do about it – arrest him? Your own clerk tried to kill himself too, but he wasn't thrown into prison – though he's ended up there just the same,' he added sarcastically. It seemed that he had no intention of letting de Wolfe inside his dwelling, so the coroner had to continue his questioning from the street.

'What drove de Capra to this desperate state?'

Adam leaned on the door and thrust his florid face almost against John's nose. 'None of your concern, Crowner. What passes between two priests by way of confession is not for the ears of you or anyone else on earth. Only God the Father knows what was said.'

'Was it truly a confession – or just the outpouring of a troubled mind? For I have heard that he had suffered a crisis of faith.'

The priest slammed his big hands on to the door top in temper. 'Ha! Almost every so-called priest in this pestilent land is suffering from a crisis of faith! A lack of faith in what religion should mean. The failure to tell sinners what lies in store if they fail to repent. These milk-sops are not proper priests, but weak-kneed time-servers, all of them!'

John groaned to himself. He had launched this madman on his favourite obsession and was about to get another hell-fire tirade. 'Then I'll go to see de Capra up at St Nicholas's,' he said hastily, and backed away to leave a puce-faced Adam waving his arms and ranting about the unrepentant and the fires of damnation.

De Wolfe strode up the uneven steps of the hill and passed both the Saracen and the end of Idle Lane, but resisted the temptation to call in for a pot of ale and the solace of Nesta's company, though he intended to come back later to the Bush. He crossed Fore Street and wended his way through the mean alleys to St Nicholas Priory, tucked away at the top of Bretayne. The prior, a sour-faced man whose cheeks were pitted with old cow-pox scars, was in the small garden, chastising a young monk for some error in the way he was weeding the vegetable plot.

When de Wolfe asked to see Ralph de Capra, the prior shook his head. 'He's not fit to be spoken to yet.

The infirmarian has given him a draught to quieten him, though it seems to have had little effect.'

'I have to talk to him now,' insisted de Wolfe. 'It is a matter of the utmost urgency.' Though the chances were slim, if the deranged priest let slip anything that identified him as the killer, Thomas would be cleared. John could not pass up even the most remote possibility of saving his clerk's neck from the rope tomorrow.

The scowling prior pulled up the cowl of his black Benedictine robe against a sudden gust of cool night air. 'If you must, then be it on your head if he goes berserk again,' he grumbled. He beckoned to a novice who was washing a pan outside the kitchen of the small priory and told him to take the coroner to the sickroom. Following him, John passed the storeroom where more than once, he had attended dead bodies from this part of town, though mercifully, it was empty tonight.

The young man led him into a passage with two cells opening off it, in one of which was locked the priest from All-Hallows. Nervously, he pulled a wooden pin from the hasp and stood aside for the coroner to enter. The moment John slipped inside, he heard the pin being hastily shoved back.

In the tiny room, with only a shuttered slit to admit a little light, he made out a skinny figure crouched on a pallet in a corner. He was stark naked and his tunic lay on the floor, torn into ragged strips. John wondered if he had been trying to make a noose, but there was nothing in the bare cell from which he could hang himself.

De Capra was shivering like a man with the ague, but not from cold. He gave no sign that he had noticed the coroner's arrival, and sat staring at the floor.

'Ralph, I am John de Wolfe, the crowner. Do you remember me?'

There was no response, so he pulled over a milking stool, the only furniture in the cell, and sat directly facing the other man. 'Ralph, you must answer my questions.'

Again there was no reaction and John reached out to take the priest's chin in his hand. He moved the man's head so that he could stare straight into the vacant eyes. 'What has happened to afflict you like this? What have you done?'

Suddenly, the other man was galvanised out of his catatonia. Shocked by the change, John fell backwards off his stool as de Capra leapt up and threw himself against the corner of the cell, standing naked on the straw mattress with his arms outspread against adjacent walls, like a living crucifix. 'I have sinned, I have sinned!' he wailed, his eyes rolling up to the wattled ceiling.

'How have you sinned? What have you done? Have you killed, Ralph?' The coroner was becoming desperate in his quest for a confession.

'Killed? I have sent a legion of souls into purgatory!'

De Wolfe's spirit leapt for a moment, in glorious hope that he had at last found his man.

'What do you mean? Were they murdered in the city?'

De Capra thumped his lean body back and forth into the angle of the wall, his nails scrabbling at the plaster. 'I stopped believing! Satan stole my mind! With no faith I shrove many, I betrayed them! I baptised babes with no belief in what I was doing! I shrove the dying without the true grace of God! They are lost! I betrayed them!' He slid down the wall on to the pallet and sat in a crumpled heap, weeping disconsolately.

With a sinking heart, John made one last attempt. 'But have you *killed*, Ralph? The old Jew, the priest at All-Hallows, the sodomite, the whore?'

There was no reply and the sobbing continued.

The door opened and the fearful face of the novice appeared, followed by that of the prior. 'This cannot be!' he hissed. 'You must leave, Crowner. This man is sick in his mind.'

Acknowledging defeat, de Wolfe nodded and, with a last compassionate look at the wreck of a man on the mattress, he followed the monks out of the room. As they left the passageway, Ralph de Capra began to scream, the high-pitched, repetitive wail of a soul in torment. It was the signal that de Wolfe's last chance of saving Thomas had failed.

CHAPTER SIXTEEN

In which Crowner John discovers the truth

The coroner left the priory of St Nicholas at dusk, going from there to Priest Street to find Julian Fulk. Matilda's news that the priest of St Olave's was leaving suddenly was curious, but John had little expectation that it was in any way connected to the Gospel killings, unless Fulk was running away in expectation of being exposed.

Most of the dwellings in Priest Street were lodging for clerics and he had to ask directions to the right house. The priest was at home, living in two comfortably furnished rooms, which suggested that he had some means of his own as well as his pittance from parish tithes.

Fulk was resting after his meal before preparing for the midnight Matins, which he insisted on holding even though sometimes he had no congregation at that hour. Confident that one day he would be officiating in some great cathedral, he drove himself to observe most of the canonical hours, even in a tiny church like St Olave's. He was surprised to see the coroner, but invited him in civilly and gave him a cup of good wine. He seemed more subdued than usual and his normal false heartiness had evaporated. As de Wolfe sat drinking his Anjou wine, he felt that whatever oddities might be in the priest's nature, he was unlikely to be a serial killer. But, for Thomas's sake, he had to pursue every chance to the bitter end.

'They say you are leaving Exeter rather suddenly?'

The plump priest gestured impatiently. 'This city is like a village. Every time you fart, the news is around the taverns within five minutes.'

De Wolfe agreed with that, but it was no answer to his question. 'Is there an urgent reason for us losing you? There is nothing wrong, I trust, between you and the Church authorities?'

The priest began to spit out a litany of complaints against the religious establishment in England – their indifference to his ability, their deliberate campaign to keep him in some ecclesiastical backwater and similar expressions of outrage that soon convinced John that he was quite paranoid about the Church's attitude towards him. But nothing in his tirade gave the coroner hope that Julian Fulk was anything but a vain, self-opinionated wind-bag.

Tiring of the repetitive monologue about the iniquities of bishops, abbots and priors, John finished his wine and took his leave, more depressed than ever that nothing now could save Thomas.

His feet took him the short distance to Idle Lane and he flopped down on his usual bench in the Bush, feeling ten years older than he had the previous day. Even the usually loquacious potman was subdued when he brought over a quart of ale, and when Nesta came in, she sat quietly by his side, with little to say once he had told her of the fruitless efforts he had been making.

He described his visit to Thomas and the clerk's apparent calm. 'I'll see him again in the morning – and, along with John de Alençon, go with him to the gallows at noon,' he said sombrely.

He saw that tears were running silently down Nesta's cheeks at his mention of the hanging-tree beyond Magdalen Street, for it brought home with awful finality the fact that this tragedy was really going to take place. 'I'm a coward, John, for I can't bring myself to visit him,' she whispered. 'I wouldn't know what to say and all I'd do is weep and make things worse for him. Neither can I come out beyond the walls with you tomorrow, for I couldn't bear to see him die. But Gwyn will be with you – he called in here earlier looking for you.'

'What did he want?'

'Only to know if you had any good news, poor chap. He said he would call to see Thomas on his way home to St Sidwell's, before the gates closed.'

He sat with Nesta a little while longer, then decided to go home. The lack of anything useful or comforting to say to each other had depressed them even further. It was now quite dark outside, but his feet knew every pothole in the twisting lanes without him being conscious of guiding them. However, he was certainly conscious of his full bladder as he crossed the rough wasteground at the side of the tavern. After two quarts of ale, he needed to relieve himself against the trunk of a gnarled elder tree that was dimly visible at the edge of Smythen Street.

As he stooped to hoist up the hem of his long tunic, a figure materialised out of the gloom behind him and struck him a violent blow on the back of the head, pitching him forward to lie stunned at the foot of the tree.

John de Wolfe was found less than ten minutes later by three men coming up from the Saracen ale-house. One, who was quite drunk, tripped over his legs and, cursing, stumbled against the elder tree. Though it was so dark, they heard a body on the ground groan, though the sounds were strangely muffled. The other two, who were less inebriated, bent over him, just able to make out the shape of a man. The groans became louder, now being mixed with slurred words, but were still indistinct.

'There's a bloody bag over his head!' exclaimed one man, feeling around with his hands. 'Let's get some light, quickly.'

The other, a porter from Milk Street, looked up Smythen Street for any glimmer of a candle behind a shutter. The street was mainly occupied by forges and blacksmiths, hence the name, though a couple of houses had lately become schools. Seeing a faint flicker across the road, the porter ran across and hammered on the door, shouting, 'Stop thief!' at the top of his voice, then ran next door and repeated the cry.

Meanwhile, the rapidly sobering drunk and his friend squatted alongside the victim, who was fast recovering his senses. His stifled groans became more strident and he dazedly lifted his hands to the covering over his head, which the third man, a weaver from Curre Street, was already trying to remove.

'There's a purse-string around his neck!' he complained, but then managed to undo the knot and pull off the leather bag. Groggily, John struggled to sit up and by this time, several people had run across from nearby dwellings. By the light of a horn lantern they propped him against the tree, at which he started to curse fluently and hold the back of his head gingerly with one hand.

As soon as the faint lights fell on his face, the rescuers recognised him. 'Holy Mary, it's the crowner!' yelled the porter. Half a dozen neighbours were now clustered around, some risen from bed and wearing only their under-shirts. A buzz of excitement went round when they realised that it was John de Wolfe, known to every person in the city.

'You're bleeding, Crowner,' said the man with the lantern. 'The back of your head has taken a nasty knock.'

De Wolfe looked blearily at his bloodstained fingers, then tried to get to his feet. He failed miserably, and fell back against the tree.

'Stay quiet, sir, you need someone to attend to that cut. We must get you to St Nicholas's, that's the nearest place.'

Though his head was throbbing like a drum, de Wolfe's senses were rapidly returning. 'Did you see anyone running away? he demanded thickly.

'Not a chance,' said the weaver. 'It's as black as the inside of a cow's stomach tonight, Crowner.'

'What was that over my face?' he demanded, his memory returning piecemeal.

The weaver held up a large leather bag with a plaited string threaded around the neck to close it. Even in the poor light, de Wolfe saw that it was similar to the one that had been over the moneylender's head, though such bags were commonplace.

'Lucky you didn't suffocate with that cutting off your air,' said some morbid Jonah amongst the cluster of onlookers.

The weaver shook his head. 'The seam around the bottom has ripped. There's a hole in it, thank God.'

'The footpad must have tugged it down too hard over your head, Crowner, and torn the stitching,' added the porter. He thrust a hand into the bag and poked three fingers through a gap in the bottom. 'There's something in here, Crowner.' He pulled out a crumpled scrap of parchment and held it close under the flickering light of the lantern. 'There's some writing on it. Can anybody here read?'

No one could, but de Wolfe stretched out a shaking hand to grab the fragment, his fury over having been assaulted fading as his fuddled senses realised what this meant. A warm feeling of relief flooded through him as it dawned on him that Thomas must now surely be saved. He slumped back and a contented smile relaxed his face in the gloom. If the Gospel killer was still active, then his clerk, locked in Stigand's foul gaol, must be innocent! As the townsfolk fussed over him, he sent up a short and rather curt prayer of thanks to the God whom he was not convinced existed. Though he had killed many men himself and seen thousands more die on a score of battlefields, he surprised even himself at the depth of feeling he had experienced over the hanging of a miserable little scribe. He knew that Gwyn felt the same and wanted to tell his officer the good news – but that was impossible until the morning: Gwyn was at home in St Sidwell's, outside the locked city gates. But at least he could tell Nesta, who otherwise would probably cry half the night.

'Help me back to the Bush!' he commanded, trying to struggle to his feet.

'You're in no fit state yet, Crowner,' protested the weaver. 'We'll take you to St Nicholas's to have your head seen to first.' A forge-master from a nearby work-shop dragged across a loose hurdle from around his yard and, though he protested, they laid de Wolfe gently on it and four of them trotted the few hundred yards to the little priory, with a posse of concerned neighbours running behind. The coroner was a respected and popular man in Exeter and his fellow citizens were determined to do all they could for him in this emergency.

As they went, he bellowed orders from his stretcher, his strength returning rapidly. 'Send for Osric the constable, and all of you be sure to tell him exactly what happened, especially about the bag and that parchment.' He wanted to make sure that independent witnesses confirmed the circumstances, so that the damned sheriff could not claim that he himself had fabricated them.

'And someone go to the castle and call out whoever they can find – the sheriff, Ralph Morin or Sergeant

Gabriel. We should have the streets searched, though God knows who we are looking for!'

He ended his stream of orders with a final demand that someone should go back to the Bush and tell the landlady what had happened.

The one person he failed to remember was his own wife, Matilda.

If the pockmarked prior of St Nicholas's was annoyed to see John de Wolfe back again so soon, he concealed it well. He immediately sent the infirmarian to deal with the coroner's head wound and, with the porter and the weaver standing solicitously by, the old monk cleaned and anointed the cut on the back of his scalp. 'Nothing terrible, Crowner, but keep this length of linen bound around your head for a day or two to keep out the dirt,' he instructed, as he wound cloth around de Wolfe's scalp like a Moorish turban.

De Wolfe thanked him, then held up his fist, in which he still clutched the fragment of parchment found in the leather bag. 'Can you tell me what is written here, Brother?'

The infirmarian took it and held it towards the pair of candles on a shelf nearby. 'A few words, but I cannot fathom their meaning.'

'What are they?'

The elderly Benedictine screwed up his eyes and held the parchment further away. 'It says, "For thou do not enquire wisely concerning this" ... whatever that might mean.'

De Wolfe looked blankly at him, forgetting the pounding in his head. 'Is that from the scriptures?'

The infirmarian looked again at the words. 'It certainly sounds biblical – but to my shame, I have no great knowledge of the Holy Book, being more concerned with potions and salves.'

The prior was hovering in the doorway, listening to what was said. He came forward and took the scrap of parchment from the monk's fingers.

'Neither do I recognise that quotation – but there are some further letters at the end . . .' He pulled the fragment towards his nose, for unlike the older man, he was short-sighted. 'They seem to be "Ecc", which must surely refer to Solomon's Book of Ecclesiastes – though it could also be Ecclesiasticus, the Wisdom of Jesus, son of Sirach, in the Apocrypha.'

John was not concerned with the academic origins of the words. As long as they came from the Vulgate, that was good enough to lay them at the feet of the murderer. At the moment, all he cared about was saving Thomas de Peyne from the gallows tomorrow and even the prospect of catching the killer took second place to that.

The significance of the quotation was at first obscure, but on thinking about it a little more, his still-shaken brain decided it was a rebuke for being too searching in his investigations. That was good, he thought, for it meant that the culprit was getting worried that the law was closing in on him.

Events moved quickly after this, as did de Wolfe's return to full activity. He was a tough old soldier who had suffered a multitude of injuries far worse than this and, within an hour, was able to stand and walk about, though his head still ached abominably. Before that, though, Nesta had arrived breathless and, ignoring the gossip that was sure to follow, threw her arms about John and tearfully celebrated both his lucky escape and the reprieve it surely must mean for Thomas.

'You could have been killed,' she snuffled. 'And almost in the backyard of my own tavern! I feel responsible for letting you walk out into such danger,' she added illogically.

'The crowner was a lucky man, mistress,' said the weaver, grinning at the sight of the coroner and his mistress showing such public affection, and in a priory, of all places. 'The knock on the head was not too bad, but that bag over his chops would have smothered him, had not the stitches given way.'

This sent Nesta into another paroxysm of emotion, which was cut short by pounding feet outside and the entry of the huge castle constable, Ralph Morin, followed by Gabriel and Osric, the town guard.

The story was told all over again and the leather bag and the parchment passed around, for de Wolfe was anxious for them to verify all that had happened, to defeat any counter-attack by the sheriff and the Justices. 'Osric, make sure that you get the name of every man who came to my aid in Smythen Street tonight. They may be needed to give testimony.' Ralph Morin, a good friend of de Wolfe and a covert adversary of de Revelle, promised he would send all the available men-at-arms from Rougemont to scour the streets, though this was little more than a gesture in the pitch dark, when they had no idea who they were looking for.

'Have you any suspects we should put our hands on at the moment?' he demanded. 'You say it must be a priest, but who are the most likely candidates?'

'There are a hundred to choose from, Ralph, and I have no evidence against any of them. One of the possibles is locked up just across the passage here, so it can't be him.'

The prior shook his head. 'No, he's not! He went out a few hours ago.'

De Wolfe stared at him. 'But he was raving mad when I came to see him. How can he have gone? Did he escape?'

The prior shook his tonsured head. 'After you left, he suddenly became calmer. He put on his clothes and asked us to send for his fellow priest and confessor, Adam of Dol. I had no reason to refuse. Adam came up and said he was taking de Capra back to his dwelling. I protested for a while, but had no power to keep de Capra against his will if a brother priest was willing to look after him, so off he went, as quietly as a lamb.' The prior sounded glad to have been relieved of the responsibility. De Wolfe walked to the doorway. 'I'll go up to Rougemont myself very soon. My clerk needs to be put out of his misery about tomorrow – and I need to have a few strong words with the sheriff. Where is he, anyway?'

'Eating and drinking with the Justices down at the New Inn,' said Morin sarcastically. 'He's not one to let slip any chance of fraternising with the high and mighty!'

John grunted. 'We'll call in on him and their lordships on the way. I'll enjoy spoiling their digestion by telling them that the hanging is off.'

De Wolfe set off for the New Inn, with Ralph Morin close by his side in case he staggered or collapsed. But his hard head and his exultation at Thomas's rescue kept him on his feet as he walked with increasing confidence through the darkened streets of Exeter. With his white bandages swathing his head, he looked more like one of Saladin's warriors than the King's coroner. At the inn, the landlord told them that the sheriff had left for Rougemont and the judges had already retired, so they carried on to the castle, although John found the temptation to drag the Justices from their beds hard to resist.

With Osric and the sergeant-at-arms following behind, they arrived at the keep. There, de Wolfe and Morin marched into de Revelle's outer chamber without ceremony. It was empty, but John hammered on the inner door to the sheriff's bedroom, remembering the time, some months earlier, when he had caught him in there with a whore.

This time he was alone, and opened the door petulantly, dressed in a gaudy silk surcoat to cover his nakedness. He stared in sleepy incredulity at his brother-in-law's Levantine headdress and was even more incredulous when he heard that the Gospel killer was still on the loose. For several minutes, nothing would convince him that this was not some underhand plot of de Wolfe's. 'But you weren't killed, were you?' he brayed. 'This was just some opportunist cutpurse in that unsavoury part of town!'

John jingled the coins in his purse to quash that notion. 'Neither was de Vallibus killed, was he? Nor that harlot in the fire – and maybe there was another who didn't die!' He winked at Richard, who understood that unless he was careful the full story of Waterbeer Street might leak out.

The sheriff weakened, but muttered again that there must be some mistake, so Ralph Morin yelled for Osric and Gabriel to come in from the hall. They told their story, listed the numerous eye-witnesses and then, as the *coup de grâce*, produced the leather bag and the parchment note.

De Revelle stared at this, then feebly suggested it might be a forgery.

'A forgery?' roared de Wolfe. 'It was found inside the bag that almost killed me. And d'you think I knocked myself unconscious, then swallowed the weapon that did it?'

De Revelle, sitting slumped behind his table in his peacock-blue robe, capitulated. 'Very well, but we'll get that canon, Jordan de Brent, up to look at it in the morning. He's the expert on writing.'

'That will tell you nothing, but if it pleases you,

do it. At the same time, you can get him to look at that ridiculous note you read to me about my clerk, to see if that was a forgery. Now I'm going below to the undercroft to tell my much-abused clerk the good news.'

The sheriff leapt up, his surcoat falling open to reveal a hairy chest and a white belly. 'He's not being released tonight, whatever you say! Not until this is put to the Justices and they agree, understand? I've suffered some of your damned tricks before, John, so keep away from him tonight, d'you hear!'

De Wolfe was not disposed to fight him for the sake of a few more hours in a cell and, gathering up his precious bag and parchment, left the sheriff to fume over yet another humiliation at the hands of his brother-in-law.

Feeling decidedly shaky now that the rush of excitement and exultation was fading, de Wolfe headed for home, Osric shepherding him as far as his front door. As he headed for the steps up to the solar, Mary came out of the kitchen-hut and almost fainted when she saw his bandaged head in the moonlight, for the silver orb had risen since the events of a few hours ago.

He turned down her offer to make him something to eat and drink, but told her of Thomas's deliverance, at which she was as overjoyed as Nesta had been, for the little clerk was an object of sympathy and affection to all the women – except Matilda. The thought of his wife sent his eyes up to the solar door.

'She's been in bed these many hours,' Mary reassured him. 'So get yourself there as well. You'll have no trouble until the morning.'

Next morning Matilda was surprisingly concerned about his head, though she cooled a little when she discovered that he had suffered the injury only a few yards from the Bush Inn. Even so, she made him promise to attend her favourite apothecary's shop in the high street that day to have the dressing changed. When he told her of Thomas's reprieve, she showed none of the scorn he expected – in fact, he sensed that she was grudgingly pleased that his obvious distress over his little clerk had been lifted.

After breaking his fast early, he hurried up to Rougemont, his legs, if not his head, back to normal. Gabriel had already told Gwyn of the night's dramatic happening and the big Cornishman was half drunk with delight and celebratory ale. He had wanted to rush over to the undercroft and drag Thomas out there and then, until the sergeant had cooled him down. 'Best wait until the crowner has sorted things out with the sheriff and the Justices,' he warned. 'We don't want to mess things up by being too hasty.'

De Wolfe was about to do this now, and all his witnesses had been gathered in the Shire Hall well before the time when the court session was due to start. They were waiting for the Justices and the sheriff to come across from the keep.

Richard de Revelle had reluctantly told them the story, and they sat down at one of the clerks' tables on the platform with solemn faces, a suspicion of a scowl on those of Sir Peter Peverel and Walter de Ralegh.

De Wolfe stood over them, told them the facts again and produced the leather bag and the parchment note. His own injury was obvious, especially as some blood had seeped through the linen, which made it look all the more impressive. A few of the witnesses from Smythen Street were called to confirm the attack, and Osric nervously added the names of others who could support the story. The judges listened in stony silence, though the Archdeacon from Gloucester looked relieved that one of his brethren looked certain to be declared innocent.

By this time the cathedral archivist, Canon Jordan de Brent, had appeared, summoned from the dusty Exchequer above the Chapter House. He sat at the table and looked at the most recent message from the Gospel killer, together with the others and the disc of hard candle-wax from the steps of St Mary Arches. He looked intently at them and then shook his head. 'The writing is deliberately disguised,' he pronounced. 'All the notes are different in style and slope and are irregular, so it was not a normal freehand.' He peered more closely at two of the notes for a moment. 'Yet I would suggest that these two notes were by the same hand,' He held up the first, found at the scene of Aaron's death, and the one from last night. 'Each of these has a strange hook on the letter T. The writer, though he has successfully varied all his other letters, must have forgotten this one quirk, perhaps in haste or panic. I think it confirms that last night's message was written by whoever killed the Jew.'

When he was shown the letter that had been delivered to the sheriff, accusing Thomas of being at the scene of the cordwainer's death, the old canon declared that the handwriting was unlike that in any other of the notes.

Though the sheriff and two of the judges argued for several minutes against Thomas's lack of guilt, they knew they were making bricks without straw and grudgingly, they had to admit that there was no reason to hold him in custody any longer. This was all de Wolfe needed and he bobbed his head in grudging deference to the Justices, gave the sheriff a look of cold disdain and hurried away, leaving them to begin a shortened session, as they had to witness half a dozen hangings at noon – thankfully without Thomas as one of the participants.

The castle constable came across with the coroner and his officer to deliver Thomas from his cell. Stigand would probably not have accepted de Wolfe's word alone that his clerk was to be released, even at the risk of Gwyn's threat to tear off his head. When they entered the cell to tell him the news, the clerk was sitting on the edge of his bed, his book open in his hands. Though the foetid chamber was tiny, he still appeared small within it, looking up at them pathetically. His lank hair hung down like a curtain from his shaven crown and his long, sharp nose seemed to dominate his receding chin even more than usual. When de Wolfe gave him the news of his acquittal and release, he seemed less exultant than they had expected and the coroner wondered fleetingly if Thomas had seen hanging as God's offering of an alternative to the mortal sin of suicide.

Yet Gwyn had more than enough enthusiasm for them all. The ginger giant grabbed the puny man in his arms and danced out through the iron gate, yelling in triumph. With his free arm, he shoved the odious gaoler in the chest, sending him sprawling into the stinking straw, then ran out with the clerk into the sunlight of the inner ward.

A few moments later, they gathered in Gabriel's guardroom in the gatehouse for a celebratory drink, where even the abstemious Thomas was cajoled into taking a cup of cider. He still had his precious Vulgate clutched in his hand and John suspected that if he had been hanged, it would have been tucked under his arm as he fell from the gibbet.

The coroner explained in detail what had happened the previous night and the clerk nodded at intervals, seemingly dazed by the speed of events. 'We'll get you back to the Bush now. Nesta can feed you and give you a bucket of warm water in the yard to wash off the filth and the lice from that damned cell,' promised his master.

'Can I start work again today?' asked Thomas. 'And go back to the canon's house to live?'

Gwyn roared with laughter, but the little clerk was serious.

'Tomorrow, certainly,' answered de Wolfe gravely. 'The court session finishes early today.' There was silence as they realised why this was so and how close Thomas had come to being part of the reason for it.

Soon Gwyn left to take Thomas to the Bush for the promised food and wash, leaving Ralph Morin and Gabriel sitting with the coroner to finish their ale.

'I'm damned if I'll attend the hangings today,' growled John. 'Let one of the court clerks take the details – we can copy them on to the rolls later.'

Later, as they walked across the inner ward, they were joined by Brother Rufus coming from the keep. He was intrigued by de Wolfe's Moorish headgear. When he heard the whole story, he congratulated John on Thomas's salvation, then listened as Ralph again broached the subject of the killer: 'He's still out there, John. Why do you think he attacked you last night? He must have been following you, to know that you would be leaving the tavern after dark.'

De Wolfe ran his hands through his thick hair, bunching it back on to his neck. 'According to the sense of that text he wrote, it seems he was warning me not to investigate so persistently. Some chance he's got of that – I'm not one to take heed of such threats!'

'Three times he's failed to kill,' mused the constable. 'Is he getting careless – or was it deliberate?'

De Wolfe snorted. 'Not much doubt about him being serious when he tied a bag over my head! That's how he killed the moneylender.' His hawk-like face, with the downturned lines at each side of his mouth, was a grim mask as he vowed to catch the maniac who still stalked the city. 'I don't know how and I don't know when, Ralph, but one way or another, this bastard has to be stopped,' he declared.

The Viking-like constable pulled at his forked beard, his favourite mannerism when perturbed. 'Where can you start, though?'

'My guts tell me that there's something very odd about three of the priests on the cathedral list. I've spoken to all of them more than once, right up to yesterday – and last night someone tried to put a permanent end to my probing.'

'Which three?' persisted Morin.

'Your namesake, Ralph, the madman from All-Hallows-on-the-Wall. Then there's his neighbour, Adam of Dol, who wants to save us all from hell-fire – he seems to have appointed himself as protector to Ralph and gets into a great fury when I question him. And lastly Julian Fulk, who is obsessed with his own importance, through somehow I don't see him as a killer.'

'Many of my ecclesiastical and monastic friends are more than a little strange,' objected Rufus of Bristol, 'but I doubt that any is a multiple murderer.'

John shrugged. 'I agree with you, Brother. But the fact remains that someone is killing or attacking our citizens and all the circumstances point firmly to it being a cleric.'

Ralph Morin stuck doggedly to practicalities. 'So what can you do about it? The bloody sheriff seems remarkably uninterested in the matter, though I suspect that the Justices, aggrieved at losing your Thomas, will soon be kicking his arse.'

De Wolfe winced as a ripple of pain shot through his head from the wound but it soon passed. 'I'm going down to aggravate those parish priests again,' he said, with stubborn determination. 'Especially Ralph de Capra and Adam of Dol. If I tweak their tails hard enough, in their anger they might let something drop. It's worth a try, for I've no other ideas to follow up.'

The castle constable and his sergeant went off about

their business, but the persistent Brother Rufus asked if he could accompany John on his visits to the parish priests. As castle chaplain, he seemed to have plenty of spare time, the coroner thought – but his tiny chapel of St Mary near the gatehouse provided only two services a day, except on Sundays so his duties were far from onerous.

'We'll wait for Gwyn and Thomas to come back, then walk down towards the West Gate to twist a couple of arms.'

Outside that same West Gate, the river Exe bulged out over an area of marsh and mud, cut through by leats that filled at high tide and during floods. This was Exe Island, covered in reeds and coarse grass, with some huts, a few small houses and several fulling mills. Every year when the river was in flood, some shacks were washed away and people were drowned, but during this particularly dry month, the Exe was behaving itself. Just upstream of the West Gate, the old wooden footbridge was still the only way to cross with dry feet. Below this was the ford, where all carts, cattle and horsemen had to cross, for the new bridge downstream was still incomplete. Its many long arches spanned dry ground on the city side, allowing for floodwater at spring tides and after storms on Exmoor. There was even a small chapel on this part, though the bridge was nowhere near complete, as the construction of the western part had stopped a year ago when the builder, Nicholas Gervase, ran out of funds.

Soon after Thomas de Peyne had washed himself down in the yard behind the Bush, another priest was slipping furtively into this tiny church. It was little more than a simple room poised on the upstream edge of one of the piers, projecting out on a buttress fifteen feet above the grassy mud of Exe Island. The interior was virtually bare, except for a stone shelf around the walls and a stone altar covered with a cloth, on which stood a wooden cross. The place was intended for travellers wishing to give thanks for their safe arrival at Exeter or to pray to St Christopher for a safe journey into the wild West Country. A chaplain had been appointed by the diocese, but he visited rarely.

The priest was carrying a large pottery flask and, incongruously in broad daylight, a small lantern. He produced a flint and tinder and, with some difficulty, his shaking hands managed to light the candle in the lantern, which he placed alongside the cross on the altar. Then he sank to his knees in front of it and, head bowed, began to gabble in a monotone that soon rose to become a frenzied supplication in a mixture of Latin, English and Norman French. This went on for half an hour, the man rocking back and forth on his knees, beating his breast. Finally, he collapsed on the floor and lay flat on his face, his arms and legs spreadeagled on the cool slabs.

He lay immobile like this for some moments, then silently got up and walked stiffly to the altar, picked up the lantern and the flask and moved like a sleepwalker to the open doorway. Outside in the sunlight, he walked down the unfinished bridge to where the empty roadway came to an abrupt end over the final pier that stood at the edge of the Exe's main channel. The water flowed smooth and deep below him, as he stood with his feet near the edge.

Setting down the flask and the lamp, he pulled his long black tunic over his head and threw it on to the ground. When he kicked off his scuffed sandals, he was as naked as the moment he was born.

Picking up the pitcher, he upturned it over his head and let about a gallon of turpentine mixed with strong Irish spirits gush over his body, holding it until the last drops of the oily liquid had coursed over his shoulders, chest, belly and legs. He threw the pot aside then picked up the lantern. He moved until his toes were curled over the very edge of the masonry, and looked down at the water, moving almost silently below. Then he opened the door of the lantern and, with a cry of exultation and despair, clasped it to his chest so that the flame almost touched his skin. The light spirits ignited into an almost invisible blue flame and flashed across his body. The heat caught the heavier turpentine alight and in seconds, the man was a human torch. With another scream, this time of mortal agony, he threw up his arms and his back arched in unbearable pain.

Just outside the West Gate, two porters with great packs of raw wool were sitting for a rest, when they saw what seemed to be a flaming crucifix in the distance. With yells of alarm, they sprang up and ran down the bridge towards it, followed by one of the gatekeepers and a few passers-by. Until they reached halfway, the astonished men could still see the writing, contorting figure, from which flame and smoke swirled into the still air. But suddenly and with a final despairing cry, the living cremation pitched forwards and fell into the river below, a last hissing and bubbling marking where the body sank beneath the uncaring surface.

De Wolfe had just crossed Carfoix when shouts and the sound of running feet coming up Fore Street told him that yet another emergency was in the offing. Gwyn and Brother Rufus were with him, one on each side of Thomas, who seemed to have recovered rapidly from his ordeal.

As they neared St Olave's church, people in the street were turning to look at three men jogging up the slope from the West Gate, shouting and waving their arms to attract his attention.

The leading man panted to a stop in front of him. It was Theobald, the town constable. 'Crowner, there's a body just dragged from the river. Can you come quickly?'

De Wolfe scowled. Drowned bodies were one of the most common type of case he had to deal with. There was usually no great urgency about viewing them, especially as now he had other things on his mind.

'Can't it wait a little? Or get a barrow and take it to the dead-house on the quayside.'

Theobald shook his head. 'It happened not half an hour ago. He set fire to himself on the new bridge and then jumped in. It's a priest, by the clothes he left behind.'

The word 'priest' instantly grabbed John's attention, but the ever-inquisitive monk got in first. 'Priest? Who was it?'

'We're not sure, his face was badly scorched, but it looks like the priest of All-Hallows.'

'Ralph de Capra?' snapped de Wolfe.

Theobald nodded. 'About his height and build. His hair's burnt off and most of his skin's gone, but it's most likely him, especially after that caper he had on the city wall yesterday.'

They all hurried down towards the river and Theobald led them across the mud of Exe Island below the new bridge, followed by a crowd of onlookers. The corpse had not drifted far: a hundred paces away from where the man had jumped into the river a dead tree had trapped his body in its branches. The two porters who had seen the conflagration on the bridge had rushed down and dragged it ashore, where it now lay on its back on the rough grass. Even in the open air, the smell of cooked flesh was distinct.

As they stood over it, Thomas and Brother Rufus competed with each other in crossing themselves repeatedly, but John and his officer dropped beside the body into their usual crouch.

'Bit of a mess, but I reckon it's de Capra right enough,' said Gwyn. The face was bright red with blackened patches, and was completely skinned, as were much of the shoulders, chest and thighs. All the hair had gone and the scalp was scorched. The burning and swelling of the eyelids and lips made the features grotesque, but there was no doubt that it was the mad priest of All-Hallows-on-the-Wall.

'He'd have been a damned sight worse if he hadn't jumped in the river,' offered one of the porters, with morbid satisfaction.

'Stark naked, he was, standing on the end of the bloody bridge like a bush afire!' contributed the other excitedly.

De Wolfe rocked back on his heels to ponder the situation. Was this a final act of contrition for killing and assaulting all those people? There was no proof of that – even priests are allowed to go mad without necessarily being serial killers.

'Shall we haul him off to the mortuary, as you said, Crowner?' asked Theobald.

John got to his feet and looked again at the scorched cadaver.

'No, he's a clerk in Holy Orders, so we must see what the cathedral wishes to do about this. The Archdeacon is responsible for the parish priests, so he must be told – and the Bishop, if he's still in the city.'

A wide circle of people had formed around the scene and as they moved to allow de Wolfe and his party to pass through on their way back to the higher ground outside the city wall, Brother Rufus reminded him of Ralph de Capra's recent movements. 'He was being sheltered by the priest at St Mary Steps, both before and after he was taken to St Nicholas. I wonder if he knows about this?'

'That's further reason to speak to him, as soon as we can,' grunted the coroner. 'He seemed quite fond of that deranged fellow, so it may come as a nasty shock.'

Privately, de Wolfe wondered if the same nasty shock might trigger some useful reaction in Adam of Dol, but when they reached the little house behind the church, no one was in. The four investigators came back down the steep cobbles at the side of the church and went in through the front door.

Inside the empty nave, they saw Adam with his back to them, up a ladder set against the blank wall at one side of the chancel arch. He wore an old black robe stained with paint, the skirt pulled up between his legs and tucked into a broad leather belt. A tray of small pots was balanced precariously on one of the rungs and he was leaning out with a small brush, meticulously putting pigment on another of his terrifying images.

He was so intent upon his artistic endeavours that he failed to hear them come in. Gwyn nudged his master and pointed to the new scene, mostly in red and black, which contrasted starkly with the whitewashed walls. It was only partly completed, but showed an angel and a winged devil fighting over an agonised human, each trying to drag him up to heaven or down to hell. The details were very well drawn and the face of the angel was undoubtedly that of Adam himself. The devil was equally clearly that of Henry Marshal, Bishop of Devon and Cornwall!

'That'll not increase your popularity in the cathedral precinct,' said John in a loud voice. The priest turned so suddenly that he was in danger of falling from the ladder, but when he saw who his visitors were, he snarled, 'I don't give a tinker's curse what they think down there! They're only interested in fancy vestments, good food and their fat tithes and prebends. Saving souls is the least of their concerns.' He turned back to his painting, deliberately ignoring the coroner and his

companions. He was adding a disembowelled corpse to
the free hand of the bishop-devil, presumably one which
Satan had already seized from the forces of heaven.

John waited patiently, while Brother Rufus stared with
rapt attention at all the other wall-paintings, and the
ever-inquisitive Thomas wandered over to the chancel
steps to leaf through a thick book that lay on a wooden
lectern.

After a little time Adam finished what he was painting
and leaned back a little to admire his work. Then he put
his brush on the tray and slowly came down the ladder.
Rubbing his hands on his grubby tunic, he came across
the nave towards de Wolfe, his red face as truculent as
ever. 'Anyway, what do you want, Crowner? I've seen
enough of you lately. Can't you leave us alone?'

The 'us' brought home to John that he had an
unpleasant duty to perform. Quite bluntly, he told
Adam of the gruesome death of his priestly neighbour
less than an hour before. If he had been hoping for a
reaction, he was not disappointed, for after a moment's
shocked inertia, the burly priest gave a bull-like roar and
charged at the coroner, his hands open as if to seize
his throat.

Gwyn, who had spent many years as bodyguard to his
master, stepped calmly between them and grabbed the
priest's wrists in a bear-like grip, forcing the man down
to his knees.

'Now, none of that or I'll have to hurt you,' he said
benignly.

However, Adam's mouth could still function and he
poured out a torrent of invective at de Wolfe, widening
it to include the sheriff, constable, bishop, all the archdeacons and most of the Exeter canons. 'If you had not
persecuted that poor man, he would still be alive!' he
raged. 'He lost his faith, as many of us do at some time or
another, but he was hounded into insanity by you all.'

Rufus tried to intervene, pointing out that though racking doubts about the very existence of God were an occupational hazard of being a priest, few were driven to madness and self-destruction. Adam ignored him and continued to rage at the coroner and the faithless world in general, his fleshy face almost purple with anger.

John let the abuse wash over him and motioned to Gwyn to let the man get to his feet, though the Cornishman kept a wary eye on him in case he became violent again.

As the priest continued to shake his fist, wave his arms and rant about the indolence of the Church, Thomas sidled up to de Wolfe and tugged at his sleeve. 'Crowner, come over here, quickly,' he whispered, and pulled him the few paces to the chancel steps where the Vulgate now lay open on the lectern. The clerk pointed a finger at one page, where John saw faint but distinct underlining in powdery charcoal beneath some of the beautifully regular lettering of the Latin text. Thomas turned feverishly to another page, which he had marked with a small feather dropped by one of the birds that nested in the roof beams. 'Here again passages have been marked – and in other places!' he hissed.

As de Wolfe stared at him with dawning comprehension, he became aware that Adam's tirade was running down in volume and virulence. The priest had noticed the activity near his lectern.

'Are these the same quotations as at the scenes of death?' he muttered, leaning closer to his clerk.

Thomas bobbed his head. 'This one is from St Mark about the moneylenders in the temple – and the first was that about the millstone around the neck.'

Adam's angry monologue had faded to silence now and de Wolfe saw that both Gwyn and the castle chaplain had turned to listen to what Thomas was saying. 'Hold him, Gwyn, I have some questions for that man!'

snapped John urgently, but he was too late. With surprising agility for one so heavily built, Adam of Dol
raced for a small door at the front of the nave, alongside
the entrance from the street. Gwyn pounded after him,
but the priest slipped through and slammed it after
him. They heard a bar being dropped on the inside
and though Gwyn crashed his great body against the
oaken door, it shuddered but held fast. The four left
in the nave clustered around the doorway in excited
frustration.

'Where does this lead?' demanded de Wolfe.

'It can only be to the bell-tower,' suggested Rufus.

Shouting over his shoulder to Gwyn to break it open,
de Wolfe ran out into the narrow street between the
church and the city wall near the West Gate. Turning,
he looked up at the squat, square tower that had been
erected only a few years earlier with funds donated by
a rich burgess in memory of his wife. Just under the flat
top, there was a small arch on each of the four sides,
which allowed the peals from the central bell to ring
out over the city. He could see no one under the front
arch so he hurried back into the nave.

Gwyn had failed to shift the door with his shoulder
and rubbing his bruised muscles, was on his way to
fetch Adam's stout ladder to use as a battering-ram.
There was silence from behind the door and John
wondered whether Adam might decide to follow his
fellow priest's example by killing himself. However, the
coroner decided that it seemed out of character with
the man's truculent nature, unless by leaping from the
bell-tower, he could land on the coroner and personally
send him to hell, having failed the previous night with
his leather bag.

As he waited impatiently for Gwyn to break down the
door, de Wolfe noticed that Brother Rufus and Thomas
were staring at the other gory scenes painted by Adam

high on the walls. They were pointing at particular parts of the murals, which were frighteningly realistic in their sharp detail. 'Crowner, look at that face – and that one,' brayed the monk. 'Can you see who they are?'

John peered up, following Rufus's finger. Though the main characters in the scenes were angels and devils, there were several smaller individuals, almost all agonised victims of sin. Suddenly, his eyes registered what the other two were indicating. In the lower corner of the first painting, one face was unmistakably that of Aaron, the Jewish moneylender, and in the next, a woman with flowing hair and prominent breasts was Joanna of London. Astounded, John moved along and found the merchant sodomite Fitz-William, then the unmistakable pointed beard and close-set eyes of Richard de Revelle.

'No sign of the crowner here, in his gallery of rogues,' chaffed Rufus. 'I suppose as you were the last victim he hasn't had time to include you.'

Gwyn had by now grabbed the ladder, letting the pots of pigment crash down to stain the nave floor. As he charged across the nave with the stout timbers held like a lance, John tried to assimilate all that the last few moments had revealed. It was patently obvious that Adam of Dol was the deranged killer and the attacker that they had been so desperately seeking – for whose sake Thomas had come so close to a humiliating death. If only he had taken more notice of these damned paintings earlier, then a great deal of trouble – and even a life or two – might have been saved.

A thunderous crashing began at the base of the tower, where Rufus of Bristol had joined Gwyn in swinging the heavy ladder against the stubborn door. While they were assaulting it, John laid a hand on Thomas's shoulder and shouted a question at him: 'Were all those quotations underlined in the book?'

'Like the faces up on the walls, all of them except the one left at your attack, master. But that was but a few hours ago.'

They were interrupted by the rending of wood and turning, they saw that the door to the tower was hanging from its hinges. With a roar, Gwyn dropped the ladder and dived through the opening. By the time John had followed him inside, his officer was still roaring, but with further frustration. A tiny room, the floor rush-covered, was empty but for a broom and a bucket. In one corner there was a square hole in the ceiling and below this a rope ladder lay crumpled on the floor, thrown down from above. They could hear heavy feet pacing up and down on the boards overhead and a muffled litany of imprecations.

'Come down, Adam! There's no way you can escape,' yelled Rufus, in his usual interfering way. Thomas scowled at him, annoyed that the chaplain had been first to notice the faces in the wall paintings, though Thomas still could claim recognition of the marked passages in Adam's Bible.

The coroner joined in calling upon the priest to surrender, but was met by another barrage of defiance, mixed with the usual commentary on the Armageddon soon to come.

'The Book of Revelation must be his favourite reading,' muttered Thomas cynically, though he made the Sign of the Cross a few times, to be on the safe side.

'Any fear of him jumping from the top?' asked Rufus, echoing John's earlier thoughts.

'Any hope, you mean!' countered Gwyn cynically.

'It would certainly solve many problems – not least those of the Bishop,' said Rufus wryly.

'What d'you mean?' asked de Wolfe suspiciously.

The castle priest shrugged. 'Unlike our little friend here, Adam is a fully fledged parish priest, still in Holy

Orders. The Bishop proscribed torture for Thomas, though technically he is a layman, so I doubt he'll withhold Benefit of Clergy for this man.'

'That's not my business, thank God,' grated de Wolfe. 'My concern at the moment is to get the swine down from up there.'

Adam's head appeared in the trap above, an almost manic leer on his face as he stared down at them. 'My work on this earth is nearly finished – but the Lord will deliver me from mine enemies!' he yelled triumphantly.

'I'll bloody deliver you, you evil bastard!' shouted Gwyn angrily. He bent and picked up the end of the ladder that was lying across the ruined door, and propped it just below the hole into the upper chamber, where the bell-rope hung. As he began to climb the rungs, John called a warning, as Adam's face vanished and was replaced by one of his feet. 'Watch your face, man!'

The furious priest above was kicking downwards as Gwyn's head reached the ceiling. A heel skimmed the red hair as Gwyn dodged and retreated a rung or two.

'Right, your time has come, unless you can get God to whisk you out of there right now!' he roared. Reaching behind him, he pulled his dagger from his belt and went back up the rungs. The foot stamped down again, but this time the coroner's officer jabbed it through the leather sole. There was a yell of pain and Gwyn dropped the knife to grab Adam's ankle with both hands and pull it with all his considerable strength.

For a second, the open-mouthed spectators standing below thought that both men were going to fall on top of them and scattered to the opposite wall. But though the priest came bodily through the trap-door, he managed to grab the edges as he fell. Now Gwyn had him around the knees and reached up to land Adam a punishing blow in the belly. The priest jackknifed down on top of

the Cornishman. Careless of any further injury, Gwyn
tipped his prisoner sideways off the ladder, letting him
crash on to the thick layer of old rushes on the floor.
Adam lay there bruised and winded – silent for once on
the subject of sin and retribution.

By the end of that week, most loose ends had been
cleared up.

The Eyre of Assize went more quickly than had
been expected and all the Gaol Delivery and criminal
cases had been finished by Saturday, leaving de Wolfe
relatively free of the court. the General Eyre, which the
sheriff was dreading, had little to do with the coroner.

The Justices were subdued when it came to acknowledging their grievous error over the identity of the
Gospel killer, though Archdeacon Gervase assumed a
rather condescending 'I told you so' manner. Walter de
Ralegh was gentleman enough to offer a gruff apology to
John in private, but Serlo de Vallibus and Peter Peverel
did their best to avoid the subject.

Richard de Revelle's main concern was to keep his
name clear of any association with the fire in Waterbeer
Street, afraid that a trial might bring out some embarrassing evidence. He was therefore overjoyed to hear
that Bishop Henry Marshal had exercised his right to
insist on Benefit of Clergy for Adam of Dol, preventing
him being dealt with by the secular courts – which in
this case would have the Exeter Eyre of Assize that
very week.

Meanwhile, the deranged priest of St Mary Steps was
closely confined in one of the cells adjacent to the
cloisters, kept for erring clerks by the proctors, the
representatives of the Chapter who, with their servants,
were responsible for law and order in the cathedral
precinct.

As John de Alençon related to de Wolfe a few days

later, Adam was first brought before the Bishop for his sins to be explored. As he was not a cathedral priest, the Chapter had no jurisdiction over him but, given the uniquely heinous nature of his crimes, a preliminary interrogation was considered necessary, before the matter went to the Consistory Court of the diocese. The Bishop led this inquisition, assisted by some senior canons. De Alençon, as Archdeacon of Exeter, was present as Adam's immediate superior, and the Precentor, Thomas de Boterellis, with the Treasurer, John of Exeter, made up the group, along with Jordan de Brent, the archivist.

The deposed incumbent of St Mary Steps was led by two proctors into the Bishop's audience chamber in the palace. Given Adam's tendency to physical violence, his wrists were shackled and a pair of burly servants stood on either side of him. As if anticipating his ejection from Holy Orders, he had been dressed in a smock of drab hessian instead of his black clerical robe, but he displayed no sign of shame or contrition. On the contrary, he glared at his accusers with aggressive contempt as he stood before the Bishop's great chair, the others hunched on stools alongside.

The cold-eyed Henry Marshal was more than equal to the challenge as he opened the proceedings. 'Are you mad, Adam, or just evil?' he asked quietly.

The priest's face flushed with righteous anger. 'Neither, Lord Bishop! I do the Lord's work in my own way, because the efforts of you and your feeble cohorts to counter the devil and all his works are futile.'

'You wretched man! How dare you insult your fellow labourers in the vineyard of God, they who use compassion and solicitude in place of your sadistic perversions?'

Adam continued to bluster about the need to warn their flocks of the torments that awaited sinners, but the prelate cut him off with an imperious gesture. 'Be quiet! Your evil obsessions weary me. Do you deny that you have been killing and attacking innocent people in this city?'

Adam glowered at the faces before him. 'I carried out the tasks that the Almighty charged me to perform.'

'And how did he call upon you?' cut in Canon Jordan, in his deceptively mild voice.

'His voice came to me in the night, clearer than you are speaking to me now. Many a time, God answered my prayers for guidance, telling me how to outwit Satan.' His voice rose. 'He told me how to make up for the weakness of our Church, for I was his appointed disciple.'

'Cease this arrogant blasphemy!' snapped the Bishop. 'You have been indulging in these abominable practices for your own depraved pleasure.'

De Alençon decided to join the inquisition. 'These killings you admit to now, they began recently. What caused this escalation in your misdeeds?'

'As I told you, it was the voice of God. I could see signs of wickedness going unchecked all around me in this city. I was called to bring retribution and convince those in power of the peril of neglecting their duty. I assumed that God was calling others to do the same in other places, as part of a great crusade against Lucifer, who was clearly winning the fight.'

The Archdeacon marvelled at the way in which a madman could rationalise what he was doing, to justify his indulgence in the very same sins against which he alleged that he was campaigning.

'Did you intend to slay every whore, every money-lender, every sodomite in the city?' enquired the Precentor in his acid tones.

Adam, who seemed to have a logical answer to every slur on his fantasies, shook his bull-like head. 'Of course not! It was but a sign, a token of warning to those who committed similar sins. And you have interrupted my work, damn you all! God will be unforgiving when you go to judgement, though you be bishops and archdeacons all!'

Henry Marshal sighed. It was impossible to penetrate this disordered mind. He turned to John de Alençon. 'Archdeacon, I gather you have some further information?'

De Alençon leaned forward and unrolled a parchment that he had been holding. 'In the last few days, we have learnt that the parish priest of Topsham, one Richard Vassallus, was a secondary and a vicar at the cathedral of Wells at the same time as Adam of Dol. This was now many years ago, but Vassallus was sent for yesterday and was able to give me some pertinent facts about his old colleague.'

The others turned to him with expectant interest, but the prisoner barked his derision. 'Vassallus was a weak-kneed fool, as well as a liar. He has hated me ever since I broke his jaw after he derided my theories about countering Satan's wiles!'

The Archdeacon ignored the interruption. 'This priest said that Adam had a reputation for outbursts of ungovernable violence when at Wells. He was known to consort with loose women – though we must accept that was not a unique crime, even among young clerics – and he was suspected of having been involved in the fatal mutilation of a whore in Bristol. The sheriff's men came to make enquiries, but nothing could be proved.'

'Liars, all of them! God had not then called me to do his bidding,' ranted Adam, until a proctor rapped him across the neck with his rod.

'Was there anything else?' asked the Bishop.

'There were two mysterious fires when he was at Wells. Part of the dormitory was burnt down and later, there was a fire in the Chapter House that damaged the scriptorium. Again, suspicion fell on Adam, but no proof was forthcoming. However, the canons had him transferred to their superior house of Bath Abbey, where it seems his dubious history was not known.'

De Alençon unrolled his scroll a little more and continued, 'By chance, I was discussing the matter with one of the Justices now in the city, Gervase de Bosco, who, as you all know, is an archdeacon in Gloucester. He told me that almost a year ago, he was one of those holding the Eyre of Assize in Wiltshire. Two deaths were presented by the coroner there, one from Salisbury, the other from Devizes, which were never solved, no perpetrator ever being found.'

The others waited with interest upon the rest of the Archdeacon's explanation.

'The victims were both harlots, mutilated in an obscene way. One had also been damaged after death by fire. Other whores who frequented the same ale-houses as the dead girls told a vague story suggesting that a man with a priest's tonsure had been the last man seen with the victims, but in the absence of any other evidence, nothing could come of the matter.'

There was a pregnant silence.

'Murdered whores, mutilation and fires seem to recur often in this sad story,' said the Bishop. 'Have you anything to say on the matter, Adam of Dol?'

The priest's pugnacious face jerked up defiantly. 'Sin is sin, whether it be in Exeter, Salisbury or Devizes! It needs to be rooted out wherever it occurs.'

'Which offers you your perverted pleasures at the same time, no doubt,' said Henry Marshal dryly. 'If that is the last of your sad catalogue, Archdeacon, then I have something to add, which I learnt only today.'

The company turned expectantly to their superior.

'Since it became public knowledge that this deranged

fellow had been apprehended, his own confessor came to me in great concern. Father William Angot, of the church of Holy Trinity, has been on a pilgrimage to Canterbury and only returned yesterday, so he knew nothing of the spate of killings during these past few weeks. Mindful of the sanctity of confession, he has been disconsolate about what to do but came to me for guidance. Though we accept that confessions are never disclosed, even to fellow priests, in the circumstances I gave a dispensation to Father William to divulge what he felt was relevant to this vile situation.'

'You had no such right!' howled Adam, his eyes bulging in a face almost puce with rage.

Ignoring his outburst, Henry Marshal continued in cold, even tones: 'Though this evil man had not deigned to make confession for almost half a year, according to William Angot, in the past he has admitted to such strange behaviour and actions that his confessor urged him repeatedly both to desist and to seek counselling from higher authorities. He had suggested pilgrimages to Canterbury and even to Rome, but Adam rejected these notions with scorn.'

All eyes and ears were now on the Bishop, waiting to hear what came next,

'From such confessions over several years, William gathered that the roots of this man's madness are rooted in his childhood. His father treated him with contempt and his mother and a sister were confined by force in a nunnery, due to distressing afflictions of the mind. In his rejection, he began to torture small animals and developed a passion for fire, causing a number of conflagrations on their estate in Totnes. Eventually, his father disposed of him to the cathedral school in Wells, mainly, it seems, as a means of getting rid of a troublesome embarrassment.'

Adam began again to shout denials and curses and

tried to move towards the dais on which his accusers sat, but the proctors and their henchmen restrained his struggles.

'His so-called confessions became progressively more like the abuse and cant we are hearing from him today – which is another reason why I have sanctioned the limited revelation of his dealings with Father William. He admitted his fornication with harlots, thankfully well away from Exeter, and he gave broad hints about the revival of his fascination with fire and torture, which seem to have been manifest in a perverse degree in his preaching and those abominable paintings that desecrate the walls of St Mary the Less. I have been myself to see them today and have given orders that they be whitewashed over without delay.'

This provoked another howl of protest from Adam, who viewed the obliteration of his artwork as an even greater tragedy than his own arrest, but the Bishop was unmoved as he brought the interview dispassionately to an end.

'Adam of Dol, it is the Consistory Court that will finally judge you, though I will appoint its chancellor and its members. At this stage, all I will do is to wonder whether you are totally deranged or totally evil. Whichever it is, there is no doubt that the Satan you claim to fight, has invaded your mind. Indeed, he seems to have been residing there since your childhood and it is a great pity that those who had the care and teaching of you in the early days of your church career did not cut out this perversity, root and branch.' With the words, 'Take this creature out of my sight', he rose and, to the bows of his colleagues, turned to leave through the door behind his chair.

'And that's that, until the Consistory Court is convened next week,' concluded John of Alençon later, over a flask of wine with his friend the coroner.

'One thing puzzles me,' replied de Wolfe. 'His relationship with Ralph.'

De Wolfe told the whole story to Gwyn, Thomas and Nesta, when they were sitting at their table in the Bush on Saturday evening. The matter had been aired again that day in the Shire Hall, when John de Alençon, as Archdeacon of Exeter, had come to deliver his Bishop's decision to the Justices.

'Henry Marshal has done this to emphasise the Church's independence of royal authority,' commented the coroner sourly, 'and I suspect he has used the opportunity to hint at his own partiality to Prince John by delivering a snub to King Richard in taking Adam out of the jurisdiction of his courts.'

'I should have broken the bugger's neck instead of his ribs when I pulled him off that ladder,' grunted Gwyn. 'It would have saved a lot of trouble.'

Nesta, resplendent in a new kirtle of fawn wool under her white linen apron, looked radiant and content, with her lover and friends around her. But she was rather hazy as to the outcome of this latest drama.

'The Bishop refused to give this "Benefit of Clergy" to poor Thomas here,' she said, 'so why is this murderer so favoured? And what does it mean, anyway?'

'Poor' Thomas, as he seemed fated to be known from now on, provided her with an explanation himself, glad to be free of competition from the erudite Brother Rufus. 'It's existed for centuries in many countries, in one form or another – mainly to emphasise the Church's superiority over kings and emperors, as the crowner said just now.'

'It just seems a way of avoiding the harsh justice that the rest of us have to endure,' objected Nesta.

Always a champion of his beloved Church, the clerk disagreed and explained further. 'It doesn't absolve priests from trial, but transfers their judgement to a different court. It had a great boost in England in old King Henry's reign, when as part of his penance for having Thomas Becket killed' – here he paused to make the Sign of the Cross – 'he accepted the Church's demand for recognition of Benefit of Clergy, which took them from the secular courts to the Bishop's Consistory Court.'

'So it's entirely up to Henry Marshal what happens to this murdering bastard,' grumbled Gwyn, wiping the ale from his moustache. 'He can let him off if he wants to.'

'It's not that simple. The Consistory Court makes the final decision.'

'Oh, come on! Who's going to be brave enough to cross the Bishop, eh? He must already have some crafty scheme to deal with this madman.'

John was massaging Nesta's thigh under the table, but he didn't allow that pleasant pursuit to distract him from the conversation. 'The Archdeacon told me that Henry Marshal is going to recommend that Adam be incarcerated in the Benedictine monastery of Mont St Michel in Normandy. It seems the Bishop is a friend of the Abbot there, and can ensure that the maniac works off his obsessions with hard labour for the rest of his life, carrying building stones up the mount for the new church on top. I think he'd probably prefer to be hanged.'

Thomas's forgiving nature allowed him to feel a twinge of pity for Adam. He crossed himself again and said, 'At least he'll be near Dol, his birthplace, which is within sight of Mont St Michel.'

Nesta's forehead wrinkled in thought. 'I've heard somewhere that even men who are not really priests have been given this Benefit of Clergy. Can that be true?'

Again Thomas was the fount of knowledge. 'It can happen, especially to those clerks in minor orders who can read but who are not yet ordained. The usual test is to give them the Vulgate and see if they can read the first sentence of the fifty-first Psalm – "Have mercy on me, O God, according to thy loving kindness – according to the multitude of thy tender mercies, blot out my transgressions."'

'That bit of the Psalms is famous,' observed the coroner. 'It's known as the "neck verse" because it's saved many a cleric from the rope – and some who weren't even in Orders of any kind!'

Gwyn snorted his disdain. 'I could learn that off by heart, without being able to read.'

'Maybe you better had – it might come in useful, in case you tumble any more priests out of their bell-towers,' said de Wolfe, with a grin.

Nesta, having been further from the dramatic events of the past week or so, had a wider perspective of the whole affair and could see gaps in the story.

'Why did Adam start on this mad crusade – and why at this particular time?' she wondered aloud.

John shrugged, as the same question had bothered him. 'Who can fathom the mind of someone as possessed as he was? As to the timing, I think the imminent arrival of the Justices triggered it. Maybe he wanted to show that his own brand of God-given retribution was more effective than man-made laws.'

'Did he kill at random, d'you think?' asked the Welsh-woman.

'He must have chosen his victims in advance,' de Wolfe replied, 'as he had to find appropriate texts. He seems to have put their faces on the wall of his church later, as he hadn't got around to mine, unless he was about to add it when we caught him up that ladder.'

The others were silent for a moment, then Thomas

asked, 'How did he manage never to be seen at any of his killings? He was hardly a skinny wraith like me,' he added.

'Apart from the attack on Justice Serlo, they were all at dead of night and this city is hardly well lit,' replied John. 'A priest with his black robe and cowl is virtually invisible after dark, and if he's challenged by the constables, he always has the excuse that he's going to some church for Matins or to give the Last Offices to the dying.'

Gwyn agreed. 'He's lived in Exeter for years, and must know every lane and alleyway. I suppose he stalked his victims and struck when the best opportunity arose.'

'He certainly stalked me to good effect!' said John, pointing ruefully to his head. His turban-like bandage was gone, but he still had a very sore spot on his scalp.

Swallowing the last of his ale, de Wolfe prepared to leave. He had spent precious little time at home this past week and wished to avoid damaging Matilda's fairly benign mood. She had been relieved that events had concealed her brother's folly in Waterbeer Street and also that her own niggling doubts about Julian Fulk had been dispelled. In addition, the public acclamation of her husband's success in unmasking the Gospel killer had significantly notched up her standing within her social circle – especially since another feast for the Justices, this time at Rougemont, had given her another opportunity to display both her finery and her famous husband.

As John stood up, he put a hand on Thomas's shoulder. 'I spoke to your uncle when he was at the court today. He'll no doubt talk to you himself, but it seems that the Bishop is a little conscience-stricken at refusing you Benefit of Clergy when you were in such dire trouble and then proved innocent. He has hinted that he might withdraw his objections to your eventual return to Holy Orders.'

The clerk's face lit up as if a shaft of sunlight had struck it. Tears appeared in his eyes and he clutched at the sleeve of his master's tunic. 'God preserve you, Crowner! But even if I am restored, I will remain your clerk for a long while yet. You may again need someone who can interpret the scriptures for you!'

Next morning, de Wolfe ambled up to his chamber above the gatehouse of Rougemont, partly to get out of the house on a Sunday and also to give Brutus some exercise: the old hound's joints were getting stiff.

With the dog resting by his feet under the table, he spent a few minutes studying his reading lessons, badly neglected during the recent busy weeks. Soon bored and thirsty, he rose to look for Gwyn's store of cider, which he kept in a large jar in the corner of the barren room. The Cornishman's frayed leather jerkin, discarded in the warmer weather, was draped over the two-gallon pot and when John pulled it off, something fell out of the large poacher's pocket inside. It was one of Thomas's little pottery jars of ink, a curious thing for the illiterate Gwyn to be carrying. Intrigued, de Wolfe dipped his hand into the pocket and pulled out a quill pen and a ragged piece of blank parchment.

Sitting back at the trestle, he felt in the pouch on his belt and pulled out the folded note with the text from Ecclesiastes that had been left at the scene of his own assault. When he put the irregular margins of the two fragments of parchment together, they fitted exactly. Staring at them with slowly dawning comprehension, John now knew why Gwyn had chosen to make his own private visit to the clerk on the last evening before he was due to be hanged. The Cornishman must have overcome Thomas's resignation to a welcome release from

this world and persuaded him to use his accomplish-
ments with a pen to forge a note in a disguised hand,
similar to that left with the dead Jew.

Slowly, de Wolfe sat back on his stool. A lopsided
grin creased his face as he put up a hand to feel the
still-tender swelling on the back of his head.

'Thank you, Gwyn,' he said quietly. 'But now I owe
you one!'

**POCKET
BOOKS**

This book and other **Simon & Schuster** titles are available from your book shop or can be ordered direct from the publisher.

Guenevere:

0 671 01812 4	**The Queen of the Summer Country**	Rosalind Miles	£6.99
0 671 01813 2	**The Knight of the Sacred Lake**	Rosalind Miles	£6.99
0 671 01814 0	**The Child of the Holy Grail**	Rosalind Miles	£6.99
0 671 03721 8	**Isolde**	Rosalind Miles	£6.99

The Stone of Light:

0 671 77371 2	**Nefer the Silent**	Christian Jacq	£6.99
0 671 77374 7	**The Wise Woman**	Christian Jacq	£6.99
0 671 77375 5	**Paneb the Ardent**	Christian Jacq	£6.99
0 671 77376 3	**The Place of Truth**	Christian Jacq	£6.99

0 671 51673 6	**The Sanctuary Seeker**	Bernard Knight	£6.99
0 671 51674 4	**The Poisoned Chalice**	Bernard Knight	£6.99
0 671 51675 2	**Crowner's Quest**	Bernard Knight	£6.99
0 671 02965 7	**The Awful Secret**	Bernard Knight	£6.99
0 671 02966 5	**The Tinner's Corpse**	Bernard Knight	£6.99
0 671 02967 3	**The Grim Reaper**	Bernard Knight	£6.99

Please send cheque or postal order for the value of the book, free postage and packing within the UK; OVERSEAS including Republic of Ireland £1 per book.

OR: Please debit this amount from my

VISA/ACCESS/MASTERCARD ....

CARD NO: ....

EXPIRY DATE ....

AMOUNT £ ....

NAME ....

ADDRESS ....

....

SIGNATURE ....

Send orders to SIMON & SCHUSTER CASH SALES
PO Box 29, Douglas Isle of Man, IM99 1BQ
Tel: 01624 836000, Fax: 01624 670923
www.bookpost.co.uk
Please allow 14 days for delivery. Prices and availability
subject to change without notice